SECOND SPRING

by

Sally Laity

**Flip over for another great novel!
THE KISS GOODBYE**

ISBN 1-55748-258-6

90000>

9 781557 482587

A BARBOUR BOOK

Published by Barbour & Company, Inc.
P.O. Box 719
Uhrichsville, Ohio 44683

Printed in the United States of America
ISBN   1-55748-258-6
Typeset by Typetronix, Inc., Cape Coral, FL

92   93   94   95   96   5   4   3   2   1

Dedicated with love to Robin—my daughter, my friend.
And to Barb, for reminding me how much
I have always loved Pennsylvania.

I wish to thank fellow writers Dianna Crawford, Debbie Bailey, Jeannie Levig, and Sue Rich for endless hours of critique and support during the writing of this novel. Their comments were much appreciated. And a special thanks to Chelley Kitzmiller, whose writing conferences got me started.

Second Spring

First spring comes softly, on tiptoe,
    A shy maiden-kiss
        That barely warms winter's cold heart.
    She runs to hide when his last breath
        Covers the crocus with a mantle
            of white, of cold.
Second spring comes dancing, laughing,
    An eager debutante
        Dressed in a gown of new green.
    Daffodils grace her sun-streaked hair
        As she waltzes across the landscape
            on breezes, in bird-song.
Winter shrivels and melts away
    As the world awakens with life anew.
        First spring whispers a promise
            of hope . . .
        Second spring comes to stay.

1

Elena Ryan balanced a bag of groceries on one hip and inserted her house key into the lock. As usual, there was no smooth turning, no resounding click. "Darn," she muttered to herself. "Why do you always have to be so obstinate?"

The sack teetered. She took a deep breath and huffed, then set her burden down for another try, debating whether to resort to the ever-popular good swift kick.

A strong masculine hand closed over hers, and a warm breath stirred the hair near her ear. "Lancelot at your service, milady."

Elena's heart leaped to her throat. Ready to scream, she jerked her arm back and spun around. The ring of keys clattered near her feet.

One very familiar grin filled her vision, and her face filled with surprise. "Josh Montgomery!" she gasped. "It can't be you!"

"Sorry, Laney," he said, enveloping her in a bear hug. "Didn't mean to scare you."

She laughed in disbelief and smiled up into his clear gray eyes. "What are you doing here already? Your mom said you wouldn't be home until sometime next week."

"Well, I finished up early and took off." After a last squeeze, he held her at arm's length as his gaze swept over her. "You look wonderful, Laney. How've you been?"

"Just fine—except for being locked out of my own house."

Josh nodded slowly. "I thought it looked like you were having a problem." He bent to retrieve the key ring, then inserting the correct one into the lock, he jiggled it until it turned. "Has this acted up before?" he asked. He opened the door for Elena and picked up the groceries.

"Only ever since we've had this place." Elena stepped inside and turned, watching him enter. "Greg did oil it from time to time and that helped some." She raised her eyebrows. "Have time for a cup of tea, or are you in a hurry?"

"I'll always have time for you," he said with a lazy wink. "You know that."

"Right. Friends forever and all that." Unexpectedly, Elena felt the warmth of a blush coloring her cheeks, and she turned and walked hurriedly into the living room.

Josh followed her through the homey house and into the bright apricot and oak kitchen.

Rays of late afternoon sunshine streamed through the frilly peach-colored Cape Cod curtains on the double window and settled invitingly on a brass bowl in the center of the round oak table. Josh set the bag on the tile counter.

"Thanks. Make yourself at home, okay?" Elena said, removing the groceries and putting them away. "I'll put on some tea." Taking the copper kettle from the stove, she filled it with water as Josh retraced a few steps and pulled out a wooden captain's chair. Out of the corner of her eye, she saw him lower himself onto the seat and stretch out his long legs, resting an elbow on the table.

"I can't tell you how good it is to see you, Josh. It seems like you've been gone forever." She turned on the burner beneath the kettle, then leaned back against the counter, her hands cushioning her spine, her head expectantly tilted to one side.

He ran his fingers through his already tousled blond hair and grinned, sharply defined laugh lines bracketing his mouth like parentheses. "I suppose. That's how the Air Force is, you know."

Elena smiled. The years had been kind to him, she noticed. He was still devastatingly handsome, sitting there dressed in soft blues and grays. She thought that he had always looked great in crewneck sweaters and dress slacks, and the checked shirt he wore complemented the colors of both. She sighed.

"I . . . um . . ." Josh cleared his throat. When he spoke again, his voice was surprisingly uneven. "I was really sorry to hear about the accident, Lane."

Elena swallowed and lowered her gaze while she gathered her thoughts. Drawing her lips together, she inhaled a long ragged breath.

"Sorry. You'd probably rather not talk about it."

"No, it's okay. I . . . need to talk about it once in a while. I've just gotten used to the way most people avoid the subject." Turning around, she busied herself pouring milk into a small pitcher, taking two mugs from a rack, and arranging cookies on a small plate.

"I would've liked to have been here for you, instead of half a world away."

She smiled to herself.

"I did try to write, actually," he continued, "but nothing looked right on paper. All I could do was pray."

Meeting his eyes as she set napkins and the other items on the table, Elena shrugged. "Well, what could anyone do but pray, really? It all happened so quickly. One day I was a wife and mother, the next . . . well, you know." Her eyes misted over, and she blinked to clear her vision. "I'm sure it was prayer that got me through it."

The kettle whistled, and she hurried to turn off the burner and fill the teapot. Returning with it to the table, she sat opposite Josh. Automatically, they reached for one another's hand while Josh asked the blessing.

"Anyway," she said afterward, filling their mugs, "thanks for the card and note. They helped more than you'll ever know. I must have read them a thousand times." She remembered clutching the treasured correspondence to her heart in her grief. He'd probably never know that she'd kept them under her pillow for weeks afterward, almost feeling the presence of her friend in the words of comfort written by his hand, she realized.

"Greg was . . . killed outright, you know," Elena said softly, "when the truck jackknifed in front of our car."

"Oh?"

She nodded. "But Stevie . . ." She stopped for a moment and swallowed hard. "Stevie lingered in a coma for two days. I thought that since he was—alive—" Pressing her lips together, she drew them inward momentarily, then released them and sighed deeply. An unbidden memory flashed into her mind: of bandages and tubes, rooms smelling of antiseptic, hushed voices, soft incessant beeps that merged suddenly into a single terrifying tone, and then doctors shaking their heads in slow finality. When she'd finally gathered the courage enough to go home, she'd found the cherished teddy bear her little "big boy" always left waiting inside the door for his return. She remembered disintegrating then. Burying her face into the fuzzy softness that had still carried Steven's scent, she had sobbed until there were no tears left inside.

She bit her bottom lip and brushed away an unwanted tear. "I guess the Lord had some things to teach me about prayer. Hard things." Elena felt the steady warmth of Josh's gaze and knew that he'd hardly taken his eyes off her for an instant. Slightly unnerved, she wondered if the wind had made a mess of her hair. She fought an impulse to reach up and check. "Listen, would you mind if we talk about this another time? It's kind of a long story."

"Sure. But when you can talk about it . . ."

"I know. You'll be there to listen, like always." She smiled and took a sip of tea. "So what's been happening with you all this time? If it weren't for your mom living right up the street, I'd have never known anything about you."

A guilty grin spread across his face, softening the strong squareness of his jawline. "I guess I did neglect you a bit, didn't I? But it wasn't on purpose. I've always thought about you and prayed for you."

Elena nodded her head, lost in his laughing gray eyes. "I pray for you, too. But it's not exactly like having you around. We go back a long time, you know."

"That we do. And speaking of time," he said, checking his watch, "I think I'd better be on my way. I have someone else to surprise. Thanks for the tea." Pushing back the chair with his legs, he stood up.

Elena rose with a smile at the same time. "How I'd love to see the look of surprise when you walk in."

Josh chuckled, and they walked to the front door. "It's been nice talking to you, Lane. Maybe I'll come by again in a day or two and take a look at the brass monster there," he said, gesturing with his thumb toward the lock. "If you don't mind, that is."

"Are you kidding? Any damsel appreciates having a knight come to her rescue. Thanks for . . . saving my life."

He grinned and stood there for an awkward second or two before they laughed and hugged again.

Elena felt him inhale deeply before he patted her back and released her.

"See you, Laney." Picking up a duffel bag outside, he strode briskly away, turning to wave at the end of the walk.

She smiled back and closed the door. An odd warmth flooded

over her. What a surprise it had been, seeing him again out of the blue. Thinking back, Elena realized that he'd gone away right after her wedding, eight years ago. Be happy, he'd said. The addition of a few lines carved by time near his eyes and mouth had only made him more handsome, she thought. His muscular six-foot-two frame sported an incredible golden tan, and his grin still held its dazzling power.

She smiled, remembering the way all the girls in school would swoon over him as he walked by. How they'd envied her living next door to him for so many years. They couldn't believe that he was more like a big brother to her than anything else and that she thought of him as just a friend.

Three years older than Elena, Josh had entered the military at the beginning of her sophomore year in high school, and the girls were left to find a new heartthrob. Oh well, so much for old memories, she told herself. Elena dismissed the vague recollection of his engagement a few years ago to a European woman and walked toward the kitchen to clear away the tea things.

She caught her reflection in the hall mirror and stopped to assess her image, wondering if she'd changed much in eight years. Squinting, she checked for lines around her eyes. She was glad that her hair had grown out of the short sophisticated style that Greg had preferred during their marriage; it was long again, the way she'd always worn it. She ran parted fingers slowly through a lock, looking for the first telltale evidence of silver.

Elena cocked her head back and forth. "I suppose you could look a lot worse," she said aloud. "Now, about those dishes. Big Brother will come another day."

The front door squeaked when Josh opened it, and he set his duffel bag down on the floor as he walked in.

"Is that you, Chris?" called his mother's voice from the kitchen. Wiping soapy hands on her apron, Stella Montgomery came through the dining room and stopped short. "Josh!" she gasped in a hushed voice. "Mercy me! What— How—"

Laughing, Josh crossed the room in three strides, picked up his slender, startled mother, and swung her around in a circle. "How are you, Mom?" he asked, setting her down gently and kissing the top of her head.

Hand on her bosom, Stella stood with her mouth agape for a

few seconds. "Better, now that you're home. Just let me catch my breath."

Josh led his mother to her favorite rocker and she settled down on the soft melon and blue floral-patterned cushions. He patted her arm and sat nearby on the couch, which had a matching slipcover. Glancing around the room, he felt at home in the familiar arrangement of furniture. "Where's Chris?" he asked.

"Helping out at a conference in Philadelphia this week. When I heard the door, I thought that she might have finished early."

He nodded. "Well, I'm the one who finished ahead of time, so I decided to surprise you."

"I'm glad you did," Stella replied with a smile. "Heaven knows there's precious little excitement around here." Her blue eyes twinkled.

Josh fidgeted in his seat and propped one ankle on the opposite knee. "Say, Mom," he began, "I sort of bumped into Laney on my way home and stopped in for a couple minutes."

"Oh?"

"Yes. She looks great, doesn't she? Says she's been doing okay. Has she, really? You never wrote much about her in your letters."

A strange smile played across his mother's face. "Oh, you know Elena. She's a trooper, always proving she can get by on her own without bothering anybody."

"Sounds like her."

"She had some pretty rough times, but the Lord's brought her through. She's coming along . . . on the surface, anyway."

Josh grew serious. "What does that mean?"

"I don't know if I can explain it." Stella thoughtfully tapped her fingers on the chair's arm. "She keeps herself busy, all the time. Too busy to think, I believe."

Josh continued to scrutinize his mother's expression.

"At least she doesn't have any financial worries. The insurance settlement left her well provided for. But . . . there's something inside she hasn't come to terms with yet, some kind of pain that she keeps to herself. Perhaps no one else can tell, I don't know. But it's all I see when I look at her. It's in her eyes. They just don't smile anymore."

A buzzer sounded from the kitchen, and his mother got up. "Good. The chicken's done. How about some supper, dear? You know I always make more than I can eat."

In his bedroom later that night, Josh rose from his knees after his prayers and turned down the fluffy homemade quilt on the single bed. He felt good to be home again.

His eyes surveyed the second-floor room. Everything was about the same as he'd left it. Sports trophies lined the built-in shelves on one wall, but his tennis racquets and baseball gloves had been put away. Much better, he thought. Not so much clutter. He climbed into bed between the cool navy blue sheets and turned off the light on the nightstand.

Restless, he rolled over to punch his pillow a few times, then settled his head back down. Maybe some music would help, he thought. Reaching for the stereo on the shelves next to the bed, his finger found the power switch, and soft music drifted from the speakers. Rachmaninoff, he thought. Perfect.

Thoughts of Elena weighed heavily on his mind. *Have I waited long enough before coming back?* he wondered. *Too long?*

A silver picture frame across the room reflected the glow of moonlight that drifted through the partially closed window blinds. When Josh had undressed and put his watch beside it on the chest of drawers, he had purposely avoided looking at it. He knew exactly who was in that photograph. His mother had taken it on one of his military leaves. He remembered standing right next to Elena while they smiled at the camera. And on the other side of her, with his eyes on Elena, was Greg Ryan. Good old Air Force buddy Greg. Good old be-my-best-man-while-I-marry-your-girl Greg. Josh's face twisted bitterly into a cynical smile.

Turning onto his side, he allowed his mind to have free rein. *Elena.* She had forever been in his thoughts. He still felt the joyous torture he'd experienced a few hours earlier, when he'd held her close in his arms. Good grief, he thought, she had gotten so thin. Her high cheekbones were more pronounced now, accenting the straightness of her nose and her small chin. She seemed almost fragile.

She's even more beautiful than I remembered, he thought, recollecting her golden strands woven by summer sunshine among her light brown silky waves. Drawing a deep breath, he inhaled the fragrance of it in his mind.

He thought of her mouth and the way that her slightly fuller lower lip had trembled when she had tried to talk about the accident. And then he envisioned eyes of misty blue fringed with long, brown lashes.

Yes, he thought, *beautiful as ever. Except . . . Mom's right. Something about her eyes. I have to see them again. I have to see her again.*

Lord, don't let me bungle it this time. Help me to tread softly.

2

Saturday's dawn was clear and crisp, with a cool breeze that hummed a definite song of fall.

The aroma of homemade bread wafted from the kitchen into the spare room, where Elena knelt sorting through the contents of her storage closet. This was her least favorite chore. Sighing, she folded a corduroy blazer and added it to the discard pile. *This may take longer than I had planned,* she thought grimly. *Why do I always save everything?*

Stacking the Christmas decorations off to the side, she picked up one of the bottom cartons and read the label: "Mementos." A chill ran through her at the thought of facing things that had belonged to Greg and Steven. She dropped the box back into place and forced her mind to concentrate on the other items before her.

At that moment the oven timer went off and someone tapped at the front door. Grateful for the interruption, Elena bolted for the stove and removed the finished bread. Then she answered the door.

"Locksmith, milady," Josh said with a grin. He held a toolbox in one hand.

"Well, aren't you out bright and early," Elena laughed, stepping aside to let him in. "I thought you'd have a million things to do once you were home."

"You're right. But this happens to be next on the list. See?" He held up an itemized column.

Smiling, Elena shook her head in disbelief.

"By the way, what smells so incredible?" he asked.

"Oh, you mean the bread?"

"Yes. This might end up costing you a sample," he said with a wink.

"Well, maybe if you do a good enough job, I'll think about giving you some. Fair enough?"

"Sounds like a deal."

Elena smiled. "In the meantime, I'll go and finish what I was doing, if you'll excuse me."

Josh nodded in answer, and Elena felt his eyes follow her as she left the room.

In front of the closet, Elena took a disgusted look at the pile and put all the cartons back inside. The rest she would get to later, she told herself. Closing the door on the whole room, she returned to Josh and knelt beside the tools. "How's it going?"

He had three screws between his lips and mumbled something that sounded like, "Not too bad." Removing one, he put it into place with his screwdriver.

"Was your mom surprised when you got home yesterday?"

"Mmmmm!" He removed another screw. "Cooked up a regular storm," he said out of one side of his mouth. "Fatted calf and all. Well, fatted chicken, anyway," he said with a lopsided grin. "I have some out in the car. Feel like a picnic?"

"Ooh, that's a tempting offer."

"Good. I meant it to be." He looked pointedly at her skirt and blouse. "We can do some hiking, too, if you put on your hiking boots. I'm just about finished."

As he gathered up his tools, Elena went to her room and changed into wool slacks and a soft pullover sweater, then ran a brush through her hair. Taking a cardigan out of the closet, she left the room.

A few moments later they stepped outside, and Josh locked the door behind them. "I don't think this'll give you any more trouble."

"Never?" She cast a doubtful look at him as they strode down the walk.

"I hope! I straightened a warped pin in one of the cylinders. The lock shouldn't be so likely to jam now."

"That'll be a welcome change."

Josh ushered Elena into his classic Thunderbird, then circled around and lowered himself into the driver's seat, slamming his door. "Thought we might go to Ricketts Glen, if that sounds okay to you," he said, turning the key in the ignition. "The leaves are just beginning to turn now, and the park'll be all dressed up for company."

"Great! I haven't been there for ages."

Pulling away from the little white cottage, he headed for Route 118 and the Pennsylvania state park situated on North and Red

Rock mountains.

Named for Civil War Colonel Robert Bruce Ricketts, the 13,000-acre park had been a favorite spot over the years for picnics Elena's family had enjoyed with the Montgomerys. Together they had hiked the glorious Falls Trail along the picturesque gorge carved by Kitchen Creek, which cascaded 1000 feet down the face of the great mountain barrier. The arresting beauty of the trail's twenty-two waterfalls, ranging in height from eleven to ninety-four feet, had never ceased to enchant them.

Easy-listening music filled the car. Under brilliant blue skies, Elena drank in the panorama of familiar rolling countryside as they sped along. She turned to gaze at Josh as he drove, noticing his strong profile and the way his beige sweater and brown slacks accented his tan coloring.

He glanced at her and smiled. "What's on your mind?"

Elena barely prevented a blush from warming her cheeks. "Oh, I was just thinking how swiftly the years have passed. And how wonderful it will be to spend a day at the park again."

"I agree. I hear it's quite a popular camping spot now. Family cabins, tent sites, bridle trails—quite a change from when we were young."

"I hope it hasn't changed too much."

"We'll soon see."

Her eyes averted to the scenery out of the side window.

"Mom said you've taken over one of the Sunday school classes at church recently."

"Well, yes, but it wasn't exactly my idea. No one else was willing to walk into that lion's den. Pastor Douglas thought that it would be 'good therapy' for me to take on some different problems. He thought it would broaden my outlook, or something."

"And?"

She shrugged. "I decided to give it a try. Truth is, no one wanted to teach the teenage girls since Priscilla Andrews got married and moved away."

"You've always helped out in the youth programs. What's the problem?"

"Well, they're not the little kids I'm used to. They're too old to play kiddie games, too young for just a basic prayer and Bible study. They're trying to grow up too fast, rebelling against traditional values. Typical teens."

"Hmm," said Josh, speculatively. "How are you making out?"

Elena smiled to herself. "You know, it's odd. At first I was terrified. All I could see was this row of mutinous eyes staring at me, waiting for me to walk out on them. Two teachers before me had done that. But I decided to stick it out, no matter what." Her voice became light and teasing. "Of course, I suppose that the prayer and fasting didn't hurt any."

Josh chuckled. "Sounds like the Laney I know." He patted her hand as it lay between them on the seat.

Elena smiled. "Well, I discovered they were afraid, too, afraid that someone was going to be there preaching at them about rock and roll or their clothes and makeup, that sort of thing. They didn't expect anyone to *like* them. And, to be truthful, I didn't think I would! But for the first few weeks, I did most of the listening. Now we all have a better understanding of each other."

"So that class has finally found the right teacher, then?" Josh said, pulling into the park entrance. He eased the car into a space and they got out.

"I knew it'd be a good day to be here." Josh inhaled deeply and stretched. "How beautiful God's character must be, don't you think? I'm in awe when I see His handiwork everywhere and hear the sound of rushing water."

"I feel the same way." Elena walked in the direction of his gaze toward the waterfall near the park entrance, where the creek cascaded and swirled over rocks and ledges and plunged beneath the overpass of the road.

Josh followed her, and for several moments they stood at the edge of the chasm, gazing down at the churning water. "Great, isn't it?" Josh shouted over the racket. "Remember when you, Chris, and I climbed out on that dry rock shelf and had our picture taken with the water thundering past us?"

She nodded. "I thought our moms would have coronaries."

"Oh well," he laughed. "We did a lot of crazy things in those days. And most of them gave me an appetite, too. Like the kind I get when I work next to a bakery." His wink made her smile. "What do you say we find a place to eat?" He offered a friendly hand, and she took it as they returned to the car.

Handing her a folded blanket to carry, Josh removed the picnic basket from the trunk, and they headed for the path.

Carved through the forest by the steps of countless feet, the trail curved and wound along Kitchen Creek. Rustic wooden bridges crossed the swiftly flowing water in places. A squirrel skittered away among the lush ferns as they approached, and overhead the wind rustled through the leaves.

"Looks like we have the whole park to ourselves," Josh said. Stopping in a shaded clearing near a small waterfall, he looked around and made a wide sweep with one arm. "What do you think? Is this spot okay, or would you prefer a picnic table?"

"It's perfect." Elena spread out the checkered blanket and sat on one corner.

Kneeling, Josh set the basket down nearby. "This is like the picnics we used to have in the backyard when we were kids, remember?" he said, removing containers of food and handing them to her.

Elena smiled to herself. "We sure had a lot of fun in those days. It was fun to eat outside on the grass."

"Right."

"Except that once."

"What once?" Josh looked up at her.

"Oh, come on. Remember that special box of 'dessert' you gave me—with the frog inside? I almost died when I opened the lid and he jumped onto my lap!" Elena could not keep from laughing.

"Hey, now, let's be fair. If I recall correctly, that *was* the day after you gave me your piece of cake soaked in Kool-Aid, wasn't it?"

"Well, it spilled."

"Besides," he continued, "I was the one who had to go through the rest of the day with only fifty percent of my hearing because of your shrieks!"

Elena raised an eyebrow. "Well, all I know is, I never did develop a love for frogs!"

Josh grinned and reached to take her hand as they bowed their heads. "Thank you, Lord, for friendship, for food, and for the time to enjoy them both. In Jesus' name." Together they said, "Amen."

The splashing waterfall and the singing birds in the treetops gave just the right musical accompaniment to their superb assortment of Mrs. Montgomery's fried chicken, fresh homemade rolls, potato salad, fruit salad, hot tea, and apple tarts.

"I don't know when I've enjoyed a picnic so much," said Elena, as they finished eating. "It was a feast. I've gained five pounds for sure."

"Oh, we'll walk it off in a little while, Laney, never fear. But let's have the rest of this tea first." He refilled their cups.

Elena changed position and folded her legs under her.

Handing her a plastic mug, Josh smiled. "By the way, you haven't told me anything about yourself. I've been away for a long time, remember?"

She wrinkled her nose and exhaled softly. "Well, I'm sure your mom has kept you up to date. It's all rather boring, actually. I work part-time in a law office in Wilkes-Barre, with Wednesdays off. Marcy works there, too. In fact, she recommended me for the job."

"Marcy? No kidding. We had a lot of good times with her, growing up on Willow Tree Lane. I'm glad you're working with someone close."

"She's a dear."

"And how are you getting by?" Josh asked. "I seem to remember a shy, timid girl who was afraid of her own shadow."

The sunlight streaming down through the canopy of leaves overhead fell like bits of shattered glass in a bright pattern all around them, touching Elena's light brown hair and picking out tiny red and gold highlights.

Josh noticed the way that the soft blue of her eyes reflected the hue of her sweater when she looked at him. A deep sadness shone from within their depths.

She sighed unconsciously and gazed off into the distance. Several moments passed before she spoke. "Well, when something happens out of the blue and shatters a person's life, it's impossible to accept right away. I couldn't believe it. I walked around in a daze for some time. Numb. Then that wore off, and I was—" she gestured helplessly, "—devastated. It was hard enough trying to cope with Greg's absence and to make some sense out of the chaos of our affairs. But losing Stevie too . . . ." Her breath caught. "I almost didn't make it through that one. I almost . . . didn't *want* to make it." A shadow of pain crossed her face, and a glistening tear traced a path down her cheek.

Josh felt a lump form in his throat.

"Sorry." Elena shrugged and tried to smile. She flicked the tear from the soft curve of her cheek with a fingertip. "Some things are still a bit hard to talk about."

"Hey, it's me, remember?" Josh said, putting a hand on her shoulder for a moment. Small comfort, he thought, when what he wanted more than anything was to wrap her in his arms and hold her forever.

"Steven lived for two days, after the accident. I think I told you that. He was unconscious, but he was alive, so I thought there was . . . hope." She smiled wistfully. "It was the end of November, and he was already excited about Christmas. Department stores were full of holiday displays. I remember him asking why *we* get all the presents if it's Jesus' birthday. And why couldn't we give Him something special. Only a few days later . . . the accident happened. And the most special treasure I ever had went to be with the Lord."

Josh swallowed as Elena's eyes turned to his.

"Before Steven was born, I gave him to the Lord, in my heart. And when he was a few weeks old, Greg and I dedicated him to God. So, you see, when he lay in the hospital, and I held him up before the Lord in prayer, I couldn't say, 'He's mine, You can't have him.' I had to hold him up with my hands open."

Her eyes misted over, and she paused briefly and looked away. "I guess that was the hardest thing I ever had to learn about prayer. We have to be ready to accept the Lord's will, even if it turns out to be the opposite of what *we* might've wanted. But when we do accept it, He gives an incredible peace, the kind that passes understanding, as the Bible says."

Josh leaned back on one elbow and gazed intently at Elena, pondering her words.

"Everyone was so kind to me," she continued. "Pastor Douglas was a real blessing. And your mom was incredible. I don't know what I would've done without her. She took me home with her, stayed up all night with me, kept me from being alone. She helped me to face going home, to face sorting through things." She sighed. "And then, time has helped a little. But there are still some things I can't let myself think about, even after nearly two years."

A long silence stretched between them, which Josh was reluctant to break. He cleared his throat. "Well, I'm glad you felt that you could tell me all this, Lane. I know it can't be easy for you to talk about."

"No, not easy," she said with a sad smile. "But it does help. Most people are very careful not to mention Greg or Stevie around me, but they were a very real part of my life."

"Well, you can talk to me about them whenever you want, friend. I won't be going anywhere for a while."

Elena leaned over and planted a feather-soft kiss on his cheek. "Thanks. I could always count on you."

It took all of his strength to respond with only a smile. His fingers traced a familiar path through his hair as he got up. "Well, listen, if we want to do any hiking, we'd better take this stuff back to the car and get going."

A short time later, picnic gear locked inside the Thunderbird's small trunk, they began their climb. The ground beneath their feet was a spongy carpet of needles from giant pines and old leaves from hemlocks, oaks, and maples. Walking along the sun-dappled trail, they passed tall formations of rock along the swiftly flowing creek.

"It's all so magnificent here," Elena said, inhaling the earthy October scents. "Look at the huge gnarled roots everywhere. The trees have grown a lot since I was here last."

"Looks like it. Some are over 100 feet tall now. Some of the fallen trees were found to be 900 years old."

"Really? Just where did you acquire that gem of knowledge?"

"Oh, I like to read about all the places around our home," he said with a grin.

Elena raised her brows and turned to him. "You don't say. Now I know where to go for all my information."

"Just check with me, I know all about trees."

"I'll just bet you do," she said with a mock frown, and they both laughed.

"Well, I don't think we're the only ones who know about this place, though," he said, stepping off the pathway. "Look at the hearts and initials carved into these tree trunks."

As they paused to examine a sample, Elena, lost in thought, traced some of the outlines with a finger and smiled wistfully. Pieces of loose bark crumbled in her hands, and she scattered them idly along the way as they turned back to the trail.

Near several of the tall, majestic waterfalls, the path was slick with moisture, and Josh offered a hand as they hiked. They stopped to watch a pair of chipmunks scurrying through the fallen leaves, and they admired a bluejay as it soared high among the branches of the tall trees. When the temperature began to cool, they headed back.

On the ride home, Elena was the first to speak. "I feel like I've been doing all the talking, Josh. And you still haven't told me what's been happening with you. Greg was your friend, too, remember? We expected you to visit us once in a while."

Josh grimaced. "I suppose so. I got sort of busy in the Air Force, cramming in as much college as I could. I ended up with a degree in engineering."

"That's great, Josh. Now I know why I've always been proud of you."

One side of his mouth twitched into a hint of a smile. "I considered making a career out of the military."

"Why didn't you?"

"Something else came along that held better prospects. One of the base chaplains introduced me to a guy with an interesting sideline: designing experimental aircraft. I started hanging around with him in my spare time and got caught up in some of his ideas."

"Experimental aircraft? Isn't that dangerous?"

Josh smiled. "No, not really. It isn't hard to make a machine that can fly. Aviation has come a long way since the days of Wilbur and Orville."

"Do you fly them too—the ones you and your friend build?"

"Sure. We can't market something we haven't tested. What Jake and I build are called hybrids. They're sort of a combined design, where a fuselage from one aircraft is used with, say, the wing style of a second and maybe landing gear from a third. You know?"

"And that's legal?" Elena asked.

"Sure. Designers of homebuilts aren't tied down to all the traditional notions of what an airplane should look like. We take the best features from several aircraft and leave out what we don't want to use. That way, there's room for new advancements in performance, too."

"Well, that sounds logical. I've seen pictures of some odd planes in the newspaper from time to time."

"Sure you have. *Voyager*, for example. Who'd have expected such an unorthodox craft to be able to fly? Yet it was designed for a certain function and ended up not only flying, but setting its own records."

Elena nodded.

"That's just one example. The smallest airplane in the world, the Stits Skybaby, is only ten feet long by five feet high. It can fly up to 200 miles an hour."

Her mouth opened in surprise. "That sounds amazing."

"It is. It's an amazing field, and I'm really glad to be part of it."

The car came to a stop in front of Elena's house, and Josh got out to assist her. At her front door, he took the keychain from her hand and inserted one into the lock. "Voilà!" he exclaimed with a triumphant grin as it turned smoothly. He opened the door. "Thanks for the day, Lancy. We'll have to do it again sometime."

Elena reached for the keys he dangled from his hand and stepped inside. "I should be the one who does all the thanking, Josh. I had a wonderful time."

He smiled and gave her shoulder a gentle squeeze with one large hand, then turned and walked back to his car.

As she watched him drive away, Elena sighed and closed the door.

3

Elena sat at the kitchen table and drank her second cup of coffee, meditating on the morning's Sunday school lesson. Her Bible and teacher's manual for the new topic the girls had chosen were spread out before her. She bowed her head. *Heavenly Father*, she prayed silently, *please speak through me to the girls in class today. Grant me the wisdom and guidance to know how to answer their questions.* After reading through the lesson one last time to fix the main points in her mind, Elena closed the books and rose to get ready for church.

Seeing the slate gray clouds outside, she dressed in a pleated, navy plaid skirt, white silk jabot blouse, and red blazer. Then she brushed her long, shiny hair, fastening one side back with a decorative comb and allowing the soft waves on the other to cascade freely to her shoulder. She donned earrings and a slender gold watch and spritzed some cologne. As soon as she heard the Montgomerys' sedan outside in the drive, she gathered her things and left.

Josh stood waiting by the open passenger's side door and winked as she approached.

She smiled and got into the front seat, and he closed the door after her.

"Good morning, Mother," Elena said, turning sideways to greet Stella, who was sitting in the back seat. "And Chris! Hi! Nice to have you home. How was the conference?"

"Great! Even better than we'd hoped," Chris answered as Josh guided the car onto the street. "I wish you all could've been there to see the turnout. I was surprised that so many young people showed interest in missions." Tall and slender, she had her mother's sparkling blue eyes, long dark lashes, and straight brows. Her ash blond bouncy hairstyle kept rhythm with her animated movements. "The students were very enthusiastic, and the workshops were packed every day."

"Really? I'm glad to hear that. How much time will you have

19

at home before you're off again?"

"Oh, about five weeks, I think. That's about how long it'll take for all the arrangements to be finalized for the medical team's departure. The year went by quickly, didn't it?"

Elena nodded. "I can't believe that in a matter of two months or so you'll be helping out at the field hospital in Peru. It's so exciting."

"And until then, we'll get to have her around," said Stella Montgomery, patting her daughter's hand. "Most of the time, anyway."

Elena smiled over her shoulder at them both as she turned to face the front. "Must be a real treat for you, Mother, having all your family home at the same time."

"That's right, dear," Stella said, reaching to touch Elena's shoulder in her motherly way. "All my family, home again."

Elena happened to see Josh wink at his mother in the rearview mirror just then. She was more than aware of how handsome he looked in his herringbone tweed sport coat and charcoal gray slacks.

As if he could read her thoughts, he grinned at her, his eyes twinkling.

She was caught off guard. She blushed as she returned the smile. "So, Chris," she said, looking again at the young woman, "tell me more about how things are coming along with the medical team. I want to hear every detail."

Upon their arrival at Hillcrest Community Bible Church, Josh pulled into a parking space. The bell in the old tower was pealing out the Sunday school hour as they entered. Once inside, all four went in different directions.

As Elena walked to her classroom, she overheard the pastor's voice. "Josh, buddy, it's good to have you back. We've been saving a spot for you in the youth ministry. Interested?" In her mind she could picture the greeting so typical of the pastor: a warm handclasp with his left hand placed on the shoulder of the person to whom he spoke.

She closed the door behind her and took her seat at the front of the room. All five regular students were present. Valerie Bancroft and Janice Harper sat with their heads together, giggling as usual.

Elena opened the attendance book and filled it in. "Valerie!"

she said to the willowy girl. "Welcome back. How was the cruise?"

"Fine." Valerie's expressive chestnut eyes sparkled against her boyishly styled honey blond hair. Dressed as usual in the latest fashion, she seemed to know she was envied and copied by other girls her age. Her tanned face grew serious as she glanced sideways at Janice. "Yeah, it was okay."

At this, the pair were overcome by some secret joke and covered their mouths to keep from laughing out loud. Elena rolled her eyes upward and shook her head.

Just then, Janice's purse plunged accidentally to the floor, scattering its contents. She laughed and knelt to gather her belongings.

Unlike the wealthy and pampered Valerie, Janice lived a much less privileged lifestyle. She and her brothers were supported solely by their divorced mother. Janice did her best to dress within the school fashion trends. Her thick auburn hair was kept trimmed by Valerie, who also taught her friend how to use cosmetics to enhance her startling green eyes.

The girls had been inseparable since their primary days at the church, which probably accounted for Valerie's parents permitting her to associate with someone who they considered less fortunate. The relationship was beneficial in other ways for Janice, too, Elena knew. Having a rich best friend ensured easy acceptance by her peers and provided access to Valerie's fabulous wardrobe.

Elena cleared her throat and distributed the new booklets to the class. "I've looked over the material we'll be covering in the weeks ahead, and it looks like we'll all be learning some new things about the validity of the Word of God. You'll find much of it to be interesting. Before we begin, are there any questions?"

"Well, yeah," said Valerie. "I think we should study something else. You know, about people."

"Why do you say that? This was a class decision. Everyone wanted to know more about the Bible and why it's so special."

"Yeah, I know," she answered, pouting. "But my parents said that even though it was valuable a long time ago, these days there are more reliable books to read. They say the Bible is only another piece of literature now, like other books full of stories and fables."

"Well, why don't we find out for ourselves if the Bible is still relevant for today?" asked Elena with a smile. "And if it should still have any bearing on our lives. Let's open with prayer."

Valerie's announcement had come as no surprise. Over the years the Bancrofts had drifted away from the fundamental beliefs that generations before had prompted them to band together with other families to start the country church. They attended regularly on Sunday mornings, but rarely came to any other services. But they never missed a business meeting; they seemed to delight in being at every one, casting "No" votes on any new idea. "We've always done it this way," was their cry.

Even after many of the other founding families had moved away or gone on to larger, more fashionable churches, the Bancrofts remained. Elena sometimes wondered if they were bound to Hillcrest Church by the hymnbooks they had bought and presented to the congregation years ago. Inside each book, in gold script, was an imprinted dedication by the Everett Morley Bancroft Family.

"Okay, class," began Elena, "let's get to our lesson. Janice, would you please read the introduction in the new quarterly?"

Janice grimaced at Valerie and opened her booklet. "Can a book as ancient as the Bible really be trusted in today's world?" she read aloud. "Are there any reasons to believe it is scientifically reliable or historically accurate? What is there about the Bible that makes it so different from other holy writings?" She set her book down and raised her eyes.

"Thanks," said Elena. She wondered if she was the right person to be in front of these girls conducting a study that might prove to be more involved than they expected; was there a way to make it simple enough for them to grasp? *Oh well, Father*, she prayed silently, *this is where You take over*.

The faces of the girls mirrored their doubts as they turned expectantly to their teacher.

"These are just a few of the questions we'll be trying to answer in the next few Sundays," she said. "What is important is that you come each week with an open mind and examine the evidence as it's presented. The Bible *is* different from other books. It *is* reliable. And it can change lives. It offers hope to those who have no hope, direction to those wandering without focus, and a message of everlasting love. In it we learn how God made it possible for us to have a personal, vital relationship with Him.

Many other religions are based on the attempts made by man to reach God. But in the Bible we find that God had a plan of His own to reach man. He alone is able to bridge the vast gap between Heaven and earth."

Marybeth Reed raised her hand. "The Bible really can change someone's life, Elena. I've seen it happen." The other girls turned to look at their friend as she spoke. "Many people who think they have no reason to believe in God find hope in His Word. It happens all the time at the rescue mission where my mom and dad are helping out."

The daughter of former missionaries to South America, Marybeth possessed a sweet spirituality far beyond her years. An inner beauty shone from her dusty blue eyes, and a mature, loving personality radiated the love of God from within her. Elena was aware that the girls respected Marybeth's gentle wisdom and her testimony.

"Thank you, Marybeth. Well, let's begin our study by turning to 2 Timothy, Chapter 3." Elena smiled at a shy class member in the back row. "Sharon, would you please read verses 14 through 17?"

At the end of the Sunday school hour the bell chimed. The girls closed their books and broke into their usual chatter, until Elena asked them to bow their heads for the closing prayer.

Valerie and Janice lingered in the room, obviously planning to finish the conversation that had them laughing at the beginning of class.

Elena headed for the sanctuary and made her way to the pew where Chris and Josh sat with their mother.

"How'd your class go this morning?" Josh asked as he stepped into the aisle to make room for her to enter.

"I'm not exactly sure yet," Elena confessed. "I'm beginning to wish we were studying something simple, like the Old Testament tabernacle or the kings of the northern and southern kingdoms!"

He chuckled.

"How'd you make out?" she asked. "I heard the pastor waylay you the moment you set foot inside the door."

"You're right about that. He asked if I'd give my testimony to the high-school boys' class."

Elena raised her eyebrows. "And did you?"

"Sure. They looked like an interesting assortment of characters, I must say. I offered to sub anytime and find some outside activities for them."

"Well, you're officially back, now." Elena smiled, and the first strains of music filled the church.

"Oh! There's a lovely sunset," Stella Montgomery said later that day as she scooped vanilla ice cream onto two slices of pie.

Dutifully, Josh got up and crossed the room to the kitchen window. "It's a real beaut, Mom. Good to see clear skies again. Here, let me get these for you." He carried the dessert plates to the table and took his seat.

Stella filled their teacups from a china pot on the table and walked to the cupboard for a third cup and saucer. "Don't wait for me. I think I'll take some tea up to Chrissie for her headache."

Josh was barely aware of his mother's return moments later, so deeply engrossed was he in studying an invisible spot on the table. Her voice broke into his reverie. "I think I'll stay home from Bible study tonight and stay with Chris. Are you and Elena planning to go?"

Josh looked up. "Huh? Yes, we're going." He gulped some of the steaming brew and forked his last chunk of pie.

"Something wrong?" she probed gently.

He propped an elbow on the table and rested his chin on his knuckles, meeting her gaze. He swallowed his last mouthful. "Mom, can I ask you something?"

"You know the answer to that, dear."

"Was Laney . . . happy? With Greg, I mean."

"I was wondering when you'd get around to that."

"I guess I can't hide much from you, can I?" he said, a sheepish smile meeting hers.

"No, and neither can she. But I'm afraid I can't answer your question."

"What does that mean?" His eyes searched her face, trying to see clear through to her thoughts.

"Only that Elena never confided in me about that part of her life."

Josh remained silent for several moments. "Maybe not, Mom. But if she could have talked to anyone about things, it would've been you. Weren't there any clues about their relationship?"

Stella took a deep breath and folded her hands in her lap. A frown crossed her features and formed a vee between her gray brows. She turned her clear blue eyes to him. "Well, I can say this. It looked to all the world like a perfect marriage. But for some reason I sensed that it was just a surface appearance."

"Why do you say that?"

"Oh, I don't know if I can put my finger on it. I know Elena. I've loved that girl like she was one of my own. I've watched her grow from a freckle-faced imp with missing front teeth to a sensitive and beautiful young woman. As you say, it was always second nature for her to tell me when something was wrong. But once she was married, a lot of things changed."

"Like?" Josh shifted uneasily in his seat.

"Well, after she and Greg married, they moved out of state and lived away for some years. When Elena's mother became ill and knew that she was dying, Elena and Greg moved back to be near her. Of course, Grace rallied for a while with her daughter and the baby around, but her days came to an end shortly after that."

"That must've been hard on Lane."

His mother nodded. "It was. Very hard. Seems Greg had it in his mind to move on again right after Grace passed away. He sold the family home, despite Elena's emotional attachment to it. But whatever plans he had must've fallen through, I don't know. He bought the little place down the street instead. Elena would come for tea quite often. I always had a feeling that there was something she wanted to talk about, but she never seemed able to bring it up."

Josh leaned back in his chair and stretched his legs under the table. "Hmm. I wonder what the problem was?"

"I've no idea. She was a different person by then. Not the little girl who would tell me her troubles anymore. And she would never come here when Greg was around. I thought it was odd at the time. But I'll tell you one thing, dear. That deep sadness that hides behind her eyes was there long before Greg and little Steven were killed—*and* before her mother passed away."

A deep breath escaped from Josh in the silence that followed. For several moments he sat thinking about what his mother had said. Then, glancing at his watch, he got up. "Thanks, Mom, for telling me what you do know about it. I guess I'd better shave and put on a clean shirt before I pick Lane up for the evening service." After kissing her forehead, he left the kitchen.

Descending the stairs a short time later, he wondered how he would ever fill the drive to church with small talk. One question nagged at his mind.

Whatever happened to you, Laney?

4

Elena shook the raindrops from her blue floral umbrella and placed it in the stand just inside the office door. Mondays are bad enough without ominous gray clouds, she thought, as she hung her navy raincoat in the closet. Smoothing a wrinkle in her skirt, she noticed a run in her nylons and groaned softly.

"Uh-oh. Sounds like normal Monday enthusiasm," said a voice behind her, as a green-clad arm reached past her shoulder and draped a silk scarf over a coat hook.

Elena flashed a smile at her friend. "Morning, Marcy. Lovely day, isn't it?" she teased.

"Well, enjoy it while you can. I just passed Webster and Lawrence out in the hall, and the fur was flying everywhere!" She ran a comb quickly through her sable brown hair and adjusted her sweater over her straight skirt.

Elena grimaced. "Wonderful."

The phone rang as they approached their desks.

"Typical start for the week, not even time to catch our breath," said Marcy. Taking her seat, her polite business voice addressed the phone. "Good morning. Webster and Webster, Marcia Brandon speaking. May I help you?" She paused momentarily. "One moment please, I'll see if he's in his office." She pressed the hold button and signaled a nearby office, but found no response. "I'm sorry, Mrs. Clancy, Mr. Webster is not available at the moment . . . . Yes, I'll be sure to have him call you when he comes in." She replaced the receiver with a sigh.

Elena smirked.

Marcy looked over her shoulder at her. "Oh, by the way, Elena, you have a run in your stocking."

"Well, it's too late to worry about it now. I'll have to get some new ones at lunchtime."

"No you won't. That's why I mentioned it. Here," she said, removing a small package from her desk drawer and holding it out.

27

"Oh, Marcy! Ever the girl scout, even after all these years! What would I do without you?"

"Let's hope we never have to find out," she giggled, as Elena dashed toward the women's room with the new pantyhose.

Returning to her desk a few moments later, Elena found Miriam Thornsby, senior secretary for Webster and Webster, waiting for her. Her foot tapped in impatience as Elena approached.

"Mr. Webster wants you in his office right away. Bring your notebook," she said in clipped tones. She fingered the gold-rimmed spectacles dangling by a cord on her chest and placed them on her beak of a nose, then walked away.

"What is it about Mondays?" Elena said to her friend over her shoulder before opening the door of the inner office.

Later, a somewhat bedraggled Elena plopped into her chair again and cast a forlorn look at Marcy, who was writing a phone message to add to the stack beside her.

The door opened, and an impeccably dressed tall man entered. "Good morning, Miss Brandon. Any messages for me?"

"Only these," Marcy replied, handing him a sizable sheaf of notes. "Oh, and Derek? Your father asked to see you as soon as you arrived."

"Thanks, Marcy," he said, shuffling through the telephone slips. "Mrs. Clancy . . . Mrs. Clancy . . . Mrs. Clancy."

"She phoned a few times."

"So I see." He picked up his briefcase and continued toward his office.

Elena's fingers flew busily over the typewriter keys as Derek approached. She barely had time to look up as she heard his footsteps.

"My, aren't we busy already," he said. "Father must be in one of his moods again."

"Good morning," she said with a smile. "Oh, don't worry about me. I'll be out of here by—" she glanced at her watch, "by midnight. One, at the latest."

His brown eyes crinkled at the corners as he laughed. "Don't overdo, Elena. You'll need a good lunch today. How does Barrington's sound?"

"Well, I—"

"Eleven-thirty. All right?"

"Yes, Mr. Webster," she answered in a dutiful tone. "That'll be fine."

She watched him disappear as he walked through the doorway of the inner office. "Good morning, Miss Thornsby," she heard him say as the door closed behind him.

"Tsk, tsk, tsk," Marcy said, teasing. "Just wait until old Eagle Nose hears that you're fraternizing with the brass again. I think she has designs on a certain young lawyer herself."

"Oh, come on, Marce. A simple lunch or two does not exactly constitute designs on anyone. I've never given Derek the impression that I'm looking for any kind of real relationship. We're just friends, that's all."

"I wonder," mused Marcy.

The phone rang again, and Elena resumed her typing. Two more calls followed in rapid succession before Marcy was free.

Elena looked at her with a puzzled frown. "Why did you say that, Marcy?"

"What do you mean?"

"Something about my having lunch with Derek. I don't remember exactly what it was. You looked like you had something to add."

"Oh, I was just going to comment on how gorgeous the boss's son is. Those big brown velvet eyes, the curly dark hair that always stays in place, . . . whoever sculpted him didn't stop until he was perfect. And his Midas touch hasn't hurt, either. Everything he does is marked for success. Even you must admit, the guy is quite a catch."

"Only you've forgotten one thing. I'm not fishing."

"Maybe *you* aren't."

Elena cocked her head to one side. "Why, Marcy. I don't know what in the world you're talking about."

"I just hope you know what you're doing, that's all."

As if on cue, the door separating the inner and outer offices opened, and the young lawyer emerged. "Ready?" he asked Elena as he stopped at her desk.

That afternoon, Mr. Webster and Miriam were in court for most of the afternoon, which gave Elena time to finish transcribing the dictation she had taken earlier. By the end of the day a neat pile of newly typed briefs and letters lay on her desk, ready to be signed and distributed.

"I didn't think this day would ever end," Marcy said with a sigh, running a hand through her chin-length hair. She stood and stretched her arms above her head. "Any hope for tomorrow?" she asked, resuming a normal pose and straightening her sweater.

"Well, I think it should be slightly calmer, at least."

"Why is that?"

"Derek said that the Lawrence case should be wrapped up by tomorrow or the day after. Their main witness couldn't appear on the stand today. He was sick. That's what the morning's fuss was about. If they managed without him this afternoon, the office might be back to normal tomorrow. If not . . . well, let's not think about that."

"Right."

Coats on and umbrellas in hand, the pair left for the day.

"See you tomorrow, kiddo," Marcy said, as they started to go their separate ways. Elena stopped and turned. "Marce?"

Her friend looked back.

"I forgot to tell you. Josh is back."

"What? You're kidding."

"No, he came home on Friday. To stay, I think."

"Well, what do you know. Say hello for me, okay? Talk to you tomorrow."

Elena smiled and headed for her car. She was glad to relax her weary body for the twenty-minute drive home. Rivulets of rain cascaded down the windows of her red Escort as she crossed the Market Street Bridge and turned toward Kingston. Dusk was already approaching. The culm banks on the west side of the valley were draped in shadow, the black mounds evidence of bygone days when northeastern Pennsylvania was a leading producer of anthracite coal. Most recently, many of the mounds had sprouted more weeds and small trees that hid the dark tailings from view. But now that summer greenery was fading, the culm banks were drab, especially in the dusky light.

Elena was always relieved to pass the old coal-mining area of the valley. She was partial to the rustic hills of Back Mountain, where she lived in the town of Dallas.

Pelted by the driving rain and chilly wind on her way from the car to the front door, Elena smiled with relief when her key turned smoothly. She felt welcomed, for a change, by the inviting, blue-shuttered house.

Inside, she stowed her wet things, lit a fire in the fireplace, and put some supper in the oven to warm. After showering and zipping on a long velour robe, she ate slowly in front of the fire and then curled up with her Bible, working on next week's lesson until she was sleepy enough for bed.

"What'll it be?" Derek asked over his menu on Friday as he and Elena lunched at Cyril's. His brown eyes wandered slowly over her slender form as she studied the list of luncheon entrees. "Have you decided?"

"Oh, chicken salad and a croissant would be fine," she answered, closing the burgundy suede menu and setting it beside her china plate on the crisp linen tablecloth.

Derek summoned the waiter who hovered an arm's length away and placed their order.

While he spoke to the waiter, Elena put her napkin on her lap and said a brief prayer of thanks, unnoticed. Derek had already told her that he felt that prayer belonged strictly in church, not in public places, and she respected his opinion without compromising her own.

"Very good, Mr. Webster," the attendant nodded. He removed the menus, turned on his heel, and walked away.

The table for two was nestled unobtrusively in a sheltered alcove of the large restaurant. The elegance of the thick plum-colored carpeting and heavy mauve drapes took Elena's breath away when she'd first seen the interior. Numerous hanging plants, discreetly placed, provided privacy from the other patrons, and the rich green hue was a reminder of the season just past. Outside the arched windows overlooking the street, trees dressed in fall finery swayed in the wind as lunchtime shoppers passed by.

"How's your day going this time?" Derek asked. "I hope Father's not being too hard on you." He took a drink of ice water from his crystal goblet.

"Actually," answered Elena, "it's been unusually quiet. Even Marcy has commented on it."

"Good. I wouldn't want you to be too tired to enjoy the symphony tonight. You did remember that it was this evening?"

"Yes, I remember." She smiled. "Pieces by Schubert, Brahms, and Debussy. I'm looking forward to it."

The young lawyer started to reach across the table, but the

arrival of their food interrupted the motion. He patted Elena's hand casually, then cleared his throat and straightened the knot on his tie. "Are you sure that will be enough to eat?"

Elena nodded. "It's too pretty to eat, but there's plenty here." She speared an orange slice from the arrangement on her plate, lifted it to her mouth, and closed her eyes at its tangy sweetness. "This is truly lovely."

"I suppose." He took an appraising look at her food.

"You really surprise me, Derek. The chef here is so artistic. I've never been to a more elegant restaurant in my life."

Derek glanced slowly around, as though he were seeing the interior of Cyril's for the first time. He nodded approvingly. "Yes, you're right. It is a beautiful place. I guess I shouldn't take so much for granted."

As soon as their plates were empty, a waiter appeared from nowhere and asked, "Will there be anything more, sir?"

"No, thank you, Blake. That will be all." After paying the bill, Derek stood and offered a hand to Elena, then drove her back to the office. "I have an appointment in Scranton this afternoon," he said as he dropped Elena off at the curb outside the Webster Building. "I'll pick you up at seven, okay?" At her nod, he drove away.

Exiting the elevator, Elena imagined trying to explain to Marcy that a night at the symphony did not necessarily constitute a date, and with a measure of dread she opened the office door and entered.

The sight of Miriam awaiting her return at the desk put her fears on hold. Marcy's inevitable lecture would have to wait until later, Elena thought.

"Mr. Webster wants you to take your notebook in at once," said Miriam. She vanished like vapor immediately after the pronouncement.

"She's a regular little ray of sunshine, isn't she?" Marcy laughed, crossing her eyes.

Elena chuckled. "That she is. See you in a while." Picking up her pen and notebook, she opened the connecting door and closed it behind her.

The while turned out to be two solid hours of dictation. Returning to her desk with enough typing to last forever, the least of her worries was having any time to listen to a lecture from

Marcy or anyone else.

That evening as she put the final touches to her hair, Elena heard someone at the door. "I'm nearly ready, Der—" she began, as she answered it.

A blond giant stood on the step. As Josh's eyes took in her emerald green velvet gown, he whistled faintly under his breath. "I was passing by and thought maybe you could use some company on such a nice night. But I see you've made other plans."

"Josh! I . . . wasn't expecting you," she said lamely.

"So I noticed. Hey, I'll be sure to call ahead next time, okay?" Inclining his head without another word, he walked away.

Elena, her mouth still hanging open, closed the door.

A few moments later, Derek's silver Mercedes sports coupe purred to a stop in the driveway, and the doorbell rang.

"Let me tell you, you look sensational, pet." Derek put her white fur jacket over her shoulders.

Elena winced, wondering why he always chose that nickname. It made her feel as though she were a cat or a dog. She picked up the evening bag lying on the table by the door. "Thanks. You look quite dashing yourself," she said, admiring his charcoal gray tuxedo. She felt a bit like Cinderella, being ushered to a silver chariot and driven off into the night.

The feeling continued as Derek opened one of the polished solid brass doors of the F. M. Kirby Center for the Performing Arts. Once one of Wilkes-Barre's most beautiful cinemas, the huge building had been completely renovated. Elena and Derek walked through the ornate archways of the rose and gold lobby and into the auditorium, which was papered in textured gold. Their feet sank into the rich crimson carpet as they made their way to the plush red velvet seats a few moments before the performance began.

The program began with several of Elena's favorite pieces, and the audience was generous with its applause. But Elena found her mind wandering, for some unknown reason, until she was only vaguely aware of the lilting music. The sound of clapping suddenly jolted her from her thoughts.

"What's the matter?" Derek asked. "Aren't you enjoying the program tonight?"

"Hmm? Oh, I'm sorry, Derek. It's a lovely concert. I've always enjoyed that last piece, by Schubert."

He shook his head and smiled slightly. "The last piece was by Debussy, pet."

Elena bit her lip, relieved that the blush on her face could not be seen in the dim light of the symphony hall. Glancing at the slender watch on her wrist, she wondered if the evening would ever end.

It seemed hours later that the silver coupe delivered her back to her home. Derek accompanied her to the door and opened it for her. His lips lightly brushed her cheek, and with one hand he turned her face so that he could look at her, his brown eyes questioning.

"It was a lovely evening. Thanks for taking me."

He nodded. " 'Night, pet."

Later, her customary Bible reading and prayer finished, Elena slowly dressed for bed. After turning down the pale blue spread and climbing into bed, she lay awake for a long time unraveling her jumbled thoughts. The concert had been filled with beautiful soothing music, but all she had wanted throughout the program was to be home. For the life of her she could not fathom the reason for her melancholy.

5

"Honestly, Janice," said Elena good naturedly, during the class hour one Sunday, "I can't see how you can be so skeptical. Don't you remember our discussion last week that the writers of the Bible wrote under the inspiration of God?"

"Well, of course it would *say* that," scoffed the auburn-haired girl, "or else no one would buy the book!"

At this the whole class dissolved into laughter, and even Elena was caught off balance by Janice's remark. That girl has an uncanny ability to interject a touch of humor into any serious discussion, thought Elena. That's why her brothers are always teasing her: She always seems to know just what to say to come out on top.

"Okay, girls, let's settle down," said Elena, tapping an index finger impatiently on the desk. "It's time to get back to our lesson."

The giggling subsided as the class turned their attention once again to the front of the room. Janice and Valerie exchanged surreptitious glances before feigning looks of innocence as they straightened in their chairs.

"I think it might help, at this point, for us to examine the character of God, as the Bible is His Word. Let's read the verses I've written on the chalkboard." Elena stood and raised the pull-down map that covered the words. "What does it say in Numbers 23:19, Marybeth?"

" 'God is not a man, that he should lie,' " quoted the girl.

Elena repeated her words and continued. "A similar thought is expressed in Titus 1:2. Do you see it? '. . . God, who cannot lie . . .' Now look at Hebrews 6:18. What important phrase do you find in that one, Valerie?"

Valerie moistened her lips with her tongue as she scanned the written verse. " 'It is impossible for God to lie.' "

"Right. God is not a man. He cannot lie. It is impossible for Him to lie. Those are very strong statements."

"But in school they say that the Bible is just a collection of stories and fables," said Valerie, "and that it's full of mistakes. How do we know what to believe?".

Elena smiled. "It's okay to have doubts. They make you want to search for answers, and that's what we're here for—to examine the evidence for ourselves and make up our own minds." She took her seat at the desk. "Man's writings are often marked by contradiction and disunity. Sometimes even books written by the same man can say conflicting things when the writer changes his mind later on in his life or finds new evidence. But the Bible is not like that."

"How is it different?" asked Sharon, the shy red-haired girl in the back row.

"Well, the Bible isn't a bunch of unconnected stories, for one thing. It has only one; the redemption of mankind. And that story runs from one cover to the other, despite the fact that the Bible was written over a period of 1600 years, by forty different men, and in three languages."

She pushed back her chair and pulled down the map to display the world as it was in biblical times. Picking up a pointer, she said, "It was written on three separate continents, Asia, Africa, and Europe. The authors were from all walks of life. Some were prophets, some were priests. There was a shepherd, a king, a doctor, a tax collector, a servant, and even a Pharisee. Yet the Bible is still one unit and has one central theme. The message is always the same."

Janice grimaced. "I don't think we could find *ten* men today who could agree on a subject, even if they had the same career!"

The other girls laughed and shook their heads.

"Well, then," said Elena, "think about that amazing unity. From Genesis to Revelation it tells a single story: the redemption of mankind from sin. Just as branches, roots, trunk, and leaves are part of one tree, the parts of the Bible make up a single unit. It agrees in doctrine, in details of prophecy, in what it says about Jesus, and in its offer to redeem man."

She raised the map again and moved back to the desk. "We have time to look at two more verses. Sharon, would you please read 2 Timothy, Chapter 3, verses 16 to 17 for us?"

" 'All scripture is given by inspiration of God, and is profitable for doctrine, for reproof, for correction, for instruction in righteousness,' " read the girl, " 'that the man of God may be perfect, thoroughly furnished unto all good works.' "

"That is only one of many places in the Bible where we are told how important God considers His Word to be. Now turn to 2 Peter, Chapter 1, verse 21, and we'll read it together."

After the shuffling of pages ceased, Elena began reading, and the girls joined in. " 'For the prophecy came not at any time by the will of man, but holy men of God spoke as they were moved by the Holy Spirit.' " The class looked up.

"Remember what we learned earlier today about the character of God, how it is impossible for Him to lie. Do you think that a God who cannot lie would give us a book that is full of mistakes or fables?"

The girls considered her question and shook their heads.

"Well, then. It must be a book that we can trust."

The room was strangely quiet when the bell sounded to signal the end of the lesson time.

"I hope that some of your questions were answered in our study today," said Elena, smiling. "Now let's bow our heads while we close in prayer."

After the church service later that evening, Josh and Elena stopped at a small restaurant for coffee. Seated in a curved booth near the warmth of a crackling fire, they had only to glance outside to see large feathery snowflakes swirling playfully in the night wind.

"So," Josh said, frowning in mock seriousness as he closed his menu, "it'll be the usual pie à la mode, I presume." He loosened the knot on his tie and pushed up the sleeves of his sweater, looking expectantly at Elena.

She grimaced. "Are you kidding? With strawberry cheesecake in the competition? That's why I brought you here!" Meeting his eyes, she was startled to see that some of the heather green in his sweater was reflected in their gray depths.

"Oh. Right." He nodded, a smile teasing his mouth. "Well, I hope you enjoy it, then."

A waitress arrived at that moment, poured coffee into their brown mugs, and left with their order.

Josh ran his fingers through his hair. "By the way, I'm afraid I won't be around to go to the next midweek service with you. Or the Sunday services. I have to go away for a little while."

Elena looked up from her coffee in surprise. The tiny glass beads on her sweater sparkled among the angora as she moved, catching the firelight. Her coat slipped from her shoulders, and she pulled one side of her fur collar closer.

Josh drank in the sight. She should always wear fur, he thought. And soft things. He cleared his throat. "My partner, Jake, phoned last night. He needs some moral support, and he thinks the time has come for us to do some selling."

"Selling?"

"He's been doing revisions on two of our models, and he says they're looking pretty good. He'd like to try to sell the ideas to some corporation with enough money to produce them in build-at-home kits."

Elena nodded thoughtfully. "Oh. And where will you go?"

"He wants to try a few places in New York and Florida first, and then the Midwest . . . Wisconsin. A few weeks from now we'll have a better idea of the market."

"Do you think the plans will sell?"

"Sure. Some of his ideas are pretty innovative, and the field is always open to new and better designs."

The waitress refilled their mugs and placed their desserts in front of them.

"Say, that cheesecake does look good," said Josh with a smile. "But not as good as my pie."

Alone in her bed later that evening, Elena's thoughts bounced like a Ping Pong ball back and forth between her two male friends, and she struggled to organize her feelings into some rational manner. Always a perfect gentleman, Derek made her feel feminine and special, she rationalized. Yet one element was lacking in his life: a religious influence of any kind. Elena knew that the Websters considered Sunday to be more of a social day than anything else, and Derek had politely refused several invitations she had extended to attend special services with her. He also seemed uncomfortable whenever she would begin to talk about the Lord, and he lightly scorned her attempts to 'convert' him, as he called it. Whenever he took her out it was to a neutral activity he knew she would enjoy.

Josh, on the other hand, was totally committed to the Lord, she reflected. She found it refreshing to be able to discuss deep spiritual concepts and experiences with him. They felt the same way about many things. She could always be herself when she was with Josh, and she didn't have to watch what she said. It was always fun to be with him. But then, he *is* family, isn't he? she asked herself. Just like a brother.

She wondered what Josh would think of Derek and if he'd approve of her relationship with him, then chided herself for the thought. What was there for him to approve? Derek was just a friend. Her thoughts continued far into the night, despite all attempts to quiet them. Toward dawn she finally drifted off into a restless sleep.

On Wednesday, Elena baked cranberry bread and decided to take a loaf to Stella. She dressed warmly against the chill and walked the short incline to the Montgomery home nestled at the foot of a tree-covered hill. Smoke curled up from the stone chimney abutting the large stone house with yellow and white awnings and shutters. Snow blanketed the neatly kept yard as she entered the gate.

"Elena, dear," Stella said, answering the door bell with a smile. "Come in, come in. I was just thinking of you. Let me take your coat." She held out a hand and welcomed Elena in, closing the door behind her.

Elena put the loaf of warm bread into Stella's hand instead, while she unbuttoned her wrap.

"Oh, cranberry bread," said Mrs. Montgomery as she opened the plastic wrap to sniff the loaf. "How nice of you. Come and sit by the fire. I'll put on some tea."

Elena removed her coat, walked into the inviting ivory-colored living room, and sank into the comfort of a blue and peach floral chair near the fireplace. She glanced around at the abundance of lush plants, admiring Stella's green thumb. The Boston fern hanging in perfect symmetry in the center of the big picture window had always been Elena's favorite. Her eyes drifted to an array of philodendron and other trailing plants, their showy foliage displayed in containers placed at various levels of a wicker étagère in the corner. Living things seemed to flourish under the care of her dear friend, she noticed.

Elena relaxed deeply in the chair for several moments. She felt at home. Her mind floated back over so many treasured memories as the maternal sound of Mrs. Montgomery's humming in the kitchen touched her ears. Elena closed her eyes against the memory of her own mother singing hymns while she worked. Had she really been gone for years? she mused. A small sigh escaped her.

Stella returned to the room with a tray of refreshments that she placed on a nearby coffee table. After pouring tea into two bone china cups, she handed one to Elena and dropped a sugar lump into her own. Then she took a seat in a matching chair opposite her guest.

Reaching across the space between them for Elena's hand, Stella offered a prayer of blessing in her familiar quiet way. Glancing up once again, she gestured toward the plate of fancy cookies and sliced nut bread. "Have something with your tea, dear," she said with a smile. "You've been losing weight again. Am I right?"

Elena laughed. "Who'd have thought I'd ever be thin, Mother? I never knew what it was like not to be on a diet." She leaned over for a slice of bread and a cookie and placed them on a napkin in her lap. "That's one of the things Greg was always—" The sentence was left dangling in the silence as she bit her lip and shook her head.

Stella watched an unexplained emotion cloud the younger woman's eyes for an instant. "Just don't go making yourself sick. A few more pounds would really do you justice, you know." She paused. "Oh, I hope you don't think I'm nagging you."

"Don't worry," said Elena. "I'd never think that." She took a bite of nut bread and sipped her tea. "Mmmm. This is good. By the way, where's Chris today? I thought I'd see her too."

"She's visiting some local churches. Pastor Douglas suggested that the missionary societies in the area might be interested in hearing about the hospital. Even if they can't give financial support, they might be willing to pray for the endeavor or provide help in obtaining supplies."

"That sounds like a good idea," said Elena. "I'd never thought of trying other churches."

"The pastor gave her quite a list of people to see. Maybe some of them will invite her to speak to their groups."

"Well, it sounds like she's going to be busy, then, on this *vacation* of hers," remarked Elena with raised brows.

Stella nodded. "In fact, she won't be home until late. Would you like to stay and have supper with me, dear? I've already gotten used to having company around again, and I rather like it."

"If you don't go to a lot of trouble."

"Oh, it's no trouble at all. I have a casserole ready to pop into the oven, and I'll get it going right now." She rose and walked toward the kitchen, disappearing through the louvered cafe-style doors.

Elena gathered the remnants of afternoon tea and carried the tray into the kitchen, where Stella was already fussing with preparations. Placing the tray on the counter, she returned the leftover cookies to the familiar ceramic cookie jar and wrapped the bread with the remainder of the loaf.

Outside the window, leaden skies were already turning darker as the last remnant of daylight faded by the moment. Elena washed and dried the teacups and saucers as she watched a few tentative snowflakes float softly to the ground.

"Looks like we're in for more snow tonight," she said as she removed plates and silverware from the cupboard and crossed the room to set the table.

"Yes, I expect so," replied Stella. She spooned some home-canned fruit into two small dishes and set them to cool in the refrigerator. "Josh phoned at noon and said that it was already snowing heavily in upstate New York."

Elena smiled, and her voice took on a sudden softness. "It's been wonderful, hasn't it, having him back?"

Stella's eyes glistened, and she stepped near enough to pat Elena's hand. "Yes," she said as a sudden tear glided down her plump cheek. "Just as if he'd never been away. I'm afraid I wasn't quite ready to give him up so soon again."

"Give him up?" echoed Elena as she looked up from the napkin she had folded and placed under a fork. "Do you expect him to be away a long time, then?" A small frown drew her brows together.

Stella dabbed her cheek with a handkerchief from her dress pocket. "No, not very long. I don't know what got into me." Smiling, she put the hanky back in its place. "He said only a few weeks. Just as long as Jake needs him for this venture."

"What's Jake like, Mother? Have you ever met him?"

"Yes." Stella pulled out a chair from the table and took a seat, motioning for Elena to do the same. "We might as well be comfortable. Supper won't be ready for a little while."

Elena sat down and folded her hands in her lap, waiting for Stella to elaborate.

"Josh took me for a drive to Williamsport one day, and introduced me to Jake Sanders and his father. When Piper Aircraft ceased operations there, Mr. Sanders retired with the wealth he had acquired as an executive with the company. He bought a large farm in that area and stayed. He and Jake converted the outbuildings to workshops, and they've worked together on the experimental planes ever since. I believe that Mr. Sanders is in poor health now, and the business is entirely in Jake's hands. Josh has spent quite a lot of time there, working with Jake and his father."

"And that's why he's Jake's partner now," said Elena, thinking out loud.

The timer sounded, and Stella got up to remove the casserole from the oven. "Well, I just pray that things will go well for them both," she said as she returned to the table, "so that Josh can come back home."

Elena was surprised at how strongly she shared the same feeling.

By the time she left the Montgomery home, falling snow had obliterated the ground that had been covered by previous flurries, and it was still coming down at an impressive rate. Heavy and wet, it fell straight to the ground in the dark and windless night.

Elena's boots left deep imprints in the slushy snow as she walked down the street to her cottage. Blinking snowflakes off her long lashes, Elena closed her eyes and lifted her face to feel the refreshing coolness as the delicate crystals melted against her warm skin. The visit with Josh's mother had refreshed her spirit. They had prayed together before Elena left. Her thoughts drifted to the Bible verse from Stella'a morning devotions that the older woman had shared with her, a favorite of Elena's from Psalm 94. " 'In the multitude of my thoughts within me thy comforts delight my soul,' " Elena quoted to the night.

Her hand brushed the taillight of her red Escort as she passed. Parked in front of her house, much of it was buried under a snowy cap. The unfamiliar shape looked a bit comical in the beam from the borrowed flashlight, and Elena smiled to herself. "You know," she said to the car, "it's always a comfort to know you're around. And I feel the same way about Josh. I hope he won't be gone long."

6

"Old Thornsby must be in a rare mood today," said Marcy as she and Elena entered the sandwich shop on the first floor of the Webster Building. "Imagine her suggesting you and I have lunch at the same time."

Elena shrugged. "Well, unexpected or not, it was nice of her. After all, Mr. Webster kept me busy through my own lunch break."

Noticing a small table near a window, they seated themselves and removed the list of luncheon specials from the silver holder.

"Whatever the soup of the day is, that's what I'm having," said Elena. "I can't seem to get warm today."

"Sounds good to me, too. Want to split a ham on rye to go with it?"

Elena nodded and gave their order to a waitress who had approached them with pad in hand. "I wonder what Miriam's problem *is*, anyway?"

"Oh, she's harmless, really. I think that she just feels a little threatened with you around, that's all."

"Threatened? By a part-time secretary?"

"Well, sure. She's been with Mr. Webster since day one. Now suddenly there are younger girls around who can cope with word processors and data entry, not to mention electronic typewriters that correct spelling and remember lines. It must make her feel like she's part of some other era, especially since Mr. Webster now depends on you to handle so many more duties."

"Hmmm. Funny, I hadn't thought of that before. I'm not here to make a career for myself, you know. This job merely fills time for me."

"I know, kiddo."

When lunch was placed before them, Marcy offered a short prayer of thanks, then sipped her tea. "Miriam's a very unhappy person."

"Why do you say that?"

43

"Well, my mom went to school with her. According to her, Miriam was jilted years ago by the man of her dreams. He pulled the classic routine and left her at the altar in a church filled with people."

"How awful! No wonder she seems so bitter. Perhaps she never got over her lost love."

"Speaking of lost loves, have you heard from Josh since he's been away?"

Elena nearly choked on a bite of sandwich, but recovered.

"Well, has he called you or anything?" her friend prompted.

"No, actually. He hasn't called me or anything. Why should you think he would?"

Chuckling, Marcy just shook her head and brushed a lock of shiny sable hair out of her eyes.

Josh stared absently at the TV set in his motel room. A complete waste of time, he thought, as he got up and turned it off. He crossed the room, lay down on the brown plaid bedspread, drew up his arms, and locked both hands behind his head. His elbow knocked the phone off the hook. He replaced the receiver, raked his fingers through his tousled hair, and lay back down.

I wonder what she's doing? he thought. *I've got to hear her voice.* He sat up and rested a palm on the telephone. *No you don't,* an inner voice challenged, *she's probably out with that bloke she's been seeing, whoever he is. What time is it there, anyway? Maybe it's too late to call.* He glanced at his watch. *No, there's just an hour's difference. It's only nine-thirty.*

Pacing the floor like a caged lion, he glanced again at the phone, that black miracle of science, on the nightstand beside the bed. *This is just like all my other nights on this trip,* he thought. *Me versus the phone.* He remembered placing calls to her from other motels, once when her line was busy, once when there was no answer, and even once just to hear her phone ring. He had hung up after the first ring.

This is insane, Josh told himself. *What's a stupid phone call?* He sat down on the bed and dialed her number. Relief washed over him like a warm South Pacific wave when Elena answered.

"Hello?"

"Hi. It's me. Josh."

"Josh! Hi. I—I was just thinking about you. Where are you?"

"In Wisconsin . . . Oshkosh." He wanted to say, *I've been thinking about you, too. In fact, you're all I think about.* But he resisted the temptation. "We got here the day before yesterday."

"Oshkosh? Isn't that where the Experimental Aircraft Museum you told me about is located?"

"Yes. We'll be talking to two of the directors tomorrow."

"You will? You mean a museum would be interested in buying your models, Josh?"

"Well, they do buy and sell planes, periodically, but most of their finest aircraft are donated or are on loan to them."

"Then you're hoping they'll want to display some of yours."

"That's one thing we'll be discussing."

"How'd the rest of your trip go?"

"Not bad. We've signed contracts to deliver final specs on two of our models."

"Well, that's an awfully good start, wouldn't you say?"

"Pretty fair." Does she know how her voice sings? he wondered. "How are you, Lane?"

"Fine, keeping busy, you know. Is it cold there?"

"Very. Especially after Florida. There's a foot of new snow on the ground and drifts about four feet high in places. How's Pennsylvania?"

"Cold, damp, dreary, the usual. We had snow a few days ago, and it's been trying to start up again ever since."

Neither spoke for a moment. Josh twisted the cord around his finger.

"Um, will you be gone much longer?" she asked.

He took a deep breath, feeling as though he'd been away for a month already, but it had been just two weeks. "Well, we have a few people to see in the next couple of days. After that we'll be in Colorado." He switched the phone to his other ear. "We should be home sometime in the next week or two."

"Oh," she said softly.

He wondered if he'd heard a note of disappointment in her voice. "How's your class going?"

"Surprisingly well. I'm learning almost as much as the girls. One week we covered fulfilled prophecies, and the next, the way God's hand has protected the Bible against those who try to destroy it."

"Its very existence is a miracle of its own. It's hard to understand how people can refuse to believe it's God's Word. And the only hope we have."

"Well, I know two new believers who'd agree with that."

"Really? Great! I've been praying every day for you and your girls." *Of course*, he thought, *most of my prayers are exclusively for you*. He smiled to himself.

"Your prayers are definitely helping, that's for sure. Now that the girls have a new view of the Bible, they want to find out what it has to say about dating, prayer, and things that concern their everyday lives."

"That should be fun."

"I'm hoping so."

"Oh well, I suppose I should let you go. For tonight, anyway. I . . . was just wondering how you were."

"It's sure been nice talking to you. I'll be praying that everything goes well for you and Jake."

"Thanks, Lane. Take care, now. God bless."

"You, too. Bye."

The following morning, Marcy set a mug of steaming coffee on Elena's desk. "That bad, huh?"

"What?" Elena asked, startled as the voice intruded on her thoughts. "Oh, sorry."

"I couldn't help noticing the quiet on this side of the room. You were so engrossed in that terminal I thought maybe your favorite soap was on."

Elena smiled. "Oh, Marce, I don't know what's the matter with me. It's awful. I have this whole stack of files and expenses to put in the computer, and I can't seem to concentrate."

Marcy raised her eyebrows and started to open her mouth, but the phone rang. Pleated skirt swaying, she crossed the office to her desk. "Good morning, Webster and Webster. Marcia Brandon speaking."

Elena sipped her coffee. Then with deliberate effort, she focused her eyes on the computer and began typing.

"Sure looks busy out here," said Derek as he closed the inner office door and approached Elena's desk. "I've signed these letters, so they're ready to go out." He placed them on her blotter.

She looked up and nodded.

"Speaking of going out," he continued, noticing that Marcy was involved in a telephone conversation, "you've turned down my last three lunch invitations. Anything wrong?"

"Not really."

"How about today, then?" he asked, sitting down on the one clear corner of her desk. "Would you like to have lunch?"

Taking a deep breath, Elena met Marcy's eyes on the other side of the room and turned her chair to face Derek squarely. "Well, thanks, but I don't think so. Not today."

The phone rang again, and Marcy's efficient response carried from across the room.

"I see." Derek frowned. "Well, look. A friend of mine is having an art exhibit a week from Friday. I was wondering if you'd like to go with me." He studied her. "You can think about it, okay? I'll check back with you."

Elena sighed unconsciously. "Oh, there's no need for that. An art exhibit sounds like fun."

"Excuse me, Derek," Marcy said, holding the receiver away from her ear. "There's a call for you. Shall I put it through to your office?"

He nodded as he stood and looked back at Elena. "Good. I'll let you know the details later."

"What was that all about?" Marcy asked, after the office door closed behind him.

"Oh, nothing much," Elena said, a spot of color rising in each cheek. "Just an art exhibit."

Marcy bit her lip thoughtfully. "Laney."

"Marce, please. Not today, okay?" she said, turning to face the computer screen. She was glad when the phone rang and distracted her friend.

Dressing with care in a pale green dress of crushed silk, Elena fastened the clasp on the silver belt. It would be a good opportunity to wear her silver heels, she thought, as yesterday's rain had washed away all traces of snow and slush.

A smile softened her lips as the memory of a second phone call from Josh two nights before drifted into her mind. How sweet of him to think of me and keep in touch while he's away, she thought. The smooth purr of Derek's car drew her out of her reverie, and she grabbed her coat of champagne and white shadow pile.

They dined in a small French restaurant with red and white checked tablecloths. Small candles in shallow red glass holders on each table cast an intimate glow around the cafe and contrasted gently with the flickering shadows from sconces on each wall. A dark-haired girl in peasant costume playing a guitar and singing French love songs added to the aura of romance. But Elena's thoughts were elsewhere.

"What are you thinking about, pet?" Derek asked quietly, studying Elena's face as she watched the singer.

"Oh, nothing, really." She couldn't remember what she'd been thinking when his voice had interrupted her train of thought.

"Would you care for some dessert?"

"No, thank you," she said, smiling. "I've had more than enough already, and it was wonderful."

"Well, then, we'd better be on our way to the exhibit, I suppose." Rising, he helped her with her coat.

Shortly, Derek steered Elena through the crowd at the gallery. "I must say, I'm really impressed," he said. "Julian's sketching hobby has gone big time. What do you think of his work?"

"I quite like the landscapes in oil. Something about them touches me." She stopped, arrested by a rendering of a waterfall cascading into a quiet, shadowed pool. "Just look at his use of color here, Derek. The greens are so fresh, it's almost like God has just finished creating this place. The shadows are cool, as though His hand is only now moving away, and everything is still new. I could pray forever in a place like that."

A slight frown crossed Derek's face, and he stepped back to gaze at the work. "He does have exceptional talent, and this is just a mere introduction to it."

"Really?"

"Oh, yes. In prep school he amazed everyone with pen-and-ink drawings of professors and classmates. And to think he once considered foregoing this to practice law."

Elena shook her head in wonder.

"Let's check out the pastels in the other room, and I'll introduce you to Julian Sinclair, my artistic friend."

Later that evening outside Elena's cottage, Derek gave her the waterfall painting she had admired. He leaned forward and brushed her lips softly with his. "I'd buy the world for you, if you'd only allow it," he whispered. "You know that, don't you, pet?"

Elena stiffened and drew a deep breath. "Please, Derek. I don't want anything, really. It was sweet of you to buy this for me. I love it. But you didn't have to. You're much too kind to me already, and sometimes it's hard for me to take. Do you know what I mean?"

Derek cocked his head to one side and studied her, a puzzled frown on his face.

Her eyes pleaded for him to understand. "I had a really special time with you tonight. But I must go in now. Thank you. I'll see you at work Monday, okay?"

He touched her cheek softly with a fingertip and, finding no response from her, smiled thinly and walked away.

Inside, Elena closed the door and set the painting against the wall as she stared unseeing at the wooded scene. Were Marcy's suspicions right after all? she wondered. Was he hoping for more than friendship? He *said* he wasn't, in the beginning, she remembered. She slipped off her coat and draped it over a chair. The house felt as cold as her heart. Moving to the fireplace, she touched a match to the logs and sat on the arm of the couch watching as the kindling blazed to life.

A soft tapping on the door startled Elena, and she jumped up to answer it, wondering if Derek had forgotten something.

Josh stood in the glow of the porch light. Elena's eyes widened in surprise.

"I know I should've phoned, but I was on my way past and thought I'd take a chance you were . . . alone. Who was he, by the way?"

Elena couldn't meet his eyes. Glancing at the floor as Josh stepped inside, she closed the door behind him. She opened her mouth to speak, but he gave her no time.

"Nice fire." A half-smile played on his lips. "Mind if I sit down?"

"Of—of course not," she stammered. "Have a seat. Can I offer you some coffee? Hot chocolate?"

"My question first." He settled back against the plump ruffled cushions of the navy calico sofa and rested an ankle on his knee.

"It was just Derek. From the office. You know, Derek Webster. He took me to a friend's art exhibit tonight." To her dismay, Elena felt herself blushing as Josh's cool gray eyes searched her face. She felt that he could see into her soul.

"Coffee," he said belatedly. His eyes narrowed as he continued to study her.

Relieved to excuse herself for a few minutes, Elena went to the kitchen to brew the coffee. After filling the cream pitcher, she turned around and bumped into Josh's muscled chest. Some of the milk splashed over onto his shirt sleeve, and Elena gasped.

"Tsk, tsk, tsk," he teased, laughing, as Elena blushed profusely. "Aren't we nervous."

"I—I'm sorry. I don't know what's come over me. Let me get a cloth for that."

But Josh was already at the sink dabbing the wet spot. "The rising young attorney himself? *The* Derek Webster?" he asked suddenly. "The one in the society columns?"

"Oh, Josh, really! He's just a friend, that's all. Just a friend . . . like you."

"That," he said, "somehow doesn't comfort me. Let's have our coffee, okay?" He poured coffee into the mugs that Elena had set out and carried them into the living room.

She hesitated, trying to still the ridiculous pounding of her heart. Refilling the pitcher and arranging the sugar bowl and spoons on a tray calmed her a bit.

Josh replaced the stoker in the rack as Elena came into the room. Their eyes met, and he winked at her. "Laney, relax, will you? It's only me. I didn't mean to come down so hard on you. Peace?" Sliding one hand casually into a trouser pocket, he raised his eyebrows in question.

Elena eyed him speculatively before allowing a smile to soften her face in agreement to the truce. Placing the tray beside the coffee mugs on the table, she sat down.

Still standing near the mantel, Josh reached for a set of pictures in a hinged double frame. "Steven?" he asked simply, after eyeing the other photo, a family portrait.

"Yes. That was taken shortly before . . ."

"He has your eyes. He looks like he must have been a very special little boy. I'd have liked to have known him." After studying the second portrait, his gaze returned to the one of Steven. He replaced the frame and walked over to the couch.

Elena sat with her legs crossed, staring into the flames. Josh took a seat near her and poured milk into his coffee, then leaned back to sample it.

"I really miss him, you know?" Elena said with a strange little smile on her lips. "The house was so full of him, of his presence everywhere, little reminders of him. Of us together."

She paused for a moment, her quiet breathing almost silent in the crackling and popping of the fire. "I rattled around in here by myself for a long time. Sometimes it got pretty bad. Once I nearly sold the house, but I had nowhere else to go. Greg had already . . . disposed of Mom's place." Her voice rang with a vague touch of bitterness, and she swallowed hard.

Josh's large hand covered Elena's as if to comfort her, and he smiled, without speaking.

Elena looked over at him self-consciously. "Sorry, I didn't mean to go on like that." She took a small sip and wrapped her fingers around the mug in her hands. "Tell me about your trip. Were you able to accomplish all that you had hoped?" In the flickering firelight, she studied the play of light and shadow on his face.

"Things went well all around. I'm glad we went out to get an idea of the market. It gave us both a new perspective. Listen," he said, standing up and stretching his long arms, "I think it's time for me to be on my way. It's sure going to feel great to sleep in my own bed again, after that long string of motels. Thanks for the visit, and the coffee."

Elena rose as he walked over to retrieve his jacket.

" 'Night," he said with a smile as he left.

"Good night," she answered. She closed the door and turned, leaning back against it, conscious of the fading sound of the Thunderbird as it pulled away. A glow of warmth flowed upward from her chest and settled softly on her cheeks.

7

The first blizzard of the year arrived the day before Thanksgiving. Snow piled high upon rooftops, softening contours and edges, all but burying fence posts and mailboxes. By late afternoon, area roads were impassable. All schools in the Back Mountain had canceled classes a day ahead of schedule because of the impending storm. Many businesses were forced to close early. Elena was relieved that Wednesday was her regular day off. This was no day to be driving anywhere, she knew, much less home from the valley in the afternoon rush hour.

The world outside was breathtaking as Elena gazed through the window at the evergreens in the front yard. Weighted down heavily by the wet snow, they resembled giant snow maidens in fluffy gowns of white ermine. Telephone lines coated by an inch of ice and snow dipped deeply from pole to pole. And still the snow fell.

At the sound of the ringing telephone, her fingers released the slats of the miniblinds. She crossed the room and picked up the receiver. "Hello?"

"Elena? It's Derek."

"Oh, hi. What's up?"

"Nothing much. We'll be closing the office early today, with the storm and all. How's everything out your way?"

"It's beginning to look like Alaska! We must have a good fourteen inches of snow already, with no letup in sight. How is it down in the valley?"

"Well, not as bad as that, yet. We have about eight or nine inches so far, and it's supposed to turn into sleet this evening. Listen, the reason I called is, Father suggested that you take Friday off too. There's nothing to do that can't wait until Monday, and the roads should be clear by then."

"That sounds good, if you're sure you won't need me. I'll see you on Monday, then. Thanks."

"Sure. Have a nice Thanksgiving."

"You, too. Bye."

Replacing the phone on the hook, Elena's mind drifted back to last year's Thanksgiving, when Derek had invited her to spend the day with his family. Needing a change, she had accepted the offer. Even now the memory held a measure of chagrin for her.

Elegantly coiffured and wearing the latest Paris original, Derek's tall, plump mother had swept into the room in a cloud of Chanel to greet Elena. Her large fingers flashed with rings, and bracelets clanged on her heavy wrists as she shook Elena's hand. Only the merest hint of a polite smile presented itself beneath a cocked eyebrow as Elena felt a sweeping glance assess her tweed suit and ruffled blouse to within five dollars of its value.

"How good of you to come, my dear," she said, in perfectly modulated tones. "Be sure Derek takes you around to meet our other guests." Then excusing herself with a slight nod of her head, she turned to greet a distinguished couple entering the foyer.

Some of the exotic dishes served during the meal were new to Elena. She sampled everything but the wine, which was poured from a crystal carafe by a servant in formal attire and white gloves. Much of the conversation centered around European travel and dignitaries whose names she did not recognize. No blessing had been asked over the food, nor was any mention made of the purpose of the holiday. The meal seemed to last forever, or so Elena thought.

Afterward, when the men retired to the library for cigars and the ladies to the drawing room for tea, Derek took Elena for a drive through the Country Club Estates before taking her home. By the time she had climbed into bed that evening, she had a headache and was exhausted.

This year would be different, she knew. Familiar surroundings, dear friends, an opportunity to share in thankfulness for blessings received throughout the year, and last of all, a candlelight service at church. Elena looked forward to it all.

There was a knock at the door, and Elena opened it to find Tommy Brent, a neighborhood boy who lived in the house that was once her mother's, standing with a shovel in his hand.

"Would you like your walk shoveled?" he asked, his pink cheeks aglow in the frosty air.

"Sure," Elena said. "But you might end up having to do it twice, with this storm."

"Yeah, looks like it, but I don't mind."

"You're always around when I need you, Tommy. I think I'll go whip up some brownies while you start, okay?" At his nod, she closed the door and went to the kitchen to preheat the oven, knowing that he'd make short work of her sidewalk and porch.

"Say, you've been busy," said Josh the next day, when he came to walk Elena to his house for the Thanksgiving meal. "I've been shoveling all day at our place."

"Oh, Tommy Brent came yesterday. He shovels the snow for me every winter," she said. "He mows the lawn in the summer and takes care of the walk in wintertime."

"I see. Gives him a few dollars, now and then, for college, right?"

"Something like that. He's a nice kid. I'm glad he lives in my old house," she said, glancing wistfully at her childhood home as she and Josh approached the Montgomerys' cottage.

Only a dusting of snow coated the front walk as Josh opened the gate, and Elena noticed that the path to the side entrance and the driveway were also cleared. A few leftover flakes swirled in lazy circles to the ground, but a break in the clouds was visible as the dull gray bank inched silently away. They stomped the snow off their boots and entered, greeted by the delicious aroma of roast turkey.

"Elena! Hi!" said Chris, rushing up to give her a hug. "Let me take your coat."

"Hi, Chris. It's good to see you." Elena removed her boots and set them on the boot tray next to the door while Chris hung her coat in the closet. "Is there anything I can do to help?"

"Sure is. You can come up to my room while I show you the clothes I've bought for my trip."

Josh winced. "Just don't keep her too long. I'm starving."

"Oh, don't worry, we'll be down in a flash. I'm expecting company." Laughing, the pair ran up the stairs and entered a bedroom at the end of the hall.

No pile of clothing was anywhere in sight as Elena scanned the room. "So, where is everything?"

"Well, I have gotten a few things I needed," Chris answered, "but I had something else to show you." She bit her bottom lip and checked over her shoulder as if to ensure herself that no one had followed. Quietly closing the door, she turned to Elena.

Elena was confused by Chris's strange expression. "Chris," she prompted, "what is it?"

"I just had to show somebody before I explode," she said, a huge smile breaking over her face. She drew her left hand from behind her skirt and displayed an exquisite diamond ring sparkling on her third finger.

"Oh!" Elena gasped. "You're engaged? I can't believe it! Josh didn't mention anything about it."

"That's because I haven't told him yet, or Mom. I wanted to surprise them."

"Boy, you and your brother are big on surprises, aren't you?" Elena said, shaking her head in wonder. "But I couldn't be happier for you if you were my own little sister. I can't wait to see the looks on their faces when you break the news. Who is he, anyway?"

"His name is Philip Taylor, and you'll meet him at dinner. He should be here any moment. That's probably him now," she said, as the doorbell sounded. "We'd better go down now. Oh, and Elena?"

"Yes?"

"Act normal, okay?" After a hug and a giggle of conspiracy, they assumed what they hoped were casual faces and descended the stairs.

Seated at the head of the magnificently laden table some moments later, Stella nodded to Josh. "Will you ask the blessing, dear?"

Everyone joined hands and bowed their heads while he prayed. Once again the memory of the previous Thanksgiving flashed into Elena's mind, and she offered her own prayer of thanks that she was with her own family and friends.

"So, Philip," said Josh, as he passed the platter of turkey to Elena, "Chris told us that you'll be part of the Peru team. Are you a doctor?"

"No, I'm afraid not. I'm an electrical engineer."

Stella Montgomery placed some cranberry sauce on her plate and looked up. "Oh, so you'll be handling the hospital power supply, then?"

"Yes, ma'am," he replied.

"Phil will be doing a lot of the wiring and circuit work during the building of the hospital, Mom," said Chris, looking at Philip and smiling. "And while we're in our temporary quarters he'll be responsible for the portable generators that supply the power for the equipment."

"Do you think it will take long to complete the hospital?" asked Elena.

Philip took a sip of coffee and set his cup down. "That will depend on the climate. The advance team has almost completed our base camp, so we'll be able to offer medical services to the area farmers soon after we arrive. We'll begin work on the hospital immediately."

"Will you be using any Indian laborers?" Josh asked.

Philip nodded. "Some have already signed on for the coming year, I've been told."

When they finished with dinner, Stella began to clear the remaining food from the table. Elena refilled the coffee cups, and Chris served the pumpkin and mincemeat pies.

After dessert, a glowing Chris got up to make an announcement. All eyes fastened upon her as expectant faces turned in her direction.

Philip swallowed his last mouthful of pumpkin pie and straightened nervously in his chair. He brushed a lock of ebony hair back from his forehead as Chris looked at him and smiled.

"Mom, Josh, Elena," she began, "I want to thank you for welcoming Philip and making him feel at home. He's my very best friend in the whole world, and without his encouragement I probably never would have qualified for the Peru team, or been accepted on it. He's a very special person."

Philip adjusted the knot on his tie and cleared his throat. Everyone applauded.

"Well," she continued, a slight flush appearing on her cheeks, "I—um—I didn't want this to be a big speech." She wilted downward to her seat.

Philip's jaw dropped open, and Elena's head tilted to one side. "Chris?" they said in unison.

Chris stood up once again. "Okay, so there is one more thing to tell you. Philip and I . . . we . . . he's asked me to marry him, . . . and I've said yes." In one fluid motion, she sat down.

Stella Montgomery's hand flew to her heart, and for a long speechless moment, no one moved. All eyes switched to Philip and back to Chris. Then Josh laughed and stood up, extending his hand to the young man. "Well, buddy, you've made quite a catch. Congratulations!"

Smiling, Stella wiped a tear from the corner of her eye and got up to hug Chris and Philip. "Chrissie, dear," she said to her daughter, "I must say, this comes as a bit of a surprise to us all. But I have prayed so often that the Lord would lead you to the one of His choice. If Philip is that person, this is a very special Thanksgiving for me."

"Thanks, Mom," said Chris, hugging her mother.

Stella turned to Philip and leaned over to kiss his cheek. "I thank the Lord that she has found someone like you. She has mentioned you often in her letters and spoken so highly of you. I often wondered if perhaps there could be more to the relationship than what she'd told us! I'm glad that we have finally been able to get to know you a bit."

"Thank you," he answered. "I feel the same about all of you."

"So when is the wedding?" Elena asked.

"Mom," Chris said, turning to her mother, "do you think we could arrange a small wedding next week?"

"Mercy!" Stella sank to the nearest chair, her hand once again on her heart. She looked helplessly at Josh, then Elena, then back at Chris.

Her daughter continued. "Philip's parents are planning to attend our farewell banquet next Saturday night, so perhaps we could have a small ceremony early that afternoon. We don't want anything fancy, just the people we love, sharing our joy." She leaned her head against Philip's shoulder, and he put his arm around her. She was beaming.

"Well," said Stella, "we'll talk to the pastor tonight after the service and see what can be arranged."

How much in love they are, thought Elena. *I wonder if we ever looked that way, Greg and I? Funny how people always start out in love. Till death do us part, we said. Only it isn't only death that parts people; sometimes it's life.*

"Isn't that right, Elena?" Stella's voice jolted her from her thoughts.

"Excuse me?" she said, a faint blush coloring her cheeks. "I'm afraid I wasn't listening."

"I was just telling Chris that you probably have some good ideas for the wedding and would help out. Isn't that right?"

Elena blinked twice and drew a deep breath. "Of course. The three of us will put our heads together and do the best we can. It'll be fun."

Only Josh had caught the way her eyes had misted when she was lost in thought. Fingers stroking his jaw line, he continued to watch her, certain that the sudden joviality she was displaying was the opposite of the way she felt. Something was definitely troubling her, and, somehow, he would find out what it was.

8

As Elena sat in the quietness of the Sunday school room, her thoughts drifted back to Chris's wedding the day before. The day had been perfect, the sky a brilliant blue against white snowdrifts, as two families gathered in the sanctuary to witness the simple ceremony uniting the young couple.

Chris had worn a tea-length dress of white chantilly lace, her blond hair shining beneath the veil she had borrowed from Elena. Philip and Josh had stood resplendent in gray pinstripe suits, and Elena's velvet dress of dusty rose had complemented the other colors. The pastor's wife had prepared a wedding tea for the gathering, served with heart-shaped sandwiches and a double-tiered wedding cake.

After the farewell banquet later that evening, the newlyweds had left for a honeymoon trip to New York City, where they would spend the next several days. The Peru team was slated to depart from New York at the end of the week.

Elena wondered what lay ahead for her friends once they were far away from their families and homeland. She breathed a prayer for their future, that the Lord would keep His hand upon them and bless their lives in His service.

The church bell rang, signaling the Sunday school hour. Almost immediately the door opened and the girls, laughing and whispering, entered and took their seats.

"Good morning, class," Elena said with a smile. "It's good to see all of you here today. I was afraid the snow would keep some of you home."

Janice cast a sly wink in Valerie's direction and looked at Elena with a perfectly straight face. "You *know* we would never miss Sunday school."

Wishing that were only true, Elena flashed a grin. "Oh, sure."

Janice laughed aloud, and the others suppressed giggles.

After taking the roll, Elena asked Marybeth to offer the opening prayer, and the girls settled down.

"I'm afraid our new manuals haven't arrived," said Elena, "so I thought we would try something different."

"Like what?" asked Valerie.

"Well, we could look up Scriptures about things you might be interested in. Several of you may have a concordance in the back of your Bible to help find what we're looking for."

"Does the Bible have anything to say about dating?" Janice asked, wrinkling her nose.

"Well, it doesn't have the actual word 'dating,' but we can look at some of the relationships men and women had during biblical times and learn from them."

Marybeth raised her hand. "Some of the verses that tell us how to live and act might be helpful in dating, too."

"That's a good point, Marybeth. Knowing what God has planned for us, and what He expects of us, helps us to live in a way that will please Him. Let's begin by opening our Bibles to Genesis, Chapter 2, and see what's in the story of Adam and Eve for us." Elena opened her Bible and scanned the chapter. "What things do you notice from verses 18 to 25?" she asked.

The rustling of pages stopped and the girls examined the passage.

Valerie looked up. "Well, God said it was not good for man to be alone."

"Right, Valerie. Imagine what it must have been like for Adam. He'd been busy naming all the animals, male and female. And yet he was the only one of his own kind. So what happened to solve that problem?"

Janice raised a hand. "God caused Adam to fall asleep, and He made a woman from his rib."

"Do you think there was any significance in that—forming a mate from his rib, instead of just using more dust and creating her the same way He had made man?"

The girls' faces took on thoughtful looks, and Susan, one of the quieter students, raised her hand, then put it back down.

Marybeth spoke up. "Maybe He wanted the woman to be part of the man, for some reason."

Elena smiled. "This is the first picture of marriage in the Bible, girls."

Janice snickered and said something under her breath, and Valerie stifled a giggle.

"Would you mind sharing that with the rest of us, Janice?" Elena asked.

The girl shrugged, and her upper lip curled sarcastically. "I was wondering where the first picture of divorce is . . . for when the marriage doesn't work out."

"Well, that's an interesting thought, Janice, and one we can talk about some other day. Right now we're concerned with relationships that do last and what makes the difference. So let's get back to our lesson, okay?"

Janice nodded sheepishly, turning her interest back to the Scripture before her.

"In God's plan," continued Elena, "man was not truly complete alone. It took a man and a woman, whom God made as one, in marriage, to make the whole."

"Well, in verse 18 it says we were made to be man's 'help,' " Janice said with a smirk. "That sounds like we're supposed to be slaves. I don't plan to spend my life catering to some guy's whims. Not in these days!"

"Oh, I don't really think that the Lord planned for woman to be a slave of man, Janice," Elena said. "Perhaps this is where the significance of the rib fits in. After all, He didn't choose to make us from the hand, you know . . . even if we were to be help meets. Instead He used something far less vulnerable, a rib. Think about it. Within the shelter of the trunk, protected by the arms, close to the heart. It's a lovely picture of the way God intended us to be . . . sheltered, protected, cherished. In a truly happy marriage relationship, each partner finds joy in serving the other."

"That does sound a bit better," said Valerie with a smile, and the other girls nodded.

"Well, since we're in Genesis," continued Elena, "let's turn to Chapter 28 and read about the love story between Jacob and Rachel."

Toward the end of the hour, a motorcycle passed the classroom, disrupting the attention of the students for a few seconds until the engine sputtered to a stop. Janice and Valerie exchanged knowing glances as the call-to-worship bell sounded.

"Perhaps next week we'll have our new manuals," Elena said.

"Oh, couldn't we please have some more classes like this one for a while?" asked Valerie.

Elena considered the suggestion for a moment. "Well, I don't see why not. The manuals can wait for another time, but I'll expect you here every week! Agreed?"

The class nodded.

"Let's close in prayer, then, and I'll see you all next Sunday," said Elena.

Afterward, Janice grabbed her purse and Bible and made a beeline for the door. It wasn't until midway through the morning service that Elena noticed Valerie sitting alone. How odd, she thought. Valerie and Janice always sit together at church.

"Is it Monday already?" Marcy groaned as she and Elena reached the office door simultaneously the following morning.

" 'Fraid so. It did come a bit fast, this time, didn't it?" The pair entered and headed for the coat closet.

"So, how was the wedding?" asked Marcy, as she hung her coat and removed her boots.

"Lovely. Touching, in fact. I wish you could have been there." Elena closed the door and sighed. "Chris and Philip looked so sweet together. It's funny how they were able to keep their love secret."

"I suppose so. But then, she's like her brother in a lot of ways."

"What do you mean?" Elena eyed her questioningly. "Josh isn't a secretive person at all."

Marcy smiled to herself as she filled the coffee maker and turned it on. Turning to face Elena, her look was casual. "I bumped into him the other day, by the way."

"Oh, really?"

"Yes. He was at the cleaners, picking up his suit, as I came out of the bakery next door. Looks great, doesn't he?"

Elena raised her eyebrows and shrugged.

"We had pie and coffee together. And a chat." Taking her seat, she glanced over her shoulder at Elena. "A nice *long* chat. Gee, he sure looks great. Better than ever."

"Marcy," Elena said, looking at her friend with mild exasperation, "is there some point to all of this?" Her index finger tapped impatiently on the desk blotter.

"Point? Hey, listen . . . I was just making conversation, that's all."

The door opened. Miriam entered with a curt greeting and crossed the room to her office, followed a moment later by Mr.

Webster.

"Marcy?" Elena said.

Her friend turned to look at her.

"I'm sorry. I've been a little touchy lately, and I don't even know why."

"It's okay. Don't worry about it."

A few hours later, Marcy and Elena lunched together, seated in a corner booth in the building coffee shop. "You never did tell me much about the wedding," said Marcy, taking a bite of her tuna club sandwich.

Elena looked up. "Well, it was a hectic week for Chris and her mom. The three of us found dresses at Hampton's, and the flowers managed to arrive on time. Mrs. Douglas took care of the reception. Everything went smoothly."

"What about Philip? Do you like him?"

A thoughtful look crossed Elena's face, and she smiled. "Oh, yes. He turned out to be pretty easy to get to know, actually. He seems very steady and reliable, and he'll take good care of Chris, I'm sure of that."

"That should put her mother's mind at ease," Marcy remarked, sipping her tea.

"You're right about that. She was a bit apprehensive about sending her daughter off to some foreign land all alone."

A waitress stopped to see if the pair wanted dessert, and Marcy ordered a fudge brownie. "I know I don't need it," she said after the waitress left, "but they're so good here."

"Just remember, you'll have to jog an extra block or two tonight. Or do you have another date with Trent?"

"No, no date with Trent. We broke up."

"Broke up? And you're asking me about the wedding? How can you be so calm about it?" Elena asked.

"Well, it wasn't so sudden. It's been coming on for a while. We've just decided to back off and give it a rest." Marcy leaned back a bit to accommodate the arrival of her dessert.

"Ah." Elena reached over to pat her friend's hand. "So that explains the brownie. You don't usually have dessert unless you're unhappy."

Marcy looked up guiltily.

"Pie the other day, brownie today, . . . and your diet was going so well, too."

This brought a smile to Marcy's face, but she composed her expression to one of perfect seriousness. "Elena, food is my friend."

"Friend. Right."

Laughing, they got up and walked to the register.

Elena stood in the shower as the hot water coursed over her slim body, rinsing the shampoo and soapsuds away. Her neck muscles were tired, so she turned her back to the spray and dropped her chin. The warmth was soothing.

So many thoughts were crowding into her mind, each fighting to dominate. Where were Chris and Philip now? she wondered. Did they find fulfillment in one another, and were they happy in their love, in their new life?

It was stupid to cry at the wedding, thought Elena. *I've never cried at a wedding before. Everyone was smiling and laughing and congratulating them, and I couldn't even talk. I was happy for them, I really was. It reminded me of my wedding, when I was the bride and Chris was an attendant: same church, same pastor, same feeling, the newness of love and the beginning of a whole new life. The two become as one.*

"It's the first picture of marriage in the Bible, girls," Elena remembered saying to her Sunday school class. "In a truly happy marriage relationship, each partner finds joy in serving the other." Her lips curved in a bitter smile. Every bride expects that truly happy marriage relationship: joy that will last forever, love eternal.

Where had Janice gone so quickly after the class? she wondered. Had she and Valerie had some kind of misunderstanding?

The water suddenly felt cool, bringing Elena back to reality. She turned off the spray and reached for her towel, wrapping her long hair turban style. Zipping on a fleece robe, she stepped into slippers and padded out to the kitchen, where she turned on the burner beneath the kettle. Then, while the water heated, she returned to the bathroom to dry her hair.

I still have to return Josh's handkerchief, she thought. *I'll iron it tomorrow with my other things. So he and Marcy had coffee . . . and a chat. A long chat, wasn't it? So what do I care anyway?* Combing out her silky tresses, she heard the kettle whistling. *Good, tea is just what I need . . . and some music. I'll put on some music.*

The novel Elena had picked up to read did nothing to distract her. The story was corny, and she was not in the mood for a typical happy ending.

Alone in her bed after her nightly Bible reading and prayer, she stared at the slits of light formed on the wall by the streetlamp shining through the partially open blinds. *How like my life,* she thought in the stillness. *Parts I can see and understand, parts that are hidden.*

Over and over in her mind her words echoed. In a truly happy marriage relationship, each partner finds joy in serving the other. *How trite,* she thought. *Who am I, to be telling anyone how to choose a life mate? Look what a mess I made with my choice!* She covered her face with both hands and felt the sting of tears.

The phone rang.

Elena sat up and dabbed at her eyes with a tissue.

There was a second ring, and a third.

She made no move to answer. *I don't want to talk to anyone,* she thought. *I just want to be left alone.*

In the middle of the fourth ring it ceased abruptly. Only then did Elena realize that being alone was the very last thing she wanted.

Odd, thought Josh, *replacing the receiver on the cradle. I know she's there. Her lights were still on last time I looked. Ever since the wedding she's been withdrawn, off in some little world of her own. I wonder what battle is raging inside that beautiful head of hers?*

9

The Christmas season was rapidly approaching. Elena's class had asked to put on a short play for the Christmas program, and she knew that she would need help sewing the required costumes. Bundled warmly against the chill December air, she walked up the street and knocked on Stella Montgomery's back door. There was no answer. Hugging herself for warmth, she rapped a second time, hesitated, and turned to leave.

Just then a finger parted the curtain on the kitchen door, then the door opened. A hairy male arm reached out to draw her swiftly through the opening and closed the door quickly against the blast of frigid air.

"Well, hello, Laney. What are you doing out so early on a Saturday?" Josh stood barefoot, clad only in jeans. He had a towel draped around his shoulders, and with one end of it he blotted moisture from his hair with a muscular arm.

A thought flashed through Elena's mind that it was disgusting for someone to be so tanned in Pennsylvania in December. Caught momentarily off guard by the magnificent sight before her eyes, she could only stammer. "I was—I mean—is your mom home?"

"No, actually, she's not. She took Mrs. Jenkins to the doctor this morning."

"Oh."

"She'll be back in a while. Why don't you wait for her?"

Elena noticed a stray drop of water tracing a path down through the mat of dark hair on his chest. With great effort, she raised her eyes to meet his, finding a sparkle of amusement there. She felt a glow rising on her cheeks that was not from the December cold or the warmth of the kitchen, and she closed her eyes for a full second before looking up at him again.

This time he was smiling. "Your coat," he coaxed, holding out his hand.

"Well, I really—"

"Oh, come on, Laney. I'll bet you haven't even had breakfast yet, right?"

"I don't eat breakfast."

"Well, we do here, and I'm about to have some. Now, your coat?"

Elena removed her scarf and unbuttoned her wrap, sliding out of it smoothly. Handing it to him, she checked to see if her boots were dry.

He motioned for her to sit down, hung her coat on the rack near the door, and excused himself for a moment. It was then that she first became aware of the music drifting softly from the direction of the stereo in the living room. She had heard it vaguely when she had first stepped inside, but the sound had not really registered. The tune was unfamiliar and sounded somewhat foreign, yet she liked it.

She glanced up from the table, out of the window. Outside, the trees rattled slightly in the cold wind, their stark bare branches stiff and resisting, moving only by force.

The sound of Josh's returning footsteps drew nearer, and she turned to smile as he came through the half-doors. He was fully dressed, having added a long-sleeved checkered shirt and crewneck sweater. His hair was damp and combed neatly into place.

"So, you still haven't told me what you're doing out so early." He grinned as he started the coffeepot and rustled around for frying pans.

"You're right. It's just girl stuff. I wondered if your mom had time to do some sewing for my class play."

"Play, huh? That ought to keep you busy." He broke eggs into a bowl, added milk, then began dicing a bell pepper and a tomato.

Elena watched him work, oddly fascinated. A memory of Greg's complete helplessness in the kitchen came to mind. He couldn't even make a decent peanut butter and jelly sandwich if no one was around to show him where the knives were, she recalled. "Need any help?"

"No, ma'am. Just someone to talk to. Oh, on second thought, you can spread these around, if you want to." He took some silverware out of a drawer, removed two napkins from a holder, and set them in front of Elena.

It felt more natural to be doing something, she thought as she set the table. When had anyone ever waited on her before? "Are there any new developments in the museum venture?" she asked

Josh as he worked.

"Yes and no. They still want only the models in the original agreement, but they've asked Jake to move there and head the department."

"Really? Do you think he will?"

"Can't say for sure. I know he's giving it serious thought."

"Well, it's a good opportunity, isn't it? Sort of a step up."

"Yes, it is that. They've offered a great salary, plus some pretty good benefits. I think he'll probably go for it."

"If he does, where will that leave you?"

"Actually, he wants me to go with him. And I'm considering it, too."

His words fell to the bottom of her heart with an almost audible thud. Elena's lips parted in surprise as she gazed at him.

Josh slid the omelettes onto warm plates, added toasted English muffins, and carried them to the table. Setting them in place, he returned for two mugs of steaming coffee and then sat down opposite Elena. Reaching for her hand, he bowed his head and said a prayer of blessing. "Everything all right?" he asked, as she stared at her plate.

Elena looked up into his warm gray eyes and forced a smile. "Yes. It all looks lovely. I . . . had no idea you were a part-time chef."

"I have a lot of hidden talents," he said with a teasing wink, returning her smile.

The omelette had been cooked to perfection, with just a touch of cheese inside and on top. Elena savored the first taste of it and took a bite of her English muffin, chewing slowly before swallowing. "Josh?"

"Yes?"

"When will Jake go, if he does go?"

"Oh, probably not until the beginning of June at the earliest. Why?"

"I was just wondering." She reached for the homemade jam between them. The feeling of relief that washed over her gave her appetite a boost.

As he refilled their mugs a short time later, Josh noticed a slight frown between her delicately arched brows. "Something wrong, Lane?"

"Oh, no. I was just wondering about the music you have playing.

It's odd."

"Do you think so?"

She shrugged.

"It's a tape I picked up in England when I was in the Air Force. Ballads that were popular at the time. Don't you like it?"

"I didn't say that. It's just that some of the songs seem so sad." Refolding her napkin, she placed it beside her plate and brushed a few stray crumbs from her gray and white striped sweater.

"Really? To me they're just relaxing. They're mostly love songs."

"Love should never be sad," she said softly. Her eyes drifted off to some vague memory.

"I think I would agree with you there." He sensed she was beginning to withdraw again.

Neither spoke for a few moments, and Josh swallowed the last of his coffee as he observed slight waves of pain crossing her face like clouds in a windy sky. "Were *you* happy, Lane?"

She looked directly at him, the merest hint of moisture shimmering against the blue of her eyes. "I . . . really don't want to talk about me," she said, abruptly, rising to her feet. "I . . . thanks for breakfast, Josh." Bolting for the door, Elena grabbed her coat and flung it around her shoulders. Grasping the door knob, she wrenched the door open.

Just one step behind, Josh fastened a hand around her upper arm and spun her around. "Don't go, Laney. Talk to me. Don't run away." But before the words were out of his mouth, she wriggled from his grasp and fled. "Don't run away from it," he repeated softly, into the emptiness. "It'll only take you longer to get back."

Watching her retreat, he clenched his fist and slammed the door.

Elena had never felt more humiliated in her life. Even after she was safely home, her cheeks still felt hot, which only added to her assurance that she had made a complete fool of herself. *I didn't even wave to Josh's mother when she had passed by in the car*, she thought with chagrin.

What is wrong with me? she wondered. *Why can't I talk about Greg and me, about our marriage?* She removed her coat, unzipped her boots, and stepped into her slippers. *I don't want to talk about us. I don't even want to think about it,* she said to herself. *I shouldn't have run away like that.* She flopped down onto the couch. *What must he think of me now?* She drew her knees up and clasped her arms around them as her mind snapped shut.

Elena was exhausted from trying to appear nonchalant all the way to church with Josh and his mother the next day, and she was relieved when she closed the door of her classroom. She was early, but she knew that soon enough the door would burst open and the noisy, exuberant girls would arrive. She took two aspirins out of her purse and drained the glass of water on the desk.

Surprisingly, the group acted subdued when they assembled. Valerie and Janice sat with a seat separating them, and one of the other girls was absent. Elena pretended not to notice the way the two best friends ignored each another, and she asked Susan to open in prayer.

"Well, class," began Elena, "so far we've looked at most of the main relationships in the Bible. Thinking about them, what would you say was the one thing they had in common?" She scanned the room. "Janice?"

Janice tossed her auburn head and shrugged.

"Marybeth?" she prompted.

"Well, I would say that God was the one who chose the partners."

Elena smiled. "That's a very good answer. And a very good thought. If He chose people who were right for each other all those years ago, does He still do that today?"

"He can," said Valerie, "but I don't know if He does."

"What if we didn't love the person?" Janice asked with a pout. "Would He make us marry the guy anyway? Even if we didn't love him?"

"Oh, I don't believe that God makes any of us do anything, Janice," Elena said. "Not really. Do you?"

Janice smirked, but remained silent.

"Then let me ask you this," continued Elena. "Looking around you, at everyone you know—all of whom have done their own choosing—which system works best?"

The girls laughed.

"Well, I just think that love is the most important thing," Janice added, petulantly.

"Then let's find out what love should be like. Open your Bibles to 1 Corinthians, Chapter 13," said Elena, "and we'll read it aloud."

After the Scripture had been read, Elena looked up at the students. "Quite a nice picture of what love is supposed to be, wouldn't you say? Kind, unselfish, patient, long lasting, true, and greater in God's eyes than either hope or faith. How do you think we can find a love that is all these things?"

Marybeth raised her hand. "By letting God choose for us."

"So we're right back where we started, aren't we?" Elena said, laughing, and the girls nodded. "I believe that God does have someone special for everyone who belongs to Him."

"So, how are we supposed to *find* this perfect person?" Janice asked, still pouting.

"Well, how do you think?" Elena returned.

"Maybe," said Valerie, "the same way we find our other friends. By being with people we have something in common with."

"I'm so glad you said that, Valerie, because now I can ask you what is the most important thing to have in common with another person, especially a partner?"

The girls considered the question quietly for a few moments before a hand was raised in the back row.

"Sharon?"

"It must mean that if we're Christians, we should only date other Christians."

Elena smiled. "It would save a lot of problems if we all played by God's rules, don't you think? Let's talk about some of the blessings we experience when we follow His plan, and afterward we'll discuss the Christmas play. I have the scripts all typed, so you can begin memorizing your parts for the rehearsal."

Once again, the roar from an approaching motorcycle disrupted the last few moments of study time before the bell sounded. Elena reminded the girls about the scheduled play rehearsal and closed in prayer. She saw Janice frown and toss a defiant look first at her then at Valerie before hurrying out of the room.

During the morning service, Elena noticed that Valerie was sitting alone again. Speculating on all the possible reasons why Janice was not there played havoc with Elena's concentration, and the service dragged on endlessly. Finally, after the benediction, she approached Valerie. "Where's our friend Janice?" she asked casually.

"Hmmph! She doesn't have time for old friends anymore. She's too busy for church. And I don't think she'll be coming to class anymore."

"What are you saying, Valerie?" Elena asked, putting a hand on the girl's forearm.

"She's got a boyfriend now, Scott Peterson. He's an atheist."

Elena stumbled to the car, her face ashen. On the brink of tears, she just wanted to be alone: to think, to cry, to pray.

Stella was still on the church steps talking to her friends, but Josh was in the car when Elena approached. He got out to open her door. "Laney, what's wrong?" He took hold of both her arms and turned her to face him.

"Everything!" she blurted out. "Everything's wrong. Boy, some teacher I am. I'm great for that class. I know just how to tell those girls how to live. All they have to do is follow my example," she said, bitterly, and burst into tears.

Josh helped her into the car, closed the door, and returned to his side. Elena rummaged around in her purse for a tissue, but couldn't find one. "Oh, darn!" She clutched her handbag and stared straight ahead. Her eyes sparked with anger.

Josh took a handkerchief out of his back pocket and offered it to her. "Want to talk about it?"

She cast a sideways glance at him and unceremoniously took the handkerchief from him. "I still have the last one you gave me," she admitted, as she dabbed at her eyes and sniffed.

"There's no shortage, okay?" He smiled gently. "Now why don't you tell me what's wrong?"

He watched her brush a lock of silky hair from her face and turn her sky blue eyes on him. Then she took a deep breath and exhaled slowly. "It's Janice."

"Janice Harper? From your class?"

She nodded.

"What happened to her?"

The words tumbled out of her mouth like water over Niagara Falls. "Oh, Josh, after all these weeks of studying God's plan for us—how to live, form relationships, date—she's turning her back on all of it and dating a nonbeliever. And not just a nonbeliever. An atheist!"

Josh contemplated her answer for a few minutes. "Lane, in the first place, she is not your responsibility."

"How can you say that?" she demanded. "She *is* my responsibility. She's one of my girls, and—"

"But she's not your child, and you're not her substitute mother."

"But I love her, Josh. I care about her, about all of them." Her voice softened. "I *feel* like they're my kids, and I feel responsible when they do something wrong."

He smiled and covered her hand with his as it lay clenched on her lap. "Of course you do. But you're not. And in the second place, if she belongs to the Lord, He will handle it and bring her back."

Her fingers relaxed, and a tear traced a glistening path over the soft curve of her cheekbone. Elena dried it with the handkerchief. "But it hurts, watching her doing something dumb."

"I know. But there's something you can do about that, and it's all you can do."

"Pray." Her eyes met his.

Josh nodded, coaxing a smile from her. "And you don't have to do that alone. Come home with us and have some Sunday dinner, and afterward the three of us will pray for Janice together."

Elena smiled thinly and nodded. Somehow things looked a touch brighter.

10

Several evenings during the hectic weeks that followed, the girls met at Elena's to work on props and to rehearse for the play. Stella provided homemade treats for everyone and assisted with the costume fittings and last-minute adjustments. The young people's enthusiasm was contagious, and Stella seemed to have almost as much fun as they did. She coached some of the girls on their lines as they went over their parts.

At last it was Sunday, Christmas Eve. Patterns of color reflected from stained-glass windows like quilt patches on the snowy ground. Snowflakes danced in the frosty air around Hillcrest Church.

Excitement mounted as the sanctuary filled to capacity. Little girls in new dresses, curls, and ribbons and boys in suits and ties, hair all smoothed into place, sat in rows with their teachers. They would turn shyly now and then to catch a glimpse of their parents and friends. Everything was in readiness for the children's Christmas program.

The nursery class stole the early part of the show. Dressed in white angel smocks and tinsel garland halos, they reminded Elena of the way her own little Steven had looked in his last Christmas performance when he wore a similar costume and stood so proudly with his group. She remembered that he had waved when he had caught sight of her and Greg in the audience. People had chuckled. Even the songs the tots sang tonight were the ones that Stevie had hummed around the house as he played during the month of December.

Christmas was so full of memories; even now, after two years, it was still the hardest part of the year for Elena. Busy working with her girls up until the last minute, she had kept the sad thoughts at bay. But watching and listening to the children was almost too much for her to bear. She nearly bit through the inside of her cheek as she struggled to contain the tears welling behind her eyes. Once the tykes returned to their seats, she breathed a sigh of relief.

The remaining classes performed smoothly, and then the congregation sang Christmas carols while the ushers carried in the props and set the stage. Elena tried not to let Janice's absence disturb her as the other girls came onstage.

In the theme of the play, women gossiped at the town well discussing the recent wedding of Mary of Nazareth: it had been pretty, but what a shame that it couldn't have been *sooner*.

Marybeth Reed was perfectly suited in her role as the latecomer at the well. She had seen Mary and her baby in Bethlehem and had heard fascinating stories about shepherds and angels, wisemen and a strange star. Present when the soldiers had come to carry out Herod's order to murder all children under two years of age, she reported how God had miraculously enabled Mary's baby to escape, as though he were special. The women at the well speculated that perhaps he was the promised Messiah who had been long awaited. After a bit of initial stage fright, the lines came off perfectly, and Elena was pleased at the success of the play.

Everyone filed into the church basement for refreshments afterward. Parents and teachers hugged and kissed the beaming children. Elena overheard many favorable comments about the evening as she made her way through the crowd. She hoped that people would understand the real significance of the birth of that precious baby so long ago.

In a Sunday school room on the lower level, Elena helped the girls change out of their costumes. After fastening the last button on Sharon's dress, she looked up to see that the class had formed a circle around her. Valerie shyly held out a small wrapped package.

"What is this?" asked Elena, smiling, as her fingers closed around it.

"Why don't you open it and see?" Sharon said.

Elena took a seat and began to unwrap the gift. Inside, nestled against folds of sheer tissue paper, lay a new Bible with a soft burgundy leather cover and gilt-edged pages. Elena's eyes widened and she gasped as she lifted the book from the box and opened the front cover. An inscription read, "Our favorite book for our favorite teacher, with love." All of their signatures followed.

"Oh! How beautiful! It's just what I need! How did you know?" Suddenly, all the tears that Elena had managed to control so well during the beginning of the Christmas program rose to her eyes and coursed down her face. She looked lovingly at the girls gathered around her. She set the book on the chair beside her and rose to thank each one in turn with a hug and kiss.

By this time, Marybeth was already passing tissues around to the group of laughing and crying young people, and she held one out to Elena just before she received her hug.

"Thanks, honey," said the teacher. "I never seem to have one of these when I need one."

Everyone laughed.

"Well, I have something for each of you, too," Elena said. She crossed the room to the closet and removed a bag of brightly wrapped presents.

After the festivities were over, Elena went home with the Montgomerys to have some hot chocolate and exchange gifts. She looked forward to this Christmas Eve tradition every year.

Coats hung, Josh and Elena walked into the living room while Stella went to the kitchen to prepare refreshments. When she returned with a tray a short time later, a fire crackled brightly in the fireplace, and the two younger people were laughing.

"I was just telling Laney about the letter we got from Chris and how she's surviving without those long morning showers she always took. Remember how there was never any hot water left by the time she was finished?"

Stella nodded and smiled. "That I do recall. Still, I do feel lonesome, sometimes, thinking about how far away she is . . . especially at Christmas." She set the tray down on the coffee table, handed mugs of steaming hot chocolate to Elena and Josh, took a cup for herself and sat in her rocker. "She's in the Lord's hands, now. I try not to worry."

"I know you really miss her, Mother," Elena said softly. She brushed a wisp of long hair away from her eyes and smoothed the nap of her black velvet skirt over her knees.

"Well, ladies," said Josh, "let's cut the chitchat and get this show on the road. Some of those packages over there look pretty interesting." He crossed the room and knelt before the tree, examining name tags on the packages. "To Mom from Elena," he read aloud as he picked up a large wrapped parcel. Winking at Elena as he passed, he gave the gift to his mother.

Stella removed the bow carefully and set it aside, then tore the wrapping paper off with the enthusiasm of a child. "Oh, how lovely, dear," she said, caressing the soft velour robe and fuzzy matching slippers. "Thank you! You must have noticed how threadbare my old slippers have gotten. I'll really enjoy these."

"I'll say," remarked Josh. "She's been hinting about needing some new ones for a month already. Let's see what else is here." He stooped and reached for a second item. "To Elena from Chris and Phil." He handed it to her and watched as she opened it.

"Oh, how sweet. The new devotional book I've been secretly coveting! I'll have to write and thank them." Elena held it up for Josh and his mother to see. "What's in the stack for you, Josh?"

He knelt down and picked through the pile until he found one. "To Josh from Mom," he said, grinning. Making short work of Stella's meticulous wrapping, he fingered the pair of laser-crafted bookends and held them up. "Thank you," he said, blowing her a kiss. "Now, let's see what else we have here."

Josh walked Elena home a short time later, his arms laden with her presents. The winter wind had grown perceptively stronger, and mists of tiny snowflakes blew like veils of dust along the snow-packed road as they neared her house. They exhaled little clouds of white all along the way.

"Would you like to come in?" she asked, unlocking the front door and opening it.

He smiled and carried her things inside. After setting them on the small table near the door, he removed his jacket and built a fire in the fireplace, then took a seat on the sofa.

Elena plugged in the Christmas tree lights and turned on some soft carols. "I sure was proud of my girls tonight. They did a great job." She sat down with one leg bent under her on the other end of the couch and turned to face him.

"Yes, I was impressed. You've got some born actresses in that group."

"It would've been better if Janice could have played lead gossip, though. I wrote in some special lines just for her."

"Well, we'll just keep praying for her. Things will work out, Lane."

"I suppose. I sure appreciate knowing you and your mom are still praying for her too. Could I offer you some coffee or something?"

"No, the refreshments at church and Mom's hot chocolate were plenty."

Elena smiled and looked away, lost in thought for a moment. "Let me show you what the class gave me." She rose and crossed the room to where she had put her gifts. Taking the Bible from the box on top of the stack, she returned and held it out to Josh.

His eyes widened as he examined the book. "Wow! This is pretty classy."

"I know. I couldn't believe it myself. They've added so much to my life already, and now this."

"Well, from what I hear, you've done wonders with that group. I think they're just returning your love in measures full and running over, like it says in the Bible." He gave the book back to her, and she returned to her spot on the sofa.

Reaching into one of his pockets, Josh placed another small gift in her hand. "This is for you, too," he said with a smile. "Nothing like a Bible, mind you, but it's something I saw once and wanted you to have. I hope you like it."

Elena unwrapped the package. Inside, in a small velvet-covered box, the gold chain of a necklace sparkled in the dancing firelight. Hanging on the delicate gold filigree were two tiny hearts of sculpted ivory. On either side of them a small cut stone twinkled softly.

"Merry Christmas, Laney," he said with a grin.

"Oh, Josh, I only gave you a sweater and a wallet. I—"

"So whoever said Christmas is a buying contest? A guy has to buy something for a beautiful woman every now and then."

Elena laughed and moved nearer, handing him the necklace and turning so that he could fasten the clasp. Then she turned to face him, touching the ivory hearts with her fingertips.

"You know," he said softly, looking at her, "I knew it would look just like that on you."

She bit her bottom lip. "Thank you. I've never had anything so lovely. But you shouldn't have, you know." She moved back to her place again facing him. "Josh, whatever happened to you— when you went away? Greg and I thought you'd come to visit us sometimes, but you never came."

"Oh, I just decided to stay in the Air Force for a while. See the world, and all that."

"Was there anyplace like home?"

"That all depends. On what—or who—comes to mind when you think of home," he added. "I saw some beautiful, incredible places, that's for sure. The countryside in England is old and charming. France is enticing. And Italy—well . . ." his voice drifted off. "But, all that aside, I'm home now."

Against her better judgment, Elena continued. "But in all that time, weren't you ever . . . you know . . . in love?"

He didn't answer at first. He stared into the flames nearby, and Elena saw a muscle move in his jaw. When he turned his eyes to her she saw a look that she was unable to fathom. For a moment she wondered if she should have asked the question at all.

His steady gaze swept slowly over Elena's face, wandering to her hair, to the necklace at her throat. So intense was his look she felt her cheeks begin to color. Then his eyes narrowed. "Yes. Once."

She sat quietly, waiting for him to continue.

He stared for another long moment, as if weighing the pros and cons of telling the rest of the story. Then, apparently deciding against it, he rose and stretched leisurely. "But that's another story," he said, "and it's getting late. Time for me to be going." As Elena watched in silence, he strode across the room, put on his jacket, and opened the door. "Merry Christmas," he said with a backward glance, and then he was gone.

Soaking in a hot tub full of bubble bath, Elena mulled over the events of the day. After toweling off and drying her hair, she dressed in a long silky nightgown and went to her room. Outside, the wind howled, and occasionally the cottage shuddered. Snow drifted like frozen waves on the sea, piling up against every structure in the way. The draft along Elena's floor persuaded her to shorten her prayers and add an extra quilt to her bed.

In her last hazy thoughts before sleep, she recalled her conversation with Josh. *Imagine,* she thought, *Josh, in love. I wonder what happened? And who would ever let him go?*

11

The snow crunched under the tires of the Escort as Elena backed out of the drive and onto the plowed and cindered roads of Dallas. By the time she was halfway to Wilkes-Barre, the pavement was completely clear and dry.

The endless clouds of a gray Pennsylvania December still filled the sky, and a voice on the car radio announced that another winter storm was wending its way slowly eastward from the Great Lakes. After pulling into the covered parking area and locking her car, Elena walked along the connecting ramp to the Webster Building and headed for the elevator.

"Hi, kiddo," said Marcy, waiting at the doors with a finger poised on the elevator buttons. "I'm surprised to see you here this morning."

Elena smiled as she approached her friend. "Oh? Why is that?"

The pair entered the elevator and the sliding doors closed behind them. Marcy pushed the button for the second floor. "Old Eagle Nose was in a huff the other day. Seems you have a few holidays to take before the end of the year, or her books'll be all messed up."

"I forgot all about them," said Elena. "I sure could have used an extra day or two before the Christmas program. Why doesn't she just count the time I had to take off because of bad weather?"

Marcy's voice comically impersonated Miriam's as she held her nose and spoke in exaggerated seriousness. "Vacation days *have* to be requested ahead of time. I simply *must* mark it on this chart so that I can plan the office schedule in an orderly manner."

Elena giggled.

The elevator stopped, and they exited toward the office door, which Marcy opened with a key. After putting their coats in the closet, they walked to the women's room to tidy their hair.

Applying lipstick, Marcy glanced at Elena's reflection in the mirror, then turned to have a closer look. "Wow. That is a gorgeous necklace, Lane. I've never seen it before."

"Thanks," Elena said casually, adjusting the collar of her open-necked silk blouse.

"Ah." A knowing smile spread across Marcy's face. "It must have been from Josh."

"Why would you think that?" Elena asked, her curiosity piqued.

"Because otherwise you would have gone into more detail. You would've said thanks and told me it was a present from Josh's mom, or Chris, or the Sunday school class, or somebody. But it definitely did not come from Woolworth's, so the girls are out. Chris needed way too much money for her trip to be so extravagant, and Mrs. Montgomery has always been into things thoughtful and handmade. So you must not want to talk about it. Which means—"

"Okay, okay," Elena confessed, her eyes rolling upward. "You're right. It was from Josh. And I didn't say it because I knew that you'd make a big deal over it, and it wasn't like that." She sighed in frustration.

Marcy put a hand on Elena's forearm. "Hey, look. If the guy wants to shop at Tiffany's for his gifts, he sure doesn't have to check it out with me first. I was just teasing. It's a very classy piece."

Elena fingered the sculpted ivory hearts and watched the tiny diamonds sparkling in the mirror. "Do you really think he found this at Tiffany's, Marcy?" she asked in disbelief. Her voice was barely above a whisper.

"Well," said her friend, with a smile, "wherever it came from, it really is beautiful. That's all I know."

Elena contemplated the reflected image of the necklace for a moment before she drew a deep breath and exhaled slowly. "Well, how was your Christmas? Did you do anything special?"

"I spent it with Mom and Dad. Todd and Barbara made me an aunt again, and they were there with the new baby."

"Sounds like fun. Their other two kids must be getting pretty big."

"Yes, they're both in school now. Anyway, we all had a good time, eating and opening presents and all."

"Did anything else exciting happen?" Elena probed, as they left the restroom and headed for their desks.

"You mean, did Trent call, right?" There was an answering

smile, and Marcy continued. "Let's just say the diet is on again."

"That's great, Marcy!"

"Sure is! And not a moment too soon," said her friend, patting a hip.

The office door opened, and in whooshed Miriam, nose in the air. She nodded to the young women as she passed on the way to her desk. "I must speak to you later," she said curtly to Elena. The connecting door closed behind her.

Elena glanced over at Marcy, and they both laughed.

Mr. Webster and Derek entered just as the phone rang. The older man greeted them and strode toward the inner office. Derek watched as Marcy answered the phone, then he stopped at Elena's desk. "Morning, Elena. How was your Christmas?"

"Lovely," she said with a smile. "How about yours?"

He cocked his head back and forth, and the shining waves of his dark brown hair caught the light. "Not bad. Are you free for lunch today? I'd like to talk to you."

Elena checked her watch automatically and then glanced at her desk calendar. "Well, I—" Then, meeting his gaze, no excuse came to mind. "I—suppose so."

He smiled. "Good. I'll see you at eleven-thirty."

"What was that all about?" asked Marcy, after his office door closed behind him.

"Oh, nothing much. I said I'd have lunch, and that's no big deal, either," she added defensively.

"Hey, did I say anything?" Marcy asked, her eyes wide as she shook her head. Expelling a silent whistle, she turned in her chair to face forward.

Elena licked her lips and removed the cover from the typewriter.

The elegant plum-colored interior of Cyril's sparkled festively with holiday decorations. Small trees devoid of foliage had been painted white and strung with clear crystal minilights and were placed at regular intervals around the room. In the center stood a huge, flocked, long-needle pine, its silver star barely missing the glitter-flecked ceiling. Bows of purple velvet accented with white Belgian lace decorated the tree, and large ornaments of transparent glass and silver were tastefully placed among the branches. Elena forcibly drew her eyes away from the beautiful sight to peruse the mcnu.

"Have you decided what to have?" asked Derek.

An ever-present waiter poured coffee from a silver pot into their china cups as Elena thought and answered. "Yes, I think I'll have cream of broccoli soup and the snow crab."

"Two of my favorites. I believe I'll have the same."

"Very good, Mr. Webster," said the attendant, picking up the menus.

Derek raised his eyebrows and smiled at Elena. "So, I hear you'll be having the next few days off."

"Oh really? No one has mentioned that to me."

"Well, I'm sure Miriam will get around to it this afternoon. You still have some vacation days left."

Elena frowned. "How can I have any time coming, when I've missed so many days because of winter storms?"

"Easy. You haven't taken any sick days, either." He patted her hand. "I've never been able to understand your dedication. You're a fine worker and a super secretary, Elena."

"Thank you." She saw his gaze drift to the decorations, and she used the opportunity to offer a brief prayer just as their food arrived. "Oh, this soup looks lovely, doesn't it?"

Derek smiled and used his spoon to remove the holiday garnish from the steaming soup. "I imagine it tastes as good as it looks, too."

She sampled hers and closed her eyes for a second. "Mmmm, it's delicious." Enjoying the soft background music, Elena met his brown velvet eyes across the table several moments later and smiled.

"Is that a new necklace, Elena? It's very lovely."

Her hand flew to her throat. "Do you really think so? I—I mean, thank you. It was a Christmas gift."

"And a very beautiful one, to say the least. An admirer?"

She was saved from answering by the waiter as he removed the bowls and set the luncheon plates before them.

"More coffee, sir?" he asked.

"Yes, thank you, Blake. That would be fine." Derek watched as the cups were refilled. After the attendant left they ate in silence before he spoke again. "I have something for you, too." He reached into a vest pocket and drew out a small wrapped package, which he placed on the table beside her.

"Derek! You didn't have to do this," she said. Her voice grew softer. "Besides, I don't have a gift for you."

He shook his head. "I wasn't expecting anything."

After wiping her fingers on the linen napkin, Elena picked up the package. "What is it?"

Derek smiled and watched silently as she removed the wrapping and opened the box.

"Oh, it's beautiful." Elena lifted the beaded evening clutch to examine it.

"The real gift is inside."

Elena looked at him questioningly and opened the purse. "Tickets?" she asked, reading the wording as she held them up.

"To the Russian Ballet? Oh, I've always wanted to see them perform!" Her gaze returned to him. "I didn't know they were going to be in town. I thought their tour only included major cities."

"That's right," he said. "I don't imagine they've even *heard* of Wilkes-Barre, much less planned to include it in their itinerary."

Elena continued to look steadily at him. "But the papers said that all their performances have been sold out for months."

"Right again."

"Well then, how could you . . ." She looked at the tickets more closely. "Derek! This says New York City! On New Year's Eve!"

"Well, you do have some days to take off, and I thought that perhaps you would enjoy doing something special. You know, see the Big Apple at the beginning of the new year, go to the best show in town . . . ."

"But I—"

"We'd have separate rooms, of course."

Elena continued to stare at him in disbelief, her mouth slightly agape.

"Listen, pet, you don't have to decide now. Take some time to think about it, okay? I have to keep an appointment this afternoon, so I'll have a cab take you back to the office. I'll phone you tonight when you get home."

Speechless, Elena rose and followed him to the cloakroom. What will Marcy think? she wondered. What would she tell Josh? How could she decide what to do?

"What's wrong?" Marcy said, frowning, as Elena passed her

desk after lunch. "You're as white as a sheet."

"What?" her friend replied absently.

"I said, you look like a ghost. What happened?"

Elena swallowed and sat down, placing her purse and the gift box in her bottom drawer. She drew a ragged breath. "Marcy, I—"

The connecting door squeaked as Miriam entered the room and spoke directly to Elena. "I must straighten out something with you before I go to lunch. Please come to my office."

Woodenly, Elena followed, glancing back just in time to see Marcy putting on her coat. It was her lunch hour, too, Elena remembered.

A large chart took up most of the room on Miriam's desktop. It was marked with twelve blocks, each representing a month of the year. Various colored strips were drawn through different weeks. "The yellow strips represent you," Miriam said tersely.

"What yellow strips? I don't see any." She rubbed her temples as her head began to throb.

"That is precisely the point," Miriam said in an irritating pitch. She adjusted the gold-rimmed spectacles on her nose and leaned into Elena's face. "There *aren't* any."

Elena was beginning to feel exasperated. Her shoulders drooped. "So?"

Miriam stared. "There is no need for you to get smart with me." Her voice seemed to rise with each word, until the door of Mr. Webster's office opened and the man stepped out, apparently on his way to lunch. Immediately, Miriam's voice took on a syrupy sweetness. "Well, obviously, you must take off the rest of the days that you have coming."

"How many are there?" Elena asked.

"Six vacation days and two sick days."

"Miriam," Elena said, her eyes squinting now against the pain of her headache, "there aren't that many work days left in the year."

Mr. Webster exited to the hall outside the office, and the latch clicked shut. Miriam's eyes narrowed, and she drew her lips into a tightly shriveled small circle. "Young lady, I am fully aware of the number of days remaining in the year."

"Of course. I'm sorry. What would you like me to do?"

Miriam's beady eyes gleamed for an instant, as if caught in

some wickedly funny thought, then she composed her face. "Do not come in for the rest of this week at all. And, after the new year, do not come in to work until you have used up the rest of the time the company owes you."

"But—"

"And when you do come back, I'll thank you to schedule your vacation time for the year, as you should have done for this one, months ago."

"Whatever you say," Elena said. "Is that all?"

"Hmmph! That is quite enough, I should say."

Elena forced a smile and returned to her desk. A few moments later Miriam left, and the office was silent. Elena rummaged unsuccessfully through her purse for an aspirin. She got up and went to Marcy's desk and opened the top drawer. To her relief, she found a full bottle. *The ballet!* she thought, as she took a drink at the water cooler. *It would be such an experience! But how could I go with him? What would people think? How could I expect the Lord to approve of it?*

When Marcy returned from lunch, she found Elena resting her head on her arms. "Are you okay?" she asked.

Elena sat up and nodded. "I borrowed some of your aspirin, and I'm feeling a bit better."

"Any calls?"

"No, it's been quiet as a tomb. Boring, in fact."

"Did you see the stuff Thornsby put on your desk to be typed?"

Elena stiffened suddenly and looked at the In tray. "No! I never even noticed it." She thumbed through the papers, grimacing. "Great. This will take me all day."

"Sorry, kid. I figured that you would check."

"It's not your fault. I guess I had something else on my mind."

"Want to talk about it while nobody else is around?"

Elena looked at the clock on the wall. Sighing, she put the papers down and turned in the chair to face her. "Marcy, I don't know how to tell you this." She took a deep breath and continued. "Derek wants to take me to the Russian Ballet on New Year's Eve."

"The Russian Ballet is coming to Wilkes-Barre?" her friend asked incredulously. "I just read an article about them in this morning's paper, and the whole tour has been sold out. There's not a ticket available for a million dollars."

"Well, Derek just happens to have two."

"The paper didn't say anything about a local performance."

"That's because there isn't one."

"Well, if it's not local, where are they dancing?"

Elena hesitated. "New York City."

Marcy's mouth dropped open. "New York? On New Year's Eve? Isn't *that* something! Do you think you'll go?"

"How can I do that, Marce? You know I don't approve of that sort of thing . . . going on overnight trips with men."

"But a ballet. The Russian Ballet, yet. It's a once-in-a-lifetime chance. I'd sure be tempted, Lane."

"That's the problem," Elena said softly.

Elena had very little appetite when she returned home. After a cup of tea, she went to her bedroom and fell to her knees. *Dear Heavenly Father*, she prayed silently, *I don't know what to pray. I know I must ask what Your will is, in this matter that's troubling me. I've been seeing Derek outside of the office, but not for dates, exactly. And now he has invited me to go with him to New York. What should I do? I've always wanted to see a classical ballet by famous dancers, and now I have this opportunity. But it is overnight, and I know people could get the wrong impression. I'm so mixed up.*

Two verses were at war in her mind. Part of her wanted to listen to 'He has given us all things richly to enjoy,' and part of her remembered, 'Abstain from even the appearance of evil.' She sighed and opened her eyes.

After a long struggle in prayer, Elena rose from her knees and checked the time on her watch: Nine-thirty. *I wonder when he's planning to call? And what will I say when he does? I've never been more mixed up in my life.* Gathering her robe and nightgown from the closet, she took them to the bathroom and turned on the water faucets in the tub, adjusting the temperature until it was just a touch hotter than she wanted. Then she added some scented crystals and watched them swirl and dissolve. Thinking that she heard a knock at the door, she turned off the taps and listened. The knocking startled her the second time. She went to the door.

"Derek!"

"Hi. I thought it would be better to call in person. May I come in?"

"Of—of course." Elena stepped aside and closed the door after him. "Please, have a seat. Can I get you anything? Coffee?"

"No, thanks," he said, crossing to the sofa. He sat down and rested an arm on the back of it. "I won't stay long. I just came by to say say I hope you're planning to come to New York. I've booked separate suites for us overlooking Central Park. I'm sure you'll like them."

Nervously Elena sat down in a chair facing him. "Derek—"

"You'll be perfectly safe, I promise."

In spite of herself, Elena could not help smiling. "I believe you, I really do. But—"

"But you're not interested in the ballet. Well, we could do something else instead. Take in a show, go to the symphony, anything you like."

She shook her head. "That's not it. I *am* interested in the ballet. It's something I've always dreamed of."

"Well, then, what's the problem?" he asked, a frown drawing his straight brows together.

"I'm not sure that I can explain it so you'll understand. I'm not sure I understand it myself." She rose and walked to the fireplace and stood before its cold emptiness, her back to him. "I can't go with you, Derek."

"Can't? Or won't?" He got up and covered the distance between them. Taking hold of her arm, he turned her around, as if to argue in his own defense. But seeing that she was in tears, he closed his mouth and put his arms around her. "You're right. I don't understand."

Elena stiffened slightly and drew away, wiping her cheeks with her fingers. "It was lovely of you to invite me to go. I know it must have cost a lot of money, not to mention all your time and trouble. And there's nothing I would rather see than the Russian Ballet. But I just can't do it. And I can't accept the evening bag, either. It's much too elegant."

"Right. Elegant. You can keep someone else's gift of fancy jewelry," he said bitterly, giving the ivory hearts at her throat a flick with his index finger, "just not anything *I* give you. Well, that's pretty clear."

"Please. It isn't like that. We're just friends—you said we'd just be friends—and it isn't appropriate for you to buy me extravagant things, or for us to go away together overnight."

"I said you'd be safe, Elena. I have no plans to seduce you while we're in New York."

"And I believe that. But I can't go away overnight with a man, Derek. It's against everything I believe. I teach a Sunday school class of teenage girls every week. What kind of example would I be setting for them if I went away with you? Who would *know* about the separate rooms? I couldn't live with myself if I did something that could lead them astray. I'm sorry. I don't want to hurt you, but I just can't go with you."

"So that's your answer?"

She nodded.

He clenched his teeth so tightly that she saw a muscle twitch in his jaw. Then his eyes lowered and he turned away. "Well, that's that, I suppose. Sorry I took up your time." He spun on his heel and reached for the doorknob.

"Wait, Derek," Elena said. "I want you to have these back." She picked up the evening bag from the table by the door. The tickets were on top, and she placed them carefully inside before handing the purse to him.

Derek gave her a long, searching look, then he shook his head and left.

12

After the Sunday morning service, on the day before the new year, Elena carried two pumpkin pies and a bag of homemade rolls to the Montgomery home. At the door, hands full, she considered ringing the bell with her nose, but it opened as if on cue.

"I saw you coming up the walk," said Stella, wiping her hands on her apron and taking the pies from Elena. "Mmmm, these look good. Come on in, dear."

Elena stomped the fresh snow off her boots and stepped inside. "What can I do to help, Mother?" She set the bag of rolls on the entrance table and hung her coat in the closet. The aroma of baked ham filled the house.

"Not a thing, except bring the rolls out to the kitchen. We have everything under control." Turning, she led the way.

Josh looked up from slicing celery at the counter and grinned. Elena smiled back. "So, the chef is at work again, I see."

"It seemed the reasonable thing to do. It's always a rush after church to get a big meal on the table, especially since we had to drop *you* off at your house," he added with a wink.

"Well, I'm here now," she said, setting the bag on top of the warming oven, "and I'm dressed to help."

"These are ready to be taken to the table," said Stella, indicating a bowl of steaming mashed potatoes. She emptied vegetables into a second dish as Elena took the potatoes into the dining room. They passed in the doorway on Elena's return. "There's a basket on the counter for the rolls," said Stella.

Elena transferred the rolls to the fabric-lined container and started for the dining table.

"I think this about does it," Josh said, putting the celery into a crystal glass and picking up a dish of olives and pickles. "If you have another hand, would you grab the teapot, Lane? Everything's ready."

The conversation was lighthearted as they ate the festive meal. "Hey," said Josh to Elena toward the end of the meal. "I dusted off the old guitar. How's about you and me whipping up a song for tonight, like old times?"

"You can't be serious!" she said, laughing.

"Oh? That's where you're wrong. We have all afternoon to come up with something. What do you say?"

Elena rested her chin on her closed fist and considered the proposal thoughtfully. "Oh well, why not?"

Instead of the regular evening service, a Watchnight program to welcome the New Year had been scheduled for nine o'clock. Elena had always loved the New Year's Eve services, and she went with Josh and his mother that evening. Even though her heart was aware of the bittersweet pain of missing the ballet in New York, she was conscious of an inner peace. She knew that she had made the right decision. Nothing could equal the joy of being with her family and Christian friends to experience the blessing of the Lord as the old year drew to a close and the first moments of a new one began.

The first section of the service was divided between a current missionary film and special music. The pastor had been delighted to add Josh and Elena's song to the list. When it was their turn to perform, they mounted the steps to the platform, and Josh adjusted the microphone. Elena caught sight of Marcy and Trent in the audience, and her friend's radiant smile calmed Elena's nerves. Josh's rich baritone voice blended perfectly with Elena's clear soprano as they sang.

The middle part of the service was a time for refreshments in the church basement and a chance to visit with friends. As soon as Elena walked into the room, Marcy ran up and hugged her.

"Marcy! I'm so glad you're here," Elena said. "And you brought Trent."

"There wasn't a service in our church tonight, and I wanted to come here and see you and Josh and everybody. Where is he, by the way? I want to introduce him to Trent."

Elena scanned the room. "I think he's talking to Pastor Douglas, up in the sanctuary. At least, that's what he was doing when I left."

"Oh, well, he'll be along soon. Come say hi to my fiancé, then."

Elena cocked her head to one side. "Fiancé?"

Marcy grinned. "That's right! I wanted you to be the first to know." She held out her left hand displaying her ring.

"Oh, Marcy! How beautiful! I'm very happy for you." Throwing her arms around her friend, Elena kissed her cheek. Arm in arm, they walked over to talk to the quiet, dark-haired man waiting on the sidelines for Marcy's return.

The final hour of the year began in the sanctuary. After a brief period for testimonies, Pastor Douglas gave a moving devotional, challenging everyone to commit the new year to the keeping of the Lord. Elena felt that the pastor was in his element when he preached a message like this. She knew he lived what he taught, and his life was an example of the Christian walk.

"In closing," he said, "I'd like to leave you with two verses from Proverbs, Chapter 3, that have meant a lot to me all through my life. 'Trust in the Lord with all thine heart, and lean not unto thine own understanding. In all thy ways acknowledge Him, and He shall direct thy path.' May this blessed promise be especially precious to you in this coming year."

The congregation joined hands in a huge ring around the sanctuary for prayer, and then sang "Blest Be The Tie That Binds." The sounds of bells, sirens, and fireworks broke forth in the countryside during the last notes of the song.

Standing in the circle between Josh and his mother, Elena felt Josh give her hand a gentle squeeze. She turned her eyes to his and saw him smile as he enveloped her in his long arms. "Happy New Year, Laney," he said. Stella smiled and wrapped her arms around both of them.

All around the circle people shared hugs and kisses and wishes for the new year, then some hurried away to the kitchen to gather up the remnants of the baked goods brought for the fellowship, and everyone left for home.

The weather on the first day of the year was typical for a Monday, gloomy and gray. Early in the morning sleet began to fall steadily.

Elena dressed warmly in gray wool slacks and a soft blue sweater and decided to take down the Christmas decorations after breakfast and straighten the house. Afraid that she was wearing out her welcome at the Montgomery home, she had declined Stella's dinner invitation. Josh and his mother deserved some time to themselves, she thought. Besides, there were several Christmas letters still to answer, and her mending had piled up. She knew that there was plenty to keep her occupied for the day.

Taking the empty box out of the spare bedroom closet, she set it by the tree, dusted the ornaments and put them away. Then she hauled the small tree outside onto her front porch. With the holiday clutter out of the way, the living room was much easier to clean, and once it had been dusted, Elena pulled the vacuum into her bedroom.

The small front bedroom, once Steven's room, had been wallpapered in a dainty, country floral print. She felt comforted without so much empty space around her. There were fewer bad memories to haunt her there. Practically the first thing she had done after the funerals was to move out of the big bedroom and, in a frenzy, she redecorated the entire house. Except for a few photographs, there was nothing in sight to remind her of her marriage. Everything looked clean and tidy after Elena had vacuumed and dusted. She partially closed the blinds and left the room.

Outside, the wind grew stronger, and the temperature dropped, turning the drizzle to ice. Setting the polish on the mantel for later, Elena turned on some music to cover the sound of the sleet lashing against the window and arranged several logs in the fireplace.

After the letters were answered, Elena stopped for a bite to eat, then tackled the mending. That chore put her to sleep, and she dozed in the warmth of the fire in the middle of the afternoon.

The ringing of the phone startled her. She answered on the third ring.

"Hi, kiddo. Happy New Year, again," Marcy's cheery voice said.

"Oh, hi, Marcy."

"I just called to see if you're getting much of this storm that's pouring all over us. Some great first day of the new year isn't it?"

Elena yawned and separated two slats of the blinds with her fingers to peer out. Stunned to see everything coated with an inch of ice, she gasped.

"What's wrong?" Marcy asked.

"It looks like the North Pole here, that's all. It's an ice palace."

"Good thing you won't be driving to work tomorrow."

"I suppose so. What are you doing today?"

"Getting ready to go out. Trent is taking me to dinner. To celebrate our engagement, and all."

"Sounds like fun. I'm glad you two finally got your priorities straightened out, Marce. He's a super guy."

"He sure is. Uh-oh, he's here. Gotta run. I'll miss you at work."

"Me too. Bye." At the buzz of the dial tone in her ear Elena replaced the receiver. She stretched the kinks out of her neck.

Noticing the furniture polish still sitting on the mantel, she decided to finish her last chore. With a sigh, she removed the pictures and vases, sprayed a fine mist of wax on the shelf, and polished it with a cloth. She dusted each object before replacing it, allowing her eyes to linger on the last item, the photographs in the hinged frame. Elena remembered Josh looking at it on one of his visits.

She studied the typical family portrait of her and Greg with their son sitting on her lap. In the other picture, Steven's angelic smile gazed back at her, and his shiny blond hair shimmered in the studio light. It had been as soft as silk to the touch, and her finger stroked the smooth surface of it in his likeness. She remembered the long red feather the photographer had given her to use to make him laugh. *Oh, Stevie,* she thought, *you had such a cute laugh . . . like musical notes on a descending scale. Such a sweet sound that used to fill my world. How I miss it. How I miss you. . . .*

Unexpectedly, her eyes filled with tears, and the clarity of the photographs became lost in a blur. Elena replaced the frame on the shelf. *All along Willow Tree Lane,* she thought, *and everywhere else, families are laughing and enjoying being together. And here I am, in this empty house, and I have no one.*

A wave of self pity washed over her. *It isn't fair,* she thought. *During family times and special days I should be able to have my little boy near. I should be able to watch him grow, to teach him about the Lord, to experience all the joys that other mothers take for granted.* She blinked hard and tried to dry her face with her fingers, but the tears would not stop.

Picking up the can of spray wax and the cloth, she heaved them into the broom closet and sank into a chair at the kitchen table. Dropping her head onto her folded arms she wept . . . softly, at first, then great wrenching sobs from the center of her being at the thought of Steven and the years of his life that were forever lost to her, of all the Christmas joys and birthdays they would never share. For an instant she was angry with Greg for having their little boy with him the night of the accident. She wished that he had been alone.

Elena was shocked at the depth of that bitter thought. She stopped crying and sat up, amazed that she could harbor such anger after two years. *Please forgive me, Father,* her heart cried out. *I didn't mean to think such a horrible thing. I know the accident wasn't Greg's fault. I'm sorry.*

The words that Pastor Douglas had spoken to comfort her in her grief reached out once again in her mind, and she could hear them as though he were standing before her even now. "There are no accidents in the will of God, Elena," he had said. "You must not blame God for this experience, but draw nearer to Him and allow Him to be all that you need. I know there is no easy way for you to get through a heartache like this, but, in time, you will be able to look back and thank Him for the years He gave you to enjoy with your loved ones while you were together."

Even now those words gave her comfort. The years she had known with her son were precious in her memory. He had given her so much joy, so much love. And he was with the Lord now, where nothing could ever hurt him. Elena dried her tears with a tissue. It had been silly to want to be alone today, she thought, when she knew that holidays always made her sad.

The telephone rang. Automatically, she picked it up. "Hello?"

"Hi, Laney," Josh said. "Want some company?"

Elena knew that if she spoke now it would be painfully obvious she had been crying, and she tried frantically to think of words without n's or m's that she could say in a conversation.

"Lane, are you there?"

"Yes."

"Well, could you use some company, I asked?"

"I . . . umb . . . no." She mentally kicked herself for her brilliant choice of words. There was no use trying to pretend any more that she hadn't been crying. She sounded awful, she knew.

"Elena, I'll be right over," he said, matter-of-factly.

"I'mb fide, Josh. Really I amb. It's not necessary."

"I'm already on my way." The click on the other end echoed in her head.

"Great!" she said aloud. "Just great." And she flew to the

bathroom to blow her nose and wash her tear-stained face.

A few moments later, she heard a soft tapping on the door. She hesitated, then placed her hand on the knob and felt it already turning. The door opened easily with their combined efforts, and Josh stepped inside. Elena looked incredulously at the ice skates he wore.

"I knew those skating lessons we took would come in handy someday," he said in mock seriousness.

She closed her eyes for a second and shook her head as Josh sat down to remove his skates. When she looked at him again his eyes were searching her face. Wondering if her nose still glowed, she took a deep breath.

Josh continued to stare as he stood and removed his jacket, placing it on the chair by the door.

Elena felt herself wilt under his scrutiny. Turning her back to him, she walked over to the window and pretended to look outside. *What must he think of me,* she thought, *a grown woman crying because she's by herself!*

Suddenly Elena felt a pair of strong hands on her shoulders, and she was being turned around again to face those deep gray eyes. Knowing that she could not meet his gaze, she stared at the middle button on his shirt and chewed the underside of her lip.

For the briefest of moments he kept his hands on her shoulders, then he drew her close to himself. "My poor little Laney," he said softly as he wrapped his arms around her. "We should never have left you alone."

Elena had almost forgotten what it felt like to be held against someone else's warmth and to feel another heart beating against hers. For a second it brought back the tender memory of other arms around her neck . . . arms tiny and strong. Her eyes brimmed with shimmering tears, and her composure shattered like a dropped Christmas ornament. "Oh, Josh, why am I still here? I should have been with them. I should have died too. I'm so tired of trying to be strong," she sobbed as she collapsed against him and wept.

Josh held her close, gently rocking her trembling form back and forth. "I know, my love. I know." His words were barely a whisper as his lips brushed her forehead with a soft kiss. "You shouldn't have to carry all this by yourself. Forgive me for not insisting that you spend the day with us." He held her next to his heart until her tears were spent, until she stopped shaking.

Elena gazed up at him, her lips quivering. She wiped her face with her hands and took a deep breath. "Seems like you've been comforting me for one thing or another ever since we were kids, and now here you are again."

He put his hands on either side of her face and smiled at her. "Hey, that's what friends are for, right?" Then he drew her close again and cradled the back of her head in one of his hands.

"I suppose. But sometimes I feel like I tax this friendship of ours to the limit." Elena felt, rather than heard, his soft chuckle. She eased back and looked up at him. "I . . . I think I'm okay, now, Josh. Really."

"You sure?"

She nodded.

He relaxed his hold and dropped his arms, but his finger lightly brushed away a tear from the middle of her cheek before he stepped away.

Elena had not even known it was there.

"Have you had supper yet?" he asked. "Or don't you *eat* supper?"

She smiled. "I wasn't very hungry before. Have *you* eaten?"

Josh shook his head and grinned.

"Well, look. I'll do what I can to make myself look human again, then see what I can fix to eat, okay? Sit down and make yourself comfortable. I won't be long."

Josh added logs to the fire and flipped through her record collection until he found some music that was cheerful but soft.

An hour later, as they were enjoying after-dinner coffee by the crackling flames, Elena turned and faced Josh. "I—I'm sorry . . . about before. Feeling sorry for myself, and all."

Josh shrugged. "No need to be sorry. We all have our low moments. I just wouldn't want to know that you were feeling down and not do something to help you through it." He reached over and took Elena's hand in his. "You've always been special to me, you know. What hurts you hurts me."

"What a nice thing for you to say."

"Hey, I'm a nice guy," he said with a grin.

Elena laughed. "That you are, all right. Sir Lancelot, always rescuing the local damsel in distress. And this damsel thanks you."

"Well, I suppose I'd better make my rounds, then, and check in on the queen," he said lightly. He went to the chair by the door to retrieve his jacket and tie on his skates. "It's really bad out there," he said with a wink. "I'd never have gotten here by car."

Elena stood by the door as he finished with the laces. Josh got up and put a hand on her shoulder, squeezing gently. "Take care, Lane. And if you ever need somebody again, give me a call, okay?"

She smiled and nodded. After watching Josh skate off toward his house, she closed the door and headed for the kitchen.

Long after Elena had gone to bed, her heart was strangely warmed by the thought of the comfort she had felt when Josh was there. Remembering it, a frown crossed her brow. Something he had said when he was holding her taunted her, like a child playing peekaboo in a hedge. What was it? she wondered, re-playing the scene in her mind. But it was no use. Whatever it was, it remained misty and just beyond her grasp. Perhaps it would come to her later.

Everyone has low moments, he had told her. Did Josh? she wondered. Surely he must. Elena remembered the expression in his eyes when he said that he had been in love once. She wondered who comforted him when he was down, and who, for that matter, could ever hurt him.

She yawned and turned on her side, closing her eyes. She was tired, physically and emotionally. But the misty memory was there again, teasing her consciousness in the last fleeting moments before she drifted off to sleep. If only she could remember his words.

13

"How's Elena?" Stella asked, coming across the room as her son took off his skates and hung his coat on a closet hook.

"Better. She shouldn't have been alone, that's all."

"I agree, but we can't force her to come here if she doesn't want to. Some of her excuses have sounded pretty convincing."

"I know. Well, I think she's okay now." He put an arm around Stella's shoulders and bent his head to kiss her cheek. "I'm beat, Mom. Guess I'll turn in, okay? I have some thinking to do."

From inside the crook of his long arm, she patted his back and smiled. "I want to finish the scarf I'm making for Mrs. Jenkins anyway. See you in the morning, dear." Crossing the room to her rocker, she picked up her knitting and sat down by the dying fire.

"Good night," Josh said, glancing over his shoulder. He mounted the steps two at a time. In his room he removed his watch and placed it on the dresser in front of a photograph of Elena he had taken at Chris's reception. After the usual formal groupings, he had filled the roll with shots of her. In most of them, Elena had smiled into the camera, and once she had sucked in her cheeks and assumed an exaggerated *Vogue* pose. But his two favorites had been taken when she was not looking. Those he had framed for his room.

He gazed at the likeness next to his watch and brushed her cheek lightly with the back of his finger. The haunting sadness reflected in her eyes seemed even more poignant with the suggestion of a smile. *My beautiful Elena,* he thought. *Will that pain ever go away? Will you ever really be free?*

Sighing deeply, Josh took off his slacks and laid them over the back of a chair. He unbuttoned his shirt and dropped it onto the floor and took off his socks. Then he knelt by his bed. He wanted to pour out his thoughts and feelings to the Lord, but when he closed his eyes, all he could see was Elena's face, her misty blue eyes, her tremulous lips.

What a joy it had been to enfold her in his arms and hold her close to his heart. It was all he could do to keep from proclaiming his love on the spot, he realized. But caution had held him back—except for one slip of the tongue. He had said it so softly that she hadn't noticed . . . or hadn't appeared to, anyway.

What if I told you that I love you, Laney? What would you do? If I'd told you years ago, would you have chosen me instead of Greg? Would you choose me now, or would you pick someone else? I've lived through that once already. I don't think I could endure it twice. No, I'll just be your friend, for a while. I have to. Until I'm sure.

He ran his fingers through his hair and climbed into bed.

The girls were already in their seats when Elena entered the Sunday school classroom and closed the door. "Good morning," she said with a smile, and they echoed her words. At her desk, she took the attendance and passed the roll book to the back of the room.

"Before we begin, let's bow our heads and ask the Lord to bless our new study. Valerie, would you like to do the honors?"

"Dear Heavenly Father," she began, "Please guide our thoughts as we look into Your Word, and show us what You have in it for us today. In Jesus' name. Amen."

The class looked up at Elena. "I'm glad that you all wanted to know more about prayer. After all, it's part of our relationship with God. These study guides will be a big help to us," she said, passing the booklets to Marybeth to distribute, "but some of the time we'll be searching for our own answers. To begin, I would like to ask, Is prayer important? Important to you?"

Sharon was the first to speak. "Well, I know it's supposed to be important to us."

"Why did you say, 'supposed to be'?" asked Elena.

"Because the pastor preaches about it, and because there's a lot about it in the Bible."

"So do you all pray a lot, then? Since it's so important?"

"Well, uh . . ." Sharon shrunk down in her seat.

Everyone laughed.

Elena continued. "Why do you suppose we don't pray as much as we should? Any volunteers?" She scanned the faces.

Valerie raised a hand. "Some people don't believe that God

really hears prayers—or answers them."

"That's a good point, Valerie. After all, why should the God of the universe care enough about insignificant humans and their problems when He is so busy running things. Right?"

The girls nodded.

"Well, all through the Bible we're told how God feels about us. But to keep it simple this morning, let's turn to the book of Ephesians. In the first four chapters, Paul gives us quite a list of the ways God sees those who believe in Christ."

The girls turned to the passage.

"Notice that in verses 3 through 8 of Chapter 1 Paul writes that we are blessed with every spiritual blessing, chosen before the beginning of time, loved, adopted, redeemed, and forgiven. What else can you find? Sharon?"

"Well," the girl answered, "in verse 9 it says that we've been given wisdom and understanding."

"And verse 11 says we have an inheritance," said Valerie.

"That's right," said Elena. "There's more in Chapter 1, but let's look now at Chapter 2. Notice verses 4 and 5. They tell us that because of God's love for us, He gave us life in Christ."

"And verse 10 says we're His workmanship," said Sharon.

Elena smiled. "To fill out the entire picture of the way God sees us, we'd have to continue on through the whole New Testament, of course. But just think about how much of God's love for us has been revealed in the few verses we've read. And now, on to *why* we should pray. Let's turn in our Bibles to Psalm 34, verse 15, and read it together."

When the pages stopped turning, Elena started to read, and the class joined in. " 'The eyes of the Lord are upon the righteous, and His ears are open to their cry.' "

"I have one more reference for you just a few books further on, in Isaiah. Turn to Chapter 65, verse 24; I'll read it while you find it. 'And it shall come to pass that, before they call, I will answer; and while they are yet speaking, I will hear.' Now, does that sound as though God is too busy to be concerned about those who love Him? To me, the verses say just the opposite. It even sounds like it's important to God that we do pray. Why do you suppose that is?"

After thinking for a moment, Marybeth answered. "Well, it's one of the ways we can tell Him we love Him."

"You mean, prayer can be more than just a 'gimme this' or 'gimme that' type of thing, then?" prompted Elena.

Marybeth nodded, thoughtfully.

"Then, let's look at the most famous prayer of all, the Lord's Prayer, in Matthew 6, verses 9 through 13. Let's examine the different parts of it and see what kinds of things we can learn to help us in our own prayers."

The whole month of January was bitterly cold. Heavy slate-gray clouds hung in the sky, and Pennsylvania shivered in the gloom.

Elena arrived at the office early on her first day back at work, dressed in brown wool slacks and a camel-colored blazer of brushed suede. As she placed her leather shoulder bag in the desk drawer, Marcy breezed in, breathlessly.

"Hi, Lane! Boy, are you ever a sight for sore eyes."

"So you missed me, then?"

"Let me tell you," she said, wagging her finger as she spoke, "missed is not the word."

"Well, I don't know if I like being back yet or not, Marce. I was getting used to the life of leisure," Elena said, watching her friend hang her coat in the closet and head for the coffee maker.

"I'll bet." Marcy filled the reservoir of the machine and set the pot in place. "I can just see you, sleeping in until seven-thirty, instead of six?"

Elena laughed. "You do know me, don't you? Well, I did make it all the way to eight, once."

Marcy groaned and took her seat. "And meanwhile, the rest of us slaves were toiling away here, day after day, without so much as the sunshine of your presence."

"Oh, right. Well, everything is still here, so you must have fared well enough."

Grimacing, Marcy nodded. "I guess. Speaking of sunshine, though, do you think that somewhere in the world the sun still shines? I can't even remember what blue sky looks like!"

Just then the phone rang, and Marcy picked it up. "Good morning. Webster and Webster."

Elena rose and crossed the room to fill two mugs with the freshly brewed coffee. After setting one on Marcy's desk, she returned to her own.

The door opened to admit Mr. Webster and Derek, obviously in the middle of a conversation.

"Well, I'll have to check it out with him, Father, and get back to you," Derek said. Walking briskly toward the inner office rooms, he nodded to Marcy and tossed a cool half-smile in Elena's direction as he passed.

The older man stopped at Elena's desk. "Good morning. It's good to see you back, Elena."

She opened her mouth to speak, but Marcy interrupted.

"Excuse me, Mr. Webster. That was Miriam on the phone. She says she is ill with the flu and won't be in for two or three days."

Glancing back at Elena, Mr. Webster rubbed his jaw line with his fingers. "I'm afraid that means we'll be keeping you pretty busy, my dear. I hope you won't mind."

"Not at all," she said, smiling.

"Well, in that case, I'll check today's agenda and let you know when I'll be needing you," he said as he walked to his office.

"You know," said Marcy, "I'm sure there's a Murphy's Law to cover this."

Elena looked puzzled. "What do you mean?"

"Mondays. There's never a calm, simple one." The ringing of the phone effectively silenced their banter.

That evening and the next, Elena stayed late, trying to make a dent in the pile of work in her tray. Both afternoons had been spent in taking dictation, and she was sure that there was no end to the correspondence or briefs in sight. Mr. Webster asked her if she could fill in on Wednesday in Miriam's absence, and she consented. Yawning as she drove home in the darkness, though, she wished that some previous commitment could have prevented having to work on her day off. Oh well, tomorrow couldn't be worse than today, she thought. At home, she fell asleep right after her prayers.

"Good morning," said Marcy, into the receiver the following morning. "Webster and Webster. Marcia Brandon speaking."

"Marcy, this is Josh."

"Oh, hi, Josh. She's not at her desk right now."

"What?"

"I said Elena's not—"

"Isn't Wednesday her day off?"

"Yes, normally, but she had to come in because—"

"Hey, I didn't call to talk to Elena, okay?"

"You didn't?"

"No. In fact, don't even tell her I phoned. I need to talk to you. Could we have lunch someplace?"

Marcy's jaw dropped. "You want to have lunch with me?"

"Yes, unless you have other plans. I'll meet you anywhere you like. Preferably someplace quiet."

"Wait a minute, here. You want *me* to meet you for lunch, behind my best friend's back, and not even tell her about it. Is that right?"

"I guess it does sound a bit underhanded, put that way. But this is important, Marcy. I wouldn't ask you if it weren't. What do you say?"

Marcy sighed as she considered his request. She glanced at the door of the inner office and then at her watch. "Well, I'll get off in about an hour. I guess I could meet you at the Coach House around eleven-thirty. Is that okay?"

"Great. See you then. Thanks, Marce."

Replacing the receiver on its cradle, she drummed on it absently with her index finger. Why the big secret? she wondered.

Elena returned to her desk just before it was time for Marcy to leave. Sinking into the chair with an exasperated sigh, Elena flopped her pen and shorthand notebook on the blotter and leaned back, crossing her legs.

"Another rough one?" her friend said with a smile.

"I may *never* finish this mess, Marce. Thank heavens he'll be in court after lunch."

Her words had barely faded away before Mr. Webster came through the office on his way out. He nodded and left, closing the outer door behind him.

Elena drew a slow breath, wondering if he had heard her last words.

"Well, I'm off, myself," Marcy said cheerily. "Hold the fort." She walked to the closet and took out her coat.

"You're not eating downstairs?" Elena asked with a yawn.

"Uh, no, actually. I . . . have an appointment." Buoyed by her fast thinking, her face brightened. "See you later." She waved from the doorway as she left.

Once at the Coach House, Marcy caught Josh's eye from the foyer. Indicating his table to the waitress, she joined him. He stood to help with her coat.

"Thanks," she said, sitting opposite him in the blue tweed booth. She picked up the menu lying on the woven placemat before her and scanned the entrees. "I haven't been here in a while."

"Neither have I. It's not bad."

Marcy smiled and looked around at the surroundings, admiring the frosted-glass panels with gleaming brass fittings separating the various areas of the restaurant. She glanced past the dark blue print curtains and out the window at the Susquehanna River, somber now with its thick layers of ice. Bare cherry trees stood like palace guards along its banks, and dismal snow hid the contours of the landscape.

A young waitress in colonial dress approached the table. "May I help you?"

"Yes, I'll have the breast of turkey sandwich on rye, please," said Marcy, "and coffee."

Josh looked up at the young waitress. "I'd like some coffee, too, with a ham and turkey club, and fries."

"I'll be right back with your drinks," she said, removing the menus. Within moments, she returned with frosted glasses of water and the coffeepot.

"What's this all about, anyway?" asked Marcy, adding cream and glancing at her watch.

"Right to the point, huh?" he teased.

"Well, I only have an hour for lunch, you know."

"I figured that."

They each took a sip of coffee.

"How's—" he paused, thinking, "—Trent, isn't it?"

She smiled and nodded. "He's good. But we're not here to discuss Trent, are we?"

The waitress arrived with their plates and left quietly.

Josh bowed his head, and Marcy followed suit as he thanked the Lord for their food.

Looking up, Josh grinned. "That looks good. They always did have pretty decent food here." He picked up a section of his club sandwich and took a bite.

Marcy drank more coffee and took stock of her companion before trying her food. She noticed that, oddly enough, they both were dressed in kelly green and gray. *We probably look like a matched set,* she thought, smiling inwardly. For several moments, they ate in silence.

Josh dipped a french fry in ketchup and bit it in half. "You say Lane is working today?"

"Yes. Our secretary is out with the flu, so someone had to cover for her."

"How's she been, since she's been back at work?"

Marcy tossed her head speculatively. "Same as always. Why do you ask?"

"I've been a little worried about her. She was sort of down on New Year's."

"Oh, really? I talked to her that day, and she sounded fine to me."

"Well, that must've been before I saw her."

Marcy shrugged. "It's not unusual, Josh, for someone to get depressed on holidays . . . being alone, and all."

"Yes, I know. But she wasn't just depressed, Marcy. She was hurting." A frown creased his brow as he spoke, and eyes as gray as morning mist searched her face. "She's *always* hurting . . . inside. I know her. I can see it."

After finishing the last of her coffee, Marcy drew her lips inward slightly and considered his words. "I know," she said softly.

"It had to be a terrible blow, losing a husband and son so suddenly. But, Marcy, I have a gut feeling there's more. There has to be something else. Do you know what I'm saying? What can you tell me about her marriage?"

Lowering her eyes, Marcy expelled a deep sigh. "I didn't see very much of her after she married . . . him."

"Why not?"

"I don't know how to explain it, Josh. She just wasn't the same. I did go over a few times, before he took her out of state. But she seemed so nervous when he was around, we could hardly visit. We could barely talk on the phone."

A muscle twitched in his jaw, and his eyes narrowed, but Josh remained silent.

Marcy went on. "When he spoke, she jumped. And nothing she did seemed to suit him. He was super critical of her: how she looked, the way she dressed, you name it. He even had her cut her hair the way he wanted it."

Josh shook his head. "I can't see that. They seemed—"

"Well, at first I think they really were happy. But, for some reason, within a few months all her happiness seemed to be put on, like an act."

"But you don't know why?"

"Not really. She never talked about it, Josh. I wish I could help you."

"So do I," he said with a sigh, then drained his cup.

Marcy studied him. "There's something else, right?"

"Yes, there is." He absent-mindedly rubbed his jaw. "But I decided not to ask. Oh, what the heck. How involved is she with Webster?"

Marcy stifled a knowing grin. "She sees him outside the office a few times a week, but she insists that it's all in friendship. Personally," she paused, wondering whether to continue, "personally, it looks to me like he's really trying to push the relationship forward."

"That's what I figured." He reached for the check.

"Can I ask you something?" Marcy asked, as she stood up and draped her coat over one arm.

"Sure." He got to his feet and took her wrap, holding it while she slipped it on.

"Why didn't you go after Elena when you had the chance?"

Josh smiled and shook his head. "That's something I've asked myself a thousand times. I guess it goes back to one thing. She was barely fifteen when I went away. She was still a young girl. I thought I had plenty of time."

"I see what you mean. And you might have had, too. If only—"

"I know."

When Marcy returned to the office, Elena was on the phone. "Yes," she said. "I'll be sure to give him your message, Mr. Franklin." After replacing the instrument, she went back to her own desk. "I'm glad you're back. I'm starved. Everything go okay with your appointment?"

"Oh, sure. It went fine." Reaching down to place her purse on the floor near her feet, she straightened in her chair and turned to face her friend.

Elena was already on her way to the door. "I'll be going to lunch, then. See you soon."

The door closed behind her.

"Oh, Lane," Marcy said into the silence, "someone besides you is hurting, and he's hurting badly."

Josh went alone to the midweek service that evening, for Elena's house was dark. He came straight home after the service and decided to turn in early. Far too restless to sleep, however, he welcomed the ringing of the bedside phone, hoping it would be her voice that he heard. "Hello?"

"Hi, buddy. It's me. Jake."

He sat up in bed and clicked on a lamp. "Jake?" Disappointment crossed his face. "What's up?"

"I'm having some problems with that new design we started on. You know? The specs just don't seem to add up, and I'm having a devil of a time trying to figure out what's wrong. Do you have time this week to take a run over and help me unravel them?"

Josh expelled a long breath through his nostrils. "Sure, pal. I'll come tomorrow."

"Thanks. Shouldn't take more than a couple of days."

"Right. See you then." He replaced the receiver and lay back down. *These are probably the plans I drew while I had my mind on somebody else,* he thought. *I'm glad the problem is just on paper, not in the air.*

On impulse, he reached for the phone again and dialed Elena's number. On the fourth ring, as he was about to hang up, he heard a groggy voice answer.

"Hello?"

So that's how you sound when you first wake up in the morning, he thought. A slight smile softened his mouth. "Oh, sorry, Lane, I didn't mean to wake you. I was just checking to see if you got home safely."

"Josh," she said, clearing her throat. "I've been working late this week."

"So I've noticed. Are you okay?"

"Sure. I'm fine. And you?"

"Same as usual. Oh, I'll be going to Williamsport tomorrow to work with Jake for a few days. I just wanted to let you know."

"Oh."

That's all? he thought. *Oh? Well, did I expect you to cry and beg me to stay?* "Well, take care of yourself, okay?"

"You too. I'll . . . be thinking about you, Josh."

That's a start, anyway, he thought. *Maybe there's hope after all.* "Good night, Laney."

"Night, Josh. Be careful, please?"

"I will. See you in a few days. Bye." After hanging up the phone, he turned off the light, lay down, and fell asleep with a smile on his face.

14

Miriam returned to the office, gaunt and pale, the following week. After a glance at her tidy desk, she set about her work and kept to herself throughout the day.

An hour before closing, Marcy glanced over her shoulder at Elena. "How can you stand all that gratitude?"

"Did you say something?" Elena asked, looking up from the computer terminal.

"I noticed that Miss Prissy hasn't said one thing about all the work that wasn't waiting for her when she came back . . . or about the flowers we sent. She has to be about the most selfish, ungrateful prude I've ever seen."

Elena shrugged. "It's no big deal, Marce. Don't worry about it."

"Sure, no big deal. You just stayed after hours a few nights, worked on your day off, and barely had lunch breaks. Who would've noticed?"

"Well, maybe I shouldn't have worked so hard. Maybe Miriam was hoping to find everything in chaos, so that she'd feel indispensable. Ever think of that?"

Marcy folded her arms and shook her head, remaining silent for a few moments. "And she isn't the only one who's been ignoring you, I noticed."

"Hmmm?" Elena rose and crossed the room to get a drink of water from the cooler.

"Mr. Junior Executive has barely made his presence known here for days. He's in his office before you and I even arrive. And he must be using the emergency exit if he goes anywhere, because he sure doesn't pass us. What in the world happened?"

Dropping the empty paper cup into the wastebasket, Elena tossed her head and turned to face her friend. "I guess I hurt his feelings, turning down the ballet. But he couldn't have expected me to go with him, could he, Marce? Not really."

Marcy didn't answer.

Elena glanced at the thick coffee on the warming plate and wrinkled her nose. "Yuck. I think we're through with this." Smiling, she left for the restroom, returning moments later with the empty pot.

"What's new with our friend Josh?" Marcy asked as Elena returned to her desk and sat down.

"He's away, at the moment." She pressed the Save button and removed the disk, then turned off the computer and put the vinyl cover over it. "He had some work to do in Williamsport, on the planes."

"So I guess you must be lonesome, then, when you go home."

Elena cast a sideways glance at her. "Why would you think that?"

"Well, you know. You must have gone to church by yourself yesterday . . . that sort of thing. You do usually go with Josh, don't you?"

"Yes, but why do you always give me the third degree about him, Marcy?" She cocked her head to one side and frowned.

"Well, you never want to talk about Josh. I just wondered what's up with him, that's all."

"Well, it's like this. He's busy doing the big brother act again, and I'm the little sister, and nothing is up. That about covers it."

"Oh." Marcy turned to tidy her desk before leaving.

Elena dozed on the sofa, her Bible and lesson manual on her lap. She awakened with a start when the telephone rang. Sitting up, she stretched and yawned, then reached to answer it. "Hello?"

"Hi, Lane. It's me. Josh."

"Josh! It's nice to hear your voice. How are you?" She closed her books and set them on the end table beside her.

"Not too bad. I was just about to turn in for the night and decided to check up on my girls."

Elena smiled to herself at his words.

"So how's everything with you?" he asked.

"Fine. Everything's normal, even at work."

"Well, that's good news. I was afraid that you were still working your fingers to the bone, day after day."

"Oh, that ended last Friday. Now it's just back to the routine. How are the problems with the planes coming?"

"Jake and I redid the specs and started to work on a mock-up of the new model. So far it's looking good. We may take our designs on the road again soon. There's a fly-in scheduled for homebuilts out on the West Coast next month, and we'd like to go."

"That sounds like fun. I hope things go well for you."

"Me too. Lane, I . . ."

"Yes?"

"Oh, nothing. I'll see you when I get home."

"Okay. Take care, Josh. We miss you."

"We?"

"Your girls—Mom and I."

"Oh. Right. G'night, Laney."

"Bye, Josh."

Several moments later, as she turned down the pale blue bedspread, Elena finally realized how empty her day had been before his phone call. *I'm getting too used to having him around,* she thought. *Funny, maybe I really am lonesome when he's away, just like Marcy says.*

The following morning Elena arrived at work early. She adjusted the vertical window blinds and peered out at the swirling snowflakes, fluffy and feathery against the grayness of the day. Traffic on the street below crawled at a snail's pace, and warmly dressed pedestrians walked swiftly against the brisk wind. Sighing, she stepped over to the coffee maker and put a new filter in place. The door opened and closed as she measured grounds and added water.

"Hi, Marcy," she said without turning around.

"Good morning," answered Derek's masculine voice.

Elena turned abruptly.

"Looks like we're the only early birds this morning," he said with a half-smile. His brown eyes twinkled.

"Looks like," she echoed, making a nonchalant sweeping gesture as she spoke. Her hand brushed the open coffee can, knocking it to the floor and spilling the remaining grounds on the tweed carpet. "Darn," she muttered, faint color rising on her cheeks as she knelt beside the mound.

Derek chuckled. "Not to worry. I'll help you clean it up. Do we have a broom anywhere?"

"Yes," Elena said, relieved. "It's in—" she finished lamely, "—

the women's room. I'll get it." She stood up and hurried away. When she returned, Derek had already scooped up most of the dry coffee with index cards and disposed of it.

"See?" he said. "It wasn't bad at all. The can must have been almost empty anyway."

"Well, thanks for helping, Derek. I'll just sweep up the rest." She bent to finish up with the broom, using the card he offered as a dust pan.

"Some things just take a bit of teamwork," Derek teased. "We do make a good team, now and then, wouldn't you say?"

Elena looked up at him curiously.

"I'm getting tired of eating by myself all the time. Would you like to have lunch today?" He raised his brows in question.

Surprised, Elena switched the broom to her other hand. "Well, thank you, Derek, but I—"

"Oh, come on," he coaxed. "We could have separate tables, if you like."

She knew that he was teasing. The ridiculous suggestion struck her as funny, and they broke into laughter at the same time.

"Well? What do you say?" he prompted.

Elena shrugged one shoulder and nodded.

"Good. See you later, then. About eleven-thirty." Turning, he tipped his hand in mock salute and walked briskly to his office.

Staring after him, she wondered briefly what had just happened. *Oh well*, she reasoned, *it's the least I can do, considering how badly I hurt his feelings over the holidays. After all, it's only lunch.*

"You what?" Marcy asked incredulously as she and Elena talked later that afternoon.

"I said, I decided to go to the symphony with him tomorrow night," Elena answered. "We had such a nice lunch, and we got to talking about music, and, well, one thing led to another."

"Oh, I'll bet." Marcy shook her head, her chestnut hair swinging rhythmically. She picked an imaginary piece of lint from her apricot sweater sleeve and, brown eyes sparking, looked across the room at her friend. "And just what do you think Josh is going to think about that?"

"Josh?" Elena asked, frowning. "What in the world does he have to do with it?"

Marcy rolled her eyes upward and gave an exaggerated shrug. "Darned if I know. I was just making conversation." Shaking her head again, she turned in her chair to face forward.

Elena rose and walked over to Marcy's desk. "Marcy, what do you think—that Josh is my keeper, or something? That I have to check with him whenever I go out with anyone?"

"No," she said softly. "I know he isn't like that."

"Well, what then?" Elena demanded. "Josh and I aren't . . . good grief, Marce! He isn't . . . interested in me. Not in that way. I mean, we've always been close friends, but that's it. I'm sure he never . . ." Grimacing at her friend, Elena walked away, her thought dangling, unfinished, even in her own mind.

That night, she slept restlessly, drifting in and out of a dream where she was parading an endless line of men past Josh as he sat on an enormous throne. Marcy was there, on the sidelines, laughing, always laughing. The sound of it woke Elena, and she sat up in bed. The laughter turned out to be the barking of the German shepherd next door.

Elena shook her pillow and lay back down again. *It must have been that chicken teriyaki I had for lunch,* she thought. *That sauce always makes me dream weird things.*

In the red plush seats of Kirby Center, Elena sat next to Derek, lost in the majestic music of Aaron Copland's *Appalachian Spring.* The concert hall was filled with people obviously awed, as she was, by the glorious talent of the American composer.

During intermission, as Elena and Derek sipped soft drinks, Mr. and Mrs. Webster approached. The older gentleman put his hand on his son's shoulder and inclined his head.

Mrs. Webster drew a gloved hand from under her luxurious sable coat and extended it to Elena. "How nice to see you again, my dear."

Elena returned the overly polite smile with one of her own. "Lovely concert, isn't it?" she said, releasing the woman's hand.

"Yes. You must come to the reception we're hosting for the conductor later."

Elena smiled. "Thank you, but I'm afraid it's not possible this evening." She wondered if the slight wave of relief that crossed Mrs. Webster's face was her imagination.

"Well, perhaps another time, then."

The lights dimmed twice, signaling the second half of the symphony. Mr. Webster smiled genuinely at Elena and nodded to Derek as they turned to leave.

The remainder of the program consisted of Copland's *Rodeo*. Dancers from the Wilkes-Barre Ballet Theater Company performed flawlessly, and Elena was intoxicated by the brilliant colors of their costumes and the orchestra's sweeping music.

"I guess I got you to the ballet after all," Derek teased during a break in the music.

Elena felt herself blush, and she was glad the only lights were on stage. "Yes, seems that way."

Her date chuckled.

"Why so quiet?" Derek asked later, as the Mercedes purred softly over the snow-packed highway.

Elena smiled. "Sorry, I didn't mean to be. I was still at the symphony, with music swimming around and around in my head. I'll probably be listening to it for days."

"I'm glad you enjoyed it. It was one of my favorite programs." He bent his head slightly, and the reflection of a streetlight danced against the soft waves of his hair as he gazed at Elena. Then his attention returned to the road.

"I have most of that music at home on records," she said, "but somehow hearing it in person makes it even more wonderful. Don't you agree?"

"And hearing it with you makes it better still," Derek said. He placed his hand on Elena's resting on the soft velvet folds of her skirt.

She stiffened, and he withdrew his hand, steering the car onto the side of the road. He turned off the motor. "Why do you always *do* that?" he asked, a note of exasperation in his voice. "Do you hate me, or what?"

Elena sat looking down at her hands, clasped tightly now in her lap. She pressed her lips together tightly and turned to face him. "Of course I don't hate you," she said, her words barely audible. "I don't hate anyone. And I don't *know* why I do that. I really don't."

"Is it that you can't stand to be with me, then?"

She looked away. "Of course not. I enjoy your company, very much."

"Then what is it, pet? Why can't I ever touch you without making you afraid?"

Neither spoke for several moments. Elena's thoughts struggled within her head. "Maybe I *am* afraid . . . that people I care about will be taken away from me."

Derek could see tears in her eyes, and they glistened in the lights of passing cars. "Elena, you can't go through your whole life all by yourself, in some safe cocoon, can you?"

Unable to answer him, she stared straight ahead into the darkness.

With a sigh, Derek started the engine and drove onto the highway again.

The remainder of the ride was silent. Elena could feel the barrier between them but could think of no way to alter her feelings or erase the things she had said. She wondered if she would make it all the way home before losing her composure.

Always the gentleman, Derek walked Elena to her door and unlocked it for her. When she attempted to thank him for the evening, he smiled a sort of cynical smile that curved only one side of his mouth. "Sure," he said. "Anytime." Then he turned and walked away.

When the evening Bible study on the Montrose Christian radio station ended with a hymn, Josh inserted a cassette into the tape player. *Another half hour and I'll be home,* he thought, as he cruised along the newly plowed country roads listening to some of his favorite European love songs. At least it has stopped snowing, he thought; there's no need for the wipers anymore.

He patted his shirt pocket through the open zipper of his down jacket, feeling the photograph near his heart. He drew it out and, in the glow of the dashboard, smiled at Elena's likeness. "If you only knew how much I miss you," he said out loud, shaking his head, "and what I'd give to be going home to you right now." Planting a kiss squarely in the middle of her face, he put the photo back into his pocket.

He barely noticed the remaining miles as his mind lost itself in thoughts of misty blue eyes, long silky waves, and the fragrance that was Elena. Making the last turn onto Willow Tree Lane, he wanted to burst into song.

That feeling continued right up until he saw the silver Mercedes driving away from her house. Then, his spirit took a nose dive, crashed, and burned.

15

As the laughing, chattering students filed out of the classroom, Elena stood at the window, awed by the beauty of the winter landscape. The clear blue of the sky was reflected in rich blue-gray shadows upon stark white snowdrifts and frost-coated trees. Someone should be here with a camera, she thought, taking pictures for next year's calendar.

"You wanted to see me?"

Elena turned. "Yes, Valerie. Thanks for staying behind. I . . . wanted to ask you about Janice. Do you still see her?"

"Yeah, we have a lot of classes together at school."

Breathing a sigh of relief, Elena smiled. "Oh, then she's okay?"

Valerie's gaze did not waver. Lips slightly parted, she chewed her gum in slow motion, as though she debated whether or not to confide in the adult before her. Then she answered. "Yeah, she's okay, I guess. Scott signed up with the Army and has gone to Alabama for basic training."

"Oh. Well, do you think Janice would like to come to our sledding party next Saturday? I could give her a call."

Sunlight glistened against Valerie's short honey-blond hair as she tossed her head. Her expressive chestnut eyes brightened as she smiled, and gold metallic threads in her aqua sweater sparkled with her movements. "Well, I can ask her tomorrow at school, okay?"

"Sure. That would be great. Thanks."

The first strains of organ music drifted softly through the closed door of the room as Valerie nodded and turned to leave. As her fingers touched the doorknob, Elena, a step behind, spoke her name. Valerie looked back.

"We'll get her back, honey. I'm still praying for her."

Valerie pressed her lips together in a smile. "Me too." Wordlessly, she reached out and hugged her teacher. Then, opening the door, she headed toward the sanctuary.

Josh rose and stepped into the aisle as Elena approached. She noticed that he did not return her smile but flashed a tiny hint of a wink instead as she stepped past him and sat down by his mother. Stella smiled and patted her hand, and the pastor opened the service in prayer.

All through the song service, Elena observed that Josh's rich baritone voice seemed subdued. He had been almost silent during the drive to church, she recalled. Later, when he helped take the offering, she watched him. Something must be wrong, she thought. Where is that twinkle in his eyes? she wondered. Where is the smile that is always such a part of him?

As Pastor Douglas announced the text for the morning sermon, Josh took his seat. Elena looked at him questioningly, but he turned his head away slightly and picked up his Bible from the pew beside him. Turning her attention to the front again, she watched from the corner of her eye as Josh turned automatically to the right page and raised his gaze toward the pulpit. She shifted in her seat and swallowed, feeling an odd tickle in her throat.

"Before we study God's Word this morning, let's bow our heads in prayer," the pastor said.

Elena's active imagination took full rein of her thoughts all through the devotional, and before she knew it, the organ was alive with the introduction to the closing hymn. Amazed, she reached for the hymnal and checked to see the page number in Josh's book. His Bible still lay open in his hand as he sat woodenly in place, staring at nothing. She looked at Stella's open hymnbook, turned to the selection, and gently nudged Josh as she moved her book over so that he could look on.

Clearing his throat, Josh closed his Bible and set it on his other side. Then he held a side of the hymnal and joined in, only to stop partway through and release his grip. Elena nearly dropped the book. *This is going to be a fun day*, she thought. *It's my turn to make the dinner*.

The table was already set when the trio reached Elena's cottage, and they were greeted by the aroma of roast beef. "Make yourselves at home," she said to Stella and Josh as she took their coats. "Everything'll be ready in a few minutes." Laying their wraps on her bed, she tied on a half-apron and headed for the kitchen to reheat the potatoes. Josh was already at the stereo, and Elena grimaced to herself when the classical music started. Today of all days, she thought, something more lively would be better. He had barely said a word all the way home.

"You've bought new dishes," Stella said, admiring the white china as they sat down at the table a short time later.

"Yes," Elena said. She checked to see that her best crystal salt and pepper shakers were there. The gold rims of the plates do look pretty against the peach tablecloth, she thought. Removing a napkin from its crystal ring, she glanced across the table at Josh. "Would you please ask the blessing?"

He nodded, and they joined hands while he prayed.

"Everything looks lovely, dear," Stella said afterward as Josh handed her the platter of beef. "And isn't it a pretty day today?"

Elena smiled. "The sunshine woke me early, streaming through the blinds. I got up to make sure it wasn't a dream." She passed the steamed broccoli to Josh, careful to avoid his eyes.

"In fact," she continued, "the blue sky inspired me to plan a sledding party for my girls next Saturday, and I mentioned it in class. It was all I could think about during the morning service."

"Sledding party?" Josh echoed, looking at her.

"Yes. Sounds like fun, doesn't it? Do you think the high-school boys would like to join us?"

He considered her suggestion briefly. "Sure. They haven't had an outing since I've been back, I know that. It could be fun. Where will you have it?"

Elena noticed that the stormy gray of his eyes had brightened to a soft misty shade. "I thought I'd ask Stan Parks if we could use that high back field of his, where we used to go when his dad owned the place. Remember?"

"I haven't seen any young people there for years," said Stella, "not since his dad passed away."

"I know, but I'm pretty sure he'll agree. He was always so nice to Mom and Dad. And if he says no, Valerie Bancroft says she has an uncle in Tunkhannock who might let us use his farm."

"We'll go to see Stan this afternoon, then," said Josh. "Maybe we can arrange all the details."

"Good," Elena answered, glad to see him smiling again. She heard Stella expel a soft sigh of relief and glanced at her, meeting the sparkle of her clear blue eyes.

Driving home from church later that evening, Josh had as many plans as Elena for the party. "If it's cold," he said, suddenly, "it might be a good idea to have a small bonfire. If Stan doesn't mind, that is."

"Yes, that way the kids could warm up before we go home," Elena agreed.

"You're planning to take care of all the food, right?"

She nodded.

"Then I'll bring hot chocolate."

"This is going to be great fun, Josh. I hope they have a good time."

"I'm sure they will. Shall we stop for coffee?" he asked as the car turned onto the Dallas highway.

"Why not?" she teased. "I'd like to ask you for more ideas. We'll need a short devotional, you know, after the party. Do you think you could work something up? It would be a treat for the girls to hear someone besides me preaching at them."

Just before midnight, Stella tapped softly on Josh's bedroom door and heard him respond. She opened it and stood in the doorway.

"Am I keeping you awake?" he asked. "Sorry." He put his pencil down on his drafting table and tried to make some order out of the chaos of papers before him.

"I heard the music. I just came to say good night. Will you be up much longer?"

He crossed the room in three strides and hugged his mother. Planting a kiss on the tip of her nose, he grinned sheepishly. "No, not much longer. I'm just trying to shorten my night a little. I'll turn the music off, though. How about that?"

"It's okay if you just turn it down a bit. I'll see you in the morning."

" 'Night, Mom." He turned and took a step back toward his work area. He glanced over his shoulder and saw his mother still poised in the doorway, and he stopped.

"Are you okay?" she asked.

"I will be. I sort of went through a bad time, but everything will be all right. Don't worry about it."

She smiled and closed the door.

Josh turned off the music, returned to the table and picked up his pencil. About to sit down, he noticed that all he had accomplished was filling numerous empty spaces on his wing drawing with Elena's name. *I might as well pack it in,* he thought. After undressing, he extinguished the light and peered out of his window at her house. It was in darkness. "Sleep well, my love," he whispered. Then he turned down his covers and got into bed. Lying on his back, he stared wide-eyed at the ceiling.

Elena awoke the following morning with a sore throat. Hoping to ease the tightness in her chest, she took a hot shower, but that only made her feel worse. Looking in the mirror at the dark circles under her eyes, Elena groaned inwardly. She dried herself in a hurry and wrapped the towel around her body. *A fresh nightgown would be just the thing,* she thought. *Then I'll have to phone Marcy.*

After finding her one and only flannel nightie in her bottom drawer, she slipped it over her head and buttoned every last button. Already she felt goosebumps. Reaching into the back of her closet, she found an old, heavy robe and pulled it on, tying the belt around her slim waist. She sat down on the edge of the bed and reached for the phone.

"Good morning. Webster and Webster. This is Marcia Brandon," she heard in the receiver.

"Marcy," she tried to say. The name came out in a near croak.

"I beg your pardon?"

Elena struggled to clear her throat. "Marcy," she repeated. Her voice sounded foreign to her own ears.

"Yes?" her friend asked.

"It's me. Elena."

"Laney! What in the world is wrong with you? You sound awful."

Elena grimaced. "I feel even worse than I sound."

"Well, get right in bed. Do you hear? I'll tell Mr. Webster you won't be coming in for a day or two."

"Marce?"

"Yes?"

"Be sure to tell Miriam to put me down for a sick day. Yellow is about my color right now."

Marcy's giggle brought a smile to Elena's face. "I'll call you tomorrow, kiddo. Take care."

"Thanks. Bye." Shivering as she hung up the phone, Elena crawled under the blankets on her bed, still in the robe.

It wasn't until hours later that a sound awakened her. Startled, she sat up and pulled the covers up to her chin.

"Do you know that your door is unlocked?" Josh asked with a grin as he peeked into her room. "I fixed it so well that I was afraid I'd have to break in."

"Josh!" Elena mouthed the name, but no sound came out. "What are you doing here?" she managed to whisper. *Great,* she thought, *I'm mad, and I don't need him here, and I can't even sound serious.* Indignantly, she put her head down on the pillow.

"I noticed your car was still out front, so I came to check on you. I brought some chicken soup. Best remedy in the world, you know."

Elena glared at him. *Checking up on me?* she thought. *I don't even have any privacy!* Then a second thought made its way through the dense fog in her brain. *With chicken soup? Just wait'll I get my hands on that Marcy!*

"It's cold in here, you know," Josh said as he removed his jacket. "Where's your thermostat?"

She opened her mouth to speak, but he continued.

"Never mind, I'll find it. And I'll get a fire going, too. Sure is nice and quiet, though," he teased.

Clenching her teeth, Elena turned her face away and stared at the wall across the room. *Keep it up, wise guy,* she thought. Still, the sound of another presence in her normally silent house grew strangely comforting as she listened to Josh chopping wood in the basement, mounting the steps two at a time, building a fire. Memories of another time came to her mind, and Elena fought against tears and lost. Sitting up to blow her nose, she reached for a tissue, but found the box empty. *Honestly!* she thought sarcastically. *Now I get to look like Rudolph, with red eyes besides.* She tried to get out of bed.

"No way, lady." Josh gently pressed against her shoulder with one hand. "Whatever you need, I'll get it. Now what is it?"

Lying down, she pointed to the empty tissue box.

"Do you have any more?" he asked.

Grimly, she shook her head.

"Laney, Laney, Laney." His head shook back and forth with each repetition of her name. "Well, this'll have to do for now." Reaching into his back pocket, he removed a clean handkerchief and held it out. "I'll get you some tissues later. Is there anything else you need?"

Her fingers touched his as they closed around the handkerchief. Self-consciously, she jerked it away and dabbed at her nose.

"You're still cold," he said. "I'll bring you an electric blanket, too."

"Please, Josh," she rasped. "I don't need anything. Just leave me alone."

"Sure," he said, his voice teasing. "The lady would rather die alone. Well, that's too bad. I have to keep you alive for Saturday. I can't handle all those females by myself, you know."

Elena rolled her eyes upward with a grimace. "I give up."

"Now, see? That's more like it. You just go back to sleep, and let me take care of everything."

She closed her eyes in obedience, surprised at how sleepy she felt.

16

Elena drifted in and out of sleep for the next two days, waking during the daytime to the soft sounds of Josh's presence as he puttered and fixed things around the house. Hearing the tapping of a hammer outside, she supposed that there was no longer a loose porch step. She wondered what other repairs had taken place.

On her way back from the bathroom during the night, she noticed Stella Montgomery sleeping on the couch. Elena smiled to herself. Not since her stay in the hospital, a few years ago, had anyone waited on her hand and foot while she recuperated in bed. A soft blue bundle had been placed in her arms then, and she remembered counting fingers and toes and caressing the tiny velvet head. Her eyes misted suddenly as sorrow clogged in her throat. *Oh, Stevie,* she thought. *I can't let myself think about you.*

"Are you all right, dear?" Stella asked in the dim light as Elena passed by.

She swallowed, nodding. "I'm beginning to feel better. I'm just sleepy all the time." She tried to smile.

"Probably the antibiotic, but rest will help, you know."

"I suppose." Elena placed her hand on the doorjamb of the bedroom and looked back. "Thanks for being here, Mother." Turning swiftly, lest she cry, Elena crept back into bed.

On Friday Elena returned to the office, only to learn that both Mr. Webster and Derek had been out of town for days and there was no backlog of work waiting for her.

On her way home from work two hours early, she removed her gloves and popped a cough drop into her mouth as the car warmed in the afternoon sun. There were last-minute details to finish for the sledding party, and Elena was glad for the extra time.

Pulling into the grocery store parking lot, she reached into her coat pocket for the shopping list she had prepared during her lunch hour. The original menu had changed drastically since the all-girl party had been changed to coed. She chuckled at the thought of serving fancy-shaped sandwiches on colored bread to all the high-school boys. And the coconut ice cream snowballs would have been a joke. Long live the ever-popular hamburger, she thought.

At home, pressing the ground beef into patties, Elena heard a soft tapping on the door. She washed her hands and hurried to answer it, opening the door wide.

"Hi, Lane," Josh said.

"Hi. Come on in. I'm just making the hamburgers so that they'll be ready tomorrow."

She turned to walk back to her chore, and Josh strode after her.

"We got all the paper plates and cups," he said.

"Good. I hope we've thought of everything." She looked up to find him scrutinizing her face. "Something wrong?"

"No. Your color is better today, that's all. How do you feel?"

"Well, after being waited on like a helpless invalid for three days, I couldn't help but recover."

"We overdid it, huh?"

"No, not really. I'm just not used to so much attention. Actually it was rather nice. Except now I'll be forever in your debt, of course," she said, a teasing note in her voice.

"I know." A slow smile played over his lips. "But remember, I need you tomorrow, so we had no choice."

"Oh, I see. Your motives were entirely selfish, then."

"Entirely."

They laughed, and Elena covered the plate of meat patties with plastic wrap. "You can take these with you when you leave, okay? How about some tea?"

"Sounds good."

Saturday dawned a most beautiful day, mild and clear, with a sky so impossibly blue that it almost hurt Elena's eyes. A fresh blanket of snow had fallen two days before, hiding the browns and grays of the long winter season. Whipped and swirled by a strong, playful wind, the new layer of white lay like an eiderdown on the Dallas landscape. *This is the Pennsylvania I missed so much when we moved away,* she thought. *Thank you, Lord.*

After finishing some last-minute baking during the morning, she delivered the food to the Montgomerys, thankful that Josh had offered the use of the downstairs recreation room for the gathering. There was no way a group of sixteen or twenty could have found enough places to sit in her little house.

"All set and ready to go?" Josh asked when he opened the door to admit her.

Elena nodded. "Can you believe this day?"

"Well, it's just what we prayed for, right? Why should it come as a surprise?"

"I guess I never thought about it. It must be human nature to ask the Lord for something and then think it's a coincidence when it turns out that way."

Pulling on his boots, Josh grinned. "When it comes to faith, some of us lack even the mustard-seed size. Well, shall we load up the van and get over to the farm before the kids arrive?"

"Van?"

"Jim Michaels owed me a favor, so I collected. It was either borrow a van or make twenty trips later to bring everyone back here."

"I see what you mean. What goes?"

"Just these." Josh bent to pick up two bags, placing them in Elena's arms. Then he grabbed two folding chairs and a large thermos. Opening the door, he called over his shoulder, "Bye, Mom. See you later."

The young people began to arrive at the farm at two-thirty, bundled for fun and toting the equipment needed for their day in the snow. Last to arrive was Valerie, driving her father's customized van, with Janice as her passenger.

Elena waved and hurried over to greet them. "Hi, Valerie. Janice, we're so glad you could come. We've missed you."

Janice smiled and raised an eyebrow, as though she found it hard to believe that anyone would notice when she was not around.

"Need any help?" Elena asked.

"I think we can get everything," Valerie said, unloading a toboggan and a large inner tube from the back. "This is it."

"Well, then, go and have some fun," Elena said. Hugging herself, she turned and walked back toward the fire site, where she sat down again to watch as the others began the long climb to the top.

Laughter and shouting drifted down the hill as the teens yelled to one another and showed off on skis, sleds, and inner tubes. Elena glanced over to one side where Josh and some of the boys were working on opposing forts for a scheduled snowball fight.

Hearing someone call out her name, Elena turned to see Marybeth waving from halfway up the hill. After waving back, Elena opened a stack of styrofoam cups and set them next to the thermos, then watched three boys in a sled race. It did not seem so very long ago since she had been part of an eager young group herself, she mused, and for a few moments memories of whisking down the three-tiered slope in the crisp winter wind replayed in her mind.

"Would you like to ride with me?"

Elena looked up to see Valerie holding the rope of the toboggan in one hand. "Thank you. I'd like that very much." Side by side, they started up the long hill.

Time passed swiftly once Elena joined in with all the activity. In the slanting rays of the afternoon sun, she swooshed downward alone on a sled. Catching sight of Josh next to the fire, she decided to veer off the worn path and head in that direction. She remembered too late the small drop-off near the bottom that had caused them to stay purposely toward the center of the hill. Knowing there was no way to avoid it, Elena clutched the sled as tightly as she could.

She closed her eyes when the sled soared over the edge and was airborne for the few seconds it took to touch down on the next level. The landing was harder than those in her memory. She gasped and lost hold, rolling over and over as she lost momentum. Coming to rest at last, she lay motionless, her face in the snow.

The sound of heavy footsteps hurried in her direction as Josh came running. "Are you all right, Laney?"

She did not answer.

He knelt and turned her over gently.

Elena could not pretend any longer. Seeing the anxious look on his face, she burst out laughing.

"What were you trying to do, kill yourself?" he said in mock seriousness when he saw that she was unhurt.

"Do you know how long it's been since I've ridden on one of those things?" she asked, laughing. "Time was when we went out of our way for that little drop-off, it was so much fun to go over. Remember?"

Josh smiled and got up, offering a hand to Elena. He brushed the snow from the back and shoulders of her charcoal gray jacket as she bent to brush off her slacks and retrieve her red and black tam. Still smiling when she straightened up to tighten the matching scarf, her face glowed from the wind. She blinked snowflakes from her dark lashes.

Hastily, Josh looked away. He stooped down to pick up the rope attached to the sled, and they walked together over to the fire, which blazed brightly in the brisk air.

"This is great," Elena said as she pulled off her gloves to warm her hands. She had a small brush burn on her wrist from the tumble, and she glanced at it absently.

Josh also noticed it and shook his head, grinning. "I wish you could have seen yourself on that landing! Arms and legs flailing about in a blur of color, . . ."

"No doubt," she answered, laughing at the thought. "Too bad we had to grow up," she added wistfully.

Sounds of laughter echoed off in the distance, and they both looked toward the commotion.

"Uh-oh," moaned Josh. "Looks like Tommy Brent and Janice are having a ski race. I was sure things would start winding down by now. I don't want anyone to get hurt."

"Well, it's getting late anyway. Let's call the group over for hot chocolate and pack up."

"Great idea." Removing a whistle from his pocket, he blew three short blasts and motioned for everyone to assemble at the fire.

A short time later, as Elena approached the van to stow the folding chairs, she overheard Valerie's voice from the other side of the next vehicle.

"You're not really serious, are you?" Her tone was demanding.

"Well, yeah! I have to. I don't know what else to do," Janice said. "Read this." She sounded ready to cry.

Elena felt guilty listening to what was obviously a private conversation, so she backed away and returned for the thermos and leftover cups. She looked uneasily toward the second van.

The soft strains of music filled the paneled room as Josh strummed the guitar and the circle of young people sang "Great Is the Lord." Elena watched the beaming faces turned toward him, each one aglow with winter's soft kiss. *He has them wrapped around his finger,* she thought, glancing around the group. *And it isn't just his authority. It's hero worship with the boys, and the girls—they're in love, pure and simple. Well, there is a lot to love about him,* her thoughts reasoned, as she returned her gaze to the leader.

He was looking at her. And so was everyone else. "Well?"

She stared at him blankly.

"I told them we'd sing a song for them. How about it?"

Elena drew a deep breath and considered the suggestion.

"We could do 'Amazing Grace.' We've sung that a hundred times."

Sure, she thought, *a hundred years ago*. "Why not?" she answered. "Play in a low key, though. I don't know if I can sing yet."

His devotional was on having friends and being a friend. "Sometimes," Josh said, "even your best friend on earth can do something that hurts you. But the Bible says that there's one Friend who sticks closer to us than a brother. We can always count on that friendship, with Jesus. Have you found that to be true?" He scanned the group.

One after another, the young people got up to give testimonies about how their lifestyles had changed since they had found Jesus. With few exceptions, everyone spoke in turn.

Elena saw Janice exit to the powder room as Josh continued. After several moments she went after her and tapped softly at the door. "Janice?" she whispered.

There was no answer.

She tried the knob, and it turned easily. Elena opened the door. Janice sat straddling the edge of the tub, her back leaning against the wall, her knees drawn up to her face. She was sobbing. Closing the door behind her, Elena stroked the girl's auburn hair. "Would you like to talk about it?" she asked gently.

Janice nodded her head, but remained as she was for several moments. Then she turned and put her feet on the floor. Raising her tearful green eyes to Elena, she said, "I feel so left out."

"What do you mean, Janice? You've always been a part of us, ever since you were a little girl."

"Well, it might look that way, but it doesn't feel like it. All of them . . . all of them talk about Jesus as though they know Him as a real friend. You know?"

Elena nodded. "He *is* a real friend, honey. The best friend I've ever had. I couldn't live without Him."

"Well, He could never want me," Janice sobbed. "I'm not good enough. I've . . . done things."

Reaching for the box of tissues, Elena drew out a few and handed them to Janice. Then, seeing a New Testament on one of the shelves nearby, she took it down and opened it as she spoke. "None of us is good enough for Him, Janice. We all have things in our lives that shouldn't be there, and there's never been a person on this earth who was ever good enough to live without Him. The Bible tells us in Romans 3, verse 23 that 'All have sinned and come short of the glory of God.' And in Ecclesiastes it says, 'There is not a just man upon earth that doeth good and sinneth not.' "

"Well, Mama says that being saved is old-fashioned, not for today. And that as long as we don't murder anyone or do something like that, we might be okay . . . since God is love, and all that."

Elena smiled. "Well, if the word of God could be trusted since the beginning of time, then we can trust it today. God is love. That's true. But He is also just, and He hates sin. It must be dealt with and punished, and the punishment is death. If there were any other way for us to have our sins forgiven, Janice, why would God's own Son have died for us?"

Janice sat silently in thought for a few moments.

Turning in the Bible to John 3, verse 16, Elena placed the book in Janice's hands and pointed to the verse. "You've been able to recite this since you were in Pioneer Girls. But did you ever really read what it says?"

Janice read it aloud. " 'For God so loved the world that He gave His only begotten Son, that whosoever believeth in Him should not perish but have everlasting life.' "

"What did that say?"

The girl's eyes brightened. "It said whosoever. Whosoever believes in Him. That must mean me, too."

"Of course it does," Elena said, pressing her hand upon Janice's where it rested on the Bible. "Would you like to ask Jesus to come into your heart and be your friend, Janice?"

She nodded, smiling through her tears, and they knelt together to pray.

"Now I have a testimony, too," Janice said afterward. A shadow crossed her face for an instant, and Elena knew what was coming. "But my mom is going to be mad."

"We'll pray for her. The Lord can change her heart just the way He's changed yours. Somehow I'm sure that everything will work out."

Opening the door to join the group, they could hear singing again. As the last word of "I Praise You, Lord" faded, Janice told everyone about her new friend. Valerie jumped to her feet and ran to embrace her. "We're sisters now, in the Lord, Val. I'm so happy."

The doorbell sounded, signaling the arrival of the first parents. Everyone scattered to round up jackets, boots, and equipment. As Janice turned to leave, she and Elena exchanged smiles, and Elena squeezed her hand. "God bless you, honey. Remember, I'll be praying with you."

Janice kissed her cheek and left.

The joy Elena felt later that evening in her own devotions poured out of her heart in praise to her Friend above all friends.

17

With Josh away at the West Coast fly-in, the next two weeks crept by slowly for Elena. How easily he had become an integral part of her life again, she thought, just like when they were children. Yet he never seemed to pry into her personal affairs. He was just there, a constant source of strength for her to tap whenever she needed him. He has so much to give, Lord, she mused. He should have someone special to love.

Elena's thoughts were so busy that she barely heard the Sunday school bell signal the beginning of class. But the door opened, and the arrival of her students brought the quiet to an end. She smiled and opened the attendance book, checking off names as the girls entered the room.

Valerie and Janice came in with their heads together, apparently in the middle of some ongoing disagreement. Taking their seats, they continued to spar in whispers as the others took their places.

Elena watched Valerie shake her head vigorously and roll her eyes upward. After passing the roll book to the back of the room, she raised her eyebrows and scanned the faces. "Would someone like to open in prayer?"

Janice nodded and bowed her head. "Dear Heavenly Father," she began, "Thank you for this beautiful morning. Please open our hearts as we study Your Word and show us what You have for us today. In Jesus' name Amen."

"Thank you, Janice." Elena felt a surge of joy each week when she saw Janice back in the group. She's almost like a new person, Elena thought, then mentally chided herself. Didn't the Bible say in 1 Corinthians that if anyone be in Christ he is a new creature, and all things become new? Still, something nagged at her consciousness as she noticed Valerie and Janice exchange secretive looks once or twice before the study even began. Elena tried to ignore a premonition that something serious was in the air. *I'll pray extra hard for Janice every day in my devotions,* she thought.

"Let's open our Bibles this morning to Philippians, Chapter 2. We'll be studying how to find God's will for our lives."

Elizabeth, one of the more quiet girls, raised her hand. "Is that something we can ever really know for sure?"

"Well, I won't say that the Bible gives us an actual map so we can go step by step through life," answered Elena, "but it does point the way for us. It's a bit like a compass. If we truly want to serve the Lord, He will guide us in the direction."

Valerie cast a triumphant look in Janice's direction, which Janice made an obvious attempt to ignore.

"Sharon, would you please read verse 13?" Elena asked. "Let's see what we can find out from this passage."

" 'For it is God who worketh in you both to will and to do of His good pleasure,' " the girl read.

"Right. God works in us, the Bible says, to do His will. In the fourth chapter of the Gospel of John, we read that even Jesus came to do the will of God. He has a plan for each one of us, and He will reveal it to us if we seek Him. In the Old Testament, we find many examples of the ways men have tried to find God's will. Sometimes they cast lots, sometimes they fasted, and many times God revealed things in dreams or performed a miracle for someone. We'll look at many of them, beginning today with Gideon's fleece. Turn to Judges, Chapter 6, verse 37. . . ."

Josh returned from his trip that afternoon and accompanied Elena to the evening service. She needed the opportunity to discuss the situation concerning Janice with him.

"Come on, Lane," Josh said lightly, on their way home afterward. "She has to be going through some changes, now that the Lord has started working in her life."

"Yes, but there's something else. I feel it inside. Something is happening that she doesn't want anyone to know about."

Josh's gaze shifted to Elena, then back to Hillside Road as he drove. Even in the darkness, winter's charm was obvious in the beam of the Thunderbird's headlights. Snow-covered stone walls, which bordered the winding country road, reflected the glow of light as Josh negotiated the snow-packed road past hilly dairy farms and an occasional farmhouse. Along the partially frozen creek on the right, low-hanging branches nearly touched the ground under the weight of snow and frost.

"You know," Elena said, "this has to be one of the most beautiful drives around, in every season. I'm glad you came the long way."

"I like it too. Many times I've had to sit on this road waiting for a herd of Holsteins to cross. It's good to know that there are still places where the pace of life has to slow down for a little while."

Elena smiled to herself and was quiet for a few moments before her thoughts returned to Janice Harper. "I don't suppose I could come right out and ask the girls what the problem is, could I?"

His silent stare was answer enough.

"Then I'll just have to wait and see."

"And pray."

"And pray," she echoed.

Josh rose from his knees and crawled into bed that night, glad to be home again. Weary from the trip, he had almost been too exhausted to even consider going to the evening service. But the thought of seeing Elena again after two interminable weeks made the decision easier. It had been hard to restrain himself from phoning her every night, but it was a last-ditch effort to see if the adage was true, that absence really did make the heart grow fonder. Surely he had not imagined *all* that radiance in her face when she had opened the door and had seen him. Her spontaneous hug and the kiss on his cheek had nearly pushed him over the edge. He could easily have crushed her tantalizing form against him and drowned her in kisses.

He drew a deep breath. *One of these days, Elena, my love, I'm going to throw caution to the wind and tell you exactly how I feel about you . . . if ever the time seems right.*

Josh picked up a letter that his mother had placed on his nightstand; it had arrived while he had been away. Noticing the foreign stamp and the familiar handwriting, he opened the envelope and read its contents slowly. Then, extinguishing the light, he lay on his back, clasped his hands behind his head, and closed his eyes.

Marcy was poring over the latest issue of *Brides* magazine when Elena passed by her desk the following morning. She stopped in her tracks. "Marce!"

Her friend looked up absently. "Hmm?"

"Tell me! I can't stand it. Have you and Trent set a date, or what?"

"Oh, this," she said, closing the magazine. "I'm just looking for some ideas." Then, seeing Elena's crestfallen face, she smiled. "But yes, we are thinking of an August wedding."

Elena's face brightened, and she bit her bottom lip. "That's great! August? That's only a few months away."

"Yes, I know. I've decided to design my own gown, like my mom did for her wedding. She showed me how to do some fancy things with seed pearls, and I thought I'd work up something really unique. Of course, I'll run out of time, if I don't get started on it right away."

"True. It sounds like a lovely idea, though, to do your dress yourself. Did you find any ideas?" She placed a hand on the young woman's shoulder. "Honestly, Marcy, how can you be so calm about everything?"

Laughing, Marcy patted her friend's hand. "I'm not, really. I'm only letting part of myself even think about it, if you must know."

"Well, that's a relief," Elena teased. "I was beginning to worry there for a minute. But now I see that you're normal after all!" They broke into giggles.

At that point, Miriam entered the office. In her usual style, her face was tight and she nodded curtly as she hurried past them and closed the connecting door behind her.

"Well, Miss Congeniality has arrived. Later I'll show you the designs I found, okay?" said Marcy. "I guess we'd better get to work."

Elena stepped to the coffee maker and filled a mug. "Would you like some?" she asked, glancing at Marcy.

"No, thanks, I've already had a cup."

"Okay, but that does me out of my good deed for the day, you know." Crossing the room, Elena placed the mug on her desk and removed the cover from the computer terminal. "Looks like I may run out of work this morning, if our executives don't come back pretty soon," she said, surveying her uncluttered desk.

Marcy glanced up. "Well, that's one worry you can put to rest. They'll both be in the office this afternoon."

"No doubt with a ton of reports and conference notes, too," Elena said with a grimace. "Oh well, I did wish I was busy, didn't I?"

The phone rang, momentarily capturing Marcy's attention.

Elena's thoughts drifted to a place filled with satin and orange blossoms, a time when, dressed in white, she stood poised on the threshold of life, of womanhood. *How innocent my dreams were then*, she thought. *How naive I was. It didn't take long for them all to come crashing down to lie crumbled at my feet. Oh, Marcy, I hope that you aren't disillusioned the way I was. I hope that Trent will always be the man you think he is.* Aware of tears welling up in her eyes, Elena fled to the women's room just as she heard Marcy hang up.

Later that day, Derek stopped at Elena's desk. "Well, well, aren't you a sight to behold. It seems like a month has gone by since the office was graced by your presence."

She looked at him disbelievingly. "Oh, really? How odd. You're the one who's been away most of that time, you know."

"Ah yes. That is true. But you must know that my days are empty without you." He placed a hand over his heart and turned soulful eyes to her.

Elena shook her head. "Be serious, Derek. Do you want Miriam to hear all this nonsense? And Marcy will be back from lunch any minute. What would she think?"

"Oh, don't worry. I have all these papers in my hand. I'd just ad lib."

"What are all those papers, anyway?" she asked apprehensively.

"Just some things I need typed for the board meeting tomorrow. Do you think you could finish them before you leave tonight?"

Elena took them from him without ceremony. After looking them over, she glanced back at Derek. It wasn't often that he joked around in the office, but she preferred that to his being overly serious. She decided to play along. "Okay, I'll do my best. But I should have known you were only interested in me for my typing."

"Ouch. You've cut me to the core." His jovial expression faded. "Really, I'd appreciate having them done today, if it's possible."

"I'll get right on them."

"Thanks. I'll take you to lunch tomorrow, okay?" he said, turning to walk back into the inner office.

She smiled and nodded. It would be good to talk to him again, to find out about the conference and his new cases. Marcy surely couldn't find any fault with that, she thought.

18

"I really appreciated the hard work you did for me yesterday, Elena," said Derek, as the waiter at Barrington's refilled their china cups with steaming coffee. "I would never have been ready for the Board of Directors this morning without those summaries."

Elena set her fork down beside her shrimp salad and looked across the table with a grin. "Well, that's what secretaries are for, you know. To be indispensable."

He grinned. "And you are, pet. Especially to me. I—" Catching sight of someone across the room, Derek rose abruptly. "Will you excuse me for just a moment, Elena? I need to speak to one of my colleagues."

"Of course." Watching him stride confidently toward a distinguished older man several tables away, Elena took a sip of ice water and blotted her lips with the linen napkin. He's the perfect picture of a bright young executive, she thought. Successful, wealthy, known in society circles, handsome enough to pose for *Vogue* beside the top models. . . . She saw him lean down to kiss the cheek of a fashionable young woman seated across the table from the older man. Her face seemed oddly familiar to Elena as she watched the trio laughing and talking.

Wondering vaguely who the woman was, Elena placed her napkin on the table and went to the powder room. As she returned the comb to her purse and removed her lipstick, recognition dawned. Of course. It was Devon—something. Marcy had pointed her out in the society columns. Devon Madison, daughter of Elliott Madison, Mr. Webster's friend and associate. Elena replaced the lipstick tube and closed her purse, then returned to the table, where Derek waited for her.

"Sorry to keep you waiting," he said. "That was Mr. Madison. Father and I are supposed to meet with him later this week on the McDermott case."

Elena smiled. "I didn't mind at all." After a moment, she spoke again. "Was that his daughter with him?"

"Yes, Devon. She's a friend of the family. I've known her all my life. Would you care for dessert? They serve an excellent chocolate mousse here."

"No, but thanks."

"Well then, I'll deliver you back to the office. I have an appointment in Scranton this afternoon." He stood and assisted Elena with her chair.

Later, as Elena sat down at her desk and placed her purse in the bottom drawer, Marcy raised an eyebrow. "How was . . . lunch, was it?" Her sable hair caught the light as she tilted her head to one side.

Elena grimaced. "Lunch was very nice, thanks."

"So where'd you eat?"

"Barrington's."

"And so casually she says it!" Rising with exaggerated grace, Marcy flung one end of her blouse's silk scarf dramatically over the opposite shoulder. "James," she said, in carefully clipped British tones, "we'll eat at Barrington's today. Have them prepare our table at once."

Elena laughed. "Marcy, you are just too much. Go have your lunch."

"Sure, kiddo. See you." She walked to the closet and got her coat.

"I saw Devon Madison at the restaurant, with her father," Elena remarked as Marcy opened the door to leave.

She turned. "*The* Devon Madison?"

"That's the one. The pictures in the newspaper hardly do her justice."

"I'm not surprised. She's a close friend of the Websters, you know."

"Yes, that's what Derek said."

"She's a close friend of Derek's, too."

"Oh, really?" Elena scratched her cheekbone with an index finger and turned in her chair to face her typewriter.

"Remember the ballet? Well, he took Devon. I thought that you would have noticed the article in the paper the week of your vacation. The clipping's in the file. Talk to you later."

The door closed behind her.

Elena sat for a moment in the silence, staring straight ahead. So Derek took Devon Madison to New York. Well, he probably had lots of woman friends, not that it was of any interest to her. What file was Marcy talking about, anyway? she wondered. Then, recalling the times she had seen her friend clipping newspaper articles related to the law firm or the Websters, Elena walked to Marcy's desk and opened the file drawer.

Her fingers brushed lightly past the tabs as she read silently: Bell Telephone, . . . Manuals, . . . News Items—that's it. Removing the folder, Elena went back to her own desk and sat down.

The first several items related to recent cases handled by the firm. Then came a picture of Mr. Webster shaking hands with the mayor. After that was the full-length photo of Derek with Devon Madison, dressed for a gala evening on the town on New Year's Eve. They made quite a couple, thought Elena. The prominent young lawyer and the society belle.

It was only one of many pictures of the boss's son in the file. She picked up a second one. Derek with Simone Fitzpatrick at a charity ball; "Is romance in the air?" the caption asked. Elena scanned several articles concerning the Webster family and then came upon another shot of Derek with Angeline O'Hara, daughter of Wilkes-Barre's eminent and esteemed surgeon. Poor Derek, she thought. He simply pines away in his lonely existence. She didn't bother to look at the remaining assortment.

Elena replaced the folder in Marcy's drawer and poured herself a mug of coffee. *Those clippings put you in a whole new light, Derek Webster,* she thought. *And if I live to be a hundred, I'll never know why you ever take a nobody like me anywhere!*

Marcy returned with an armful of packages a half hour later, her chestnut eyes dancing with life. "Is it dead here, or is it my imagination?" Setting the things on her desk, she returned to the closet to hang her coat.

Elena sat filing her nails with an emery board. "Oh, it's dead here, all right. There hasn't even been a phone call since you left."

"Good. You won't believe the things I found at the lingerie shop down the street. Are you ready for . . . this?" she said, whipping out an ivory peignoir and holding it against herself as she whirled over to her friend.

"Oh, Marce. It's really beautiful." Elena reached out to finger the shimmering blue satin trim.

"I'll admit it's a touch daring," Marcy said, caressing the cluster of satin rosebuds in the center of the empire waist, "but I figured, what the heck? I've waited a long time to be sexy."

Elena had to laugh. "Oh, right. You're almost over the hill, I forgot."

"Well, he makes me feel like a teenager, Lane." Her voice grew soft as her smile faded. "I really love the guy."

"I know. I hope . . . I hope that he makes you happy."

"I'm sure he will. Now, wait'll you see the other things I bought."

On her way home after work, Elena unbuttoned her coat in the warmth of the red Escort and turned down the volume of the radio. A few solitary snowflakes swirled lazily in the air, but not enough to matter. It was barely cold enough to snow.

Her thoughts drifted back to her first day at the law firm. *Marcy must have really done one fine selling job, recommending me for the part-time position*, she thought. *I wasn't anything more than an automaton then; an empty, numb shell programed to drown myself in work while I got through one day at a time.*

She remembered how gallant and dashing Derek Webster had been from the first, making sure that she had eased gracefully into the routine. He had apologized for the tough job involved in converting the office files to computer data. But she had needed to work hard, to have no time to think, let alone feel. Worried that Elena wouldn't even stop to eat, Derek had taken Marcy and her out for lunch and had made them laugh. That was the beginning of friendship for Derek and Elena.

One day, he had even played the knight, Elena recalled with a smile, her mind drifting back to that day. As they had finished lunch and risen from their table, an old buddy of Greg's had approached them. Not having heard of her husband's death, he'd asked Elena jokingly if she were out "two-timing the old man." Elena had stared at him, speechless with fresh grief, as her knees buckled. If Derek hadn't wrapped both his arms around her and prevented her from falling, she thought, he might have decked that guy instead of only calling him a choice name. Derek had held her until her shaking had subsided, Elena remembered. Then his lips had brushed hers so softly that she'd thought she must have imagined it.

Elena guided the car onto Willow Tree Lane and slowed down as a German shepherd ran across the road. A moment later, after parking in the drive, she unlocked her front door and stepped into the house.

Well, Derek, she thought, *we really are friends. Strange ones, perhaps, but friends nonetheless. It doesn't bother me that you have relationships with other women. After all, I have no intention of ever falling in love again.* She opened the refrigerator to see what there was for supper.

The following evening, Elena smoothed a navy cashmere sweater over her gray skirt and ran a brush through her hair. She knew Josh would soon arrive to take her to the midweek service. She spritzed perfume behind each ear and fastened the clasp of her Christmas necklace just as she heard his car in the driveway.

He rapped on the door with his knuckles and opened it to look inside. "Anybody home?"

"Hi," she called out from the bedroom. "I'll be right there, Josh. Make yourself at home."

Sitting down on her sofa, Josh stretched his long arms and drew a long deep breath. "So how was your day?"

"Not too bad," she said, peeking around the doorjamb. "How about yours?" She stepped into gray heels and picked up the matching shoulder bag from her bed before leaving the room.

"Fast. I logged a few hours of flight time today, for fun."

Elena smiled. "Fun? I should think flying is more work than fun."

"Why? Don't you like it?"

"I wouldn't know." She sat on the other end of the couch and turned toward Josh.

He stared at her. "Are you kidding? You've never flown? I can't believe that someone—" He sat there with his mouth open, the sentence unfinished.

"—My age?" she prompted.

Josh laughed. "That about says it. I can't believe that someone your age has never flown."

"Well, we never had anyplace that far to go, know what I mean?"

"Ah, Laney, Laney," he said. Then his surprise turned into a lazy smile. "Actually, that's good. Great, in fact."

"Oh? And why is that?" She was almost afraid to ask.

"I have Jake's Cardinal sitting at the airstrip in Tunkhannock. I'll take you flying the next time we have a clear day. Okay?"

Elena swallowed nervously. "Why not?"

"And in the meantime," Josh said as he checked his watch, "we'd better leave for church." He stood up and reached for his jacket on the armrest. "Where's your coat?"

Just as Elena opened her mouth, the phone rang. She picked up the receiver. "Hello?"

She heard a sniffle on the other end of the line before anyone spoke. "Elena?"

"Yes."

"It's me . . . Valerie. I'm . . . sorry to bother you at home, but I didn't know who else to call."

"It's okay, honey," Elena said, feeling a sudden heaviness and dread inside. "What's wrong?"

"Oh, Elena," the girl sobbed. "It's Janice. She's going to run away to be with that Scott Peterson."

"What?"

Valerie sniffled. "Yeah. She took all her savings out of the bank today. She's on her way to the bus station right now."

"Does her mother know about this?" Elena asked.

"No. I tried to call her, but she must be out with one of her boyfriends or something. Please, you've got to stop Jan from going."

Elena bit her lip in thought and frowned. "Well, I'll sure try, Valerie. Thanks for the call."

"What's up?" asked Josh as Elena hung up the phone.

"Oh, Josh, it's Janice Harper. She's going to run away. I have to try to stop her."

"Are you sure she'll listen to you?"

Elena stepped around him to get her coat. She looked over her shoulder at him. "I don't know, Josh. But I love her. I have to try."

"Then come on. I'll drive," he said. "You pray."

19

Father, please let us get there in time, Josh prayed silently as the car raced along the highway to the bus station. He stepped on the accelerator and pulled into the passing lane. Out of the corner of his eye he watched Elena's fingers twist the folds of her skirt while she stared intently ahead.

Elena drew a slow deep breath and bowed her head.

Josh wished that he could reach over and draw her against his side to impart some of his strength to her. He settled for less. His hand covered her clenched fist and gave a comforting squeeze.

The neon bus station sign glared just ahead. Josh maneuvered the Thunderbird into a parking space. Before he killed the engine, Elena jumped out and headed for the double glass doors.

Josh hesitated only for a moment. Brushing past an unshaven man in faded gabardine, he followed. Inside, he unzipped his brushed suede jacket and remained at a discreet distance.

The man had stepped inside now and leaned against the peeling yellow paint of one wall. In the center of the room two heavy-set women in adjacent molded plastic chairs were knitting. To the left of the ticket counter, Janice was slumped on a wooden bench staring at her feet, her hands in the pockets of her jacket. Her small figure looked lost in the garish room.

"Janice," Josh heard Elena say.

The girl looked up with a start. "Oh, great. What are *you* doing here?"

Lips closed, Elena smiled thinly and sat down next to her. "I wanted to talk to you."

"Yeah, I'll bet." Janice rolled her eyes upward. "You mean you want to stop me." Folding her arms, she turned away.

Elena took a breath and moistened her lips. "Well, of course I don't want you to go, honey. Did you think I would?"

"I really didn't care one way or the other."

"I don't think you mean that."

"Don't I?" Janice cast a defiant glance over her shoulder.

SECOND SPRING   143

"No. And I'm sure your mother would want you to come home, too."

"Shows how much you know about it," Janice said, her voice rising. "She doesn't care what I do, as long as the dishes are done and the house is clean. In fact, she won't even notice I'm gone until no one clears the table after the next meal." She pushed a stray lock of auburn hair behind her ear.

Glancing around at the gawking eyes in the room, Elena laid a hand on Janice's shoulder. "Let's go outside and talk, okay? At least would you listen to what I have to say?"

The girl turned her head toward Elena and shrugged. Rising, she picked up her purse and followed Elena outside. They sat on the worn bench facing one another in the frosty air.

Josh slipped out behind them and stood in the shadows, silently praying that Elena would find the right words to say.

"Janice," Elena began, "why are you doing this . . . turning your back on your family, your friends . . . going off all alone?" As she spoke, her breath formed little clouds of mist that floated upward.

"Oh, don't be so dramatic, Elena. That's not what I'm doing at all. I'm just going off to live my own life. Everyone has to do that sometime."

"But not like this, honey. Not before you've finished school."

"Hey, they have schools in Alabama, you know."

"And you expect to enroll there, once you arrive?"

Janice shrugged. "I haven't decided yet."

"No, because you don't even know where you're going to live, do you?"

Eyes downcast, Janice shivered in the silence.

Josh blew into his cupped hands and put them into his pockets.

Reaching out, Elena took Janice's hands into hers. "Please, Janice. Think about what you're doing. Don't go. Not like this."

Janice pulled her hands away and stood up, her back to Elena. "You don't understand. I have to go. I just have to. Everything will be okay, once I'm there. He'll see that I'm better than she is."

"Are you saying that Scott doesn't even know you're coming?" Elena asked, rising to her feet. She stepped around Janice and faced her. "He doesn't even know?"

Janice drew a deep breath and expelled it all at once. "He sent me a—what do you call it?—a 'Dear Jane' letter. He says he's going out with some girl he met there. And I don't want him to. It's not fair. He said he loves *me*."

Elena took hold of the girl's arms, but before she could speak, Janice interrupted.

"Don't you see?" Her eyes shimmered with tears in the light of the neon sign. "If I go there, he'll want me. We can get married. Everything'll be okay."

"Janice," Elena said. "Marriage isn't something you can use to solve a problem relationship. It has to be based on love. You can't pretend it's like glue, something to bind someone to you who doesn't want to be there. That wouldn't make your life better. But it could make it worse, a lot worse."

"Yeah, well I don't see it that way. It's almost time for my bus." Pulling away from Elena's grasp, she avoided her look. "I might as well tell you the rest. You'll find out anyway. I—I'm pregnant." She glanced back at her teacher, as if to gauge her reaction. "So, you see? It'll be all right."

Time seemed to stand still in the velvet night. Josh watched Elena shake her head and close her eyes. When she opened them again, tears traced a glistening path down her face. He swallowed hard.

"So you think a baby will solve everything, then?" she asked softly.

"No, not exactly. But he'll have to marry me, won't he? And after the baby comes we'll be a family."

Elena brushed the tears away with her fingertips, but they continued to flow as she spoke. "You know, there was a time in my life when I felt the same way you do. I was so sure that a sweet little bundle from Heaven would make all my problems go away. But I was wrong." Her voice broke, and she struggled to go on. "I learned the hard way that sometimes a baby only makes things worse. Sometimes they make a man feel more pressured than ever, and sometimes you and the baby have to pay the price . . . unless the man decides that you're the one to blame and takes it all out on you instead."

Josh felt his stomach knot, and he clenched his teeth. At his sides, his hands curled into fists. Hatred and anger coursed through his veins, and he wished for one brief moment that Greg Ryan had not died in the accident. He would have enjoyed ending that cur's life himself.

The roar of a bus engine grew louder as it approached. Over the loudspeaker, the ticket agent announced its arrival, along with the departure time for Washington, D.C., and points south. People filed out of the bus and stepped around the two heavy-set women and the man in gabardine who were waiting to board.

Crying, Janice reached out and put her arms around Elena. "Well, that's not the way it'll be for me, you'll see. I . . . have to go now." She drew away and turned to leave.

"Janice?" Elena called out after her.

The girl hesitated, then turned back. "I'm really sorry, Elena. I— I have to go. Thanks. For coming, and all. . . ." Pivoting swiftly, she almost ran to the bus. With one last backward glance, she handed her ticket to the driver and boarded.

Josh watched Janice collapse, sobbing, into a seat near the back of the bus. He strode over to Elena and, as the bus pulled away and faded into the distance, stood behind her with his hands on her shoulders.

"I failed, Josh," she said in a very small voice. "She wouldn't listen to me." Turning to him, she buried her face against his shoulder and wept.

Conscious of her trembling, he wrapped his arms around her, cupping the back of her head in one of his hands and pressing her closer. "Oh, I'm sure she'll have plenty of time to think about all the things you said to her, Lane. She heard more than you think." *And so did I,* he thought as he rocked her gently back and forth. *So did I.* "Come on, I'll drive you home."

Later that night in his bed, Josh mulled over the scene in the bus station. Janice would probably come to her senses sooner or later, he was sure. But she was not his concern. It was Elena who tugged at his heart. He recalled every word she had said, remembered her crying softly for most of the drive to her house afterward, drying her tears with his handkerchief. She had wanted to be alone. And he had needed to be alone, too.

How was it be possible that a man he once considered his best friend could have had a side to him that was so unspeakable? He tried to imagine something in Elena's character—anything— that could possibly override a man's basic need to protect and shelter her . . . and love her. Greg had professed to be a Christian in the Air Force, had attended all the Bible studies, had spoken the language. But it says in the Bible that only God can see into a person's heart. *Well,* he thought, *it also says that God renders to every man according to his work. I just hope that Greg got what he deserved.*

Elena's face filled his thoughts once again, and he could still feel her in his arms. "Well, my love," he said in the stillness, "at least I know what I have to deal with now, what hurt you so deeply that you had to keep it all inside. What you need is someone who loves you the way you were always meant to be loved. And I happen to have just the perfect chap in mind." Smiling, he rolled onto his side and closed his eyes.

20

During the latter part of the week, a warm front moved gradually into eastern Pennsylvania, bringing clear skies and mild temperatures to the winter-weary landscape. On Saturday morning, Josh knocked on Elena's door.

"Oh, hi, Josh. You're out early."

"I thought you might be interested in a walk to the old quarry."

Her face brightened. "Sounds good. I don't have much to do around here." She donned a three-quarter coat and grabbed a knitted tam from the closet shelf. Outside in the warmth, she removed her gloves and put them into her pockets as they walked toward the hill just beyond Willow Tree Lane. "What a treat, a day like this," she said. "It's been gloomy forever."

"You're right. Winter won't be around much longer now."

"Well, I won't miss it. For all its glorious whiteness, it leaves twice as much brown and gray behind. It must be great to live in a warm, sunny climate."

"So I hear."

In the forest behind Josh's house, their booted feet left imprints in the spongy cushion of old autumn leaves. Most of the winter snow had melted under the touch of sunshine's warm fingers, leaving crusty mounds of gray in the shadows of rocks and trees. They inhaled the moist woodsy fragrance around them and listened to the silence. A dog barking in the distance was the only other sound besides their footsteps.

In a few moments they reached a small deserted clearing. A low stone wall of flat rocks hewn from the shallow excavation rimmed the area, providing a natural seat.

Josh snapped a twig from a small tree next to him and absently peeled bark from it. "I haven't been back here for ages," he said. "The pond seemed so big years ago. And now look at it—it's hardly more than a puddle. Remember when we used to skate here?"

Elena smiled. "Yes. It was our secret place, until the day Jimmy

Bradshaw followed us and told his friends about it. We did have a lot of fun, though." Her smile faded. "I thought I would always be that happy."

"Ah, the innocence of children. Doesn't last very long anymore, does it?"

She shook her head and looked off into the distance.

"When did it change for you, Laney?"

"When I grew up," she said, her voice brittle.

"It was Greg, wasn't it?"

Elena turned and looked directly into his eyes, then she lowered her gaze.

He felt her withdraw. "Look, I know he must have done something that hurt you very badly. I was there when you talked to Janice the other night. So I know some of it."

Elena picked up a small rock and rolled it back and forth in her hands. "I don't even remember what I said to Jan. I honestly don't. All I know is that none of it made any difference to her. And that I failed."

He wrapped one of her hands in both of his and smiled. "No, you're wrong. I'm sure that everything you said helped her. She had a long trip ahead, with nothing to do but think. I believe she'll be back, sooner than you know."

"I only hope you're right."

"Anyway, you're the one who's hurting right now. And until you open up to someone there's no way that pain will ever go away."

Elena exhaled slowly and rose. She turned her back to him and with one arm made a gesture of helplessness. "Oh, Josh, don't you understand? I don't want to talk about it. I don't even let myself think about it."

"You've made that abundantly clear. But look at what it's doing to you. You've gotten bitter. You've built this wall around yourself that nobody can get through. Are you going to let him make the rest of your life miserable too? Talk it out. Get rid of it."

Elena swallowed and turned to look at him. "I don't know if I can," she said, her voice barely more than a whisper. "I had no one *to* talk to, for a long time. No one I wanted to burden with my unhappiness, anyway."

"Well, there was a time in your life when you used to confide in me, remember? And I'm here now. Talk to me, Lane." He brushed her cheek with his fingertip.

Elena averted her gaze, then looked back at Josh. Resignation and pain clouded her eyes. "I know you're right. I do need to talk, to let go of it."

Josh nodded encouragingly into her haunted eyes as she sat down beside him.

She dropped the stone she'd been fingering to the ground and pressed it into a spot of old snow with her boot. Then she drew a long, ragged breath. "I don't know where to start. It wasn't all bad. We were pretty happy for a while, in the beginning."

"So what happened?"

"Oh, little things, at first. Greg grew very possessive. He didn't like me spending time with my mom, Marcy, friends at church. He didn't want to, well, share me. With anyone. I got a job to fill the time, you know? And then he was upset because it put me with people he didn't know. He decided that he had no use for church, so he stopped going. He hated for me to go. But I went anyway."

"Hmm," Josh said in wonder. "It doesn't even sound like him."

Fingering the fringe on her scarf, Elena did not respond.

"It gets worse," Josh said, brushing a lock of silken hair over her shoulder, "doesn't it?" When she turned to look at him, he felt the whisper-soft splash of a tear.

"Please, I—can't—"

His arm encircled her shoulder, and he hugged her to him. "It's okay. Take your time." He felt her struggle to keep her tears at bay. When she regained her composure, he relaxed his hold.

Elena blotted her face with the end of her scarf and took a deep breath. "Mom figured out what his problem was." She looked away with a shrug. "I thought he was going through some kind of personality change or something."

"What was wrong?"

"He drank." Elena turned, and her eyes searched his. "Did you know he had a problem with alcohol?"

Josh's lips parted. "No. I never would've guessed it."

"Neither did anyone else, until Mom saw through the cracks in his facade and discovered what caused them."

Josh shook his head in wonder. "I never even saw the guy take a drink, all the time we were in the service together. He wouldn't even go to the canteen for a soda."

"Well, I didn't see it for a long time myself. But once it started, he became a whole different person."

"How was that?"

"He was paranoid that somebody would discover his drinking. As soon as Mom knew his secret, he lost control. He wanted me to choose between them. Can you believe that? Choose between the two people who should mean the most to me?"

"So that's why you moved away, then?"

One side of Elena's mouth curled into a bitter smile. "Partly. More like he wanted to . . . punish . . . Mom and me. By moving, he'd have me all to himself again. And no one would notice if he never went to church." She sighed. "He needed help. I tried to get him to go to my pastor there . . ." she sobbed and bowed her head.

Josh reached for her, but she stood up and moved beyond his touch.

"That's when—when he—" Hugging herself, Elena surrendered to her tears.

Josh shook his head. Concern etched lines into his face. He got up, placed his hands on her shoulders, and turned her around. "He hit you, didn't he?" Josh said through clenched teeth, his words more a statement than a question.

"Th—that was . . . the first time."

Crushing her against his chest, her slender form almost lost inside his arms, he echoed her statement one word at a time in disbelief. "The *first* time?" *Dear God,* he prayed. *I can't be hearing this.* A wave of nausea washed over him, and he looked upward as if to find some answer written against the blue. "You stayed with him? Even after he hurt you, you stayed there?"

Elena sobbed. "He—he s—said he was s—sorry."

"I'll bet," Josh groaned.

"He w—was always sorry. So I—I—never told anyone."

"Grief, Lane. You should've told someone. Don't you know that? You should've gone for help yourself."

She eased away and sat down on the stone wall, wiping her tears away with one hand. "Probably. But I thought . . . you know. If—if I were—more submissive, like the Bible says, . . ." she waved vaguely in the air, "things would be okay."

Josh didn't know what to expect this time. He sat down beside her.

"I—got pregnant." Her voice was flat. "I was afraid to tell Greg. When I couldn't hide it any longer—" Elena hid her face in her hands and cried. "Are—are you s—sure you want to hear this?" she sobbed, turning tear-streaked cheeks to him.

Josh nodded grimly, his jaw muscles taut.

"Well, he raged at me. I . . . fell."

Josh stood up, took two steps away, and then stopped. The fingers of one hand kneaded the hollows of his cheeks. His other hand flexed and relaxed several times as he breathed slowly, regularly.

"At least, I . . . think I fell."

He turned and stared at Elena. It was all he could do to keep silent while she went on.

"It happened so fast," she said, wiping her face with the scarf. "Greg sobered and got help for me, then stormed out. He was gone for days."

"Just like that!" Josh said incredulously. "He left you. Hurt. Alone. It's a good thing he's dead, Lane. If he weren't—"

Elena exhaled slowly and shook her head. "Well, he was sober, anyway, when he came back. He tried to make up for . . . everything."

"He stopped drinking?"

Elena nodded. "Things improved between us, for a while. Once the baby was born, Greg tried to be a good father."

"How big of him," Josh sneered.

"When Mom was . . . dying, I begged to go back home. So he took us. But before I got too comfortable, I began to see signs of his problem again. Then when Mom passed away, he couldn't sell her house fast enough. Part of me died then, too. I decided that if love could be like that, could cause so much pain, so much heartache, well, I wanted no part of it. Ever again."

Neither spoke for several moments. Elena slipped her gloves on and stood up. Hands in her pockets, she circled the edge of the tiny frozen pond.

Contemplating the acrid story of Elena's marriage, Josh watched her press the toe of her boot into some of the dry, white edges of the ice, making soft crunching noises. The thought of her suffering physical abuse at the hand of someone he had called his friend clogged in his throat, choking him. Almost without thinking, he punched a fallen limb propped against the stone wall.

It splintered and fell in two pieces.

Elena looked up. "You okay, Josh?"

"What?" He glanced at the bruise already purpling the side of his hand, the pain strangely comforting. "Sure."

"What happened?" she asked, walking over to him and taking his hand to examine it.

"I slipped." *I could have felled the whole stinking tree,* he thought. "Just caught myself in time."

"Oh, it looks nasty, Josh. Come home, and I'll put some witch hazel on it for you."

"Don't worry about it, it's okay. Anyway—"

Elena tilted her head back and looked up at him.

Josh glanced around the clearing. Her painful words still seemed to echo from tree to tree, clanging around like the peal of an old bell. "Let's get out of here. It's still early. What do you say we go flying?"

"Are you serious?"

"Why not? Jake's been having some mechanical work done on his Cardinal in Tunkhannock. Now that the weather's breaking, I'll be returning it. We might not have another chance like this."

"Well, . . ."

"Oh, come on, Lane. You'll love it. Trust me." He held out his good hand to her.

She hesitated, then shrugged and took it.

Within moments they were in Josh's car for the half-hour drive to the Tunkhannock Airport. Noticing that Elena seemed preoccupied with her thoughts, Josh traveled the distance in silence. It took miles for the knot in his own stomach to ease. Occasionally glancing her way, he noticed a change in her. She sat with her chin up, watching the scenery as they drove, her hands relaxed in her lap. If he hadn't seen her so many times with her head bowed and her eyes downcast, the contrast wouldn't have been so obvious.

Elena felt oddly light, as though a tremendous weight had been lifted from her shoulders. It hadn't been easy to tell her secrets to Josh, but now that she had talked to him about Greg, she could almost feel the healing process at work within her. Josh, being the friend he was, would always make her pain his own. She was thankful he'd kept after her and convinced her to share her burden. It wasn't so heavy now.

"Here we are," Josh said as he turned onto the airport road. Elena looked around. "Where's the airport?"

"You're looking at it. See?" He pointed at a cluster of buildings ahead.

"But there's no tower! No terminal! In fact, there's not even a runway!"

"Sure there is. See that grass strip over there?"

Swallowing, Elena felt a twinge of panic. "But—"

"Hey, you were going to trust me, remember?" he said, patting her hand. He stopped the car by an old hangar and got out.

Elena opened her door and peered at the cinder block building with its huge multipaned door. Along the roofline, birds chattered and skittered about. She took a deep breath and followed him.

Josh heaved the heavy door and it slid off to one side, exposing a single engine plane. "Pretty, isn't she?"

The white paint of the Cessna Cardinal gleamed in the burst of sunlight. Two-toned red trim graced the sides and the wing tips, and on the tail was painted a red cardinal.

Nodding, Elena stepped closer to have a better look. "Are you sure you—"

Josh clamped a hand on her shoulder. "Relax, okay? You don't think I'd let anything happen to you, do you?"

If only he hadn't winked when he said that, thought Elena, *his statement might have had some credibility!*

"Just stand right here," said Josh, guiding her off to one side, "while I do my preflight check."

Elena watched him run a hand along the leading edge of each wing, and then along the propeller blades. He reached inside the cowling with one hand, then checked the movement of the ailerons and flaps.

She watched as he drained a sample of fuel from each wing tank into a small cup, held it up to the light, and spilled it out.

Noticing her puzzled expression, he smiled. "Have to see if there's any water in the fuel. Then I'll check the oil and a few other things."

"My word, Josh. Do you have to do this every time you want to go flying?"

"Yes. Even pilots like to get back to the ground safely, so we make sure that all the equipment is working. Otherwise, you know what they say—about that first step."

"I guess I expected it to be like driving," Elena said sheepishly. "You know, get in, turn the key, and drive away."

"Not quite." Using a tow bar, he pulled the craft outside, away from other planes, and opened the door. "Okay, Lane. Come here and I'll help you in." He buckled her seat belt and gave the shoulder harness a firm tug.

"Is that everything, then?" she asked, her voice wavering slightly.

"Everything outside." Josh slammed her door and walked around the plane. Once in his seat, he pulled his own door closed and locked it, then reached over to lock hers. Handing her a headset, he tapped the mike. "Put this close to your mouth so you can talk." He put on his own headset and checked the radio controls. After priming the engine, he advanced the throttle and turned the ignition key. The motor sputtered to life. He checked the gauges to see if their indications were normal, then revved the engine a few times. "Well, kid, this is it," he said, squeezing Elena's hand.

With her heart in her throat as they bumped along the taxiway to the end of the runway, Elena swallowed and tried to smile.

"Tunkhannock traffic," said Josh into the radio mike, "Cessna Cardinal 16172 departing runway three-six, straight out departure." At full throttle, they raced down the runway.

Elena held her breath as the countryside sped by. Then a sudden floating feeling announced that they were airborne. She watched the trees shrinking beneath them as Josh banked the plane and they crossed a bend in the Susquehanna River. "How beautiful! Look at everything!" she gasped, straining to see out of every window at once.

Josh smiled, pointing with his finger. "Over there's the town."

"It's so breathtaking! I never realized that so much of the area was covered by forest. I mean, I see trees from the road, and all—"

"I know. There's a lot of bush. Lots of pretty lakes, too. Look over that hill," he said, indicating with his finger where to look. "You can see the paper company in Mehoopany."

She nodded. "I can't believe there's still so much snow."

"See, I knew you'd like it," he said with a grin. "There's more to see this direction." Banking the plane, he made a wide sweep over the landscape.

Elena felt her spirit glide and soar as the Cessna climbed toward the sun. In the light and warmth of its rays, she felt the heavy chains of the past fall away. She was free at last. Beholding the glorious beauty of God's handiwork all around them, she turned and smiled at Josh.

She never did figure out how he was able to find the tiny airport in the vast world below, after the flight, but when the wheels touched down on the runway once again, she breathed a sigh of relief.

"That was lovely, Josh. So much fun," Elena said on the way home in the car.

"We'll do it again, then, if you'd like. Another day."

"Really?"

"Sure. It—uh—won't be for a while, though."

Elena glanced at him questioningly.

"I've been meaning to tell you. A friend from Europe is coming for a visit."

"Oh, how nice."

He shifted in his seat as he turned onto Willow Tree Lane. "I'll be meeting the plane in New York tomorrow. I get to be tour guide for the next several weeks or so."

"Well, I hope he enjoys his visit."

Josh cleared his throat and looked out of his side window.

Outside her house, a few moments later, Elena took the key from her purse and turned. "I had a really great time today."

"Good."

"No, I mean it, Josh. I feel a lot better . . . about my life. Thanks for listening. I'm beginning to feel that I can . . . forgive Greg."

"Well, that's the first step, I guess." Josh toyed with the zipper on his jacket, pulled it down a few inches, then looked at Elena for a long moment. "The guy was a jerk, Lane. He didn't have a clue about how to love someone like you." Lifting her chin with the edge of his index finger, he leaned down and planted a feather-soft kiss on her lips. Then, with the tiny hint of a wink, he turned and strode back to his Thunderbird.

Elena stood staring after him, her lips parted in delicious surprise.

21

The following Monday morning Elena sat at her desk, lost in thought. She stared straight ahead, her palms resting on the edge of the computer keyboard, her fingers relaxed.

"You haven't heard a single word I've said, have you?" remarked Marcy from across the room.

"Hmm?"

"I said—oh, what's the difference?"

"Sorry, Marce. I guess I have a few things on my mind." Elena took a sip from the coffee mug beside her and made a face. "Yuck. It's cold."

"Well, no wonder. You haven't touched it since I put it there. What's got you in such a state, anyway?"

Elena raised her brows and shrugged. "It's nothing." *Nothing!* she thought. Her mind had been in chaos since Saturday. She could still feel the soft touch of Josh's lips, still smell the clean musky aftershave he'd worn. Her heart quickened at the memory. Who would've thought—

"Well, you look like it's nothing, I'm sure," Marcy said, shaking her head. "I happened to see that smile just now."

Elena felt a flush of color warm her cheeks. "Don't be silly."

"Silly? Right. Uh . . . did you and Josh go to church last night?"

"No. I went alone, actually."

Marcy tucked her chin and stared incredulously.

"Josh had to go to New York to meet a friend coming in from Europe. He'll be gone for a few weeks, that's all I know." She eased her chair back and walked to the coffee maker with her mug. "Want some?"

"Sure. Thanks." Marcy held out her mug.

Elena filled it and handed it back, then returned to her own desk with a fresh cup just as the phone rang.

"Good morning. Webster and Webster," Marcy said, then paused. "One moment, please, Mr. Franklin. I'll ring his office." She buzzed the intercom. "Mr. Webster, Mr. Franklin's on line 1."

156

She replaced the receiver and sipped her coffee. "Looks like our day has begun."

"Looks like," echoed Elena.

"I don't know if I can stand it for two weeks."

Elena glanced up. "Stand what?"

Her friend's eyes sparkled. "Oh, you know. You go all mopey and dreamy whenever Josh goes away."

Elena cocked her head to one side and glared.

The playful smile melted from Marcy's face. She cleared her throat and turned in her chair to face her own desk.

Mopey and dreamy, Elena thought, smiling to herself. *I don't know about mopey, but for the first time in ages I think I could believe in dreams again. On the other hand, it was only a kiss, and not even a real one. Just a peck. After all, he did say that he once loved somebody. Maybe he still has feelings for her.*

"Ahem."

Elena blinked and looked up to find Derek smiling down at her. "Sorry. Did you say something?"

"No, I just brought these letters by. They're all signed and ready to go out."

"Thanks. I'll take care of them."

He nodded, but made no move to walk away.

"Was there something else?" Elena asked, a perplexed frown on her face.

"Yes. Um . . . there's a special concert coming up. On Friday night. I was wondering if you'd like to go with me."

Elena considered the invitation with mixed feelings. "Well, I—"

"It's the last of the season. You always said *Scheherazade* was your favorite work."

"That's what they'll be playing? *Scheherazade?*" She drew a deep breath and raised her eyebrows. It really was her favorite. *What a treat it would be*, she thought.

Derek nodded and smiled. "Would you like to go?"

Marcy coughed and craned her neck from across the room to peer around Derek's back at Elena.

Catching the look, Elena pursed her lips defiantly. "Why not? That would be really nice. I'd love to."

"Good," he said. "I'll check back with you later, okay?"

Elena smiled and inclined her head. As the inner door closed behind him, she eyed Marcy. "Coming down with something, are you?"

"Who me? No. It's just that sometimes I . . . have a hard time figuring you out, that's all."

Don't feel bad, Marce, thought Elena. *If you want to know the truth, I don't understand myself either.* She flipped the power switch on the computer and started working double-time.

On Wednesday, her day off, Elena decided to tackle the closet that she had been avoiding since early last fall. Now that she had begun to deal with the painful memories of her past, she knew that it was time to sort through the things which had belonged to Greg and Steven, mementos she had clung to since the accident. The task went slowly; Elena had always been a compulsive saver of all things sentimental. Mustering all her strength, she packed the few items that had been Greg's into a box to mail to his kid brother, if she could manage to locate him. Steven's things she hugged to her heart and, after a short cry, placed them in a smaller carton with his teddy bear, to keep forever. After the remaining items were restacked in the closet, she picked up the last box, marked "Photo Albums and Treasures" in her mother's handwriting. Elena carried it in to the kitchen table so that the contents could be spread out on the table as she sorted through them.

Two albums had been compiled by her mother over the years. Elena sat on a kitchen chair and opened the first one, which contained mostly pictures of relatives and friends of her parents. Flipping through the worn pages, she smiled at the black-and-white snapshots of aunts and uncles as she remembered them from her childhood days. Most of them had passed away. She wondered what had become of her favorite cousin. Family members don't seem to stay close anymore, thought Elena, the way they used to. Young people can't wait to spread their wings and go as far from their roots as possible.

She sighed and picked up the second album. It began with a wedding picture of her parents, which she gazed at for several moments, tracing the images with her finger. *Oh, Mom, you were so beautiful in white lace. And how handsome Daddy was. He was so proud of you. It's lonely here without you,* Elena thought, sighing unconsciously. *I miss you both. But at least you're with the Lord, now, and someday we'll all be together again . . . you, me, Stevie*— Her eyes misted, and she turned the page.

So many memories had been captured in the flash of a bulb. There was the birthday dress with red polka dots she'd loved as a child, and her first pair of red shoes. Even though the pictures were black-and-white, her mind's eye remembered their vivid color, and a wistful smile crossed her face.

It was fun watching herself grow with each turn of the page, watching her father's hair lighten at the temples and turn a distinguished silver. There was the first new car they'd ever owned. Elena could still remember the smell of its new leather seats, the shiny gearshift knob, and how her father had taken them for a drive around Harvey's Lake every Sunday.

In most of her childhood pictures Elena was forever with a young boy. *Josh,* she thought, *were we ever so young?* There were scenes from her teenage years with Marcy, her graduation, and several of her standing with two men in military uniforms: Josh and his best friend from the service, Greg Ryan. She recalled the day those shots had been taken, when Josh brought Greg home with him on leave. It was the first of many visits. Later Greg wrote her dozens of letters from overseas. *If only Josh would have kept in close contact that way,* mused Elena, *perhaps— Oh well, the past is over.* She skimmed over the photos from her wedding, the day that Josh vanished from their lives.

Closing the back cover of the album, Elena set it down and opened a large envelope filled with yellowed newspaper clippings that her mother had saved. One headline after another proclaimed Josh Montgomery to be the star of the football team, the swimming team, tennis champ. *No wonder all the girls had been in love!* Elena thought and smiled. There were honor roll lists from high school with her name circled in ink and notices of her classmates' engagements.

The last clipping was a small news item from *The Dallas Post* announcing the engagement of the town hero, Josh Montgomery, to Gina Maria DiAngelo from Milan, Italy. Elena caught her bottom lip between her teeth and read the article over a second time, wondering about Gina DiAngelo. Returning the clippings to the envelope, she put everything back into the box and carried it to the closet. Feeling a slight headache beginning, she glanced at the clock and decided to go for a walk in the fresh air.

Friday evening arrived with a crisp, soft wind and a sky full of stars. Elena fastened the wrist buttons of her lace-sleeved violet gown and surveyed her image in the full-length mirror. Her grandmother's diamond ear clips sparkled back at her; she swept her curls upward and fastened them with a matching diamond comb. As she pushed the lace away from one wrist to glance at her silver watch, she heard Derek's car pull into the driveway. She opened the door, and Derek stepped inside.

"You do have a way with clothes, pet," he said, giving her a long look of approval. "You look sensational."

Elena smiled and picked up her evening bag. "Thank you. You look quite dashing yourself."

After helping her with her white fur jacket, Derek locked the door behind them and ushered Elena to the waiting Mercedes. They drove off into the night.

In the grand concert hall entranced by the beauty of *Scheherazade*, Elena's mind flooded with memories from her childhood. Often, during a quiet evening at home, her mother would put on the haunting music they had both loved. Elena would sit at her knee and listen to the story of the Persian princess who enchanted the king with tales of one thousand and one Arabian nights. The Wilkes-Barre Ballet Theater Company, in their vivid costumes, performed flawlessly, and Elena felt her imagination come to life.

All too soon it was intermission, and the house lights went up. Derek got up and offered his hand to Elena. Smiling, she accepted his assistance and stood.

At that moment, Elena heard the lilting sound of an unusual laugh, almost like music, from several rows behind them. She turned and her gaze fell upon a strikingly beautiful young woman who was wearing a simple gown of ivory satin that draped her slender form in elegance. Shining, waist-length raven hair flowed gracefully over her smooth olive-toned shoulders. Her expressive brown velvet eyes sparkled above high cheekbones as she laughed lightly and spoke with a rich European accent. She turned her luminous eyes to the man who smiled up at her from the next seat, a handsome man whose fair coloring bore rich contrast to her exotic beauty.

Josh! Elena was weak in the knees and her heart stopped for a few seconds, as the concert hall took on a nightmarish quality.

"Are you all right?" Derek asked, putting his arm around her.

She looked up at him gratefully. "Yes, I—I'm fine. I just need some fresh air."

As Derek led Elena up the aisle Josh glanced at her, but only the barest hint of recognition registered in his eyes. For a brief moment, she feared that she would be sick. Breathing deeply, she continued out of the auditorium.

The second half of the program seemed interminably long. Gone were the magic and the charm of the story, and to Elena's dulled senses even the most brilliant costumes looked faded and flat. The colors ran together like watercolors in the rain. Stealing a glance over her shoulder, she felt the final blow. The two seats were empty. Josh was gone. Through sheer force of will, she turned and faced forward again.

Derek nudged her elbow. "Are you sure you're okay?" he whispered.

"Well, I—" To her dismay, her eyes brimmed with tears, and she bowed her head.

"Come on, pet," he said, tugging gently on her arm. "I'll take you home."

Wordlessly, she followed.

The refreshing cool night air restored her composure, but she didn't feel like talking. Except for the soft music on the car stereo, they drove in silence. "I'm really sorry, Derek," she said as he unlocked her front door. "I didn't mean to spoil the evening."

"Oh, don't worry about it," he said, but his tone verged on anger. "I've seen it before, anyway. I would like to know what happened, though. Up until intermission you seemed to be enjoying the program."

Elena didn't answer. She stood with her eyes downcast.

"I looked forward to this evening, you know? I wanted to take you somewhere special. And I wanted to be alone with you afterward, so I could tell you how I—" He took her forearms and drew her close, and his lips sought hers.

Elena turned away and stepped back out of his grasp. "Derek, don't. Please. I just can't deal with . . . whatever it is right now. I just want to be alone."

A muscle twitched in his jaw as Derek expelled a deep breath. Then after a moment he spoke again in low, clipped tones. "I don't understand you, Elena, I really don't. But I'll tell you one thing. I do not intend to give up on this. One of these days you *will* hear me out. Good night." Shaking his head, he walked back to his car and got in, slamming the door after him.

Elena stepped inside and closed the door. Leaning against it for support, she barely heard the purr of the Mercedes as Derek drove off into the darkness. That he had wanted to tell her something barely penetrated her consciousness at the moment. All she could think about was Josh. He was her friend, wasn't he? *They didn't have any secrets . . . did they?* she questioned. Why had he spent so much time and effort getting her to bare her entire soul if it was all to end with him walking out of her life again? Just when she was beginning to think that perhaps . . .

Perhaps what? Elena drew a ragged breath. Still echoing in her ears was a laugh that sparkled like crystal. Even when she closed her eyes she could see the beautiful olive-skinned woman in ivory satin gazing adoringly at Josh. *Her name must be equally lovely,* thought Elena. *Something as lovely, perhaps, as . . . Gina DiAngelo.*

22

Derek swore under his breath as whirling red and blue lights flashed in the rearview mirror. *Just what I need,* he thought, *to make the night perfect.* He pulled over onto the shoulder and lowered the power window before killing the engine. "What's the problem, officer?" he asked, squinting against the glaring flashlight beamed at his face.

"Step out of the car, please."

"Yes sir," he said, opening the door to comply with the order.

"Let me see your driver's license," the stern voice instructed.

Reaching into the breast pocket of his tux, Derek withdrew a leather billfold, removed the license, and handed it to the officer.

The man rocked back on his heels as he glanced from the picture to Derek's face and then returned the card. "Derek Webster," he said. He bent and scanned the interior of the car with his flashlight. "Hmmm. Don't suppose you're any relation to Mitchell Clark Webster, Wyoming Valley's finest attorney. It's not often we get anyone well known up in these parts." He walked to the back of the vehicle to copy the license plate number.

"Yes sir," Derek replied. "He's my father."

"Well, what do you know? That's very interesting. Two months ago, my sister lost her kids to her rat of a husband, thanks to your father." He handed Derek the ticket and started back for his car. "It's a pleasure doing business with you, boy. But from now on, keep an eye on your speedometer, okay?"

Derek stared after him and watched the patrol car drive away, then got back into the Mercedes. *At least it took my mind off Elena for a little while,* he thought. *I wonder if I'll ever understand that woman.* He pulled onto the highway toward Wilkes-Barre. *She's like no one I've ever known. She's . . . different. She has qualities about her that are so fresh, so vulnerable. She's never superficial or impressed by wealth or a person's importance. When I'm with her I notice things that I've always taken for granted.*

He sighed. *Mother certainly has fits whenever I take Elena anywhere. I know she prefers Devon or Angelique. But I . . . I think*

163

I'm falling in love with her. I nearly told her tonight. I would have, too, if she hadn't acted so strangely during the performance. Maybe next time, Elena, my pet.

After escorting Gina to her suite at the Heritage House Hotel, Josh drove home slowly. He passed the silver Mercedes at a traffic light along the way and smiled smugly. Webster must not have stayed very long at Elena's, he surmised.

What a stroke of bad luck it was for her to see me with Gini. It never entered my mind that Laney'd be there—though I might have figured as much, he thought. *From the way she dresses when they go out, he must take her to all the classiest places in the valley, and the Kirby Center is about the top of the line here. It burns me up whenever I see her with that guy, especially now. After the plane ride, I was sure that she was beginning to see me in a whole new light . . . or so I hoped. That's just what she needed, to see me with Miss Italy of all people.* He whacked the steering wheel with the palm of his hand. *Nothing like being set back to square one,* he thought.

As he passed Elena's house, he saw that it was dark. If some lights had been on he might have stopped to explain. *Oh well, we'll have Lane over for Sunday to meet Gini and her aunt before I take them to D.C.,* he decided. *Everything will be okay then . . . I hope.*

Saturday morning Elena hung up the phone and glanced at her watch. Although she had felt guilty for asking Pastor Douglas to find a substitute for her class the following day, she was glad that at least she'd be spared having to face Josh and his fiancée. That was the last thing she needed right now, she realized. It would be a treat to have the Sunday off. A Bible college chorale was scheduled to sing at one of the churches in the Poconos, and Elena had booked a cabin at Swiftwater Ridge Resort. With her plans settled, Elena took a suitcase from the spare bedroom and packed the things she'd need. Then, turning down the thermostat and glancing around the cottage one last time, she was on her way.

By late afternoon, Elena stood at the door of a rented cabin. *It's definitely still winter in the mountains,* she thought, blowing into her hands to warm them. She unlocked the door and carried her suitcase inside. She ignited the logs already stacked in the fireplace and put the kettle on. Clouds hung low, and an occasional snowflake floated lazily in the air, but as the firewood hissed and popped, warmth spread through the room. Curling up on the couch with a comforting cup of tea, Elena rested her head on her hands and fell asleep.

In the gloom of early darkness, she awakened and stretched. A snowplow roared by in the distance. Elena glanced out the window and saw a fresh layer of snow sparkling in the light from the manager's office. The world needed this new beginning, she thought. All the ugliness of winter's end,—the piles of cinders along the roads, the ashes outside in the driveway, the mud everywhere—was hidden in white, and everything was cloaked in beauty.

She turned on the kitchen light and removed some convenience foods from the refrigerator. *Guess I'll see what's so great about TV dinners,* she told herself, reading the directions and sliding one into the oven. *And after that, I have some thinking to do.*

After eating, Elena put fresh logs on the fire and took another look outside. The office light illuminating the snow cast a pale glow over everything, and the folds of the newly fallen blanket shimmered like ivory. *Ivory satin,* she thought, as a forbidden memory chilled her heart. *Oh, Josh, will this be a new beginning for you, too? For you and Gina DiAngelo?*

That thought sickened her as she released the curtain and flopped on the couch, drawing her knees up to her chest and hugging them. *Why did she have to come back into your life . . . or has she been there all along?* she wondered.

Listen to yourself, Elena's conscience warned. *What's it to you if he still loves her? What's he to you? Just a friend . . . isn't that what you told him? Just a friend. If you recall, you told him that you wanted nothing to do with love ever again. You should be happy for him. Didn't you pray that the Lord would send him somebody to love?*

Elena moaned and put her head down on her knees. She remembered with startling clarity telling him how she'd learned that when a person prays, she must be willing to accept God's will. If Gina DiAngelo were part of God's plan for Josh's life, what right had she to object?

But Gina had hurt him, Lord, she reasoned. *I can't even imagine anyone doing something to hurt Josh. Why did she come back now? And why am I jealous of her? I don't even know the woman.*

She's so beautiful, so perfect. How could he not be in love with someone like that? How could I ever begin to compete with her elegance? I've treated him like he was my brother, no less. But he's

*not. He's more . . . so much more. He's the very dearest friend I've
ever had in this world, and I don't want her to hurt him again. I'd
never hurt him if I loved him. If I loved him, I'd—*

As suddenly and as surprisingly as the first rays of sunshine after
rain, the realization of the deepest feelings in her heart dawned on
Elena, and she stood up, eyes wide. "I love you, Josh Montgomery,"
she whispered, and the words sounded astounding to her own ears.
Hugging herself, she smiled. Then, Elena dissolved into tears, sure
that she had lost Josh forever.

Monday morning found Elena subdued and hard at work before
anyone else arrived at the office.

"Look at you," exclaimed Marcy, noticing the time as she came
in. "Did someone dump some extra work on you, or what?"

Elena grimaced. "No, I just thought I'd get some of this out of
the way. How was your weekend?"

"Great. How 'bout yours? How was the concert?"

The reality that Elena had struggled so hard to keep from her
thoughts crashed in on her again. Tears threatened, and in an effort
to keep them at bay, she didn't answer.

"Lane?" Marcy crossed the room and sat on a corner of Elena's
desk, coffee mug in hand. "Are you okay?"

She nodded.

"Do you want to talk about it?"

Elena shook her head. "I—can't." Tears won out, and sobbing,
she put her head down on her folded arms.

Marcy patted her shoulder. "Hey, I'm sorry, kid. I didn't mean
to be nosey."

"It—it's n—not your fault. Oh, darn, I'm out of tissues," she said,
opening and closing desk drawers, "and I'm going to be a mess when
everyone comes."

"I'll get you some from my desk, okay?" Marcy crossed the room
and returned with tissues, which she handed to Elena.

"Thanks, Marce."

"Go into the women's room and fix yourself up. I could tell Miriam
you're not feeling well and had to go home."

"Oh, I'll be all right. I'm just having a bad day. If I keep busy,
I'm sure everything'll be okay." Rising, she mopped at her face and
left the room. When she returned a few moments later, she was
composed once again and resumed her work.

"Morning, ladies," said Derek cheerily, as the inner office trio passed en masse. Mr. Webster nodded as though he agreed with his son's assessment of the day, and Miriam inclined her head slightly. The door closed behind them.

Marcy stared after them, then looked at Elena, carefully scrutinizing her face. Whatever it was, it must not have had anything to do with the boss's son, she thought. Maybe she'll open up later.

The opportunity arose at lunch time. The Websters and Miriam were scheduled for court at one o'clock. Mr. Webster buzzed Marcy on the intercom and suggested that she and Elena take the early lunch together.

In the coffee shop of the Webster Building, Marcy watched Elena peruse the limited menu. "Anything look good?"

Elena looked up. "Well, I haven't had a pork barbeque for some time. I might have one of those." She smiled and put her menu back in the stainless steel holder at the inside table edge.

"Sounds good to me, too. Make that two, please," she said to the waitress. "And we'll have tea."

The waitress nodded and left.

"Feeling better?" asked Marcy.

Smiling, Elena nodded, and a tiny blush colored her cheeks. "I had a lot on my mind."

"Oh?"

"Mm-hmm. I spent the weekend at a cabin in the Poconos. I needed to do some thinking . . . and I had to get away to do it."

"Did you . . . go alone?"

Elena frowned. "Of course."

"Well, I thought so," said Marcy, sheepishly. "I don't know why I even asked."

Neither spoke for a few moments. The food arrived, and Marcy asked the blessing. "So, did you think everything through?" she probed.

"You've known for a long time," Elena began, studying her friend's face as she spoke.

Apprehensive, Marcy glanced up from sipping her tea. "Known what?"

"What I didn't know myself. That I'm in love with Josh."

She set the cup down, her expression brightening. "Well, praise the Lord! The light has finally dawned!" Her smile dimmed when Elena's face remained serious. "So what's the problem? You can finally be with the man you were destined to love all along. You can stop messing around with Derek Webster."

One side of Elena's mouth curved in a small, bitter smile. "At least it sounds good, even if it isn't possible."

"What do you mean, not possible, Lane? Josh loves you, too. I know it," she said, taking a bite of her sandwich.

"Maybe he does, but not in the way you think. So maybe Derek Webster will be an alternate choice after all."

Marcy stopped eating and put her sandwich on the plate. "Now, wait just a minute. I think you've left out a few minor details, Lane. What are you talking about?"

"Just this. Remember that girl from Italy who Josh was engaged to? Gina DiAngelo?"

Marcy nodded.

"Well, she's here. She's the friend from Europe he went to meet. I saw them together at the concert Friday night."

"You can't be serious."

"I've never been more serious."

Shaking her head, Marcy frowned. "Gina DiAngelo has come all the way to America? She's here now?"

Elena's nodding head confirmed the statement.

"Well, what's she like?"

"Beautiful. Perfect. No flaws at all. None."

"Why would she come here?"

Elena gazed steadily into Marcy's eyes, her own face expressionless. "Why do you think, Marce? Use your imagination."

"You think she's after Josh."

"I'm positive. And he knew she was coming. If it was just a friendly visit, Josh would have told me. Don't you agree? We were together the day before he went to meet her. And he did more than not mention her. He let me think that some *guy* was coming to visit."

"I see what you mean."

"It's too late, Marcy. I've lost him for good, this time."

The waitress appeared with the teapot and asked if they wanted dessert.

"No, I don't think so," Marcy answered. "All of a sudden, I'm not hungry. Would you please wrap up my sandwich?"

Elena picked up her own barbeque and ate it slowly.

23

The week passed in a blur. Josh was away most of the time, and Elena imagined him escorting his true love up and down the entire Atlantic coast, around the Great Lakes, to Niagara Falls, and on to the nation's capital. Even in her dreams she saw them, laughing, embracing, and happy to be together again, as Elena stood on the sidelines, an unwilling spectator to it all.

She could hear Josh's voice clearly as he whispered to the beautiful woman in his arms. "I tried to write," he was saying, "but nothing looked right on paper." And then Gina DiAngelo laughed, that tinkling crystal sound. In her dream, Elena had turned to walk away, but his words to Gina followed. "You've always been special to me. What hurts you hurts me." How could he use the exact same words? Elena thought miserably. Or was it all just a line, always a line?

It took an extra touch of makeup to hide the dark circles under her eyes as Elena dressed for church. She wished that she could have found another excuse to be absent, as she had the previous Sunday, but the responsibility of being an example to her class weighed heavily upon her. *Well, at least I can spare myself one indignity,* she thought, as she pulled on her coat and walked to her car. *I won't be here when the Montgomerys and their guest come for me.*

A full hour early for Sunday school, Elena shivered in the deserted building as the furnace chugged away the remaining chill of the night. She read and reread the same paragraph in her lesson manual, somehow never seeing the words. Was it too much to hope that Josh would have made plans to attend a service somewhere else? she asked herself. She'd just avoid him as long as Miss Gina Maria DiAngelo was around, that's all there was to it.

The students trickled into the room at the beginning of the Sunday school hour, and Elena checked off each name in the attendance book. "Does anyone know where Valerie is today?"

"I think she's got the flu," answered Sharon. "She's been out of school the last two days."

"Oh, that's too bad. I'll have to send her a card." Elena sighed inwardly. She really needed Valerie and all her input this morning. "Well, let's open in prayer. Marybeth, would you mind?"

Elena barely heard the prayer. In her heart she silently voiced a plea of her own, that the Lord would take control and somehow speak to the class in spite of the conflicts going on in her head. In the silence, she looked up with a smile. "Thank you, Marybeth."

"In our character-building lesson series, we've learned quite a few ways in which God uses us as examples to the unbelieving world around us. Today we'll be looking at Scriptures relating to pride. Do you think there's a difference between feeling good about yourself and being proud?"

Nodding, Sharon raised a hand. "Well, I don't know if I can explain it, but yeah, . . . there's a big difference."

"It is a bit hard to put into words, I agree. Turn in your Bibles to Psalm 100." Seeing that one of the quiet girls in the back row was first to locate the Scripture, Elena smiled at her. "Carol, would you read verse 3 for us, please?"

The girl returned the smile and read the passage. " 'Know ye that the Lord, He is God; it is He who hath made us, and not we ourselves; we are His people, and the sheep of His pasture.' "

" 'It is He who hath made us,' " Elena repeated. "That's an interesting thought, isn't it, since we are all different. Each of us came into this world in pretty much the same way, and yet we have our own set of talents, our own interests. You and I may not share the same likes or dislikes, we may not feel the same joys or be hurt by the same experiences, but we were all made by God."

"That must be why we can feel good about ourselves, then," said Sharon. "Since the Lord made us the way we are and all."

"Right. But it doesn't really stop there, you know. As someone said, what we are is God's gift to us; what we become is our gift to God. We can develop the abilities we were given and do something with our lives that we can feel good about. But when does the good feeling become pride?"

"Well," said Marybeth, "when we decide we did it all ourselves."

Elena nodded. "That's the difference. Sometimes only a very thin line separates the two. Think of it this way. Say you have final exams to face tomorrow in school, and you haven't exactly been hitting the books this term."

The girls grinned and squirmed in their seats.

"But," continued Elena, "you really need a good grade or you won't graduate. So you pray that God will help you to remember all the facts you have to cram into your head before the test. Then, miracle of miracles, when the teacher hands the tests back, you see that you did very well. The first thing you do is breathe a sigh of relief and thank the Lord, right? You feel good about yourself. But then you find out that your score was even higher than the one Amy Smith, the principal's daughter, received. Sound familiar? All of a sudden you begin to think that you're even smarter than you thought you were. Do you see the difference in attitudes there?"

"Yeah," said Sharon. "We forgot that it was God who helped us."

"Right. Let's turn to the book of Proverbs, Chapter 16, verse 18, to see how God views pride . . . ."

Try as she might during the morning service, Elena could not prevent her eyes from wandering to the dashing couple several rows ahead and to the right of her. Gina DiAngelo looked stunning in her olive crepe dress and silver fox coat, her hair in a long french braid. Josh, in his charcoal gray herringbone sport coat with pale gray slacks and tie, complemented her perfectly.

Perfectly, Elena decided grimly, looking down at her own dress. It was the best silk creation she owned, but it felt like a thrift store bargain at the moment. Directing her gaze back to the pulpit, she forced herself to concentrate on the pastor's sermon.

"We, as believers, should never allow things to divide us or come between us," he was saying. "It was the Lord's fervent prayer that God would keep the disciples together, united in spirit, as one. This is found in today's text, John, Chapter 17."

He continued speaking during the rustle of pages as members of the congregation turned to the New Testament passage. "The evil forces of the world will do whatever it takes to cause strife between Christians, to prevent God from being glorified in the lives of His children. We must not allow things to come between God and ourselves, no matter how important—or how trivial—they might be. It is our responsibility, instead, always to seek

His will, and then to do it."

Elena wondered what God's will was, for Josh, for herself. Was it all for nothing that after so many unhappy years Josh had come back into her life, only to make a quick exit again? Was she destined just to know that there did exist a love that was not merely as she had always dreamed, but even better? Was she only to see love, but not to touch it? To touch, but never to have it? A quiet, shuddering sigh escaped her as a tear made its way over the crescent of her cheekbone. Hurriedly, Elena wiped it away and looked around. Everyone's head was bowed. The pastor was offering the closing prayer.

Intending to be among the first out the door when the service ended, Elena rose and turned, but a hand on her arm stopped her in her tracks.

"Elena. I've been wanting to tell you how much I appreciate your work with the teenage class. Sharon talks about nothing but you and how she looks forward to the lessons each week."

Elena smiled. "Thank you, Mrs. Whitney. Sharon has truly grown spiritually in the last few months. I've enjoyed having her in the class."

"Well, keep up the good work," Mrs. Whitney said.

"Thank you, I'll try."

"Lane?"

Elena could not ignore the familiar voice and the tapping on her shoulder. Her heart sank. She closed her eyes and swallowed, then turned to face him. "Josh. How nice to see you."

"I have someone here who wants to meet you."

"Oh, really?" She wondered if the pounding of her heart could be seen throbbing in her neck and temples.

"I'd like you to meet Gina DiAngelo," he said.

The beautiful Gina stepped from behind Josh with a dazzling smile and offered her hand. "You must be Elena," she said, her accent rich and lovely. "Josh has told me all about you."

I'm sure, thought Elena, gluing a smile in place as she shook Gina's soft, perfectly manicured hand. She could just hear it: This is our little Laney . . . friend of the family . . . the poor girl with no one.

"Hey," Josh said, "we'd like you to come for dinner. Mom's expecting you, as always."

"Well, I—I—"

"Please, Laney," Gina DiAngelo interjected. "You don't mind if I call you that, do you? Why, I may not have another opportunity to get to know you. You'll come, won't you?" The woman turned pleadingly. "Say something to her, Josh. Use those awesome powers of persuasion of yours. Make her come."

The way Josh returned that look, irritated Elena to such a point that she heard herself actually agreeing to have dinner with them. She had no idea why she was irked, but she was. All the way to the Montgomery home, obediently following the sedan in her Escort, Elena called herself every idiotic name she could think of.

Once inside the house, she immediately excused herself to help Stella while Josh and his—his date? his love?—sat talking and laughing in the living room. They were not alone. Gina's aunt, striking like Gina, occasionally joined the conversation with a mixture of Italian and heavily accented English. Elena had been introduced to her upon her arrival.

"I missed you this morning at church, Mother," Elena said in the kitchen as she arranged pieces of chicken on a china platter.

"Well, I decided to keep Mrs. Santelli company, since her command of English is somewhat lacking."

Elena smiled. "So, what do you think of . . . your guests?" She couldn't help asking.

"Oh my, we've had such a charming time. I've found Gina to be a lovely person, and her aunt has a delightful sense of humor. We've so enjoyed having them."

"Oh." Elena's heart plummeted as her spirit deflated.

Dinner was even worse than church. Josh presided at the head of the table, with Gina DiAngelo, in all her perfection, seated on his right. Next to her was her aunt, and Stella was at the other end of the long table. Directly across from Gina, on Josh's left, Elena seethed uncomfortably, and an empty space was left between her and Stella. She knew that this was going to be one very long meal.

After the blessing, Josh passed the platter of chicken to Gina, who smiled graciously at Elena. "I'm so glad we've finally had the chance to meet you. Josh has spoken often of you."

"Well, I've been curious to meet you also." *I could almost say morbidly curious,* Elena thought. She wished that Josh had told her something—anything—about Gina so that making conver-

sation would have been easier. When Gina turned to pass the food
to her aunt, Elena glared in his direction and saw a twinkle in
his eye. She returned her attention to Gina. "You speak English
marvelously well."

"Oh, thank you. I had the privilege of attending university in
London for two years."

"That's where we met, actually," said Josh. "I was on leave
there while Gini was a student."

Gini, is it? How cute, thought Elena sarcastically. She smiled
politely. "How interesting."

"Gina's also fluent in French," Stella added.

University of Paris, no doubt, thought Elena waspishly.

Gina's words echoed her thoughts. "I had a year of university
in Paris, as well."

"Why, how fortunate. You've really seen the world. Is this your
first visit to America?"

"Yes. Josh has extended invitations several times, and the
opportunity finally presented itself. We've been having a marvelous time. I don't know if I'll ever be able to tear myself away."

"Josh is a wonderful tour guide," Elena said. "He's very knowl-
edgeable about the area." She looked again to her right as she
toyed with her food. She noticed that Josh seemed to be enjoying
her discomfort immensely. *Was she so transparent,* she wondered? The least she could do was try to be nice to his . . .
girlfriend, she decided. "I do hope you enjoy the sights while
you're here."

"Oh, I'll make sure of that," Josh said. "Don't worry. She'll
have the time of her life."

At this, Gina put her hand on Josh's arm where it rested on
the table and smiled sweetly.

Hours later, curled up on her couch at home, Elena stared
miserably at the logs snapping in the fireplace. Pleading a splitting headache, she had excused herself from enduring further
agony by attending the evening service with Josh and Gina
DiAngelo. Elena had decided to stay at home instead and study
ahead for the next class.

Unexpectedly, the telephone rang, and she picked up the receiver. "Hello?"

"Hi, Lane," said Marcy's cheery voice. "I know you're probably ready to leave for church, but I thought I'd try to catch you."

"Actually, I'm skipping, so you're in luck."

"Skipping? Hey, now, that's a first."

"I suppose."

"Listen, I called because there's going to be a sale in the wedding department at Hampton's. I thought that maybe tomorrow we might take a run over there after work. What do you think?"

"Sounds fine to me. I guess we should start looking for my bridesmaid dress, too."

"Good. I'll let you get back to . . . whatever, then."

"No, wait, Marce. Do you . . . are you too busy to talk?"

"Why? Something wrong?"

Elena sighed. "Yes. No. Oh, *I* don't know. I made an absolute idiot of myself today."

"How?"

"Well, to start with, I got out of bed. Does that give you a clue as to how the day went?"

"I think so. Would you like me to come over?"

"Well, I appreciate the offer, but tonight I don't feel worth the effort."

"You are to me. Put on the kettle, and I'll be there in a little while."

"Are you sure you want to do this?"

"I'm sure."

True to her word, Marcy knocked at the door within half an hour. Elena hung up her friend's coat and led the way into the kitchen, where a pot of tea sat brewing on the table.

"Ahh . . . the bone china cups," Marcy said, taking a seat as Elena did the same.

Smiling, Elena nodded. "They were the first ones in my Windsor collection. Remember the day we bought each other a cup and saucer for our hope chests?"

"And every birthday thereafter," Marcy laughed. "Mine are still new."

"Well, they'll be used soon enough." Elena smiled wistfully and poured the tea. "Thanks for coming."

"Well, you are my best friend, you know. Tell me what happened."

Elena shook her head and closed her eyes, then looked up. "Oh,

Marce . . . it was awful."

"It can't be that bad, kiddo."

"You're wrong. I . . . don't even know who I was today. It was like someone spiteful and mean was wearing my body. Saying things . . ."

"So, who were you mean to?"

"Josh. Josh! Can you believe it? And Gina DiAngelo. I didn't want to be anywhere around them, even. I tried to avoid it. I drove by myself to church, sat alone, and tried to leave at the last amen." She sighed.

"And?" Marcy prompted, taking a sip of the hot tea.

"You're never going to believe this. I had dinner at his house after church. I can't believe it myself."

"You met her? What's she like?"

"Oh, where do I begin? Do I even know enough adjectives to describe her? She's so . . . elegant." Elena paused, searching her thoughts. "She must be rich. She's gorgeous, she speaks at least three languages fluently, and she's traveled all over the place. On top of all that, she fawns all over Josh, batting her long eyelashes, calling me 'Laney.' I thought I'd be sick."

Marcy smiled, reached for Elena's hand and examined it.

"What are you doing?"

"Just checking. Thought I might find some claws showing."

Elena pouted and huffed as she pulled her hand away.

Neither spoke for several minutes.

"You're right, Marce." Elena's voice was softly contrite. "I have no cause to dislike Gina DiAngelo. She's everything I've always wished I could be: warm, gracious, intelligent. It's no wonder Josh loves her."

"And if he didn't, then you'd really like her, right?"

Elena studied her for a moment, then nodded.

"Then I imagine the patient will live," Marcy said. "No point in my hanging around any longer. Thanks for the tea."

The pair rose and hugged, and Elena retrieved her friend's coat. "I really appreciated the 'mirror' of your friendship. I needed that look at my worldly side. Thanks."

"Well," Marcy said, pulling on her wrap and opening the door, "don't be too hard on yourself. Maybe you'll have another chance to show her what *you* are really like. Oddly enough, you are gracious, intelligent, warm, elegant, and beautiful yourself. Ever think that Josh might have been attracted to her in the first place because she had all of *your* qualities?" The door closed behind her smile.

Elena stared after her in shock for several seconds, then smiled to herself. It was a nice thought—or would have been, if there had been any truth to it. No sense wondering about it now, though, she thought, walking back to the kitchen to rinse out the dishes.

Moments later, she returned to the couch, tucked her feet under on the cushion, and picked up the teacher's manual. It fell open to the morning's lesson, and Elena felt a twinge of guilt as the memory of it came to mind. She did not feel proud at the moment, or very good about herself, either. She turned past the latest page marked with her notes. The title of the new lesson seemed to leap from the heading as though it had been lettered in flashing neon. It was called "Dealing with Jealousy."

Elena closed the booklet with her index finger still inside and bowed her head. "I knew there was one more thing I needed to do, Father," she prayed out loud. "I was wrong to be so wretched and unloving to Josh's friend. Please forgive me. If I ever see Gina DiAngelo again, I'll be an example of Your love to her."

Opening to the lesson again, she took a second look at the page before her. It would have been funny if she hadn't felt so humiliated by her own actions, she mused. Pressing her lips together, she turned to the Scripture passage listed, determined to apply the lesson to her life.

Josh glanced at Elena's house as he drove by on his way home later that night. The only light on was the one in her bedroom, and he thought of her there, warm and relaxed, her long silky hair splayed across her pillow, her eyes closed. It was the way he remembered her from the days when she had been sick. Even in sleep her lips curved in the hint of a smile, he recalled. Inhaling slowly, he pulled into his garage and turned off the engine.

Her light was out by the time that he had undressed, he noticed as he pulled the blinds away from the window slightly. Then, allowing them to fall back into place, he knelt by the side of his bed. She was hurting again, and he knew it. Even more, he knew that he was responsible for it. He had practically set the whole thing up, even after vowing she'd never be hurt again.

Would he ever forget the pain that clouded her eyes when she left today? he wondered The thought was a knife that twisted mercilessly inside of him. It had taken months—months!—to get her to share the painful memories of her marriage. Gradually, patiently, he'd watched the transformation as she emerged from the cocoon of her past . . . watched as the happy, smiling glow returned to her eyes, the glow that had been part of her youth and innocence. Now, he realized, it was gone again.

Kneeling there, he wondered if the disciples might have felt such a sinking, gut-wrenching feeling when they betrayed the One who had called them His friends, had walked upon the earth with them, had broken bread with them, had taught them, and later had died for them.

Dear Lord, he prayed, *there's no excuse for what I did tonight, tromping all over her heart with combat boots, trying to make her jealous. It was like forcing the petals of a rose to open in the frost when, with just a little sunshine and time, all the glory and beauty of the flower would have burst forth on its own. If I've ruined everything, it's no less than I deserve. But I'm asking for another chance . . . .*

24

The following evening, Elena tried on every style of bridesmaid dress that Hampton's bridal department had in stock, twirling before Marcy and waiting for her opinion.

"This is going to be harder than I thought," moaned Marcy from the velvet settee. "I was going to plan everything in mint green and white, but the peach tea length you had on last was beautiful. So was the orchid gown before that, and now this blue one. How will I choose? Which one did you like best, Lane?"

Elena surveyed herself in the triple mirror, turning slowly this way and that, her eyes lingering on the back view. "Well, they're all so pretty, but for an August wedding, I'd probably eliminate this eyelet one. It's too springish."

"I think you're right. But it'll be the first week in August, remember. So I don't want dark colors, either. Let me see the front of that one again."

Elena turned and stepped closer to Marcy, her head cocked to one side as her friend examined the gown.

"Oh, I don't know. Would you mind trying on the peach lace one again? The cut was elegant, and I especially liked that one."

"The dressing-room attendant wasn't too fond of all those cute little covered buttons down the back," Elena said with a half-smile.

"Maybe she wasn't, but I was. It looked stunning on you."

"Well, then, I'll be right back." Gathering up the long skirt with one hand so that she could walk, Elena stepped inside the dressing area and closed the louvered doors. She returned a few moments later.

Marcy joined her at the mirror. "The more I look at it, the prettier it gets, Lane. Do you like it?"

Elena's gaze swept over all three views, then she nodded slowly. "It's really beautiful. It's the nicest one here. But you really don't have to decide today, you know. There's still time to look around."

"Yes, I know. But I've already been to a few other shops, and

179

I don't think we'll find another one this nice."

"The attendant said it comes in mint green."

"No, it's perfect in peach, and you look gorgeous in it. In fact, I'll really have to work hard to make my wedding gown even noticeable next to it."

Elena laughed and returned to put on her street clothes, and the pair went to a small restaurant on Public Square for coffee.

"Looks like you're feeling better now . . . about yesterday," said Marcy. "You were pretty quiet at work."

"Well, the Lord has forgiven me, I'm sure. But it'll take a while for me to forgive myself."

"Are you sure that whatever you said at Josh's was all that bad?"

"Oh, it wasn't so much what I said. Heaven knows Mom taught me always to be polite to everyone. But I wanted so much to hate her. I wasn't very friendly."

"That's all? You weren't very friendly?" Marcy eyed her in disbelief.

Setting her cup down, Elena shrugged. "Well, that was enough, considering that Josh loves her and probably wanted my approval, know what I mean? I probably hurt his feelings, being so cool to Gina. She couldn't have been nicer to me."

"Oh well, it's over and done with. How much longer will she be here?"

"Who knows? I wasn't about to ask, and no one volunteered. I believe Josh took Gina and her aunt someplace again today."

Josh was still mentally lashing himself as he drove his guests to their hotel after touring historical Philadelphia. Stella Montgomery had accompanied them on this trip, and the three women were deciding who'd be first in line for a bubblebath.

Alone in his hotel room a short time later, Josh showered and lay on top of the bed with his eyes closed. His thoughts were with Elena over a hundred miles away. It was probably more like thousands of light years away, he was sure, farther than when he'd been on the other side of the world in the Air Force.

"Josh, old buddy, when you blow something, you blow it big," he said, with one punch to the mattress. He'd never seen Elena so stiff and rigidly polite in all the time he'd known her. He wished that he could call her and apologize for being such a jerk, but some things were better done in person. He would have to wait.

At least Gina had graciously understood the situation when he had explained it to her on their way to church, he realized. More observant than he'd given her credit for, Gina had already put the pieces together by the time she and Elena were introduced, so the cool treatment hadn't really affected her. One more week and she and Mrs. Santelli would be off to L.A. on their own. Now, if he could only last the week.

Derek fingered the velvet box in his pocket and waited for Elena to return from the powder room at Cyril's. It had been like pulling teeth to get her to agree to have lunch again, but he would not be dissuaded by that. *Most women made a game of playing hard to get, didn't they?* he rationalized. He was sure that once she realized his intentions were entirely honorable, after all, she would see him in a different light. He knew that he'd figure out a way to deal with his mother later.

"Oh, the food has arrived," said Elena as she breezed up to the table and took her seat. "Sorry I took so long."

"It wasn't you. They were just faster than usual today."

Elena smiled. "This is lovely. I've been hungry for quiche for ages, and no one makes it like the chef here."

"Good. I hope you enjoy it, then."

"Your steak looks wonderful, too."

He cleared his throat and took a sip from the goblet beside him. A waiter approached and refilled their china cups with coffee.

Derek adjusted the knot in his tie and observed Elena as she ate. "You're aware that Father's been successful in the Fisher and Manfield cases he's been working on for so long," he began.

"Of course. He bought roses for our desks... Miriam's, Marcy's, and mine."

"Well, we're planning a celebration at home, too. Nothing big, mind you, just a few of Father's colleagues and some friends. I'd like you to come and be part of it."

Elena set her fork down and looked at Derek, then her gaze shifted off into the distance.

For a brief moment, Derek remembered the Thanksgiving fiasco at his house and his mother's arctic treatment of her. "You'll come, won't you?" he asked.

"Oh, Derek, it's very kind of you to invite me, and I really appreciate it. But no, thank you."

"Why not?"

Elena shrugged. "I don't fit in with your family's set of friends, Derek. You know that. I don't have the right clothes, I don't know the right people, and I barely speak the same language."

"Nonsense. You're a wonderful person."

"Well, you're my friend. Of course you'd say that. But I can't consider going to your home again."

Derek was stunned. "What are you saying? Of course you can come. Father thinks the world of you, and I'm sure that, in time—"

"I don't belong there. In fact, I'm beginning to think I really don't belong here, either. It was wrong of me to think we should see each other outside the office. I'm really sorry."

"But you don't have to work in the office, Elena. That's the point." He looked around with a frown, then withdrew the tiny container from his pocket. "I would have chosen a different time, a more romantic setting for a proposal—"

Elena nearly choked on the last of her coffee as he placed the open jewelry box before her. Under the crystal chandelier of Cyril's, an exquisite diamond solitaire sparkled with tiny glittering rainbows. "It's beautiful," she said, her voice in a whisper.

"I love you, Elena Ryan. I would consider it an honor if you would become my wife."

"I—I don't know what to say." Taking the box into her hands, her finger lightly traced the prismatic sparkles of the pear-shaped stone. "I'm really touched, Derek. I've never seen such a beautiful ring, and any woman would be fortunate to have you for a husband. I mean that." She paused as she set the treasure down in the middle of the table. "But . . . we could never be happy together, you and I."

"I think you're wrong about that."

"No, I'm not. I could never be the kind of society wife a man in your position needs. We have nothing in common at all."

"Oh, hang society," he said, a note of exasperation in his voice. "Elena, you are a beautiful, charming, and intelligent woman. You intrigue me with your sensitivity, the depth of your wisdom, and your feelings about life. Why, I even enjoy some of those theories you have about that antiquated Bible of yours!"

Elena's eyes turned helplessly upward for an instant, and then she looked directly at him. "There, now, you see? If there's one thing that the person I marry must absolutely agree with me on, it's faith in the Word of God. The Bible isn't a theory, nor is it antiquated. It's living and it's real. If it weren't for the relationship I have with the Lord, there's no way I could have gone on after losing my husband and my son so suddenly. Only God has made my life worth living. Can't you see that?"

Elena watched Derek shift awkwardly in his seat and look around nervously as his expression darkened. She knew that it made him uncomfortable to speak personally about religion in public. She nearly smiled when he glanced around to see if anyone was listening.

"No. There we disagree." He glanced around once again. "But we can work it out. I know we can. You . . . you do have feelings for me, don't you?"

"Yes. I think a lot of you. You've been a wonderful friend, and I would do almost anything for you. But that's not enough for us to build a life together. Not really. When you've had time to think about it, I'm sure you'll come to the same conclusion."

Derek picked up the velvet box, snapped down the cover, and returned it to his pocket. "I think you're wrong. Honestly, Elena, you are without a doubt the most exasperating woman I've ever known. No matter what I do for you, it's never enough to make you warm up. You never let anyone near you. I give up."

Elena felt the color rise to her cheeks under his tirade. "I'm sorry you feel that way," she said lamely. "I never meant to hurt you. I really didn't."

One side of Derek's mouth curved sarcastically. He placed a twenty-dollar bill on the table and got up, and Elena followed. Outside, they drove back to the office in silence.

When Derek left for an appointment an hour later, Elena removed all the personal items from her desk drawers.

"What are you doing?" Marcy asked, watching her.

"Something I should have done a long time ago. I'm going home, where I belong."

Marcy's jaw hung open as she watched Elena go into the inner office, knock on Mr. Webster's door, and enter.

"Well, young lady," Mr. Webster said, flustered, after Elena had explained her intentions. "I wish you'd have given us some warning that you were thinking of resigning."

"I can understand that, sir. And I regret that it cannot be helped."

"Well, you've been a great asset to our staff, and I've appreciated the quality of your work. I'm sorry to see you go, but I wish you every happiness."

"Thank you, sir," she said, shaking his outstretched hand. Then she turned and left his large, book-lined office.

Next she approached Miriam's desk. "Miriam," she said with a smile, "you can draw a long yellow line through the rest of the year for me."

Her gold-rimmed spectacles slipped from her nose when Miriam looked up, and they dangled on her chest by a maroon cord. "I beg your pardon?"

"This will be my last day with the firm. I won't be coming back. I'm leaving. It's been a pleasure working with you, though. Do have a good day."

"But—I don't—"

Elena smiled over her shoulder and returned to the reception area she shared with Marcy.

Her friend was crying. "You can't do this, you know," she said. "The sun won't shine here any more, without you."

Elena leaned over to hug her, fighting tears herself. "Sorry, Marce. This is something I have to do. Trust me. I'll call you later and explain."

"Well," said Marcy, smiling through her tears, "at least now we can have lunch together whenever we want."

Elena laughed. "That's right. Well, I have to go now. Here," she said, removing the office key from her key ring and placing it on Marcy's blotter. Elena piled her possessions into an empty box and put on her coat.

"I'll miss you, kid," Marcy said.

"I'll miss you too," Elena said, waving with a nudge of one shoulder. She carried the box out into the hall and closed the office door for the last time.

As she drove homeward, Elena's thoughts returned to Derek and his proposal, and she smiled. Dear Derek. For all her poor treatment of him, she really did love him as a friend. He'd been there for her when she had needed someone to help her through a rough time. She was sure that in time he would see that she was right, and if he wanted to marry, there was a long line of society belles who would jump at the chance. He'd be okay, she knew.

If he'd been a Christian, she thought with a toss of her head, *it might have been another story.* She might have given some thought to committing her future to him; he did have some very endearing qualities. But never again would she hand her life away as casually as she had when she was young. Marriage is difficult enough when two people share the same faith in the Lord, she thought. She knew that she would rather live alone for the rest of her life than live through another bad marriage.

She sighed and steered her car onto Hillside Road. She decided to take the scenic route, even though it brought back memories of the last time she'd been on it, with Josh.

The rest of my life alone. Would it come to that? she wondered.

Gina turned to Josh as the ticket agent put her luggage onto the conveyor belt. "Well, I can't thank you and your mother enough for the wonderful hospitality. It's been marvelous seeing you again."

"Same here. I hope things go well for you in L.A." Putting an arm around her waist, he guided her to a nearby row of chairs, where her aunt and Stella Montgomery sat waiting.

When the flight to Los Angeles was announced over the intercom, the four stood at once, each hugging the other in turn. Josh walked with Gina and her aunt until they reached the boarding gate. Mrs. Santelli squeezed Josh's arm gently and smiled, then she gave her ticket to the uniformed man and walked up the ramp.

Gina hesitated and turned to Josh, and he pulled her into his arms. "Saying goodbye must be the saddest thing we do in this life," she whispered against his chest as he patted her back. "It was unfortunate, you know—"

He straightened slightly and looked at her questioningly.

"—That things didn't work out for us, when we had the chance," she continued.

He smiled.

"You've always loved Elena, haven't you? She was the reason."

Josh nodded slowly. "And I wanted you to be free to live all of your dreams."

"*Si,* I know," Gina said with a tiny smile. "You always believed in me and in my dreams. Well, I'm off to try another one. I'll never forget you, you know that." She stood on tiptoe and reached to kiss his cheek.

Josh groaned and pulled her close, kissing her softly on the lips. Then, after a last hard hug, he released her.

Gina brushed a tear away and smiled as another rolled down her other cheek. The final boarding call was announced. "I'm sure Elena loves you. Everything will turn out all right."

Josh watched her open her purse and frown, and he chuckled despite a heaviness in his heart as he handed her his handkerchief.

"Dio sia con tè," she said, turning away.

"God be with you, too, Gini," he called out softly as she walked up the ramp. *"Arrivederci."*

At the top she turned and waved.

Swallowing the lump in his throat, Josh waved back, then turned and strode back to where his mother waited.

"She's a very special young woman, isn't she?" she said, smiling at her son.

"Yes, that she is." He exhaled in a deep sigh and glanced back at the boarding ramp. "Let's go home, Mom. I have a bridge to repair."

25

The temperature had been gradually growing milder over the last few weeks, and March was drawing to an end. As Elena opened the door to get the newspaper, she inhaled a fresh scent of spring. Tiny green crocus shoots were peeking through the earth in her flower bed.

After scanning the headlines on the front page and reading the local news section over a second cup of coffee, she pushed the paper aside and reached for the Bible school catalog she'd brought back from the church service she had attended in the Poconos. She'd just about memorized the campus photos inside and the list of available courses, but she leafed through the pages one more time. Then, after setting her cup into the sink, she ran a brush through her hair and put on her coat. A drive would help to clear her mind, she thought. Grabbing her purse she locked the door behind her.

As Elena neared Wyoming Avenue, she decided not to drive directly into Wilkes-Barre, the route she had taken to work day after day for so long. On a whim she turned left and detoured idly through historic Forty Fort, the site of the famous Wyoming Valley Indian massacre of 1778. Forty Fort was now a charming place to live, and she admired the stately homes as she passed.

Just after the small shopping center off to her right, Elena noticed a new restaurant, The Village Grille, just ahead. She decided to stop for an early lunch and pulled into the parking lot.

Inside, she took a seat in one of the booths and removed the laminated menu from its holder to look over the items. As a waitress approached from behind, Elena replaced the menu and put her hands onto her lap so that the waitress could set the silverware and glass of water in place unhindered. Their eyes met at the same moment.

"Janice!"

"Elena!"

187

They stared at one another in speechless surprise and shock.
A small spot of color rose on the girl's cheeks. She ran her tongue
nervously over her lips.

"I—I can't believe it's you!" Elena said. "I didn't even know
you were back."

Janice shrugged. "Well, I am." She held up her pad. "Um . . .
what can I get you?"

"Oh." She smiled. "I'm so surprised to see that you I've forgotten what I wanted." Grabbing the menu again, she pointed
to the list. "I guess I'll have a . . . Number Three."

"Sure. One Number Three coming right up." She turned and
started to walk away.

"Janice," Elena called after her.

The girl stopped and looked back.

"I was wondering if you had a few minutes . . . to talk."

"You want to talk to me?" she asked incredulously.

Elena nodded.

Janice glanced around the deserted coffee shop and expelled
a deep breath. "Sure. It's time for my break anyway. I'll just give
your order to the cook."

Elena heard her tell the other waitress on duty that she was
going to take her break, then Janice returned with two mugs of
coffee and sat opposite Elena.

"It's really good to see you again," said Elena, after a short
awkward silence. "I think about you a lot."

"You do?"

"Of course. Does that surprise you?"

"Well, yeah," Janice said, nodding.

Elena hesitated. "I still pray for you every day."

Shaking her head slowly back and forth in wonder, Janice
emptied two packets of sugar into her mug and added cream.

She looked older somehow, thought Elena. Older, wiser, as if
life had already hurt her. "How've you been?" she asked.

"Okay." She took a sip of her coffee, and her green eyes studied
Elena for a moment. "How's Val?"

Elena frowned, perplexed. "Fine. She stays mostly to herself
since you left. You . . . haven't told her that you're here?"

Sunlight streaming through the window danced over the girl's
auburn hair as Janice shook her head. At the sound of a bell from
the kitchen, she excused herself and returned with Elena's plate.

Elena smiled and bowed her head momentarily while Janice sat down. Looking up once again, she motioned to the food. "You know, I don't need all of this. Why don't you have the other half of the English muffin?"

"Thanks." She reached over and picked it up. "I . . . um . . . mind if I use your knife?"

Elena nudged it and the tub of jam from her plate in her direction and watched as Janice made a project of covering the muffin with strawberry preserves. "Is your mom glad to have you home?"

"Now that would be something," Janice blurted, one side of her mouth curled sarcastically. "She doesn't even know I'm here. Not that she'd care one way or the other."

"Oh. I'm . . . sorry to hear that."

"Yeah. Well, I'm used to it. It's no big deal."

Elena nodded sadly. "It would be to me. Too bad. She's the one who's missing out." Spearing a small slice of omelette, she put it into her mouth and ate it slowly.

Janice cocked her head to one side with a puzzled frown.

"She doesn't know how really special you are."

With a bitter smile, Janice shrugged. "I've never been special to anyone in my life."

"Yes, you have. To me."

"Maybe before, when I was in the class, but now—"

Elena shook her head. "Just because you've been away for a while, doesn't mean that you don't matter to me anymore. I'll always love you and care about what happens in your life."

Janice's eyes misted over, and she blinked the tears away. "You always said that to all of us, but I didn't know if you were just being nice, or what."

"Well, I meant it. I hoped to be more than just a teacher. I wanted to be your friend, too."

Janice looked at Elena and then back down. She toyed with the knife for several seconds, twirling it around with a finger as it lay on the table between them. "I . . . came right back, you know."

Conscious of a difference in the atmosphere between them, Elena breathed a small sigh of relief. "You did?"

Janice nodded. "I thought about all the things you said. Seemed like I was on that bus forever, and it almost felt as if you were there, too, nagging."

Elena smiled, a little embarrassed.

"Only it wasn't nagging . . . I see that now. I thought of everything I've learned in class since I accepted the Lord, how Christians should only date other people who believe. Then I remembered the way Scott was always trying to pull me away from church. What you said at the bus station made sense, and I figured you were probably right about a lot of it. Marriage *is* an important step. And he wouldn't have married me anyway, I'm sure."

"Did—did you see him, after you got there?"

"Only from a distance. He was with some girl. He had his arm around her just the way he used to hold me. Funny," she said, shaking her head, "I believed all the things he'd told me. I sure was gullible."

"We're all a little gullible, I'm afraid. It's part of needing to love, and needing someone to love us."

"I guess."

"Well, where are you staying now?"

"At my grandmother's."

Elena raised her brows.

"Yeah, I went there as soon as I got back. She said it was okay."

"So you've never tried to contact your mother?"

Shaking her head, Janice looked away.

Drinking the last of her coffee, Elena set the mug down again. "Do you have any plans?"

"Well, I guess I won't graduate with my class, the way I had hoped. But I'm enrolled in the high school here. Grandma made me," she said with a smile. "In fact, if there'd been classes today, I wouldn't have been here. Funny, huh?"

Elena returned her smile. "Yes. I didn't plan to come here, now that you mention it. But maybe it wasn't a coincidence. Perhaps the Lord knew that I needed to find you again." Reaching across the table, she gave Janice's hand a squeeze.

The girl closed her eyes tightly, obviously fighting off tears. Then she blinked and looked up again.

"We miss having you in class. Do you think you'll be coming back?"

Janice shrugged and released a deep breath. "Maybe. I don't know. I—I'm . . . not ready to face everyone yet."

"I understand."

"By the way," the girl said, fidgeting a bit in her seat, "I . . . um . . . wasn't really pregnant. I think that's probably something else the Lord did for me."

"Well," Elena smiled, "I can't say I'm not relieved to hear that. I'm glad you told me."

"Yeah. I wasn't quite as ready as I thought I was, somehow, to give my life to some guy, to be responsible enough to raise a child. I . . . almost called you one night, after I got back. To thank you for trying to stop me from making the biggest mistake of my life."

Elena stared, lips parted. "I wish you had. Called, I mean."

"Well, I was afraid that— Oh, I didn't want to bother you anymore."

"After all the time we've known each other, do you really think I'd consider you a bother, honey?"

"No," Janice said reluctantly, "I guess not."

"Then I hope you know that you never have to be afraid to come to me when you need a friend or just want to talk. I'll always love you, Janice."

Her green eyes perused Elena for a moment before she smiled. Then she glanced out the window and at her watch. "Two cars just turned in. I guess I'd better get back to work. Did you want more coffee?"

Elena shook her head. "No, thanks. I have to run."

They stood at the same time and hesitated for a second before they stepped toward one another and hugged.

"Oh, I'm so glad you came by," Janice said, tightening the hug. "It's been a treat to see you again."

"For me too. I can't tell you how glad I am to have you back."

Janice smiled as she released her hold. "Stop in again if you're ever out this way."

"I will. And you keep in touch, okay?"

She nodded and walked away in her crisp candy-striped uniform, removing an order pad from her pocket as she approached a couple who had just sat down in a booth across the room.

Observing Janice's efficient manner momentarily, Elena smiled to herself and slipped into her coat, then headed for the door. As she reached for the handle, she turned and caught Janice's eye. The girl smiled brightly and waved, and Elena returned both as she left.

A blast of cool air caught her off guard as she stepped outside, and Elena noticed that heavy clouds had all but obscured the blue of the sky. She unlocked the car door and got inside, sitting for a few minutes while she debated whether to continue on or go home instead. She gazed absently at The Village Grille. *Thank you, Lord, for taking care of her, for bringing her home. She still needs Your help, though. Stay close to her, keep her safe.* Elena turned the ignition key and headed back home to Dallas.

Over the car radio, an announcer reported that a late-winter storm trekking eastward from the Great Lakes was expected to hit the area by nightfall. *Great,* thought Elena, *so much for spring.*

In the waning light of late afternoon, the wind picked up considerably as the temperature fell, and occasional snowflakes dotted the view from the picture window of Elena's cottage. The evergreen trees in the front yard swayed and dipped as the last cold breath of winter swished through their branches, and gossamer veils of tiny snowflakes blew along the street like handfuls of dust.

Elena closed the blinds and turned away from the window to make supper, but the weather looked the same from the kitchen window. After several moments of watching the ever-increasing particles of snow carried aloft by the wind, she noticed that the feathery flakes were becoming smaller and heavier with moisture. Snow began to gather in low, sheltered areas. She pulled the curtains closed.

Curled up on the sofa with a bowl of soup, Elena watched tentacles of smoke inch their way up the chimney as flaming fingers of blue and orange cradled and stroked the logs in the fireplace. The cottage shuddered against the icy blasts, but the music from the stereo helped to mask some of the sound of winter's wrath.

Elena's heart was still aglow with warmth as she thought back over her chance meeting with Janice. She wanted to run to Josh and tell him about it, but knowing that he was away with Gina dampened her enthusiasm. The days when she could share things with him were over for good, she knew. What had been the beginning of another chance for happiness was now lost forever. Those dreams might as well be buried with the fragile spring flowers that had tentatively sent the first shoots through the cold earth outside. Sighing, she set her empty soup bowl on the coffee table and picked up the phone. Her fingers automatically punched in Marcy's number.

"Hello?"

"Hi, Marcy. It's me."

"Oh, hi, Elena. It's good to hear your voice."

"Yours too. How's work?"

Her friend groaned. "It'll never be the same. Ever."

"Well, leaving was something that I had to do. I really messed up, you know. I've messed up everything."

"Don't say that, kiddo. I'm sure no one else—"

"Oh, Marcy. For the past two years of my life I've been a washout. I've made all the wrong decisions, I've gotten involved in a relationship I've taught my class never to get into, and I've ignored your advice. Everything I've done is stupid. I've been too blind to recognize the kind of love that comes along just once in a lifetime. And I closed that door forever. All by myself."

"Well, I don't know what to say. I'm praying that the Lord will still work things out for you. It's not impossible, you know."

Elena smiled. "Ever the loyal friend. I don't deserve you anymore. But I did want you to know that I've finally come to my senses."

"What do you mean?"

"Well, do you remember that weekend I ran off to the Poconos a while back?"

"Yes . . . ."

"It's the strangest coincidence, or providence, or whatever. But there was a Bible school chorale visiting the church I attended that Sunday. I picked up one of their catalogs on the table before I left. I never really intended to open it, but now I can almost recite the entire thing by heart."

"So?"

"So I think I may yet be able to salvage some good out of all this chaos. Beauty for ashes, like the Bible says."

"Oh, Lane, I hope you're not saying what I think you are. Please tell me you won't go away again."

"It's only Virginia. It's not the end of the world."

"But—you don't have anyone in Virginia."

Elena shrugged. "I don't have anyone *here,* Marce; no family, no ties, no reason to stay. I've been all wrapped up in my own little world and my own sorrow and pain long enough. Isn't it time I start thinking about someone else for a while? Find something to do with the rest of my life? Something that counts?"

"But your house," Marcy blurted.

"I'm not worried about my house. Look at it this way. You and Trent might like a place in the country when you get married, right? If not, I should be able to sell it or rent it out."

"You're really serious, aren't you?"

"Well, I haven't made any concrete decisions yet. But there's a career planning weekend coming up in a few weeks at the school. I've sent away for the details already. If there's any kind of course still open for the summer session, I'll probably sign up."

The phone lines were quiet, neither spoke for a moment. Then Marcy sighed. "Well, I can't say this doesn't leave me with a really heavy feeling in my heart, but I'm not about to try to hold you back from something you feel is right, either."

"Thanks. I'd really like you to pray about it with me. Somehow I have to get my life back on track."

"Sure, kiddo. I'll pray with you."

"Well, I'll let you go, then. Thanks, Marce, for being there." Not hearing a response, she spoke again. "You are still there, aren't you?"

Marcy sniffed. "Yes. I just have to go cry for a while."

"I love you, Marcy. Bye."

"Bye."

Replacing the receiver, Elena decided to check out the window once more. In the glow from the streetlights, she could see that several inches of snow had already accumulated. She drew a hot bath and soaked until the water cooled. Then she went through her entire closet and scrutinized her wardrobe, mentally noting which outfits would be suitable for Bible school. There'd be time enough later, after she was busy preparing for a new life, to think about people left behind in Pennsylvania.

26

Sunlight streaking through the miniblinds was warm on her face the next morning as Elena stretched languidly in bed and yawned. *I must have slept forever,* she thought, glancing at the clock on the night stand. *I've never felt so rested.* The world outside was unusually still after the forceful sounds of the night before. Stepping out of bed and into her warm slippers, Elena pulled on a robe and went to the bathroom to shower and dress.

Starting a pot of coffee afterward, she opened the kitchen curtains and gasped. More than two feet of snow had fallen during the storm, she calculated, judging from the few inches of stump still visible from the old apple tree.

Against the startlingly clear blue sky, the crisp white snow was incredibly beautiful. The wind had whipped high drifts against trees and buildings. Branches and utility wires were coated, and small birds flitted playfully among them, bumping off tiny clumps of white with each movement. The German shepherd next door was licking an icicle that had formed from the drain spout on her neighbor's garage.

Thank you, Heavenly Father, she prayed, *for all of this beauty, for keeping me safe through the storm and the wind. Thank you for showing me that I have the capacity to love again . . . even though I blew it,* she added sadly. *Oh well, I know that I've lived through disappointment and loss before. You'll take me through this time, too. At least I'll have the dreams for a while.*

So engrossed was she in her thoughts and her prayers that she barely noticed an odd scraping sound from outside. But three taps on the door magnified her senses, and she flew through the living room to answer it.

A blond giant stood there with a lopsided grin.

"Josh!"

"Gonna hang me without a trial? Or do I get to say a few words in my defense?"

Elena's heart pounded within her breast, and she found it hard to breathe. She swallowed.

"I brought along a witness," he said as he motioned with one arm in the direction of her yard.

Elena gazed out over the freshly shoveled walk. She couldn't believe the size of the snowman standing there dressed in Josh's hat and scarf. "Oh, Josh, will you be serious?" she said with a smile. She stepped aside to let him enter.

He was covered with snow, and with every move he made, bits of white fell onto the carpet and quickly melted in the warmth of the room. "Couldn't resist bringing along a few snow angels too," he added sheepishly.

Shaking her head helplessly in disbelief, Elena was afraid that she'd cry if she tried to speak. She had no control of her emotions, so she said nothing.

"Yes, I'll be serious . . . if that's breakfast I smell."

His smile was so disarming that she could have melted as easily as the new snow. The sight of him had caught her off guard, and she was as nervous as a teenager, wondering why he'd come. *Should she brace herself for the big goodbye?* she wondered. She watched a droplet of water fall from the damp strands of his blond hair onto his shoulder.

"Am I invited, Laney? I thought maybe we could talk." At her answering smile and nod, he removed his wet jacket and set his boots by the door.

"I . . . um . . ."

"Don't usually eat breakfast," he finished, "I know. Well, coffee will do just fine."

"Well, I have lots of eggs. You deserve something to eat, after all that . . . hard work you did outside. Come have coffee while I whip something up."

Josh followed her into the kitchen and sat at the table. Elena poured fresh coffee into a mug and brought it to him, then she busied herself preparing breakfast. As she spooned pancake batter onto the griddle and turned sausages, she heard Josh shift in his chair, and she watched him out of the corner of her eye.

He changed positions again and ran his fingers through his hair. He seemed to be studying her. His stare added to her discomfort, and she almost dropped an egg she tapped against the edge of the pan. Conscious of a rosy flush on her cheeks, she caught her bottom lip between her teeth.

For a few eternal moments, neither spoke.

"You look . . . different," he said.

"Oh?"

"Yes. I can't figure out what it is, but there's definitely something about you that's changed."

Elena glanced at him questioningly, then returned her attention to the stove as she divided the food onto two plates.

"I think I know what it is. In fact, I'm sure of it. There's a new glow in your eyes. I could even say that you look positively radiant."

Elena smiled to herself while her back was still turned. Then she composed her expression and carried the plates to the table. As she took her seat, they reached automatically to join hands for the prayer. Elena felt waves of warmth course upward from her fingertips in the strength of Josh's big square hand on hers.

She was relieved that he prayed; she still didn't trust her own voice. She wondered if it was her imagination or if he had indeed held her hand for several extra seconds before releasing his grip.

"This looks wonderful," he said with a grin. "I'm glad you've decided to have some too."

Elena smiled, but didn't quite look at him as he ate. "It smelled good," she said simply.

After a silent moment, Josh cleared his throat. "That was some storm, last night, wasn't it?"

"Mmmm. I heard one of the shutters banging in the wind. Must've come loose."

"I'll take a look at it."

Elena glanced up and met his gaze, then toyed with her food. "So when did you get back?"

"Last night, actually. We drove up the street right behind the snowplow. Mom was glad to get home."

"She went with you?"

"Yes, she did." He took a sip of coffee, then chuckled.

Elena raised an eyebrow in question and cocked her head to one side.

"I had this big speech prepared, you know? Planned just what I was going to say to you . . . but I can't remember a word of it." Spearing the last chunk of his stack of pancakes, he mopped syrup from the plate with it and ate it. Chewing slowly, he watched Elena make tiny pleats in the napkin beside her untouched plate.

"Now, why do you suppose that is? We always used to be able to say whatever we wanted to each other."

A nervous half-smile played on her lips as Elena shook her head and shrugged, avoiding his gaze. She rose and picked up her plate, but Josh's hand covered hers and guided it back down to the table as he stood up.

"Let's worry about these later. It's time we had a talk. A real one, like we used to. No secrets." Still holding her hand, he led her into the living room, where they sat in their usual spots, on the ends of the sofa, facing each other. "There's something I have to tell you," he said.

Elena's heart pounded as she took a shaky breath and expelled it. *This is it,* she thought. *The end of everything.* But she forced a smile.

"And I have to ask you a few things, too . . . if you don't mind."

"What would you like to know?"

"Well, about you and Derek Webster . . ." he began. "I have to know—"

Elena laughed. "There's no such thing as Derek and me. There never was, really. Never could be. He was just a friend . . . and now he might not even be that."

Josh looked at her questioningly.

"I've quit my job." She tried to be serious, but a stubborn smile insisted on taking over. "Any day now, I'll be destitute, hungry. . . ."

Eyeing her speculatively, Josh opened his mouth to speak.

"Hey, not so fast," Elena interjected in a sudden rush of courage. "I have a few questions myself."

"Fire away."

"About you and Gina DiAngelo . . ." *I might as well get it over with,* she thought.

"Isn't she a beaut?"

"Oh, Josh." There was a note of sadness in her voice.

"Sorry. I was trying to be—" He shrugged. "She's gone," he said simply.

"I don't understand."

"She only came over here to do some modeling for an international fashion magazine. It's what she's always wanted. She and her aunt just came to America for a visit and to see some of the country I'd talked so much about."

Elena wondered how he could discuss it all so calmly. "But you . . . loved her, Josh. Won't she be coming back?"

"Correction, Lane. I *thought* I loved her. Me and a thousand other guys. To tell you the truth, she reminded me of—" Rolling his eyes upward, he drew a deep breath and expelled it. "I was never in love with Gina."

"Now I really don't understand," Elena said with a frown. "You said that you were in love once."

He grinned. "I remember. I did say that. And I still love that girl, too. Always will."

"Oh." Elena's heart sank to her toes; she almost expected it to be visible as she looked down at her feet. *It's worse than I thought, then,* Elena's mind convinced her. *Now I'm dealing with an unknown.* She didn't want to hear any more. The plans for Virginia at once became a certainty, and she was determined to start packing as soon as Josh left. Rising swiftly, she turned to make a quick exit.

Josh got up, too, and caught her wrist so smoothly that she spun around, right into his arms.

Breathless from the attempted escape—or was it from being held so tightly? she wasn't sure—Elena curved her arms around Josh and tilted her head back to look at him. She felt as though she were drowning in the smoldering gray depths of his eyes.

His heartbeat raced steadily against her own as his head shook back and forth. "Laney, Laney, Laney. You've always been pretty bright. Do I have to spell it out for you? I'm looking right at the only woman I have ever loved."

Elena's lips parted in wonder as the full realization of her wildest dreams became reality.

"I love you. That's why I went away right after your wedding. I couldn't stand the thought of seeing you with Greg when I wanted you for myself. I had to get as far away from here as possible. Permanently. I was never going to come back."

Elena stared at him wordlessly, trying to believe that her ears were hearing what her heart so desperately wanted.

"I've waited a lifetime to hold you like this. So many times I came close to throwing caution to the wind and telling you how much I loved you, wanted you. But you had to be free from your past. Do you understand now? I hope you will forgive me for ͜ing Gina to make you jealous. It was stupid and, worse yet, insensitive. I know that now."

Still mildly stunned, Elena's eyes misted over as she finally found her voice. "I—I thought you only felt a brotherly kind of love for me. I never—"

Josh chuckled and silenced her words with a kiss of gentle passion.

She trembled in his arms. "I always wondered what that would be like," she whispered, shyly meeting his gaze.

"Oh? And what was it like?"

She smiled. "Well, not very . . . brotherly. But what can a girl tell from one kiss, anyway?"

Josh groaned softly. With a hand on either side of her face, he kissed each eyelid, then the tip of her nose. Then he covered her mouth with his, in a kiss that told her all she needed to know. "Elena." It was the first time she had ever heard him say her whole name, and the timbre of his voice made it sound like music. "Dare I even hope that you have any feelings for me?" He searched her face.

"Oh, Josh." Looking steadily at him, Elena smiled. "I have always loved you. My whole life. I don't know why it took so long for that to sink in. But by the time it did, I thought it was too late. I thought that you were lost to me forever."

"Never," he whispered, drawing her close again. "I'll never let you go again."

For a few moments they stood as they were, entwined in each other's arms, their hearts beating almost in unison. Then Josh glanced outside. "Laney, put on your boots. My snowman is lonely."

"What? You can't be serious."

"Now, that's where you're wrong," he said, grinning. "Come on. Hurry."

Moments later, they stepped outside into the blazing sunshine and sparkling day. "I ask you . . . is there anything so fickle as April snow?" said Josh, raising an arm in a gesture of helplessness. "Hurry, Lane. My snowman is melting."

Laughing like kids, they soon had a snowmaiden in Elena's hat and scarf, standing next to the shrinking snowman.

Elena spread her arms wide and twirled around in joy. "Oh, Josh, it's spring. I feel it."

"My grandmother always called the first warm days after winter the 'first spring,' " Josh said. "After that, she said, winter throws one last tantrum. Then the 'second spring' comes to stay. It's the second spring that really counts, you know," he said softly.

"Yes," she said. "It's the one that lasts and brings new life, new love."

"Ah. Then, would you do me the very great honor of becoming my wife? Will you marry me, Lane?"

"Oh, yes. A thousand times yes." Elena looked at him, her heart brimming with happiness as his lips claimed hers. And neither of them even saw the robin that had perched on the snowman's hat, until he began to sing.

Elena gazed out the church window at the magnificent day. Pennsylvania had never known one so perfect, she was sure. Her heart beat a little faster as the door opened to admit Marcy.

"Hi, kid. Beautiful day for a wedding, isn't it?"

Elena smiled. "I'm glad you came early. I can't seem to get my hair the way I want it." She sat down at the dressing table in the bride's room and stroked a touch of blush over each cheekbone.

"Let's see what I can do with it. What did you have in mind?" Marcy stood behind her and picked up the comb.

"Oh, I wanted to wear it up, but soft and casual. Do you know what I mean?"

Marcy nodded. "I'll do my best." With skillful fingers, she twirled and tucked, pinned and fluffed, until moments later Elena's hair was a mass of soft flowing curls entwined with pink ribbons, tiny roses, and baby's breath.

"You're really wasting your time at Websters, you know," Elena said, teasing. "You should have had your own beauty shop all this time."

Marcy laughed. "It's all that practice we had doing this for each other as kids, remember? I often think of the hours and hours we spent doing makeovers for fun."

"Mmm. We sure had a happy childhood."

"Well, I'm glad you'll finally have some happiness now, after all these years. That's as close as I ever hope to come to seeing you walk out of my life. You were always meant to be with Josh, you know."

Elena sighed. "God has given us a second chance, and I'll be eternally grateful for that. Two weeks ago I was certain that I'd lost Josh forever, but the Lord has given him back to me."

"There were a few other people who were praying about it too, kid," Marcy said with a smile.

"I know." Elena turned and hugged her friend. "Thanks."

"Where's your dress?" Marcy asked, brushing a sudden tear away.

"Over behind the screen."

Marcy crossed the room and reached behind the folded dressing screen for the hanger. "Ohh," she said softly. "It's lovely. You could have worn the peach lace, though. I would have understood."

"That's one thing I like about you, Marce. You're sweet. But that one is for another very special wedding. And this one caught my eye at Hampton's that day too. Anyway," she added, a slightly wicked sparkle in her eye, "the peach lace had too many buttons."

Marcy giggled. "I see." She held the dress for Elena to step into, then she zipped it up the back. "Well, he shouldn't complain about this one."

Elena gazed down at the shimmering ivory textured silk and ran her fingers lightly over the bodice with its wide lace trim. "Does it look okay?"

"Are you kidding? You look gorgeous."

The door opened quietly, and Stella Montgomery entered the room.

"Hi, Mother," Elena said with a smile, crossing the room to hug her.

"Elena, dear," she said. "I have prayed for this day for so many years. And now, think of it. You will be my real daughter at last."

Elena's eyes misted over, and she blinked a few times. "Now, let's not get too sentimental you two or you'll have me in tears. This is going to be a happy day for all of us. Let me get your corsage, Mother." Elena pinned it on and stepped back to make sure that it was straight.

"And I have something for you, too, my dear." Stella held out a white handkerchief edged with soft lace. "I carried this when I married my own dear Cameron, and I had a whole lifetime of happiness. I'd like you to have it."

"Oh, thank you," Elena breathed. "It's lovely."

"And this is from Josh." Stella handed her a velvet jewelry case, which Elena opened to find a strand of perfect pearls. "Something new," Stella said.

Speechless, Elena removed the necklace almost reverently and hugged it to her breast. Then, handing it to Marcy, she turned so that her friend could fasten the delicate clasp adorned with diamonds.

"How beautiful," gasped Marcy. "They're a perfect match for my earrings you asked to borrow."

"And I'm wearing the ever-popular blue garter already," Elena added. "So I guess my tiny little wedding will be steeped in tradition."

"Well, I for one couldn't be any happier, dear. I pray that the Lord will give you and Josh every happiness."

"Thank you, Mother," Elena said, hugging her.

The first strains of music wafted softly from the sanctuary, and Stella turned. "I do believe I hear my cue," she said with a smile. She kissed Elena and left.

"Well, pretty soon you'll have a whole new life," Marcy remarked.

"I'm almost afraid to believe it," whispered Elena.

There was a soft tapping on the door, and Josh peeked in. "I've come to escort my bride," he said, drinking in the vision that met his eyes.

Marcy smiled. Picking up her bouquet of pink roses, she handed a second one of pink orchids and white roses to Elena, then ascended the stairs to the sanctuary.

Elena placed her hand on Josh's arm, and together they mounted the steps. As they stood on the threshold of the aisle, Elena looked at her beloved Josh and saw the promise written in his eyes. The promise that the winter of her life was over, that love, too, had a second spring.

Dear Reader:

Please let us know how you feel about Barbour Books' Christian Fiction.

1. What most influenced you to purchase **Romance Reader** #1, #2, #3, #4, #5, #6, #7, #8, #9, 10, #11, #12?

   _____ Author   _____ Recommendations

   _____ Subject matter   _____ Price

   _____ Cover / titles

2. Would you buy other books in the **Romance Series** by this author?

   _____ Yes   _____ No

3. Where did you purchase this book?

   _____ Christian book store   _____ Other

   _____ General book store   _____ Mail order

4. What is your overall rating of this **Romance Reader**?

   _____ Excellent _____ Very good _____ Good _____ Fair _____ Poor

5. How many hours a week do you spend reading books? _____ hrs.

6. Are you a member of a church? _____ Yes _____ No

   If yes, what denomination?_____

7. Please check age

   _____ Under 18   _____ 25-34   _____ 45-54

   _____ 18-24   _____ 35-44   _____ 55 and over

Mail to: **Fiction Editor**
Barbour Books
P.O. Box 719
Uhrichsville, OH 44683

NAME _____

ADDRESS _____

CITY _____ STATE _____ ZIP _____

Thank you for helping us provide the best in Christian fiction!

THE KISS GOODBYE

by

Sally Laity

Flip over for another great novel!
SECOND SPRING

ISBN 1-55748-258-6

9 781557 482587

90000>

A Barbour Book

All Scripture references were taken from the Authorized King James Version.

Published by Barbour & Company, Inc.
P.O. Box 719
Uhrichsville, Ohio 44683

Printed in the United States of America
ISBN   1-55748-258-6
Typeset by Typetronix, Inc., Cape Coral, FL 33904

92   93   94   95   96   5   4   3   2   1

To Wendy . . . my other daughter, my other friend
and to Julie
with love

The author would like to express her sincere appreciation to Joan Diana, head librarian, Pennsylvania State University, Wilkes-Barre Campus, for the invaluable research material she located and forwarded concerning President Rutherford B. Hayes and his presence at the centennial anniversary of the Wyoming Valley Massacre and for historical information on the states of Pennsylvania and Wyoming.

The Kiss Goodbye

How did it happen

    that we kissed goodbye?

  We knew it was forbidden. . . .

And yet, the look on your face,

  The thought that soon you'd be gone,

    Made me forget all the rules.

Little did I know a kiss would only

    make it worse,

  That it would make me realize

    How much I loved you.

We can never go back and undo that moment. . . .

  We must go on as if nothing ever happened.

    But inside, in the treasure house

      of my mind,

    I will always feel the touch of your lips

      And know you loved me too.

1

Wyoming, Pennsylvania, July 3, 1878

"Ah, now. Ye've gone an' taken yerself a wife, Rhon Banister!" said the woman as she answered the door.

Holly Grant giggled, amazed that anyone would consider eighteen-year-old Rhon suitable husband material. With a quick glance over her shoulder at him, she stepped inside the kitchen of Alma Preston's rambling, two-story house.

Managing to contain their own laughter, Rhon and his father, Matthew Banister, followed Holly. "No, Alma," Uncle Matthew assured their hostess. "This is my niece, Holly Grant."

"Oh." Mrs. Preston looked somewhat deflated as she peered from one to the other.

"She's also my best friend in the world," said Rhon. A smattering of light freckles sprinkled by the summer sun across his face were displaced by his grin as he pulled Holly close.

Holly's lips parted in surprise. She flicked a gaze upward, meeting the twinkle in his green eyes. The thought struck her that somewhere along the line her auburn-haired cousin had gotten rather tall without her ever having noticed. She felt him release her abruptly.

Alma Preston tilted her gray head, and a slight flush spread over her already rosy cheeks, making her pink nose look like an almost-ripe cherry. "I thought fer sure . . . well, he's so growed up, an' all."

Matthew chuckled. He reached for Mrs. Preston's shoulder and gave a squeeze. "Holly's Will and Sarah's girl."

She looked taken aback. Taking one of Holly's hands, Mrs. Preston wrapped it in her plump, cushiony ones. "Oh, honey, please forgive an old lady's foolishness. 'Twas a mighty sorry day when yer mama an' daddy was lost in that flood. Terrible thing it was, God rest their souls."

Holly managed a faint smile.

1

The corners of the woman's hazel eyes crinkled with concern as she continued to stare. "Well, how've ye been gettin' by, sweetheart? You an' yer baby sister, I mean."

"Fine, thank you," Holly answered. "Beth will be fifteen soon. We live with Aunt Priscilla and Uncle Ethan, now."

"Oh." Mrs. Preston tipped her head to one side. "Ye must be close to Matt and Rhon, then."

Holly nodded, and her forearm brushed against Rhon's. Unconsciously she moved half a step away.

"Ah. Well, thank the Almighty ye're gettin' by, I always say. We often ask the good Lord to look after ye." She leaned toward the door and opened it a crack, peeking out. "Hannah didn't come fer the celebration, then?"

Matthew inclined his head. "She planned to. Looked forward to it for weeks. But she caught a bit of a cold and decided to keep out of the night air."

"She sent her regrets," Rhon added with a shrug. "At least it left room for Holly." He slid a glance at his cousin.

"I see." Mrs. Preston shifted from one foot to the other and curled the edge of her apron absently with her fingers. "Well, makes no never mind to me . . . 'cept with the fuss over President Hayes's visit, the extra rooms is all promised. There's but one left."

"Oh. Well," Matthew's brows knitted in thought, "I suppose we could stay someplace else."

Alma Preston shook her head, the little gray bun at the nape of her neck visible on every other turn. "Fiddle. With tomorrow's goin's on fer the centennial, there's narry a bed to be had in the valley. We'll jest make do, I always say." For a few silent seconds her ample bosom rose and fell with her breathing. Then her demeanor brightened. "Say, a drop of iced tea might go down smooth after such a warm day." Gesturing for the three to take seats at the big kitchen table, she removed some tall glasses from the pine cupboard and filled them from a jug on the sideboard. After setting one before each of them, she drew out a chair for herself.

The cool liquid tasted refreshing, and Holly sipped it slowly, avoiding Rhon's eyes across the table. She wondered at the strange new feelings of discomfort that tickled her consciousness. Maybe wheedling permission from Aunt Priscilla to come to the centennial hadn't been such a good idea after all, she thought.

Matthew gulped some of his drink. "Guess Rhon and I could sleep out in the wagon, after we unload the shingles."

Holly put her hand on his arm. "It's late, Uncle Matt. You and Rhon take the bedroom. I'm sure I'd be fine on the couch—if that's all right with Mrs. Preston." Questioningly, she turned to her hostess.

The plump woman pursed her lips and grimaced. "Well, now, any other time 'twould be. But me Charlie's needin' it, with his room taken up. He's out in the barn, ye know. He'll be glad to help with the unloadin'. Reese would'a been here, too, but he's still workin' on the platform for tomorrow's speech."

Matthew drained his glass and set it down.

"Well," Mrs. Preston continued, "there's but one solution. Ye'll all three use the bedroom. Menfolk in the bed, an' little Holly on the floor. The matter's settled." With a final nod, she finished her drink.

Holly swallowed quickly and almost choked, her eyes watering from the struggle. She blinked against her blurring vision.

Rhon gave a pat to her hand as he tipped his head with concern. "You all right?"

Nodding, Holly felt a blush warm her cheeks. She had no idea why she suddenly felt embarrassed at the thought of sharing close quarters with him. After all, they'd spent a lifetime of summers swimming together, confiding in one another, and going for walks. He'd even taught her to shoot a rifle and throw a knife. Yet now, when his eyes met hers, she had to look away.

Rhon watched the play of emotions on his slender cousin's face and noticed the pink glow that had settled softly upon her fine features. Odd that she looked everywhere in the room but at him, he thought. They'd always been able to express thoughts and feelings with the merest glance. Why couldn't he read her now? He smiled to himself. Funny how Mrs. Preston had figured they were married.

Holly'd make someone a fine wife, one of these days. One of these days? he thought with a jolt. She was sixteen already. Some of her friends from school were married and starting families of their own. He cocked his head and studied her, noting her alluring young curves, her graceful posture. Now that he thought about it, she was more than pleasing to the eye. Flickering light from the kerosene lamps above danced over her brown-black hair in

shimmering copper and violet. Her wide, chestnut-colored eyes were hidden by lashes long and dark, closing off her thoughts from him. He drew a deep, silent breath as Alma Preston's voice drifted across his consciousness.

"With Charlie helpin', ye'll be finished in no time." Gathering the empty glasses, she ambled over to the sink. "I'll jest rustle up some quilts, an' Holly can help fix an extra bed on the floor whilst ye fetch yer things. She can change in my room. Once the two of ye turn in, she can go to bed. How's that?" Her hazel eyes looked hopeful.

"Fine, Alma." Matthew nudged Rhon with an elbow. "Let's go empty the buckboard, then, and get the bags." He stood, giving the chair a backward push with his legs. His limp barely perceptible, he crossed the room and preceded his son outside.

Holly let out a small sigh of relief as Rhon closed the door behind them. She hadn't realized that she'd been holding her breath.

Dawdling as long as possible in Mrs. Preston's room, Holly meticulously folded her clothes, then shook them out and started all over. She tied the satin ribbon at the front of her nightgown and examined the ends to be sure they were even. Then she pulled it loose and redid it. What was the matter with her? Why was she wishing she hadn't even come? Finally resigned to facing the inevitable, she lifted her chin, picked up her things, and tiptoed across the hall to the closed bedroom door.

No sound came from the other side, so she quietly opened the door and slipped in, not daring even to look around. Setting down her clothes, she extinguished the dim kerosene lamp and crawled between the sheets on her pallet.

Rhon smiled when the light went out. He'd watched Holly from beneath lowered lids as she'd come in wearing a flowing white nightdress, her waist-length hair now in a loose braid over her shoulder. He'd seen her in the simple shift a hundred times, when he'd thrown pebbles at her attic-bedroom window and she'd leaned out to hear the latest secret. But he'd never noticed the delicate pastel flowers embroidered on the front, the little blue bow at her throat, her graceful neck. He swallowed and turned over.

Holly lay on the makeshift mattress beside the big double four-

poster bed for a long time, staring into the darkness. She wished that she'd stayed home and done the baking like Aunt Priscilla had wanted. Something precious had been taken from her within the last few hours—the easy camaraderie that she'd known with Rhon all her life. She hoped that it wasn't gone forever. His quick hug in the kitchen, although quite innocent, had shaken her. And what she was feeling now was altogether unthinkable. After all, they *were* cousins. And besides, that prissy Jenny Spencer had designs on him.

The sound of Uncle Matt's snoring erupted from the far side of the bed.

Holly's heartbeat tripped over itself at the realization that very near, and only slightly above her, lay a most treasured friend . . . whose soft green eyes held a perpetual twinkle and whose mouth had corners that always turned up just before he spoke.

She squeezed her eyes shut and prayed fervently for sleep. Tomorrow things would be back to the way they were before. They just had to be.

Rhon watched the shadows dissipate over the lithe form of his sleeping cousin as the early morning sun, peeking over the distant hills, gradually filled the room with light. His gaze traced the sable braid draping her smooth arm, and he exhaled slowly. He needed to take a walk in the stillness and talk a few things out with the Lord. He reached for his jeans, pulled them on quietly, and left the room without a sound, carrying his shirt and boots with him.

Several hours later, after one of Mrs. Preston's sumptuous breakfasts, Rhon elbowed a path for Holly and his father through the vast throng that had congregated near the new monument commemorating the 100-year anniversary of the infamous Wyoming Valley Massacre. Blinding dust, stirred up by thousands of feet, filled his nostrils and made his eyes itch. It dulled some of the festive flags and banners that decorated nearby trees, homes, and businesses. Rhon led the way along Wyoming Avenue to a spot within hearing distance of the platform where President Hayes was scheduled to speak. There, in the broiling sun, the tightly packed crowd swayed in the heat and the pressure, waiting for the ceremony to begin.

Feeling confined, Rhon stretched and shifted to a more com-

fortable stance. He peered over Holly's dark head at the people everywhere. A pair of flirty young ladies off to the left lifted their chins and smiled coyly; his mouth twitched. They weren't nearly as enchanting as Holly, he thought. He looked away, wondering when he'd begun comparing other girls to her.

He checked to the right. Some young bucks were giving Holly the eye, and he glared at them. Returning his attention to his cousin, he cast a lingering gaze over her, noticing the flush of excitement on her expressive face. She had drawn the sides of her hair up to her crown and tied it with a light blue ribbon. The bright sunshine accented the glossy shine of her thick tresses and touched the tips of her lashes with gold. Rhon watched her rise up on tiptoe to scan the stage. He was glad she'd come. Easing behind her, he shielded her from the shifting, jostling crowd as it strained forward.

Matthew smiled at Holly, and the neat, graying mustache above his mouth widened. "Your pa and I saw him once, you know. Mr. Hayes."

"Really?"

"Yep. In the war. The man fought like a real hero, almost reckless, they say. Got himself wounded at Shenandoah." Removing his wide-brimmed tan hat, he ran his fingers through his pepper-and-salt hair, then replaced it, looking toward the platform.

Holly stared at her uncle's profile for a moment, noticing the similarities shared by father and son. They had the same straight nose and strong out-thrust of chin. And, both had clear, compelling eyes, although unlike the tranquil green of his son's, Matthew's were bluish gray. The two had muscular builds from years of hard work, but Rhon stood a head taller than his father.

Holly's gaze drifted as she tried to find familiar faces among those nearby, but she saw not a one. She studied the elaborate gowns worn by the ladies, feeling somewhat faded by comparison in her blue linen Sunday dress. Although it was the best she had, it paled next to the elegance all around her. Hearing new sounds toward the front, Holly turned.

A group of officials mounted the stage and took their seats on a row of chairs. A dignified, richly dressed man stepped forward.

"Who's that?" Holly whispered.

"Colonel Charles Dorrance, I believe," Matthew answered. "Paper

says he's chairman of the celebration's executive committee."

"Ladies and gentlemen," Colonel Dorrance said with a wide smile, "we welcome you to our centennial celebration. I know many of you have traveled great distances to hear our guest of honor, so without further delay, it is my distinct honor to present to you the President of the United States," he motioned with one arm to his right, "Mr. Rutherford B. Hayes." Bowing his head slightly amid profound applause, he returned to his seat.

A second gentleman rose and stepped to the podium.

Holly looked at the long-faced leader with his deep-set blue eyes, large nose, broad, smooth forehead, and full beard. She tried to picture how he might have appeared to her father by thinking as a foot soldier might in viewing an officer. He certainly had a commanding way about him, yet he stood and quieted the crowd in a manner that seemed quite jovial.

The President smiled. "Ladies and fellow citizens," he began. "It will be impossible for me to make myself heard by any considerable part of this great assemblage. I do not think, however, that it is of any great importance, as I have not been set down for any formal speech on the program." He smiled again, scanning the audience. "But the Battle of Wyoming 100 years ago today was of national importance, and being a citizen of our great republic, I claim some of the glory and endure some of the sorrow that attaches to any of its citizens."

Stories Holly had been told about the Wyoming Massacre filtered through her mind, of the way so many settlers had been tortured. She swallowed and forced herself to concentrate on the here and now.

The President removed a handkerchief from his breast pocket. "But this grand ingathering of the people here today is a peculiar one in many respects," he said, blotting his forehead and returning the cloth to his pocket. "It is not the celebration of great military achievements or wonderful statesmanship. It is a pioneer demonstration in honor of the men and women who settled this valley, reclaimed the wilderness, and fitted it up for the habitation of a civilized people." He paused. "Almost every part of these United States has its similar celebrations in honor of the pioneers, and most of them have passed through the same bloody experience in their contests with the wily savages of the forest."

Holly blew stray hairs away from her eyes. What must it have

been like to have been alive during that night 100 years earlier? She tried to imagine a meager group of untrained settlers huddled inside the fort, while outside the walls more than 500 Indians led by a Seneca chief, and 300 Tories under the command of British Major John Butler attacked mercilessly. Even after Colonel Nathan Denison had signed the terms of surrender, the Indians had not ceased their murdering rampage, leaving ruin and desolation throughout the valley. Thinking of the mutilated mothers and children, Holly shuddered, barely aware that the tears brimming in her eyes had spilled over.

Rhon felt his cousin tremble in front of him and put comforting hands on her shoulders. He thought of the valiant souls who had died fighting unsuccessfully to protect their families. He thought of how 160 bodies, maimed and dismembered, lay unburied for three months, until people finally arrived and gathered the remains, burying them in a mass grave. How many women had there been, he wondered, who were as young and lovely as . . . ? A whoosh of breath escaped in a silent whistle. Tightening his hold a fraction, he drew Holly back.

She relaxed against him.

Matthew reined the team of sturdy horses to a stop in front of his white farmhouse in Huntsville and wearily climbed down, favoring his lame leg. His old battle wound always ached after hours on the hard wagon seat. He bent and scratched behind the floppy ears of Rhon's big black dog, Shadow, who had bounded down the lane from the front step to meet them. "Go ahead and drive Holly on home, son," he said, straightening. "It's too late for her to have to walk."

"Sure, Pa."

Holly stood up in the wagon bed where she'd been dozing and moved to the seat beside her cousin. "Thanks for taking me, Uncle Matt. It was a wonderful day."

He smiled. "You'll have lots to tell Beth tomorrow. And your young'uns, someday."

Rhon clucked his tongue and gently snapped the reins. The wagon lurched into motion again in a wide turn back onto the narrow lane that led from the house to the road. Shadow ambled along beside as the wheels crunched over the gravel.

Matthew waved after them. Then, turning, he limped quietly

into the house and up to the second-floor bedroom.

Hannah rustled the sheets on the big bed and yawned as he entered. "Ya made it back, I see," she said, squinting without her spectacles in the dim lamplight, her voice still a bit hoarse from her cold.

"Yep. Quite a day. Never saw such a crowd in my life." Unbuttoning his shirt, he pulled it out of his waistband and slipped it off, then removed his trousers. He chuckled. "Alma thought Holly and Rhon were married. Can you believe that? Almost wasn't room for us to stay the night. Ended up all in the same room."

"What?" Hannah sat up, her tired blue eyes wide in her puffy face. "That's hardly fittin'. Not proper a'tall." She flicked a thin, brown night braid over her shoulder.

Matt turned. "Oh, it was proper enough, you can be sure of that. We just laughed it off." He felt her eyes boring a hole clear into his back as he sat on the bed and raised the coverlet, then swung his legs up. "Funny, though. They acted awful quiet after."

"Well, I don't see no humor in that tomfoolery a'tall. Sleepin' two growed cousins in the same room. I been thinkin' fer some time they been spendin' too much time together."

"Aw, Hannah. Close as those two are, there's not much chance of separating them at this late date. Even if they took a notion to get married, it's not against the state law, you know." He sighed. "And what harm could that do, anyway, 'cept for a little gossip?"

"A little gossip, Matthew Banister," Hannah gasped. "I wouldn't be able to show my face in church again." With a huff, she slumped against her pillow and pulled the cover up to her chin. "I s'pose ya think it's okay if yer son sows some of them wild oats, too." She blotted sudden tears with the edge of the sheet.

"Sorry." He sighed wearily. "I was just . . . ." Extinguishing the light, Matt lay down and closed his eyes.

After a long silence, Hannah said, "Here tell that purty little Jenny Spencer's got her eye on him. Oughta do what we can to push that along."

The night breeze wafted past the buckboard as the horses, with Shadow shuffling happily alongside, plodded toward the next farm. Making the left turn at the end of the lane, Rhon brushed

away a wisp of hair that feathered across his cheek on the wind. It smelled of honeysuckle. In fact, he thought, the whole night smells like honeysuckle. He watched Holly turn and smile, the moon casting a silver glow over her head and shoulders. For one brief second he wished that they weren't cousins.

"It was a glorious day." Her voice soared with the same joy that filled him.

"Mm." Drawing the horses, Nan and Bert, to a stop in front of Aunt Priscilla's ramshackle house, Rhon jumped down and held his arms out toward Holly. As he swung her easily to the ground, a noise carried from the side yard where a hulking shadow lurked behind the well. A low growl rumbled from deep within Shadow's chest as he tensed beside Rhon's leg. "Good old Uncle Ethan," Rhon muttered sarcastically, his mood turning grim. "As usual. Maybe I should walk you to the door."

"No," Holly said quietly. "I'll be all right. Aunt Pris would fix him good if he ever tried anything, I'm sure."

"Well," Rhon said, raising his voice to be certain it carried to the well, "I'm thirsty. Think I'll go have a drink of water." He flashed a smile at her and lowered his voice. "Night, cousin."

"Good night," she whispered, running softly up the worn path and into the house.

Holly unbuttoned her dress in the brightness of the moonlight that filtered in through the plain muslin curtains of the cramped attic room.

Fourteen-year-old Beth sat up on the low-post bed and lit a candle. The flickering shadows danced over her amber hair. "I thought you'd never get here. I've been waiting forever." She blinked her wide, brown eyes. "Aunt Pris was mad as a plucked hen all day."

Holly smothered a yawn with one hand. "Shh. Then let's not make it any worse by waking her up."

"Did you have a good time?"

"Sure did. An extra special one," Holly answered dreamily as she slid off her linen dress.

"Well, aren't you going to tell me about it?"

Holly's expression softened. Beth, being younger than Holly, always seemed to have to stay behind. Holly moistened her lips and tilted her head. Eyes wide, she leaned forward slightly and

THE KISS GOODBYE   11

rose on tiptoe to speak in her best storytelling voice, her words
soft and expressive. "It was a grand, sunny day." She gazed
dramatically toward the ceiling, then back at her sister who
watched in fascination.

Her petticoats swirled about her as she made a wide arc with
one arm. "Hundreds of people—almost everyone in the whole
world—gathered to see him, the President of the United States.
They came from everywhere and stood in the heat, and the dust,
for hours. Some of them waved flags. And the ones who didn't
have any didn't care because there were flags and banners all
over: in windows, on the trees and bridges, and even on the trains
and coal breakers. They knew that it was a special day. One that
would come only once in a lifetime."

Beth leaned forward, her elbows on her knees. Enrapt, her
lissome body tensed with expectation, and a smile spread over
her rose-petal lips.

"Someone had built a great stage, and we all waited there until
it was time for him to come. It seemed to take hours, almost
forever. And finally, he walked up the steps," she gestured with
her hand, "and took a seat. And we all stretched tall to see him."

Craning her neck unconsciously, Beth followed Holly's every
movement in silence.

"He gave a wonderful talk about how special, and how sad,
the day was, about the settlers at the fort who'd been massacred
there 100 years ago, about how we should honor their memory.
And then—"

Beth tilted her head.

"Came the *Indians*!" She jumped forward and poked her sister
playfully in the shoulder.

The girl's dark eyes nearly burst from her face as her lips parted
in surprise.

"They had paint on their faces, as if they were going on the
warpath again!"

"Wasn't it scary?"

Holly settled back down onto her bare feet. "No, not really,"
she said nonchalantly. "They just sat down on the floor of the
stage, and everyone looked at them."

"Oh, you!" Beth giggled and wrinkled her nose.

Holly grinned and ruffled the top of her sister's straight, long
hair before untying her own petticoat strings. "We didn't go to

the parade, though," she said in her normal tone of voice. "It takes too long to get home in the wagon." She kicked off her underthings and tugged on her nightgown. "The Wyoming ladies gave the President an elegant buck-horn cane with a gold head. And there were so many beautiful, fancy gowns all around me, in all the pretty colors of the rainbow. I couldn't stop looking at them."

"Wish I could've been there," Beth said wistfully.

"Me too. Thanks for doing my chores so that I could go, Bethy." She hugged her sister and blew out the candle. Then, remembering her cousin, she crossed to the window and parted the curtains with a finger, peering outside.

"What's the matter?" Beth asked.

"I'm just seeing if Uncle Ethan is still by the well. He was hiding there when we got home. Rhon pretended to be thirsty and went over for a drink while I came inside."

Beth sighed in the darkness. "No."

"I wish Aunt Pris would notice the way he's always lurking around, leering. He gives me the creeps."

2

The big white rooster crowed from its perch on the fence as the morning sunlight stretched over the treetops and spilled radiant warmth onto the rolling, wooded countryside of Huntsville. Holly crept silently downstairs, her Bible and journal in hand. After a quick trip to the necessary, she slipped away to her special place, a shaded glen tucked within the groves just beyond the house. Her bare feet tingled from the cool, silvery dew as she hurried toward the spot where the flow of the creek diverted in a half-moon curve and spread out languorously in shimmering shallows at the base of a wooded hill.

Brushing aside the large fronds of a lush fern, Holly sat with her back against the huge, flat-topped boulder that had been a fort, a pirate ship, and many other imaginary delights throughout her childhood. The last soft mist of morning was already vanishing. She inhaled the woodsy fragrance and sat in the solitude for a moment, then opened the worn book to the Forty-sixth Psalm. Her father had underlined several of the verses, and her eyes were drawn to them:

> God is our refuge and strength, a very present help in trouble. There is a river, the streams whereof shall make glad the city of God, the holy place of the tabernacles of the most High. God is in the midst of her . . .

Leaning her head back against the rock, Holly admired the beauty of the sparkling, bubbling creek cascading down the gentle, shaded rock terraces to her left. Its sweet music caressed her soul, and she sighed in the quietness. Were her mother and father sitting even now by the stream that made glad the city of God? Smiling sadly, she tried to imagine how lush, cool, and peaceful it must be there. Surely that would be her favorite place in all of Heaven.

A flower-scented breeze whispered through the leafy canopy

overhead, stirring stray hairs around her face. From the branch of an oak tree on the other side of the stream a fat robin sang its morning song, and a young gray squirrel scampered up the trunk. Holly opened her journal, noticing that the last entry had been made several weeks ago. She took her pencil from her pocket and began writing.

> Yesterday I went to Wyoming with Rhon and Uncle Matt. It was ever so exciting being at the centennial and seeing the President with my own eyes. Mrs. Preston thought Rhon and I were married. We all laughed. But I must admit he really has become quite handsome. And I've always loved being with him. Perhaps if we weren't cousins . . .

Holly caught her breath and blinked in surprise. She couldn't even think such things! She wouldn't. Rising, she tore the page out, crumpled it into a ball, and threw it into the water. Without waiting for the current to carry it away, she hurried back to the house. She smelled the aroma of coffee even before she reached the back door, which opened on the kitchen side of the large common room.

Aunt Priscilla looked up from the coal stove and stopped stirring the contents of a big iron pot.

"Morning, Auntie," Holly said brightly.

"You been out already, I see." Although her aunt's sharp, discordant voice had frightened Holly when she was younger, it now seemed familiar and unthreatening. Aunt Priscilla rested the knuckles of one hand on an ample hip and shook her braid-wrapped head. "Jest like yer daddy. He was an early bird, too, always traipsin' off first thing, with nary a thought to a day's work. When we was kids, Hannah an' me, we used to wonder if he'd ever git to what needed doin'. But he done his chores somehow."

Holly smiled. "It's a real pretty morning."

"Well, jest remember, there's more to mornin' than purty looks. There's work to be done. An' no time to waste, neither."

"Well, I'll take my books upstairs and wake Beth. We'll help with breakfast." She hurried to the attic bedroom.

Her sister lay sleeping, one hand flung above her golden head in peaceful bliss. Not a care showed on the childlike face with alabaster skin. Holly gently shook her.

Beth wrinkled her thin, little nose and yawned, then raised her lashes. "Hmm?"

"It's morning. Time to get up."

"Oh. I was having such a nice dream. Mama and Daddy were—" Rubbing her eyes, Beth sat up. "Sometimes I forget."

"I know," Holly said, brushing the younger girl's hair away from her sleepy pink face. "Me too. It's nice to see them again, though, even if it's only in our dreams." Crossing to the dressing table looking glass, Holly undid her night braid and brushed her thick, long hair, tying it back with her worn, sky blue ribbon.

"Do you think they ever think of us? Or wonder how we're doing?"

Turning, Holly saw that Beth's expression was quite serious. She pressed her lips together and grinned. "I'm sure they do, Bethy. Maybe even more than we know." She took an apron from a peg on the wall and tied it around her waist, then checked to see that her sister had started dressing. "Hurry, now."

"I will."

Holly ran down to the kitchen and gathered dishes and tableware from the cupboard. Quickly she began setting places at the knotty pine table, hoping to be done before Aunt Priscilla finished sweeping the porch.

"Mornin', lass." Ethan's gravelly voice behind her startled her; his breath was hot on her neck. He brushed against her hip. "Oops," he remarked.

Regaining her balance, Holly shot him a sideways glower and grimaced. He'd been having more and more "accidents" lately, coming a bit too close, bumping into her with that odd gleam in his eye. She frowned tightly and plunked the plates onto the table one by one.

Beth came into the room still yawning. At the back door she picked up a basket and headed outside.

From the corner of her eye, Holly watched her uncle lower his imposing bulk onto his chair and rub a hand over the gray and white stubble on his chin. She could feel his ferretlike eyes following her every move as she fussed about in the kitchen. Even as he offhandedly rolled up the sleeves of his faded work shirt his gaze did not waver.

When the door opened to admit Priscilla with the broom, followed by Beth with the basket of eggs, Holly breathed a sigh

of relief. She saw her uncle turn his attention to the plate in front of him. Idly he traced the upper edge of it with a thick index finger.

"The chicken house needs seein' to," Priscilla announced, nodding in her husband's direction as she lay a cloth over the pail of milk that he'd brought in earlier. "Looks like somethin's been at the chicks. I been tellin' ya an' tellin' ya that the one side needs shorin' up, an' the pen needs mendin'. Ya know we need them chickens an' the money from the eggs to git by."

"I'll look at it after the stock's fed," he said. "Wolves're bad this year. Might be them botherin' 'em."

"Wolves!" Her aunt's voice rose to an even higher tone than normal. "That's more'n a peck of trouble. Last year weasels was after the chicks. Now wolves. How's a body ever to make a livin' with critters always interferin'?"

Ethan shook his scraggly head. "Spencer's organizin' some men to hunt 'em down. Reckon we could use some o' that bounty money as much as anybody."

From a room adjoining the kitchen, the baby cried.

"I'll dress him and Amy Sue, Aunt Pris," Beth said, pouring warm water into a basin. Taking a washcloth from the sideboard, she carried them to the little room as Aunt Priscilla's two children began jabbering and giggling to one another.

Priscilla absently wiped her hands on the sturdy apron covering her dull gray cotton dress. She broke eggs into a pan beside slabs of sizzling bacon while Holly sliced bread and put it on the rack to toast.

Within a few minutes the family had gathered around the narrow table, Uncle Ethan and Aunt Priscilla on opposite ends and the children on wooden benches on either side. They folded their hands and bowed their heads.

"Thank ya, Lord," Priscilla said, "fer the food ya saw fit to provide fer us. Amen." Looking up, she passed the plate of eggs to Holly. "How was all the doin's yesterday?"

"Oh, we had the best time! All the towns along the way were decorated in honor of the President, and it seemed like a million people had come to see him! And—"

Her aunt's plump face took on an indulgent look. "Well, the chores piled up while ya was gone. After ya churn the butter ya can take some over to Aunt Hannah."

Feeling as though she'd been dismissed, Holly's shoulders slumped. She nodded.

"Can I go too?" Two-year-old Amy Sue tipped her blond head.

"Oh, no," Beth said gently. "Don't you remember?" Spreading jam on some toast, she handed it to the toddler. "You and I have to pick berries for supper."

"Oh goody!" The tot clapped her hands together, and a dollop of sweet preserves slid down the front of her pinafore. Her eyes grew wide. "Uh-oh."

"Mind ya be more careful," Ethan scolded, setting down his mug. He wiped his mouth with the back of his hand.

The child's big blue eyes brimmed with tears.

"It's all right, Uncle Ethan," Beth said. "I'll help you, Amy." Starting to get up, she tugged her skirt free and moved to the sink.

From the devilish spark in her uncle's eye and the curl of his mouth, Holly knew that his knee had pinned Beth's dress to the bench purposely. Anger rose within her breast. She cast a quick glance at Aunt Priscilla to see if she'd noticed, but the woman was handing a crust to the baby. Holly glared at her uncle.

Returning with a wet cloth, Beth wiped the jam from Amy Sue's pinafore, then playfully tapped the child's nose. "See? All better."

The tot smiled. "All better."

Priscilla got up and set the baby down on a blanket, toast still clutched in his tiny hand. "Keep an eye on Aaron, Beth. I'd best git to the bakin'."

"An' me to me chores," Ethan said, gulping the last of his coffee. He shoved his chair back and strode across the room, removed a worn hat from a peg, shoved it on, and left.

"Don't forget the chicken house," Priscilla called after him as the door slammed shut. "Beats all how a body can take his good-natured time tendin' to things what need fixin'. That man's ornery as the devil's off ox."

"Cuz'!" Rhon's deep voice competed with the loud, high-pitched trill of the cicadas as he hurried across the meadow between the two farms toward Holly.

Watching her cousin approach, Holly removed a clothespin from her teeth and pinned the last diaper on the line. With a sigh,

she lifted her damp hair away from the back of her neck.

Rhon and Shadow took the shortcut and bounded over the stone wall at the property line with all the ease of white-tailed deer. Her cousin waved a paper high in the air as he closed the distance between them. "I have something to show you!" Panting, he slowed down and stopped when he reached her side. Shadow nuzzled Holly with his cold wet nose.

She knelt and kissed the top of the dog's soft head. Stroking his long, silky coat, she lifted her gaze to Rhon's. "I thought you had a delivery to make in town today."

He grinned. "I've already been and back. There was a letter for Pa at the post office. From Uncle Zed. Thought you'd want to read it." He held out a crumpled envelope, then drew a sleeve across the tiny droplets of perspiration on his forehead. Shadow ambled to a shady spot beside the porch and lay down, head on his paws.

"A letter from Uncle Zed!" Holly took it from his hand as they walked to the rickety porch steps and sat down. Zed Banister, Matthew's brother, had been the adventurer, a jovial jack-of-all-trades with a flair for building fine wooden furniture and cabinets. And even though he was Rhon's uncle, but not hers, he had always treated Holly and Beth as family, and the girls easily called him Uncle Zed, just like Rhon did. Uncle Zed had been the first person she knew to actually pick up and leave Huntsville for good.

Rhon nudged his broad-brimmed hat back a few inches with one finger, and a wavy auburn lock tumbled over his forehead just short of his eyes. He shook it aside with a toss of his head and watched Holly examine the ornate script written in Zed's hand. Her skin looked creamy and soft in the sunshine, and her dark lashes made spiky shadows on the crests of her cheeks. He cleared his throat and frowned. "Well, aren't you going to open it?" She made a face at him. "Of course. I just want to enjoy it, that's all. We hardly ever see any letters anymore. Since, well, you know. Mama and Daddy."

"Mm." He nodded. "Lot of people knew your dad, what with the sawmill and all. He made the best shingles in these parts."

Taking out the folded paper, Holly read slowly.

Cheyenne, Wyoming Territory
15 June 1878

Dear Matt and Hannah,
I am writing to you from the wooden walkway in front
of my shop, watching the steady stream of "boomers" pass
through town on their way farther west. It is hard to believe
that some of them would not see fit to settle here in such
a fine place.

I miss the family and hope all is well back home. Tell Rhon
to be sure and keep up the whittling like I taught him. If
he ever takes a notion to hop a train and come out for a
visit, I left a box of tools and things in your shed I sure
could use. Have him tote it along.

I pray for you every day. In spite of the miles between
us, I will endeavor not to lose touch. Hope you do the same.
You can write to me in care of General Delivery, Cheyenne.
Give everyone my greetings. God bless.

Your brother,
Zed

Holly looked up, disappointment clouding her eyes. "I hoped
he'd say he was coming back. I really miss him." Returning the
letter to her cousin, she watched him stash it inside his blue cotton
shirt.

Rhon smiled gently. "I know how you feel. He left a big hole
in the family when he went away last winter. Must've been hard
for him to stay after Aunt Ellen died." Leaning back against the
riser, he rested his weight on his elbows and stretched out his
long legs. "Sometimes when I pass his old place I almost expect
to see him sitting on his porch, whittling some toy or other."

"I think I miss his Bible stories most of all," Holly said wistfully.
"He always brought the characters to life." She chuckled. "And
we couldn't even go for a walk without him telling us the names
of all the trees and birds and flowers along the way. He always
had time for us."

"Well, he said it's up to us, now, to tell the stories to the younger
ones."

A slightly wicked smile spread across Holly's face. "So, you're

planning a passel of young ones already? You, and Jenny Spencer, perhaps? Or is it Maybelle Patterson?"

Reddening, Rhon sat up. "Now where would you get an idea like that?"

"I have my ways." She laughed lightly. "There's not much about you I don't keep track of, cousin dear."

Rhon eyed Holly suspiciously, and the corners of his mouth curved up. "I see. Well, not that it makes much difference, but I was only at Jen's place once. And I'm not planning to return."

"Time will tell."

With a lopsided grin, Rhon shook his head.

"Hey," Aunt Priscilla called from the doorway of the weatheredboard house.

Shadow lifted his head, his tail whacked the ground several times, but he remained in the shade.

"What're the both of ya doin' lollygaggin' around this time of day?" Their aunt leaned against the uneven doorjamb, holding Amy Sue by the hand. In the woman's plump arms, baby Aaron pulled at a lock of brownish hair that had dislodged from the straggly braids wrapping her head. She moved his tiny hand away. "I'll wager to bet you're needed up the sawmill, Rhon Banister," she said, mixing idioms in a way all her own. "An' Holly, girl, the wash needs bringin' in. Ya need to git up off'n yer back porch. We don't have no servants, ya know, to be doin' things fer us. I declare, the day's half gone already. Afore ya know it, it'll be dark, an' a body won't see to git their chores done."

Holly pursed her lips at Rhon, trying to keep a straight face, and they got up.

Shadow ambled over and settled his rump at Rhon's feet.

"Rhon was just showing me a letter from Wyoming, Aunt Pris. From Uncle Zed."

"Zed, indeed. It's no never mind to me. 'Twas him took it in his head to go off an' leave. That's water behind the bridge. I got too much to do to bother wonderin' over him if he didn't care to stay here." She turned with a huff. "Nothin's gonna git fixed again with him gone," she muttered to no one in particular, her words growing fainter as she stepped inside. "Beth!" she called in her shrill tone. "Where'd ya go off to?"

Holly smiled wistfully. "Well, like she says, there's the wash to take down. Thanks for the visit."

Rhon shook his head, his gaze steady and level. "You don't have much idle time anymore, do you?" It was more statement than question. "Wish I could take you away from this broken-down place."

Still smiling, Holly tilted her head. "Oh? And where would we go, I ask?" Blushing at her own rash thoughts, she moistened her lips and forced herself to sound casual. "It's not so bad, really. Aunt Pris means well."

"But she's such a grump," he said with finality.

"Well, true. But I'm sure we try her patience sometimes. It was nice of her to take Beth and me in, you know."

"Maybe. It was probably as much for her own benefit, if you ask me." He frowned in the direction of the doorway, then looked back at Holly. "I, um . . . . Would you, um . . . . That is—" He coughed.

Holly stared, puzzled.

Clearing his throat, Rhon continued. "The fair's this weekend. Would you, you know, go with me?"

"The fair? Me? Why? Is Jenny sick?"

Rhon gave her arm a teasing nudge. "Don't be looking for trouble, cousin."

She couldn't resist one last jab. "Oh, I know. You want me to keep you safe. So Jenny can't get near you. Right?"

"Confound it all, Holly. I'm serious. Will you go with me or not?" His eyes, soft and green as the early kiss of spring, pleaded with her.

Holly's expression sobered. "Well, it sounds like fun. I'll ask."

"What do you mean, ask?" He gestured helplessly. "You're sixteen, now, for crying out loud. Seventeen, come Christmas. You shouldn't have to ask permission to go to a fair. Not with me and not with all the work you do here all the time. Seems to me that Aunt Pris does have a couple of servants, whether she admits it or not."

Raising her chin, Holly studied him. "Well, we did promise to work for our keep. She'll probably let me go."

"Good. I'll check back with you, then."

Holly nodded. Turning with a smile, she headed for the clothes-line, where sun-bleached baby things hung beside stiff, worn work clothes in the stillness of the summer day. As she took the items down, Holly watched Rhon until he and Shadow crossed

the meadow and disappeared into the grove that partly hid the Banister house from view.

A fair! The thought of it brightened her day, until she looked down at her threadbare calico dress. Then her smile wilted.

Walking home, Rhon chewed on the end of a long piece of timothy and absently watched Shadow scamper off through the tall weeds after a rabbit. There had to be a way to get Holly away from that house. Aunt Priscilla was sure that she'd done her Christian duty, taking Holly and Beth in three years ago after Uncle Will and Aunt Sarah had died. They were her own brother's kids, after all. Where else could they have gone? he wondered.

Too bad Pa couldn't have built on an extra room at our house, he thought; *we took over running Uncle Will's sawmill. But our little place has always been crammed to the rafters with just the three of us.* He smiled to himself. Girls would've been real interesting to have around, too, he thought, especially Holly, with all her impulsive ways. She needed somebody to keep her out of trouble. Besides, she was nice to be with. With a sigh he flicked the sprig of grass away.

Yep, there's gotta be a way. I'll get her out of there somehow. For good. The sawmill rightly belongs to her anyway, and I plan to see that someday she gets it back.

Cleaning up after supper that night, Holly couldn't keep her mind on her task. A soapy pewter plate slipped from her grasp and clanged to the floor, rattling in ever swifter circles until it clattered to a stop.

"Come on," Beth said, nudging her in the ribs. "We'll never get done if you keep dropping things."

"Hm?" Retrieving the dish, Holly dipped it into the rinse water again.

"What's wrong?" asked Beth.

Holly sighed. "Oh, Rhon wants me to go to the fair this Saturday. I don't know how to get Aunt Pris to let me go, especially since I just went off for two days last week with him and Uncle Matt."

"Why don't you try asking her?" Beth said with a practical shake of her head.

"You know that Saturdays are always so busy. I can barely find

a minute to go to the necessary. How could I expect to have the whole day to myself?"

Beth shrugged. "Seems like if you ask just right she lets you do anything you want. I wish I were older like you."

The door opened, and Aunt Pris strode in with a pail of purplish black elderberries, which she placed on the sideboard. "These need washin' up. Think I'll make a couple a' pies."

The spark of an idea brought hope to Holly's heart. She flashed a secret smile at Beth and cleared her throat. "Yes," she blurted, "you sure do make a tasty pie, Aunt Pris. Folks always say they're the best around."

"Aw, don't be foolish, girl. Where'd ya be gettin' a notion like that?"

"Oh, I heard Maddie West talking to Charlotte Benson after Sunday meeting last week. They're both entering pies in the fair. They didn't want to let on to you, so that you wouldn't send one to the contest."

"Is that right?" she asked, each word slow and distinct.

Ignoring the frown on her sister's forehead, Holly took the iron kettle that Beth had just finished rinsing and dried it. She composed an expression of feigned innocence. "And if you make a real special one, Beth and I could take it to the fair. I'm sure that Rhon could drive us in Uncle Matt's wagon. You'd be sure to win the blue ribbon. I just know it."

Aunt Pris cocked her head and narrowed her squinty eyes, but the way she leaned nearer to Holly more than showed she was interested. She crossed her arms over her bosom, and her finger tapped her mouth in contemplation.

Holly bit hard on the tender inside corner of her lip to keep from smiling.

3

"That wasn't very nice, you know," Beth said quietly, her airy, breathless voice now stern with reproach as she and Holly dressed for bed.

"I don't know what you mean." Holly's tone was equally hushed as she avoided her sister's accusing eyes.

"Oh, yes you do. You pretended to Aunt Pris that you'd just thought of going to the fair when you'd already made plans to go with Rhon. That isn't honest. It's not even right, even if you did suddenly think to take me along."

Holly hung her head. "Well, I knew she wouldn't let me go just to have a good time again. There'd have to be a good reason, with the washing and all." She sank down on the dressing-table stool. "And I thought if I went, so should you. You shouldn't always have to stay home. I'll just say an extra long prayer tonight to make up for it, okay?"

Unbraiding her silky blond hair, Beth shrugged. "I don't see how that will make it right."

Guilt spread across Holly's face. "It wasn't on purpose. I didn't mean to give her the wrong impression. The words just slipped out."

"Oh, I know. But don't you see, Holly? Someday you just might say something in a hurry that you'll live to regret, if you're not more careful."

"Well, I'll try to think before I speak from now on." She tried a little smile. "With a little sister like you around to remind me, I shouldn't get into trouble, right?"

Beth grinned and picked up the hairbrush, stroking in long, smooth movements the amber waves made by her braids.

"But, I sure hate the thought of going to the fair in my old dress. I wonder if we could dye it before Saturday. Jenny Spencer is sure to be there in some new frock from New York or Paris. I always feel so . . . homemade, next to her."

Setting the hair brush down, Beth turned. "Why don't you check

Mama's trunk? Maybe there's something in there that you could wear."

"What?"

"That trunk of Mama's things Aunt Hannah saved for us. Remember? The one in the corner."

Sad memories crept into Holly's heart at the very thought of it. "I've never looked inside," she said softly. "I couldn't bear to."

"Sure you can. Come on, we'll both look—together."

They crossed the tiny room and, kneeling at the hinged chest, removed a pile of folded blankets and the quilted dust coverlet that kept it hidden from view. Holly swallowed hard, and hesitantly she pressed the latch. It sprang open with a snap. The lid squeaked softly as both girls raised it and peered inside.

The sweet fragrance of dried roses, the scent Sarah Grant had loved, wafted upward in a dreamlike caress. Holly's breath caught in her throat, and sudden tears blurred her vision. Sitting back on her heels, she glanced at Beth, who was brushing away unbidden tears of her own.

"I'd forgotten already," Holly whispered. "I don't think I can do this." She reached to close the lid.

Beth stopped the action in midair. "No. If there's something in here you could use, Mama would want you to."

Frowning, Holly considered her sister's words. "Well, I suppose it wouldn't do any harm to look anyway." She took a deep breath and scanned the contents.

Neat piles of folded clothing and small objects wrapped in muslin awaited their inspection. Holly picked up the jasmine-colored dress on top and stood to shake it out. She held it against herself. "This always looked so pretty on Mama," she said wistfully. "She kept it for church. What do you think?"

Shaking her head, the younger girl scrutinized her sister. "No, not that one." Moving aside the next item in the stack, she drew out the one beneath it. "Try this."

Holly handed back the yellow dress and smoothed the creases in another dress. Made of lined ivory tiffany with splashes of watercolor violets, it had delicate lace trim around the high collar and sleeve edges. "She had her likeness done in this one, remember Beth?" As she spoke, Holly's hand brushed against a pocket in the side seam, and a necklace tumbled to the floor. She bent

and picked it up.

"Mama's locket?" Beth gasped, brushing a strand of hair away from her eyes.

Holly reverently opened the golden oval. Inside were miniatures of their mother and father. After allowing Beth a moment to examine them too, Holly closed the locket and hugged it to her heart. "Oh, Bethy, this is too precious. I thought it was lost forever." Opening the clasp, she fastened it around her neck and gazed down where it rested between the small swell of her breasts. "We can take turns wearing this when we go someplace special."

Beth's eyes shone as she gazed lovingly at the newly found treasure.

With a sad smile, Holly sighed. "I don't know. Perhaps I shouldn't wear any of these clothes. What if I tear something?"

"Oh, come on Holly. Remember what Mama always said? Be practical. You need a dress. Wear one."

"Maybe you're right. I'll only borrow one of them and leave the rest alone." Holly held the ivory-colored dress out and eyed it lovingly. "I'll try it on tomorrow, to see if it fits."

"If it doesn't, I'll take it in for you," Beth promised. "I'm getting pretty good at my stitches, Aunt Pris says."

Holly nodded. "Well, it's late, Bethy. We'd better say our prayers before she starts wondering what we have to talk about that's so interesting."

Early the next afternoon, Holly crossed the sunny field toward the Banister house with a tub of fresh butter in her hand. The long meadow grasses, rippling like ocean waves in the wind, felt silky against her bare legs as she walked. She picked a black-eyed susan and threaded the stem into the hair behind her ear.

The distant rhythm of chopping grew louder as Holly passed through the grove of white birch trees that jutted into the field. She could see Rhon splitting logs on the stump by the house. A twig snapped under her foot as she emerged from the woods. Shadow barked, joyfully bounded up to her, and accompanied her the rest of the way.

Rhon put down the axe and removed a kerchief from his back pocket to wipe his forehead. He smiled as he buttoned the gray checkered shirt that hung open over his muscular chest. "Hi, cousin."

Holly smiled back as she approached. "I see you don't have much idle time yourself," she said, setting the container on a stack of wood.

"Can't blame a guy for keeping on top of things, now, can you?" He reached for the flower in her hair and sniffed it. "Too bad these don't smell as pretty as they look. He tucked it back into her sable locks.

Feeling a blush swiftly coloring her cheeks, Holly knelt to hug the dog, making finger trails in his black shiny coat as she stroked him. Shadow licked her face. She wrinkled her nose and looked up at Rhon. "Your mother inside? I was supposed to bring this butter over yesterday."

"Yep. She was scrubbing the kitchen floor, a while ago. Pa and I had orders to keep out of the way."

"She sure likes to keep things clean, doesn't she?" said Holly with a soft laugh. "It's hard to believe that she and Aunt Pris are sisters."

"Ma must've ended up with all the gumption in that family, that's for sure," Rhon grinned. "But things got more normal at Aunt Pris's once she got herself two maids, didn't they?"

Holly grimaced and shrugged. "Well, it's more pleasant to live where things are orderly." With a last hug for Shadow, she crooned softly into his ear and stood to reach for the tub of butter.

Rhon was nearer. He picked it up and put it into her hand. "Say, did you find out about Saturday yet?"

The memory of Beth reproaching her for manipulating Aunt Priscilla came to mind, and Holly felt a second flush. "Uh, yes. Aunt Pris said that Beth and I could both go."

He raised his eyebrows, and an odd expression crossed his face like clouds scudding over the mountains. "Oh. Well, good. The more the merrier. It should be fun."

Holly nodded and said. "We're looking forward to it. Well, I guess I'll take this in." She turned and headed for the porch.

Rhon watched his cousin walk away, caught momentarily by the gentle sway of her calico skirt as she moved. A breeze feathered a wisp of long hair forward over her shoulder, and he noticed the soft curve of her arm as she brushed it back. When she stepped out of sight he smiled to himself. Holly sure was a pleasure to look at and getting prettier by the day, he thought. Someday some young man would be proud to have her around,

lighting the whole place with the sunshine of her smile. With a sigh he picked up the axe and reached for another log. One well-placed stroke split it in two.

"Aunt Hannah?" Holly called from the open doorway as she entered the bright, gleaming kitchen with its starched curtains and smooth plank floor.

"That you, Holly?" came her aunt's shrill voice from the parlor. "Be right there."

Holly drank some water from the dipper at the sink and took a seat at the shiny maple table.

"Land sakes, what a hot day," exclaimed Aunt Hannah as she came into the room with a scrub bucket. Setting it down by the door, she also drew a dipper of water and took a drink. Her hair was frizzled and clung to her forehead in several places, forming tight little curls around her face. She wiped her hands on the cleaning apron that covered her sensible dark brown dress. "What brings ya by, honey? Beth need more mendin' to do?"

"No, she's still working on that last batch you sent over. Aunt Pris wanted me to bring you some fresh butter."

"Good. Jest used up the last of what we had at breakfast, we did." Plopping down in a chair opposite Holly, she absently mopped perspiration from her neck. "Take Pris some apple jelly. I made it yesterday."

Holly nodded. "You shouldn't be working so hard in this heat. You'll be making yourself sick."

"Hmmph. Don't know who'd scrub up after the menfolk if I didn't." She adjusted the gold-rimmed spectacles on her nose. "How 'bout a sugar cookie?" Removing the lid from an earthenware jar in the middle of the table, she pushed it toward her niece. "Baked fresh."

Holly removed one and tasted it. "Mmm. Yours are the best, Aunt Hannah."

The older woman sampled one herself, then brushed sugar granules from her generous bosom. "Always need somethin' around fer the men. A body can't hardly keep a step ahead of 'em."

Holly laughed and took another bite.

"So, Rhon's takin' ya to the fair, huh?"

Holly noticed a strange tightness in her voice. "Mm hm. Beth,

too."

Her aunt's normal tone returned with force. "Good. Good. Let's hope the sun holds out."

Holly popped the last of the cookie into her mouth and chewed slowly. "Aunt Pris is baking a pie for the competition. Would you like us to enter some of your jelly?"

She shook her head. "No, not this time. Didn't take no special pains with it. You kids jest go an' have yerselfs a good time. I'll git twice as much work done around here with nobody interruptin' me."

"Well, speaking of work," Holly said, rising, "I'd best be getting back. I still have chores to do."

"Don't we all," chuckled her aunt, looking past her out the door. "I wanna air the quilts in that good breeze."

"Thanks for the cookie, Auntie."

"Sure thing, child. Good to see there's somebody who can eat jest one. Rhon gobbles 'em by the handful."

Nodding, Holly smiled. "We grew up on these."

"Don't I know it? One of these days that boy's like to take a notion to git hisself married up, an' I'll have a new batch of young'uns to bake fer."

Holly found that thought somehow unsettling, and she drew a deep breath. "Well, let's hope that's not for some time." Bending to her aunt, she gave her a quick hug and kiss and turned to leave.

"Don't forget the jelly fer Pris. Take one of them jars on the counter."

As Holly stepped outside she saw Rhon at the rain barrel, splashing water over his face, neck, and chest. Shadow lay in a cool spot beside him.

"Leaving so soon?" Rhon asked.

Holly nodded, watching him pull his shirt on. The checkered shirt clung to his chest and back in several spots that darkened with moisture. She tried not to notice the rugged contours his lean body, acquired since he'd been helping out at the sawmill. But her eyes lingered, tracing his broad shoulders and strong arms. "Yes," she blurted, "I have some things to finish before we go tomorrow."

"Ah." The edges of his mouth tweaked. "I'll come by early. Be ready."

"I will."

"See you then." He looked down at the dog at his feet. "Go with her, Shad," he motioned.

Obediently, the dog ambled over to Holly and kept her company as she started toward the birch grove.

"Holly!" Rhon called after her.

She turned.

"Wear another flower tomorrow. It looks nice."

Holly smiled, aware that for the third time that day, her face had turned the same shade as Aunt Pris's summer roses.

"Well, what do you think?" Holly said, twirling in her mother's dress.

Sitting cross-legged on the big bed, Beth laid her sketch pad aside and scrutinized her sister. "Maybe it needs another tuck at the waist."

"Oh, I don't think so. It feels fine. Think I'll look all right for the fair?"

The younger girl nodded. "Better than that. You look . . . grown up. Mama'd be proud." Blinking rapidly, she turned her head.

"Fudge," Holly muttered glumly. "I wish we had a looking glass big enough to see how we look. And what'll I do with my hair? My old blue ribbon is so frayed."

"Don't fret. Take off the dress and get out the rag strips. I'll curl your hair for you." Beth's down-to-earth tone seemed soothing.

"You will?" Holly asked, looking up suddenly as she gently laid aside the ivory frock. "Are you sure that you remember how?" She slipped into her nightgown and removed a small box from the commode beside the bed.

"Of course. I watched Mama do it hundreds of times. It looked easy enough."

Holly handed her the container and sat on the edge of the bed, back turned, brushing the tangles from her dark hair. "It's probably too long to curl all over, the way Mama did when we were little. But waving the ends would make it look different, don't you think?"

"Mm hm," Beth answered. "I'll try my best. Just make sure you sit still."

"Yes, mother," Holly teased, holding out the first rag strip.

Beth took a lock of hair and began winding it around the bottom half of the cloth in a smooth ringlet. Then, apparently satisfied

with it, she wrapped the top half of the cloth over the curl and tied it at the bottom. "How's that?" she asked with a pleased smile.

Holly glanced at the bound coil resting on her left shoulder. "You *do* remember. I can't wait to see how I'll look tomorrow." She smiled as Beth continued making curls. "What are you going to wear?"

Parting another section of hair, her sister reached for another strip and worked smoothly. "Oh, I got out your maroon skirt. Remember? The one you grew out of?"

"That old thing? I tore it at school playing tag."

Beth shrugged. "Well, I mended it. It wasn't such a bad tear after all. You'll see."

After the last lock had been wrapped, Holly sighed and lay back on the bed with her hands cradling her head. "Remember how Mama would stay up nights making us new dresses, Beth? Now we have to make do with the few we have. I wish she were still here."

"Me too. But we do have a roof over our heads," Beth answered in her sensible tone. "We should be thankful that we didn't have to go to a foundling home somewhere."

"I suppose you're right." She paused. "But wouldn't it be nice to have all the pretty things we dream of, Bethy? Fine clothes and matching velvet capes, shoes with silver buckles and high heels. Can you imagine?"

Beth flung herself down on the feather tick in a swoon, her wide brown eyes bright and shining. "And rings and sparkling jewels for our ears—"

"And our hair would be all done up in curls, and we'd wear elegant hats."

"With feathers—."

"And birds!" Holly threw an arm over her sister's slight shoulder, and the girls dissolved into giggles.

Beth was the first to sober. "Oh well. It must be something to have money to buy anything you wanted. But," she added, crinkling her nose, "we'll never get that way by dreaming. And whoever heard of a rich orphan anyway?"

Holly sat up. "I hate that word. And I hate being poor. If I had a lot of money, I just *know* I'd be happy."

"I'm sure you don't mean that," Beth said, studying Holly momentarily. Then her solemn expression faded, and an impish

sparkle filled her chestnut eyes. She grabbed Holly's sunbonnet from the spindle on the dressing table and held it above her amber head in a dramatic pose. "A fine parasol to shade your fancy hair tomorrow, my lady."

Holly snatched the coverlet at the foot of the bed and flung it around her shoulders, twirling across the floor and back. "And a lace shawl to chase the evening chill." Her voice trailed off, and the pair broke into another round of giggles as they flopped onto the mattress.

"Oh well," the younger girl said several moments later, her smile fading. "We'd best say our prayers and get some sleep." She climbed off the bed and knelt on the floor.

With a sigh Holly followed. Rich people probably didn't have any troubles at all, she thought. How could they? She smiled to herself. *Tomorrow I'm going to pretend that I'm rich.*

4

Priscilla rested the baby against one wide hip and watched from the doorway as the laughing young people climbed aboard the wagon.

Beth smoothed her maroon skirt as she sat down in the wagon bed, then looked back toward the door and waved. "Bye, Aunt Pris."

Nodding, Priscilla smiled affably.

On the seat beside Rhon, Holly gingerly held a golden-crusted elderberry pie on her lap. Below her wide-brimmed straw sunbonnet, her softly curled hair trapped bits of the early sun and glistened. She turned and smiled. "I hope you win the ribbon," she said to her aunt.

Priscilla nodded again. But, taking note of the appreciative gaze Rhon swept slowly over his cousin while Holly's head was turned away, she frowned. All the young boys was sure to be noticin' the girl an' buzzin' around her one of these days, she thought.

Rhon dipped his head and grinned at their aunt, then flicked the reins. "Giddyup, Nan."

"Bye, Aunt Pris," the young people chorused, "bye!"

With the harness jingling, the sturdy brown farm horse clopped toward the rutted trail, wheels crunching over small stones and clumps of dirt as the wagon lurched along the uneven road to Dallas.

Priscilla watched the youthful forms on the seat disappear into the dappled shade of the maples, elms, and evergreens in the distance. *Jest lookit them two young'uns,* she thought, shaking her head. *Always together, always makin' some big plan, ever since they's kids. Why, them two's always been close as two peas.* Suddenly she frowned. *They're gittin' older now. Holly's lookin' real growed up in Sarah's summer dress. An' why is it I ain't took notice b'fore 'bout how tall that Rhon's been gittin'? Mebbe it ain't fittin' fer 'em to be spendin' so much time together nowadays. I jest might have me a talk with Hannah today while*

we're workin' on them chickens an' see what she has to say about it.

An hour later, fanning herself with one hand, Priscilla headed across the meadow toward her sister's place. "What a hot day," she grumbled as she pulled Aaron's thumb from his mouth. "Hot 'nough to melt the bark of'n a tree." She glanced back at Amy Sue, who ran playfully among the field flowers along the way, picking a raggedy bouquet.

Before they'd emerged from the trees, Shadow barked a welcome and jumped to his feet. In a flash he loped to Amy Sue's side, his long ears flapping, and licked her face. She giggled and hugged his hairy neck.

"That you, gal?" Hannah called from the doorway as she peeked outside.

"Sure is, gal. A mite hot to be doin' much work today, ain't it?"

"Oh, I can't be bothered worryin' none about heat. Not when I have me a day without the menfolk around. Why, I already scrubbed the kitchen walls an' the floor in the boy's room, an' I put a new quilt in the frame. When I seen you comin', I went out back an' caught the chickens we'd be needin'."

Priscilla shook her head in disbelief as she spread out a small blanket on the grass and set the baby down. Her sister's house never had time to get dirty. It was a wonder the floors weren't worn clean through, with all the scrubbin' they got all the time, she thought. She reached for Amy Sue's hand and said, "Now, mind ya watch the baby while I help Aunt Hannah." Then, trudging up the porch, she slumped down on a chair and fanned her flushed face and neck exaggeratedly with her worn calico bonnet. "I declare. Makes no sense a'tall fer a body to be workin' hard on a day hot as this. Why, I had me half a mind to—"

"Well, there's a big pot o' water boilin' on the stove, gal," Hannah remarked. "We'd best start pluckin' them hens. I'll go scald the first couple an' bring 'em out."

Priscilla watched her sister enter the house. The door slammed behind her, then opened again moments later as she returned carrying a tray on which lay two dead chickens. She set it on the small porch table between them and picked up the first hen, working over an empty tub at their feet. They worked in silence, clumps of wet feathers clinging to their hands as they cleaned

the chickens.

"How many are there, gal?" Priscilla asked, blowing straggly hairs from her eyes.

With the back of her wrist, Hannah pushed her spectacles higher on her round nose. "Five. The preacher's comin' by fer two of 'em. Thought mebbe ya'd take one by the Widow James's place after while. Other two's fer us."

Priscilla nodded. "Well, shouldn't take us too long, then. I'm ready to start on another'n." She slapped the first bird onto the tray and cast a cautious glance toward the blanket where Aaron had fallen asleep, thumb in his mouth. Amy Sue happily picked dandelions beside him.

Hannah went inside and returned a few minutes later with the remaining chickens. Sinking into her seat, she moved closer to the tub and worked nimbly. "I wonder what the kids is doin' right now?"

"Oh, walkin' their feet off, I expect, an' stuffin' their faces, like we'd do if we was with 'em. Wasn't too awful long ago we was their age. Land sakes, beats all how time scoots by."

"Rhon was sure lookin' forward to havin' two purty girls in tow," Hannah commented.

Priscilla shook the last few sticky feathers from her hand and looked into her older sister's face. "That's somethin' we need to be talkin' about, gal—"

Frowning, Hannah cocked her head to one side, and her eyeglasses slid askew. She scrunched her nose twice to inch them back into place.

"—them two peas of ours," Priscilla continued.

Hannah's frown deepened. "Rhon an' Holly?"

"See?" Priscilla said. "Ya knowed who I meant, b'fore I even got round to sayin' it."

"What're ya gittin' at?" A note of wariness crept into Hannah's voice.

"Same thing you're thinkin'. Ain't fittin' fer them two to be keepin' such close company now that they're growed. Ever'time I turn around he's over at our place makin' moon eyes at Holly. Not that anythin's goin' on, mind ya. But who knows? And with them bein' cousins, an' all, it jest ain't seemly. He needs to start seein' there's other fish in the stew."

For several moments Hannah remained silent, her eyes crinkled

in thought. Then, remembering her task, she grasped a damp tail feather, nodding slowly as she tugged at it. "Ya know, I been givin' it a bit of thought myself, lately . . . how it's time to sort a' ease the boy toward some other little gal. Someone from a good family."

"An' I'm gonna' keep my eye out fer a good match fer Holly," added Priscilla.

Rhon applied pressure on the brake as the wagon jostled down a steep part of the road. At the bottom, he saw Holly relax her grip on the pie. He glanced over his shoulder at Beth, who smiled and yawned. Turning to a clean page in her sketchbook, she began sketching. He nudged Holly and pointed off to the right where a doe and fawn stood motionless, blending with the mottled light patterns in the woods.

Her lips parted softly.

"You look real pretty," he said. "That a new dress?"

Casting him a sidelong glance, she blushed. "It was Mama's. Beth fixed it so that I could wear it today."

"It's nice."

A rabbit hopped across their path, and a cardinal darted among the high branches, its feathers a bright flash of red against the green boughs.

The wagon lurched over a deep rut, and Holly gripped the pie tighter.

The sun was high in the sky when they finally descended the last long hill on Huntsville Road and headed toward the vast clearing where the annual fair was already in full swing. Groups of people in bright clothes milled about the row of canopies and tents. Vendors called out above the noise, tempting the throng with freshly baked goods and cool drinks, candies and souvenirs. Quilts and other handmade items were piled high on the counters around them. Bouquets of bright summer irises, roses, and daisies emitted a soft, sweet fragrance everywhere.

Reaching the outskirts of the fairgrounds, Rhon guided Nan into some shade and tied her to a post as Beth jumped out of the rear of the wagon. He turned to Holly. "Come on, cousin. I'll help you down."

Rising, Holly set the pie on the seat. She leaned into his upraised hands and felt herself lowered gently to the ground. Her bonnet

slipped backward and was caught just below the nape of her neck by the ribbon ties at her throat. Laughing lightly, she reached to pull it up again, careful not to flatten the pink rose Beth had fastened at the crown of her head. The flower was held in place by a blue ribbon woven into the braid that lay among Holly's curls. She could tell by the twinkle in Rhon's eyes that he had noticed the flower.

"Well, we'd best hurry to the baking tent," she said to Beth.

"I'll walk you both over," Rhon said, reaching up to the seat of the buckboard. He handed the pie to Holly, and they headed in that direction.

"Will you be competing in anything this year?" she asked as they neared the huge canopy that emitted delectable aromas.

"Oh, I might see who's pitching quoits. I'm not sure what's on the schedule yet. I'll check while you wait for the outcome of this, okay? And, we wouldn't want to miss the wagon race. I'll find out when it is."

She nodded. "I'll be here."

"Beth!" called a voice nearby. The girls turned.

"Oh, it's Lydia and Meg from church," Beth said. "Could I tag along with them for a while? I know I'm supposed to stay and watch the judging, but . . ."

"Oh, I can see to this by myself," Holly assured her. "Go have some fun."

"Thanks!"

"If you get hungry, remember that the sandwiches are in the wagon. And act like a lady."

"I will," Beth quipped over her shoulder.

Holly felt a prick of guilt as she watched her sister lift her skirts and race like a tomboy toward her friends. Beth had hardly had time to be a child. Her own childhood had also come to a sudden halt when she'd been just a little younger than Beth was now, halted the day that Uncle Matt and Uncle Zed had come with the awful news about their parents. Then, remembering where she was, Holly drew a fortifying breath and strolled into the tent, barely in time to fill out the entry form.

Filled with anticipation, she watched the judges walk along the table tasting each entry in the pie contest while a sizable crowd looked on. When Priscilla's was selected to be in the finals, Holly felt tingly with excitement. *Please let it win, Father,* she prayed

silently.

The officials sampled the entries once more, then gathered to confer. The head judge, a rotund man dressed in black with a matching bow tie, stepped forward. "Ladies and gentlemen, we have a winner here." He held up Priscilla's elderberry pie. "Will the entrant please step forward?"

Holly's heart skipped a beat as she approached him.

"This your pie, young lady?"

"Well, it's my Aunt Priscilla Quinn's, really," she answered. "I brought it in for her, since she wasn't able to come herself."

"Well, you tell your Aunt Priscilla Quinn that we send our congratulations. We'd like her to have this blue ribbon." Extending a hand, he held out the prize.

"Oh, thank you, sir, thank you," said Holly. She grinned with joy and took the blue satin ribbon from his hand as the onlookers applauded.

"Congratulations," said a syrupy sweet voice at her elbow.

Holly looked up to see Jenny Spencer and Maybelle Patterson at her side. "Oh, hi. Did your mothers enter something in the contest?"

Jenny's face remained composed. She rarely smiled for the benefit of other girls, but when she did, it was more of a smirk than anything else, her lips drawing up on just one side. "Of course not." She toyed with the lace trim on the front of her elaborate blue dress, a hint of the smirk appearing. "We just came to watch."

"Oh."

"Did you come alone?" Maybelle asked. With a loud crunch, the plump brunette bit into a large red apple.

"No, my sister and I came with Rhon."

Jenny suddenly seemed disinterested with the cooking contests. Her pale blue eyes darted from one group to another until one seemed to catch her attention. She smiled to herself. "Well, we'll see you around. Come on, Maybelle. Oh, by the way, Holly, that's a cute dress. Really cute. Haven't I seen it somewhere?" In a toss of red-gold curls, she turned and walked away without waiting for an answer.

Holly stared after the pair. Her heart sank. Jenny fairly sparkled in her new silk creation with ruffles, puffed sleeves, and lace and a blue parasol dangling from one hand. Even her shoes reflected the sun as she walked. Although somewhat less fash-

ionable than Jenny, Maybelle also wore something new. Holly gazed lovingly at her own ivory frock and defiantly raised her chin. Rhon had liked it and said that she looked pretty. Who cared if it lacked flounces and French lace? She looked for him, but he was nowhere in sight. Leaving the shade of the baking tent, Holly stepped out into the sunshine in search of her cousin.

"Forty-nine, all," the official announced to the spectators at the horseshoe court.

Rhon stepped up beside the edge of the pitching box, horseshoe in hand. He raised it to eye level and concentrated on the spike at the other end of the dirt court.

"Good luck, Rhon," called Jenny. She smiled sweetly across the open space between them.

He looked up and his eyes momentarily caught the splash of blue. Her red curls shimmered like gold as she lowered her parasol and blew him a kiss. Smiling slightly, he concentrated on the job facing him. A movement in the distance caught his eye, and he saw Holly walking gracefully toward the onlookers, swinging her bonnet lightly by its strings. With a deep breath he aimed the horseshoe again, fixing his gaze on the spike.

"Ever gonna throw that thing?" asked the official.

Rhon grinned broadly and sent the horseshoe clanging against the stake. The circle of watchers applauded.

Sam Daniels, an old school chum of Rhon's, stepped up for his turn. He tossed a ringer too, canceling Rhon's points.

A groan of disappointment rose from the spectators.

Sam swaggered off to the side as Rhon toed the mark again and took aim. This time the iron thumped against the dirt and rolled, coming to a stop as it leaned against the peg.

The crowd held its breath as Sam Daniels smirked and shrugged. He lifted his horseshoe and stared at the peg in concentration. He tossed the iron easily. It thudded to the dirt a hair's breadth away.

"Fifty, forty-nine," the judge said as the crowd cheered and applauded the victory. Rhon strode over to receive the envelope with the five-dollar cash prize, then returned and shook hands with his mildly disappointed opponent. "Good match, Sam. Now we're even from last year."

"Get you next time," his friend said. "Best two outta three."

"Right."

Jenny ran up and took hold of Rhon's arm. "Oh, Rhon," she crooned. "That was so exciting."

For a second he feared that she might try to kiss him. Drawing back slightly, he noticed that Jenny's dress had more fancy gewgaws on it than he had ever seen at one time on one person. A few too many, he thought. He turned to search the crowd for Holly.

"Rhon, could we—" Jenny began.

"Thanks, Jen, but I came with someone else."

"Oh, you mean your cousin," Jenny said. Her voice was high and sweet, and very polite, and it rankled him sorely. "Well, I'm sure she won't mind. She'll find her sister or somebody to walk around with. It's nearly time for the race." She tried to draw him along with her.

Then Rhon's eyes met Holly's soft chestnut ones across the way. Standing with her hands behind her simple ivory frock, her head tilted slightly to one side, Holly raised a hand and waved. "Sorry, Jen," he said. "Another time." He was almost sure that he saw Jenny's eyes narrow as she raised her chin and pouted into the distance. Then she turned and tramped off toward a shade tree, where Maybelle stood eating cookies.

Rhon strode over to Holly. "Hi," he said as he approached. "How'd you do at the competition?"

"Almost as well as you." She smiled, showing him the blue ribbon. "You were wonderful. I'm really proud of you."

A warm feeling flowed through Rhon, but he managed to push it aside. "Oh well, it seems like Sam and I have been doing the same thing every year. He's not an easy one to beat." He took Holly's hand in his. "The crowd's gathering for the race already. Let's go find a spot."

Tyler Harris scanned the onlookers from his seat atop his rig as he waited for the other entrants to line up on the oval track. Many fashionable young women were strolling on the sidelines, he noticed. He returned quite a few lingering smiles. One young woman dressed in pink blushed and turned away. He chuckled.

Firmly securing his charcoal felt bowler, he leaned forward, the traces draped loosely over the tops of his long fingers. This would be an easy victory for certain, he thought. No one had a

rig as fine as his. And his matched dappled grays were faster than any he'd ever seen.

His gaze settled on a girl in a pale blue dress. The sun turned her strawberry blond curls to fire as they stirred on the breeze. In his twenty-six years he'd never seen hair of quite such a vivid color. He kept his eyes on her for several moments, acknowledging her coy smile with a nod before glancing farther down the line of spectators. Another young woman, dark-haired, willowy and dressed in ivory, caught his eye, then just beyond her, a girl somewhat younger with wheat-colored braids. He studied her guileless face for a few seconds.

An official's voice interrupted his thoughts from the podium. "Get ready," the man said as he raised the starter's pistol.

Taking firm hold of the reins, Tyler Harris stared intently ahead.

A gunshot cracked into the air. Harris snapped the leather smartly against the backs of the grays, and the horses shot forward.

As the other wagons rumbled off, an immense cloud of dust filled the summer air.

Holly stood on tiptoe to watch the speeding teams as the crowd shouted encouragement to the drivers by name. Each one had a group of supporters cheering him on—all except the young man in the fancy new wagon. No one knew who he was.

"That guy has the race in his pocket," her cousin said, watching the galloping grays several lengths ahead of the rest. "Did you see those incredible horses?"

"They are beautiful," admitted Holly, "and sure to win."

At the far turn the grays lengthened their hefty lead. "Here they come!" someone shouted. Then, seeming to forget their old favorites, the crowd roared in appreciation as the stranger's wagon passed in front of them and crossed the finish line. As the rest of the contestants slowed their horses, the crowd burst forward toward the winner.

"See?" Rhon said. "I knew he'd do it." Putting an arm around Holly's shoulders, he turned her away from the swirling dust. "Come on, cuz', let's go watch the greased pigs, and then I'll buy you some lemonade."

A short while later, Holly sat curled up under a shade tree while Rhon went for their drinks. Seeing Beth and the two girls from church off in the distance, she waved. They waved back.

"I see you made it to the fair, Holly," said Reverend Dixon, the pastor of Holly's church. At his side stood the stranger from the race.

She came to her feet and brushed the grass from her skirt. "Yes. It's been lovely."

The minister patted his broad girth with a chuckle. "I know what you mean. We've been sampling some of the lovely goodies ourselves. I have someone I'd like you to meet."

Holly turned her head with a snap and met two slate gray eyes in a tanned oval-shaped face. The young man's neatly trimmed, narrow mustache, the same rich black as his hair, formed an upside-down vee above his upper lip that widened as he smiled. He had an attractive cleft in his chin, she noticed, and he was quite fashionably dressed in a three-piece buff-colored suit that fit his wiry build to perfection.

"Holly, my girl," continued the pastor, "this is Tyler Harris, the grandson of an old family friend. He's just recently moved back into the area. I've been introducing him around, since he'll be coming to our services in the future. Tyler, this is Holly Grant."

"How do you do," she said softly, not quite meeting his eyes.

"My pleasure, miss."

The minister nodded. "Holly and her family are among my most faithful members. They've been coming to the church for as many years as I've been here."

Mr. Harris turned to Holly and smiled, displaying strong even teeth as he stared unabashedly.

She blushed at his boldness.

"What did you think of the race, Miss Grant?" His deep voice had a slight hoarseness to it, the way her father's had once when he had a sore throat.

"Oh, I'm sorry. Congratulations on your win."

"I noticed you watching from the sidelines." He peered at her as if waiting for a reply.

Holly wondered how he could possibly have seen her among the large crowd at the race.

"We're just going for some punch," he said. "Would you care to join us?"

"No, thank you. I'm—"

"With me," Rhon finished her sentence as he approached from her other side, standing closer than usual. He held out a glass

of lemonade, and she took it.

Reverend Dixon beamed. "Oh. Rhon. I'd like you to meet Tyler Harris, a family friend. Tyler, this is Rhon Banister, another member of my flock."

"How do you do, Rhon?" He dipped his head.

"Harris," Rhon said with a nod, then turned to the pastor. "Nice to see you, Reverend."

The older man pushed his rimless spectacles higher on the bridge of his large, bulbous nose and clamped a hand on Rhon's shoulder. "And you as well, lad. Guess we'll move along. I've more introductions to make. See you two tomorrow. Enjoy the fair."

"Well, it was a pleasure meeting you both," Mr. Harris said smoothly, inclining his head in Holly's direction. Then he turned and followed the minister.

Holly watched as Rhon shot an unexplainable glare after him. Its harshness shocked her. And, for some strange reason, she found it sent a rush of excitement through her. Rhon looked almost . . . jealous. She smiled up at him. "Thanks for the drink."

"Anytime, cousin." A grin softened his expression. "Let's sit for a while." Taking her hand, he drew her down beside him on the grass.

Rhon caught sight of Tyler Harris again moments later, as he and Reverend Dixon approached Maybelle and Jenny. Maybelle, as usual, appeared all giggly and flustered, but Jenny acted as if she were quite impressed. Oh well, he thought, at least the rover isn't bothering Holly.

He raised the glass to his mouth and gazed across the rim at the comely girl beside him. Holly was relaxed now against the tree trunk, her eyes closed. The slanting rays of the afternoon sun spun silver and violet highlights among the dark curls spilling over her shoulders as she rested.

A grim realization inched its way into Rhon's heart: All too soon men would be coming to call on his long-haired beauty, and one of them would take her from him. He studied the curve of her cheekbones, her smooth, creamy complexion, and he memorized her lips, soft and full and so inviting. He swallowed the last of his lemonade in one gulp.

5

"Thanks for the ride," Holly said as she and Beth jumped down from the wagon and straightened their skirts. "We had a wonderful time."

"Sure. Anytime." Accompanied by a vague smile, Rhon's quick wink was unconvincing. He pushed back the brim of his hat with one finger, and his adam's apple bobbed above his red neckerchief. "Night." He flicked the reins against Nan's broad back, and the horse plodded slowly toward the Banister farm in the waning light of early evening.

Beth frowned as she watched the buckboard leave, then turned to Holly. "What happened? Rhon was so cheerful this morning, but he barely said a word all the way home. Did he mention what was wrong?"

With a shake of her head, Holly sighed. "No. I noticed that he grew quiet late in the afternoon." But neither had she felt much like talking herself for some reason. She gazed thoughtfully after him.

The girls mounted the porch steps. Crossing to the door, Beth opened it and entered.

Holly lingered. She glanced one last time across the meadow, then stepped inside, bumping into Beth.

"Look at this place!" her sister gasped. "It's . . . back to normal, the way it used to be. And in only one day!"

Holly's eyes made a wide circuit of the room from the doorway, and her shoulders sagged. At the open windows, the bottoms of the curtains dangled half inside, half out, billowing softly as she closed the door. Discarded clothing lay heaped near the bedroom door. The table was strewn with soiled dishes and scraps of uneaten food, and pots and kitchen utensils, obviously left by the children, cluttered the floor.

"Well, it isn't normal for us." From a peg by the door Holly grabbed an apron and tied it around her waist. She lit a candle from the glowing coals in the stove and touched it to two oil

lamps in holders on the wall, then headed for the table and began clearing away the dishes.

Beth sighed and pointed to four newly pieced quilt blocks from the arm of the worn, overstuffed settee. "Aunt Priscilla must have whiled away the time sewing. I wonder where everyone is."

"She said something about going to see the Widow James sometime today. But wherever she is, she'll probably be back soon enough."

Beth picked up a basket. "Well, I'll bring in the wash." Opening the door, she went outside toward the clothes, which flapped haphazardly in the wind.

"They left us some chicken soup," Holly called after her. "I'll warm it up while we work."

Later, in the golden lamplight, the girls ate in silence. Beth playfully touched a smudge on Holly's cheek. "You missed a spot."

Holly pushed Beth's fingers away with a smile and shook her head. "I didn't think we'd ever get done. I don't know how Aunt Pris can endure living in such untidiness. I'd almost forgotten that that's how it always used to be here."

"Guess she's always preferred quilting to housework. Well, one thing is certain. We'd better not ever go away at the same time again. The house might not survive."

Holly nodded. "True." How awful it would be to live here forever, she thought grimly. For a brief moment she imagined caring for a home of her own, waiting for her husband to come through the door at suppertime. But in the daydream, the silhouette in the doorway was her cousin's. Shaken, she banished the forbidden thought and glanced toward the kettle of water heating on the stove. "Well, I suppose we can tackle the dishes now. Then I'm going to bed."

Rhon brushed Nan's russet coat and put fresh straw in her stall. At the sound of approaching footsteps, he looked up.

"Ma says come for supper," his father said, poking his head through the doorway. "It's ready now."

"Be right up. Thanks." Leaning the hayfork against the wall, Rhon sighed and headed for the rain barrel. He filled the basin on the washstand, scrubbed his face and hands, and flung the used water into his mother's flowerbed. Then, he went inside and

quietly took his seat.

Matthew Banister limped to the table, favoring his left leg. After he sat down, the family bowed their heads. "Thank you for our food, Lord," he said, "and all our other blessings, in Jesus' name. Amen."

Hannah ladled stew into three bowls and handed them around.

Studying Rhon, Matthew scratched his temple. "Somethin' wrong, son? Thought you'd be talkin' our ears off 'bout the fair and all the goin's on."

Rhon flashed him a half-smile and shook his head. "We had a fine time. Aunt Pris's pie took the blue ribbon."

Hannah cocked her head, and her spectacles slid out of place. She straightened them with a finger. "Ya don't say. Well, she always did have a way with them pies o' hers."

Something must have happened to upset the boy, Matt thought as he spread butter onto a steaming biscuit. "Pitch quoits again with Sam Daniels?"

Rhon nodded and grinned.

"You win?"

He nodded again. "It was my turn. He won last year."

"Did . . . um . . . ." Hannah cleared her throat. "How 'bout the girls? Beth an' Holly have a good time too, did they?" Nervously she tucked a few hairs behind the side pieces of her glasses.

Rhon shrugged a shoulder and frowned slightly. "Sure." He licked his lips and blew on a spoonful of stew.

Hannah turned to Matthew, her expression serious. She nodded toward Rhon.

Matt cast her a warning look. She glared back at him with a huff.

Watching the mysterious exchange between his parents, Rhon wondered what was up. Maybe it was just his mood, but it seemed he could feel an unusual tension between them.

"The little Spencer girl go, did she?" his mother asked. "Always did like her. Purty little thing, don't 'cha think so, Rhon?"

He barely heard her. He raised his brows in question.

"I said, that Jenny Spencer is purty as a bellflower. Ever'time I see her, she's all dressed up in blue."

"Yeah, she has some fine clothes." He pushed away his bowl. "Mind if I go feed Nan and Bert now?" His father excused him

with a nod of his head.

In the barn, Rhon stroked Nan's velvety flank and leaned casually against the side of the wooden stall watching her eat. Of the two horses, she was his favorite, and he always gave her extra care. He picked out a strand of hay and snapped it in half, then broke it again and again, until only a small piece remained to crumble between his fingers. Tossing it, he turned and gave a goodbye pat to Nan's rump.

Outside, he climbed onto the corral fence and sat on the top rail, not really listening to the crickets chirping in regular cadence. There wasn't much of a moon. The clouds clumped together like a bouquet of flowers. He sighed.

Bluebells were pretty, like his ma said. That much he could admit. But he was drawn more to rich-colored black-eyed susans. An unbidden smile made its way across his mouth as he thought of Holly's beautiful, wide-set chestnut eyes . . . the way they sparkled when she laughed and glistened with tears when she was sad. Too bad we're cousins, he thought bitterly. The smile dulled. *If we weren't* . . . . The thought dangled in his mind even as the faraway cry of a wolf pierced the night.

Holly raised the hem of her nightgown and ran barefoot over the dewy grass in the cool, gray quiet of Sunday morning. Reaching her secret place, she sat down by the boulder and opened her diary.

> I was too tired to write last night. The house was a frightful mess when Beth and I got home, but we had a glorious time at the fair. There were so many pretty things to see, such good things to eat. Aunt Pris's pie won the blue ribbon.
>
> Rhon beat Sam Daniels in quoits. He didn't seem very excited about it, though. He hardly talked on the way home. Something is troubling him. Things haven't quite been the same between us since the centennial. I feel shy around him now and must force myself to act natural. I don't understand the strange new feelings I have inside. I watch the meadow for him every day, hoping he'll come over. But I know this is foolishness. After all, we're cousins. How can I feel the way I do?

Leaning back against the stone, Holly sat with her Bible unopened, staring up at the heavy gray clouds dragging the treetops, while wisps of white mist rose from the ground to merge with them. Shivering in the morning chill, she bowed her head. *Father, I'm so mixed up. I used to be able to come here and think, and everything would start making sense. Whatever happened to change that? Only days ago my life was so simple, and now my thoughts are one big jumble that I can't even sort through. Please help me.*

The nearby buzz of a bumblebee interrupted her thoughts, and she jumped up. Glancing nervously around, she ran back to the house to dress for church, knowing that Uncle Matt would soon swing by in his wagon for them.

Nestled in a grove of trees by a secluded pond, the square, clapboard church stood alone. The fading whitewashed building looked dismal under gray skies as the Banisters' buckboard stopped alongside. A light drizzle touched the surface of the small lake and turned misty in the unseasonable coolness.

Rhon and his father climbed down first. Matt assisted the women. Rhon helped Beth and Amy Sue, then took Aaron from Holly and handed him to Beth. He didn't quite meet Holly's eyes as he took her waist and swung her to the ground.

"Thanks," she whispered. She felt tingly where he'd touched her and knew that she was blushing.

He tipped his head, and they joined the others.

Inside, the window shutters remained closed against the nippy weather, and oil lamps burned brightly from sconces along the walls. Warmth radiated from a pot-bellied stove in the right front corner of the room.

Holly sat with Beth and Aunt Priscilla to help tend the children, as Uncle Ethan had neither the time nor the inclination to join the "Sunday hypcrites," as he called church-goers. She glanced around for familiar faces and met Rhon's across the aisle.

He winked.

Her returning smile suddenly felt out of place, wrong. She turned her attention to the pulpit.

"Good morning," said Reverend Dixon. With one hand he smoothed the already slicked gray hair on his head and adjusted his round spectacles. Unconsciously patting his portly stomach above the gold chain of his ever-present timepiece, he beamed

at the congregation. His wide, round nose still glowed red from the cool nip of the outside air. "It's good to see so many of you here on this rainy morning. Let's open with 'A Mighty Fortress Is Our God.' "

With a flourish, the matronly organist, Miss Penelope Scott, pumped the pedals and played the introduction, then everyone joined in on the first verse. Her light blue eyes rarely left the pages of the open hymnal, but whenever they did, she'd lift an adoring gaze to the pastor, and her cheeks would glow. It was common knowledge that Miss Penelope had designs on the jovial pastor, although he himself never seemed to encourage her attentions, at least not in a way that was apparent to Holly. She wondered if her own feelings were as obvious to other people. Did they notice the way she blushed every time Rhon looked her way?

When Aaron fussed, Holly was more than glad to carry him to the back and walk to and fro with him in her arms. At least she didn't have to worry about her face betraying her unthinkable feelings. Stroking his silky brown head, she snuggled him against her shoulder. She almost tripped over her own feet when her idle glance fell upon the young man she'd met at the picnic. She hadn't given him a thought since their introduction. He gave a barely perceptible nod, and Holly turned to walk in the other direction.

At last the sermon ended, and the preacher gave the closing prayer. He then looked at the congregation with a smile. "Friends, I'm most happy to announce that we have a new member in our midst." Directing attention to the back row, he motioned for the stranger to stand. "I'd like you to meet Tyler Harris, son of one of my oldest friends. He's just inherited his grandfather Rafferty's farm in Sweet Valley and moved back from New York. He'll be attending services regularly. I know you'll all want to give him a taste of real Pennsylvania hospitality and make him feel welcome. Again, thank you all for coming to worship in spite of the weather. The Lord bless you all." With an upraised arm, he dismissed everyone and made his way toward the door, where he always shook hands with the congregation.

Holly watched the people approach Tyler Harris, who stood impeccably dressed in a store-bought brown tweed suit. The single women especially seemed eager to linger and chat, and as he talked, a chorus of titters would follow his every smile.

Typical behavior around a bachelor, Holly thought as she observed them making fools of themselves.

After watching Aunt Priscilla make her way over to the dark-haired newcomer, Holly turned to Beth. "I think it's time to take the children outside, don't you?" Glancing back, she caught Mr. Harris staring after her.

He dipped his head slightly, and his mouth quirked with a polite smile.

"Oh, honestly," she muttered under her breath, "I've never met anyone so forward."

"I think he's kind of cute," her sister teased, "and so do most of the other girls." She smiled shyly at him and lowered her gaze.

"Come on, Beth." Escaping his unwelcome attention, Holly ran with Aaron in her arms to the wagon. Hannah waited alongside while Matthew and Rhon removed the large canvas covering that they'd draped over the wagon before the service. Holly watched as Rhon assisted first his mother, then Beth and Amy Sue.

"Where's Pris?" Matthew asked, pulling Holly's attention to himself.

"I'm sure she'll be along," she answered, handing the baby up to her sister.

"Here, cousin," Rhon said at her elbow.

Startled, Holly jumped.

"Sorry," he said with a nonchalant smile. "Here, I'll help you up." Lacing his fingers together, he lowered his hands.

"My feet are muddy."

"So are mine," he shrugged. "Up."

Her cheeks were flaming, but Holly placed a slipper gingerly into his hands and accepted his boost, and he followed right behind. They chose opposite sides.

Priscilla came hurrying their way. "Mercy," she exclaimed. "Look at all the mud. Sure rained hard while we was at services."

Matthew climbed out and helped her up beside his wife.

"What'd ya think of the new young fella, gal?" Hannah asked her sister.

Priscilla gave a soft chuckle. "Funny ya should ask, gal, when I was jest thinkin' on him. I invited him to Sunday dinner today."

Holly's mouth dropped open, and she glanced at Rhon.

Anger sparked in his eyes. A muscle twitched in his jaw as he turned away.

At home, Priscilla fussed over her cooking as the girls rushed to straighten the house for company. "Be sure an' put a fresh cloth on the table," she said.

Holly tossed her head and mouthed the same words exaggeratedly, her hands on her waist.

Turning, her aunt caught Holly's sour expression. She raised her brows. "An' use the good dishes. We don't want that elegant Mr. Harris to think we ain't got nice things."

Biting back her displeasure, Holly removed a white linen tablecloth from the chest of drawers and shook it out in silence.

"An'," her aunt shook a finger at her, "mind yer manners. I won't abide none o' that poutin'."

Holly stiffened her chin and forced a smile.

"That's better."

"He's coming, Aunt Pris," Beth said in an excited voice, looking out the window. "I see his carriage down the road." Her eyes shined, and she nibbled her lower lip.

Hastily removing her work apron, Priscilla hung it on its peg. "Hurry an' help with the table."

"Yes ma'am." Beth crossed to the corner hutch and removed the company dishes.

Holly finished placing the eating utensils beside the ivory-colored glazed plates as Beth set them out. This would be only the second time they'd used these dishes since she and her sister had come to live there. She admired them as she put the saltcellar on the table. "I think everything's ready." She cast a helpless look at Beth.

Smoothing her emerald linen Sunday dress and giving a pat to her hair, Priscilla opened the door just before Tyler Harris knocked. "Saw ya from the window," she said. "Come in, come in."

"Why, thank you kindly, ma'am." Removing his hat, he held it in his hands. The vee of his mustache widened with his smile, and he smoothly brushed one side of it with the back of a finger.

"I'll take your hat," Beth said, a rosy flush accenting her fair coloring.

Mr. Harris inclined his head with a nod. "Thank you, missy. I don't believe we've met."

"This here's Beth," said their aunt. "My brother's child."

"I'm very pleased to meet you, Beth," he said warmly.

"How do you do," she whispered, lowering her lashes.

"An' that's Holly, his other girl," she added, motioning in her direction. "She's the oldest. I believe I mentioned her earlier. They live with me, now he's gone, God rest his soul."

He smiled at Holly. "Oh yes. I've already had the pleasure of being introduced to this lovely young lady at the fair. Hello again."

"Hello." She smiled tightly and jammed a spoon into the bowl of mashed potatoes.

"Mr. Harris," said Priscilla, "we'd be pleasured if you'd have a seat." She motioned to the threadbare settee and watched as he complied, then she turned. "Beth, go out to the barn an' see if Uncle Ethan's finished cleanin' up for dinner. An' call Amy, too. She's out playin'. I'll help your sister finish up."

"Yes ma'am." Her tone betrayed her reluctance to leave, and she returned with Amy Sue in hand in record time.

Moments later, Ethan stomped off the barn dust at the door and sauntered in. With a nod in the stranger's direction, he removed his boots at the bootjack.

Priscilla sighed. "Ethan, this here's Tyler Harris." She looked at the attractive visitor. "Mr. Harris, my husband, Ethan."

"How do you do, sir," Mr. Harris said, extending his hand as he stood.

Crossing the room, Ethan grasped his hand and pumped it once. "Harris. Glad to meet ya. Saw yer wagon draw up. Fine lookin' pair ya got there."

Smiling, Mr. Harris nodded. "I'm a bit proud of them myself."

"Well, ever'thin's on the table," Priscilla announced, fidgeting with a handkerchief from her pocket. "Let's not let the food git cold. Mr. Harris, take that there chair on the end. Beth, scoot down a bit, so's I can sit by ya."

Oh, wonderful, Holly thought. *That puts me all alone on my side. With him. Well, I just won't look at him, that's all.*

As the family gathered around the table, Priscilla glanced at her husband with another sigh and turned to Tyler Harris. " 'Round here, we let the company do the prayin'," she said.

"Company," Amy Sue echoed, beaming shyly at him.

"Thank you, ma'am. I'd be honored." He bowed his head. "Our gracious God, we do thank you for the kind hospitality of these

folks. We ask you now to bless our food, and the hands that prepared it. Amen." He cocked a smile at Holly.

She felt uncomfortable with his boldness. She turned her attention to Beth.

Her sister mirrored her stare with a puzzled frown.

"Help yourself," said Priscilla, handing their guest a bowl of boiled carrots. "Don't go bein' shy."

Ethan forked a slab of roast pork onto his plate and passed the platter. "Hear tell ya own the Rafferty place now."

"Yes sir, that's right. My grandfather willed it to me. He used to talk about raising some fine horses there. I thought I'd carry on his dream."

"Well, ya have yerself a good piece o' land, anyways."

"I hope so."

"Hope so," Amy Sue echoed.

"An' how's yer wife like yer new place?" asked Priscilla a little sweetly, spooning potatoes onto the little girl's dish.

If Holly's teeth hadn't been clenched, her jaw would have dropped open at Aunt Priscilla's more than obvious question. It wasn't any of her business, Holly thought. She didn't have to pry.

A shadow crossed Mr. Harris' features. "I'm afraid I've been too busy to marry, actually. And I wasn't in a position to consider it. Until now." He forked a chunk of meat into his mouth and chewed slowly.

"Oh. Well, a prosperous young man such as yerself won't be alone fer long. Not around here."

The hint of a smile on her aunt's satisfied face was not lost on Holly. A vague feeling of dread began to surface deep inside.

Aaron cried from the bedroom, and Holly rose.

"Sit down," Pris ordered in her no-nonsense tone. "Let Beth tend the baby."

Engrossed in the visitor, Beth glanced at her aunt and stood up with a perplexed expression. "Oh. Excuse me." She tossed a frown of disappointment back at Holly from the doorway of the children's room.

Holly raised her shoulders in a helpless shrug. It shouldn't have made a difference which of them had tended the baby, Holly reasoned. What had gotten into Aunt Priscilla, anyway?

"This sure is tasty, Miz Quinn," Tyler Harris said, turning

politely to Priscilla. "I appreciate your kind invitation. You have a fine family."

She nodded. "The girls is a big help. An' we like to git to know our neighbors. 'Specially the new ones, such as yerself."

Turning to Holly, Mr. Harris smiled. "So, Miss Holly. Are you in school?"

She forced down a mouthful of food. "No. I'm helping Aunt Priscilla at home."

"The gals is more needed 'round here," Ethan stated.

"Some people think schooling is very beneficial, you know," Mr. Harris retorted evenly. "Even for young ladies like Holly and Beth. City schools are including all children, now, in their programs."

At least he approves of schooling for girls, Holly thought; he must have some other good qualities as well. "My mama taught me to read and write. Her father was a schoolteacher, you see. I have all her books, and I read whenever I can." She lifted her chin. "Beth and I have both had some schooling in town, though," she blurted defiantly.

"Oh, I see."

"Well," Priscilla said, rising to clear the table. "Think we'll have some pie, now. I can use some help with the coffee, Holly girl."

"Yes, Aunt Pris."

Some time later, Holly and Beth cleared the table while Ethan and Priscilla showed Tyler Harris around the farm.

"I'm glad he's gone," Holly confessed.

Beth looked at her quizically. "You are? Why? He seems awfully nice. Handsome, mysterious . . . but you sure act strange around him."

"I don't know him, that's all. It makes me uneasy not to know what a person is thinking. But, know what?" She paused, hoping to control the tremor in her voice.

Beth tilted her head.

"I think I know what Aunt Pris is thinking, and I'm really afraid of that."

"We sure do hope you'll come callin' again," Priscilla said, walking Tyler Harris to his fine carriage while Ethan stayed behind in the barn to milk the cow.

"Why, I'd like that, Miz Quinn. Truly." He climbed onto the leather seat. "It was real kind of you and your husband to have me to dinner. I don't have any relatives in the area, you see. And you made me feel quite at home."

Priscilla felt her face warm. "Well, we'd be pleasured to have ya come by anytime. An' ya might enjoy gettin' to know our niece Holly better, too. She's a fine girl. Right friendly, an' all. Ya could call on her, if ya like."

Tipping his head thoughtfully, he reached for the reins. "Thank you kindly. I just might do that. Good evening." With a flick of the leather, he pulled away.

Priscilla nodded to herself in satisfaction as she watched him leave, then she turned and walked toward the house, a slow smile spreading her cheeks.

A chorus of tree frogs shrilled their song into the dark night. Matthew closed the corral gate and turned to face his wife. "Look, Hannah. You've had a bee in your bonnet since I got home from the valley, and I don't know what you're so worked up over. I really don't see the problem here."

"Then you're blinder 'n a fence post," Hannah said with disdain. "Them two ain't kids no more. I'm seein' all sorts of strange looks pass between 'em. We gotta do somethin' to prevent 'em from gittin' any closer."

Matthew ran his fingers through his graying hair and shifted his weight to his strong leg. He looked deep into his wife's eyes, but saw no compromise there. He knew he never would. "Well, Zed did ask the boy to go out for a visit. I'd be hard pressed without him helpin', bein' good workin' weather, and all. But I'll see if I can get him to give it some thought."

Hannah smiled triumphantly.

6

Holly leaned on her elbows against the bedroom window and stared blankly as rivulets of rain distorted the landscape. Rhon hadn't been by for days, and even his house was hidden from view by the sodden maple at the edge of the yard.

A nearby rustle announced her sister's presence as Beth tapped gently on her shoulder. "Holly?"

She turned with a sigh.

"Would you try this on?" Beth held out an indigo batiste dress she had been altering.

With a grimace, Holly shook her head. "I said I didn't want to use any more of Mama's things, remember?"

An amber braid fell forward over Beth's shoulder as she nodded, and her moist eyes sparkled in the window light. "But Aunt Pris says you need some nice things for church and the like."

"I don't see why my clothes should seem so important to her all of a sudden. She never cared before if we had any clothes at all."

"Well, *I* think you should be glad about it." A pout crinkled Beth's thin nose. "At least *you're* getting some new dresses to wear, you know."

Holly felt that guilty flush rise in her cheeks. She let her gaze wander over the dark blue frock. Her mother had only worn it a few times, and it was almost like new. Lovingly she fingered the white piping and lace on the bodice and remembered how pretty it had looked against her mother's shiny brown hair and ivory skin. *Oh, Mama,* she thought wistfully, *how proud you looked the day you finished it.*

"Come on, Holly, try it on, so I can see what else I need to do to it."

"Oh, all right," Holly moaned. "We're supposed to obey our elders, and I guess that includes Aunt Pris, too." Unbuttoning her plain cotton work dress, she slipped it off her arms and down over her slim hips.

"I sure hope it fits. Bustles are out of style, so I shortened the back, but I still have to fix the sleeves." Beth held the garment up while her sister pulled it on and smoothed it over herself. Then she stepped back to admire her work. Her mouth fell open.

Holly tilted her head. "What's wrong?"

Beth's hand rose to her throat. "You . . . You look just like Mama!"

Frowning, Holly turned and crossed to the mirror above the dressing table. The reflection that met her eyes caused her to blink and look again. Only by chance had she braided her dark hair and wrapped it in a coronet around her head to keep it out of the way while she cleaned cupboards. Now it was as if a young version of her mother were staring back from the glass. She reached out to touch the image, then realized what she was doing and pulled back her hand. "I . . . I don't think I want to wear this one, Beth. Anyway," she added, fingering the sleeves which bloused out at the elbow and were gathered again at the wrist, "no one wears these any more."

"But I can fix them, you'll see," Beth said. "I'll take them out and make them short and puffy."

Holly turned and smiled thinly. It was hard not to appreciate her sister's hard work. "You know, if I'd have spent at least half as much time practicing my stitches as I did tagging along after Uncle Zed and Rhon outdoors, I'd be doing my own sewing." She didn't speak for a moment. "It did feel strange, seeing myself like that."

With an odd little smile, Beth nodded. "Daddy always thought you favored Mama, but I never really noticed how much until now." Her voice grew wistful. "I thought she was the most beautiful woman in the whole world."

Holly stepped nearer to the looking glass and examined her reflection with a critical eye. "But a lot of Mama's beauty came from inside. I could never be that good."

"Oh, I don't know. We're supposed to be the best we can be, Daddy said."

"But he's not here. We have to make our own way in this world now. And that's kind of hard to do." Holly removed the dress and shook out the wrinkles. "It wouldn't be if we were rich."

With an indulgent shake of her head, Beth raised her brows. "I'm beginning to think you really mean that."

Holly shrugged. "You were right about one thing, though," she said, putting her old dress on again. "I shouldn't be getting all the new clothes." She took Beth by the shoulders and pushed her toward the mirror. "You're getting almost as tall as me. And," she continued, flicking a teasing glance at her sister's chest, "you're even starting to turn into a young lady."

Beth's cheeks betrayed her obvious embarrassment. She crossed her arms over her blouse self-consciously. "So?"

"So, little sister, my clothes should about fit you now. If you want to wear any of them, I don't mind."

"Oh," Beth gasped. "Then I guess I should stop being mad at you, huh?"

Holly giggled. One quick little jab sent her sibling sprawling down across the bed.

Rhon stroked Nan's rust-colored coat with the grooming brush until she glistened just like Bert in the lantern light in the next stall. Hearing his father's footsteps nearing the barn door, he leaned against the gate and relaxed, one ankle crossed over the other.

Matthew stomped the mud from his boots and set down a crate from the shed. He dusted his hands on his trousers. "Was just going through the things Zed left behind."

"Oh?"

"Yep." From his pocket he removed a handkerchief and rubbed it back and forth across his nose, then stuffed the cloth back into place. "Don't know how he's gettin' by without some of 'em. Been givin' it any thought, about goin' out to Cheyenne to see him?" He coughed nervously.

With a frown, Rhon closed Nan's gate. "Now and again." He cocked his head. Why did it feel as though he had little choice in the matter? "He'd probably rather see you, you know. After all, you're his brother."

His father studied him for a moment then idly picked up a rope from the floor and began wrapping it around an end post in neat, precise loops. He cleared his throat. "But you're freer than I am, son. Don't you see that? And this'd be a good time to go, too, before winter."

Grimacing, Rhon cast a glance up toward the sloped ceiling and back. "But how would you get by without me, Pa? It's all

we can do to keep up with the orders for shingles now, not to mention the barrels and buckets that folks always need."

Matthew averted his gaze. "Well, we're caught up for now. And you wouldn't have to stay a year, you know, just a few weeks. Just time enough to have a good visit, maybe help him out some, get a feel for the place."

Rhon shook his head. "Costs money for train fare, you know. And we just spent a passel on supplies." He reached past his father for the hayfork.

Matthew handed it to him, looked him straight in the eyes, and said, "We'll get by." He squeezed his son's shoulder.

Turning back toward the horses, Rhon brushed the old straw away from the stalls. Why did his father seem so set on sending him away? He opened his mouth to ask, but when he glanced over his shoulder, he was alone.

Two days later the large, dark clouds broke up and drifted eastward over the mountains. In the sun's shining warmth, steam rose from the water-laden trees, and the deep puddles evaporated rapidly.

Holly blew the hair from her eyes as she rubbed a flour-sack kitchen towel over the washboard then put it into the rinse water. She scrubbed the next item. It would take her until dinner to finish the laundry that had accumulated during the rainy spell. And she hadn't even had her quiet time in the glade yet, the only part of the day that was her own, away from the noise and endless chores. She looked toward the porch, where Beth sat playing with the youngsters. "I sure could use some help down here," she said pointedly.

"Oh." Guiltily, Beth ducked her head. "The baby goes down for his nap in a few minutes. I'll come then."

Holly smiled and wrung out the things in the rinse tub. Then, stepping gingerly across the soggy ground, she carried the basket to the clothesline. Jenny Spencer had been quick to let everyone know about the fancy washing machine they'd bought from Sears, Roebuck ages ago. Although Holly had never let on to Jenny, she'd heard about all the incredible things it could do. As she hung the wash, she tried to imagine what it must be like to own such a wonder. Surely a machine like that would cost a fortune. All rich people probably had those machines, though. With a sigh

she picked up the empty basket.

Beth came out to the washtubs just then, a kerchief tying back her shoulder-length hair. She glanced toward the porch. "Amy Sue, you play with your dolly until I finish helping with the wash. If you're good, I'll take you for a walk after a while."

"Walk. Goody," the tot said. Sitting on the steps with her legs curled under her, she clumsily began taking off the doll's clothes.

"I finished the blue dress for you," Beth said as they started to wash the next pile of clothes.

"Oh, thank you, Bethy. I'll try it on after chores."

Immersing a stained pinafore into the sudsy water, Holly squeezed it in her fingers, then rubbed it together. The sound of an approaching wagon carried on the breeze. She looked down the lane, where a dappled horse came into view, pulling the now-familiar black carriage with red-spoked wheels. "Fudge. Tyler Harris. I wonder what he wants." Hurriedly, she dried her hands. "Listen, I'm going to the necessary so that I don't have to be the one who talks to him. I'll be back soon as he's gone."

Frowning, Beth shrugged and watched her sister run out of sight. She did not understand Holly at all. The young, handsome Mr. Harris was not the worst of those who could be calling. Trying to still the quickening beats of her heart, she turned her attention to the nearing visitor.

"Good day, Miss Beth," Mr. Harris said. He smiled warmly as he stopped the rig and stepped down with obvious care not to soil his gleaming boots. He reached for a parcel on the floor of the buggy. "Your Aunt Priscilla at home, perhaps?"

"Yes, Mr. Harris," Beth whispered breathlessly, wiping her hands on her apron. "I'll tell her you're here."

"Thank you, miss."

She smiled coyly then ran up the steps, watching Amy Sue peer at the man from behind the rails. The front door gave an embarrassing squeak as Beth went inside.

The door hinge screeched even louder when she followed Aunt Priscilla out again. Beth cringed, wondering what the elegant Mr. Harris thought of their sad, ramshackle house.

"Well, I'll be," her aunt said, beaming as she patted her straggly hair with one hand. "If it ain't Mr. Harris. Sorry Ethan's off huntin' today, or he'd come to greet ya too."

Doffing his black bowler, Tyler Harris mounted the steps and

bowed gallantly. "Well, good day to you, Miz Quinn. And please, call me Tyler. I was going through some things at my farm and came across something I wanted you to have. Here," he said, holding out a wrapped package, "in appreciation of the wonderful Sunday dinner I shared with you. I shall never forget it."

"Weren't nothin' special . . . Tyler," Priscilla said, her round face still aglow. Suddenly taking note of Beth's presence and obvious interest, she nudged her arm. "Get on with your chores, now."

"Yes ma'am." Beth smiled at Mr. Harris, and his mouth broadened into a grin. She hurried past him toward the tubs, but strained to hear as he continued his conversation with her aunt.

"That's where I disagree, my good lady. You made me feel right at home from the start. Please, accept this humble gift in return." He handed the package to her.

Even from the side yard Beth could see her aunt's expression of pleased shock as she opened the wrapping and drew out a fine linen tablecloth with a woven lace border. "Oh, it's the purtiest thing I ever seen." She looked up at him. "I couldn't." Wrapping and all, she hugged it against her ample bosom.

"Nonsense. I've no use for such a thing myself, on my own and all. But it would give me pleasure to know it graced the table of such a good neighbor."

Priscilla beamed. "Well, that's right generous of ya. We'd be pleased to have ya come to supper again tonight, seein' as you're here already," she said, raising her eyebrows hopefully.

He smiled. "Oh, I'm afraid I have another commitment this evening. But, I was hoping to take your niece for a drive this afternoon." He glanced around. "Is she here?"

"Well. . . ." Priscilla stepped to the edge of the porch and searched in every direction, her hands on her hips. "She was here jest before ya come. Don't know where she might'a gone to. It's the durndest thing. Hol-ly," she shrilled, the second syllable nearly an octave higher than the first. "Hol-ly!"

Beth tried to appear nonchalant as her aunt sent a questioning gaze in her direction. She turned her head and pretended to look for her sister, then she shrugged.

"Hmph." Aunt Priscilla frowned. Her expression softened as she turned back to her visitor. "Well, I don't rightly know where the girl's disappeared to. She's always goin' off by herself like

that. I'll give her a good talkin' to once she's back."

"Oh, don't bother, Miz Quinn. It was an idea I had on the spur of the moment. There'll be other opportunities, I'm sure."

"Jest the same, I'm sorry the girl put ya out. But, say . . . ya could come in the morning an' drive her to church, if ya like."

"Splendid." Tipping his dark head, he drew a small packet from his inside breast pocket. "I brought this along for the three lovely young ladies of the house. I'll trust you to distribute the contents for me."

Priscilla smiled and put the package with the tablecloth she already held in her arm.

Tyler Harris bowed slightly. "See you then. Good day. My best to Mr. Quinn." He turned on his heel and strode back to his buggy. With a wave he pulled away, smiling warmly at Beth as he circled the horse.

Priscilla stared after him, her mouth agape.

"Oh my," Beth whispered as she wrung out the shirt she'd been washing. "What's Holly going to say about this?"

Fingering the five-dollar cash prize he had won at the fair, Rhon took one more turn around Ryman's General Store deciding what to purchase for his trip. He barely noticed the tinkle of the bell above the door as it opened and closed. He kept going back to the row of shiny folding knives inside a glass case, trying to choose the one that would be the handiest. As he perused the selection, he noticed a perfect ivory cameo in a tiny box to the right of the knives. It would look lovely on Holly with its rich black velvet ribbon against her throat, he thought. "I'll take the necklace, Mr. Ryman," he said. "Put it with the rest. I'll see what else I need."

The jovial storekeeper nodded. "Take your time."

In a swish of frothy ruffles, Jenny Spencer sidled up to him. "Hi, Rhon," she said sweetly. "I saw you from Daddy's window next door and thought I'd come and say hello."

"Hi, Jenny." He quirked a smile at the sight of her. In filmy pale lavender, she looked dolled up enough for the weekly barn dance, he thought and wondered if she even owned any everyday clothes.

"What brings you to town?" she asked.

"Nothing much. I'm just taking a trip, and I have to pick up

a few things."

A frown clouded Jenny's soft features. She twisted a red-gold curl around a graceful finger. "Will you be away long?"

"No. But I'm in kind of a hurry right now. Mind if I talk to you about it when I get back?"

"Not at all," she answered, but her disappointment was obvious. "Don't let me keep you. Have a good trip, Rhon." With a forced smile she walked nonchalantly around the store, lingering near the glass display case by the register before making her way over to the fabric bolts.

Rhon watched her for a moment, then turned, and his gaze fell upon a new doeskin jacket hanging on a stand against one wall. He thought of the worn sleeves of his brown wool coat and knew it would be entirely unsuitable for a summer trip. Drawing out the money his father had given him, he added the cost of his train fare to the other items he'd picked out. There just wasn't quite enough, he realized. He'd have to eliminate something. With a regretful sigh, he took the jacket to the register. "I've changed my mind about the necklace, Mr. Ryman. I'll take this instead."

Teeth clenched, Holly paced back and forth beside the stream, her hands on her waist. She huffed. Why had Aunt Pris arranged for Tyler Harris to take her to church in the morning? It wasn't fair. She didn't even know him. Shaking her head, she paced even faster, almost tripping on a small rock in her path. She kicked it, and her slipper flew off. She snatched off the other slipper and threw it after its mate. That ridiculous action made her giggle and relax slightly. With a sigh, she turned and walked more calmly along the edge of the water, trying to gather her thoughts.

The indigo dress she'd been trying on when Aunt Priscilla had told her about tomorrow rustled with each step. She looked down at the delicate lace on the bodice as small bits of sunlight danced over it. Beth had matched the now-fashionable sleeves with the same trim that she'd taken from the extra frills of the bustle. Her sister should be wearing the new gown after all her hard work. *Oh, Bethy, what would I do without you?*

"Lose something, cousin?"

Holly spun around and found Rhon relaxed against the boulder, dangling her slippers from two fingers. Her heartbeat quickened. "I didn't hear you come up."

His green eyes twinkled with obvious mirth. "Now aren't you a pretty sight."

Her expression eased, and Holly tilted her head and curtsied. "Beth fixed it for me. Do you like it?"

He nodded and set her shoes down.

"Thank you." She examined him more closely. "You have on a new shirt. That shade of green goes nicely with your eyes. What brings you by?" She noticed that his jeans were new also and his boots had been shined. Apprehension surfaced within her. "Um . . . we're all dressed up. Are we going somewhere?"

Rhon gazed off into the distance for a moment, then shrugged a shoulder nervously and turned back. "One of us is. I hoped I'd find you here. I . . . came to say goodbye."

Holly gasped and she stared at him.

"Pa wants me to take Uncle Zed's things out to him in Cheyenne. I'm leaving at first light."

Struggling to remain composed, Holly pressed her fingers against her lips, then flung her hand away. "Oh. Wonderful. Just wonder—" She burst into tears.

In two strides, Rhon stood before her. Gently he took hold of her shoulders. "Hey, what's wrong? I'm only going for a few weeks, you know. It isn't like it's forever."

Holly lifted her damp lashes. "Oh, yes it is. Mama and Daddy expected to return when they went away, you know. I didn't want Uncle Zed to leave, but that didn't stop him. And now you. Who else is left? Beth? I guess I'm lucky that she's younger than me." Pulling out of his grasp, she turned her back and hugged her upper arms, her eyes downcast.

Rhon hesitated before responding. Then, lifting a lock of hair from her neck, he toyed with it as he tipped his head around and grinned. "I take it this was not an especially good day for you, huh?"

With an exaggerated sigh, Holly ran her tongue across her lips and shook her head sadly, her eyes brimming. "One of the most terrible of my whole life, if you must know."

"Sorry I had to make it worse."

She brushed away her tears and sniffed, then smiled sheepishly. "Oh, it isn't you. You always make my day better, somehow. Your news was just the last straw."

"Want to tell me about it?"

Averting her gaze, Holly debated whether or not to confide in him. Would it do any good if he knew that Tyler Harris seemed to have his cap set for her? Could he do anything about it? There was no point in spoiling his trip. "No," she quietly answered.

Rhon searched her face. A heavy ache flooded his insides. She'd never kept a secret from him before. He could feel her slipping away, and he didn't know how to stop it. Could he bear it if he learned that someone was going to take his place in her life, that he would no longer be included in all her private thoughts and dreams? What would it be like to be shut off from her forever? He let out a hopeless sigh and cleared his throat. "Well, I guess I should get back. Finish packing, and all."

She nodded. "I suppose."

"Bye, cousin." On impulse, he drew her into his arms for a quick hug. "Keep safe."

"I will. You, too."

But she didn't let go. Instead, she rose up on her toes. "This is for Uncle Zed," she whispered, kissing his cheek.

Rhon felt his heart lurch inside his chest. He could barely resist the overwhelming impulse to crush her to his chest.

"And this is for you." She brushed her flower-soft lips on his, smiled through new tears, and backed out of his arms. "God be with you." Stooping to retrieve her shoes, she ran back toward the Quinn house.

His pulse pounded crazily in his ears as he watched her leave. He swallowed the lump in his throat and stared long after the far boundary of the trees that hid her from view. Then, shoulders sagging, he turned for home. The ivory cameo would have looked lovely on Holly, he thought. He should've bought it for her. Why did he have to go?

But even as he asked the question, deep inside he knew the answer.

Beth held up her hand, and the rainbow of ribbons trailed from her slim fingers. "I've never seen anything so pretty."

Holly glared silently and pulled on her nightdress.

"Don't you think they're beautiful, Holly? It's been forever since we've had new ribbons for our hair. And now to have so many colors to choose from!" She sighed loudly. "I love this rose-colored one. I'm going to sleep in it. And even Amy Sue

wanted me to tie a green ribbon in her hair at bedtime." She plopped down on her feather pillow in a dramatic swoon.

"Yes, they're pretty," Holly said grudgingly.

"It was thoughtful of Mr. Harris to buy them for us, don't you think?"

With a nod, Holly yanked the brush through her hair and began to plait it for night.

The younger girl sat up cross-legged on the counterpane. "Why don't you like him? I think he's quite dashing. And I love the color of his eyes."

Holly closed her eyes against the memory of Tyler Harris's piercing gray ones, then opened her own again. She rose and leaned forward on her toes. "You know," she said in a conspiratorial tone, "he's not really a man at all. In truth he's a . . . a fidgety rabbit that some evil witch cast a spell on. Now he has to spend his days calling on every pretty girl he can find. And everywhere he hops, he has to bring presents," she said making a wide gesture. "Hundreds of fine presents! Thousands of them!"

Beth giggled.

The smile on Holly's face slowly faded. She tied the bow at her neckline. "He must be at least twenty-seven, you know."

"Really?" Beth answered dreamily. "How romantic, to attract an older man." Putting the bouquet of satin strands on the bedside table, she unbuttoned her dress and changed into a nightgown. She tied her hair back at the nape of her neck with the dusky pink ribbon, studying her reflection in the mirror with a critical eye. She pinched her cheeks and thrust out her chest, then, with a dismal pout, stepped back. "I couldn't imagine any of the clumsy, awkward boys we know coming to call."

Holly cast her sister a miserable gaze. "Oh, Bethy, the problem is I'm not ready for *anyone* to come calling right now. I have so much to think about. I can hardly find the words to pray about it. I'm all mixed up."

"About what?"

Holly shrugged. How could she tell her sister that it wasn't really Tyler Harris who bothered her at all. It was her new feelings for Rhon. How could Beth possibly understand, when Holly didn't understand them herself?

With a sympathetic smile, Beth nodded. "Then I'll say a prayer for you tonight. At least you're watching what you say these days.

That's one good thing." She knelt beside the bed and bowed her head.

Holly watched her absently for a moment, then reached under the bed for her journal. Yes, she was ever so careful not to blurt out impulsive things nowadays. Her thoughts went back to the glen, and she warmed with the remembrance. *And this is for you*, she had said. Rhon had gone white with surprise, and her own feet had almost turned to lead. She'd never know how she had been able to pull herself out of his arms. She could still feel his heart, strong and fast, thundering against hers. Swallowing, she opened her book.

> Tyler Harris came by this afternoon. He brought some beautiful ribbons for each of us girls and was very polite. In the morning he's coming to drive me to church. I hope tomorrow never comes.

The words blurred before her eyes as a tear splashed onto the page.

> And Rhon's going away.

7

"Hol-ly." Priscilla's shrill call reverberated up the staircase. "Mr. Harris come to fetch ya to church."

Holly closed her eyes for a second. If only her aunt hadn't arranged this. She cast a frightened glance at Beth.

The younger girl, buttoning the front of her yellow muslin dress, raised her head. "He seems really nice, you know," she whispered with a sad smile. "Just be polite. Remember," she added with a playful wrinkle of her nose, "he's only a rabbit."

As she reached for her Sunday bonnet and tied it on, Holly couldn't help but smirk over the rabbit remark. She gazed at Beth one last time, then hurried down the steps, wishing she might turn an ankle or something. But childhood summers in the woods with her uncle and Rhon had made her too sure-footed for that. She stepped onto the landing.

"There ya are." Priscilla grabbed Holly's forearm and tugged her into the dilapidated parlor. She sneaked a glance toward the overstuffed settee, where Tyler Harris sat stiffly at one end. Ethan slumped in the big, worn chair to the right. "See? She most always comes on the first call."

Mr. Harris rose and inclined his head with a friendly smile. "Good morning, Miss Holly."

Aunt Priscilla frowned slightly and jabbed Holly with a sturdy elbow.

"G—Good morning," she said nervously.

With an angry, dark scowl on his unkempt face, Uncle Ethan narrowed his eyes and rubbed the stubble on his chin with work-hardened fingers.

Tyler Harris cleared his throat. "Lovely day, isn't it?" he said pleasantly, striding to the stairs and offering his arm.

"Yes." Tentatively Holly placed her fingertips on his tweed sleeve and swallowed. "Lovely."

"We'll be off, then," he said with a bow of his head toward the lady of the house, then one to Ethan. "Goodbye, Miz Quinn,

Mr. Quinn." He opened the door and held it for Holly.

Priscilla glowed with satisfaction. "Ya have a good drive, now. We'll be along ourselfs in jest a few shakes o' the cat's tail."

Her aunt's butchery of the old saying in front of the obviously cultured young man sent a twinge of embarrassment through Holly. She was relieved to step outside.

A mild breeze caught the trailing ribbons on the back of her bonnet and ruffled them softly against her curls. The shiny black carriage stood in readiness at the end of the front path, and Holly felt a flicker of excitement at the thought of riding in such elegance. As Mr. Harris assisted her up the step and onto the rich leather seat, she caught a glimpse of Beth at their bedroom window and forced a smile toward her.

Donning his buff felt hat, Mr. Harris climbed in beside her and gave a soft snap to the reins.

Holly gripped the side of the seat, her fingers making indentations in the upholstery. She inhaled a shaky breath and hoped she wouldn't embarrass herself by babbling, or even worse by not being able to think of anything to say.

Mr. Harris's arm brushed against hers lightly as he turned the horse. "You look quite beautiful this morning, Holly. May I call you that?"

She glanced at him and quickly looked away. She nodded.

"Good. Then you must call me Tyler."

"I . . . I couldn't."

"Don't be silly. Of course you can. Don't you call your other friends by their first names?" A teasing note muted the huskiness of his voice.

Cautiously, Holly looked at him again, more fully this time. She saw no threat in his deep-set gray eyes or in his pleasant manner. Perhaps, in time, they might become friends. "Yes."

He smiled and his mustache splayed with the movement of his firm, well-shaped lips. "Good."

The buggy traveled faster, yet far more smoothly, than those she was accustomed to; its red-spoked wheels made only a slight crunch over the ground. When they passed the worn, narrow lane to the Banister farm, Holly couldn't stop herself from gazing toward the house for some sign of Rhon's presence. Uncle Matthew and Aunt Hannah were just getting into their wagon. Shadow stood at their feet, his black feathery tail wagging. But there was

no Rhon. Unconsciously she sighed.

Tyler Harris followed her gaze. "Good friends of yours?"

Holly turned her head to look forward. "My aunt and uncle. The Banisters."

"Oh. I think I've met them at services. Are they related to that young man with the same name who accompanied you to the fair that day?"

"Rhon?" Holly tried unsuccessfully to prevent the warm glow that took swift possession of her face. "They're his parents. He and I grew up together."

"Hm. You're cousins, then. He gave the impression that . . . . Well, no matter. You're very fortunate to have family nearby."

She nodded and wished she could think of something intelligent to say as they went down one small hill and up another through the woods, but her thoughts kept drifting to Rhon. How many miles already separated them? she wondered. How many interminable weeks would pass before his return? Becoming conscious of her grip on the side of the seat, she relaxed her hand and idly tapped a finger on her skirt while watching the scenery. She had never realized before that such an incredible distance lay between her church and home.

At long last she thought of something to say. "Do you have any family around here, Mr. . . . um . . . Tyler?" she corrected.

"No, my grandfather was the only one who settled in this area, and that was just a few years before my grandmother passed on. I haven't been in these parts for years. I've been living up north."

"Oh."

"Yes. A remote little settlement in a northern corner of New York. New Thomasville. You've probably never heard of it."

Tyler stifled a smile as he saw Holly shake her head. She looked quite fetching this morning in her dark blue gown, he thought. Even though he could feel her tenseness, he was hopeful that she'd soon begin to warm toward him. Most of the other young ladies in the area already had, but he had found their endless babble to be silly and tiresome. However, being the object of such a flurry of interest was a new experience for him—that and having enough money to buy anything he wanted, after apprenticing in a leather shop for the last few years and existing on his earnings.

He glanced in Holly's direction. Neither she nor her enchanting younger sister prattled on like the others, fawning over him and

batting their lashes. In fact, at the moment, this young lady even seemed distracted. Strange that she had blushed at the mention of her cousin's name, he thought. Young Rhon Banister had made him feel like an unwelcome intruder into their own private world that day he'd first seen them together at the fair. Yet they were just cousins, weren't they?

Holly saw a few heads turn their way as the carriage drew up before the whitewashed meetinghouse.

Tyler jumped out, offering Holly a well-groomed hand. Lightly grasping his fingers, she was surprised at their cool firmness; they were not the sort of hands obtained in running a sawmill, she thought. She lifted a curious gaze toward him, catching the shock on Jenny Spencer's pouty face just beyond his shoulder.

For one brief second Holly felt like giggling. Never before had she been in a position to make prissy Jenny envious. She mentally surveyed the attractive, well-mannered gentleman at her side who spoke intelligently and carried himself with grace. Except for a small scar that marred the center of one dark eyebrow, his features were amazingly flawless. His deep-set, clear gray eyes contrasted with his immaculately kept black hair, and his nose and chin were perfectly proportioned. Assessing his fine brown tweed coat and sharply pressed chestnut trousers, Holly wondered if she looked elegant enough in her made over dress. Maybe this wouldn't be such a bad day after all, she thought. She smiled to herself and held her head high as they mounted the steps.

Reverend Dixon beamed at them from the top step and, extending a chubby hand, clasped Tyler's warmly. "Good morning, lad, good to see you." He nodded at Holly. "And Holly, my dear. Welcome. The service will begin shortly."

Tyler nodded and opened the door, escorting Holly to a middle pew.

As they took their seats, Jenny and Maybelle sashayed into the empty row just behind them and sat a bit to Holly's right, whispering and tittering.

"Oh, Jenny, I just love your new dress," Maybelle gushed.

"Do you? My aunt sent it from Philadelphia."

Holly glanced slightly to the right, and out of the corner of her eye she noticed shiny blue taffeta ruffles edged with pink satin.

"And that cameo," Maybelle continued, "is that new, too?"

Jenny's tinkling laugh grated across Holly's nerves like a rake across gravel. Jenny's voice became syrupy sweet as she said, "Actually, Rhon Banister bought it yesterday when he came to town."

Holly's heart lurched.

"Oh, how exciting. He's such a dream," Maybelle whispered.

"I know. He said he wants to talk to me when he comes back from the Wyoming Territory. I can hardly wait."

Holly's spirits sank. Closing her eyes against the pain inside, she drew a shaky breath, then lifted her chin and looked up again.

A few moments later, Beth and the rest of the family came in and entered a pew directly opposite Holly and Tyler. Beth sat down and glanced at Holly. She forced a smile and turned her face toward the front of the sanctuary.

With the usual flourish, Miss Penelope pumped the organ and played the call to worship, all the while adoringly gazing toward the pastor, her cheeks aglow.

Reverend Dixon took his place at the pulpit. "Good morning, everyone. Let us bow in prayer . . . ."

Rhon dozed fitfully in the monotonous clicketyclack of the steel wheels upon the train tracks. If this trip had come up at any other time in his life—a year ago, even a month ago—he'd have been caught up in the excitement. But going away now seemed all wrong. If his father hadn't seemed so all-fired anxious for his Uncle Zed's crate to be delivered by him personally, they could've just shipped the fool thing and been done with it. But there was nothing to do now but see it through.

He stared out the window of the wooden passenger car. This part of Ohio looked much like Pennsylvania, with its lush woods and rolling hills. Soon autumn would paint the mountains with all the bright shades of the palette. Autumn was his favorite time of year, even though he and Holly no longer compared their annual leaf collections as they had throughout their childhood.

He yawned and shifted positions on the hard bench seat, taking note of the other travelers in the narrow car. He grinned at a thin, freckle-faced little boy about five years old, who sat two seats ahead on the other side of the aisle. When the youngster peeked shyly from between his parents, Rhon smiled to himself and took a chunk of wood and his knife out of his pocket.

Memories of his own youth floated across his mind as he whittled, days when he'd roamed the woods near the farm with Uncle Zed and Holly, the two of them enthralled by Bible stories the gentle man would make as exciting as any yarn. By the hour they would listen to his voice, and all the while Uncle Zed would be whittling some new toy for them.

Thinking again of Holly, he sighed. What a beguiling young woman she had become, sensitive and impulsive, with luminous eyes that haunted his soul. She'd probably gone to church yesterday in that pretty new dress, he surmised. She'd looked so beautiful in it, her hair brushed and shining and tied back with a ribbon to match her gown. And her lips. . . . He'd never touched anything as soft as her lips. Even now he could feel their light imprint on his mouth. Why had fate, in all its cruel ironies, made them related? If ever there were a woman he could envision spending all his days with, caring for, and providing for, it was Holly. He inhaled and exhaled slowly and deliberately, then, with renewed vigor, continued the task before him.

By the time the five-year-old lad had awakened from his nap, Rhon had finished whittling. He smoothed the toy with his fingers and smiled softly. He hoped the boy would like it: a dog in a seated pose, its head slightly tilted, its mouth open in friendly greeting. Removing his neckerchief, he polished it a bit, then glanced two seats forward.

The child met his gaze and ducked out of sight, then one very round eye slowly peered around his mother's arm.

Rhon winked.

The boy blinked back in surprise and giggled.

Grinning, Rhon held out the gift, palm open.

"For me?"

"Sure is, pal."

"Can I, Mama?" he asked, tugging at the sleeve of his mother's dove gray traveling suit.

Nodding, she smiled gratefully at Rhon, and her son jumped down from the seat and dashed over for his treasure. "Thank you." His small fingers closed around the carving.

"My name's Rhon. What's yours?"

"Rusty." Removing his cap, he displayed a mass of soft, short curls. "See? I have red hair."

"Well, mine's a bit on the red side, too," Rhon said with a grin,

doffing the wide-brimmed hat that rested on his auburn head.

Rusty giggled. "We're on va—va—" he looked over at his parents. "What's that word again, Mama?"

"Vacation," she supplied.

"Vacation," he repeated triumphantly. "My Daddy's takin' us to Yellowstone Park."

"You don't say." Rhon patted the empty seat beside him and watched the boy check for permission before hopping onto it. "That's in Wyoming, where I'm headed."

"Are you on va—cation, too?"

"Sort of. I'm going to visit my uncle in Cheyenne. That comes before Yellowstone, but we can be pals until then."

The boy nodded and shifted his attention to his new possession, turning it around and around as he examined it from every angle.

"Like it?" Rhon asked.

He nodded.

"I have a dog who looks just like that. His name is Shadow. We have a lot of fun together."

"Daddy says I can have a puppy someday, when we get back home and move into our new house. I think I'll name him Shadow too." His big eyes glowed as he smiled at Rhon.

A sweet pain tugged at Rhon's heart. They were the same rich chestnut color as Holly's.

While Priscilla poured another cup of coffee for herself, Holly rose to clear the breakfast dishes. Ethan got up at the same time, purposely bumping against her at the corner of the table.

"Oh. 'Scuse me," her uncle rasped, with a chuckle only her ears could hear.

Holly scowled at him and sighed. Why did Aunt Priscilla never see these actions? she wondered. "My fault. I'll have to be more careful." She glanced over her shoulder at Beth, but her sister was busy helping Amy Sue down from the bench. With a bitter shake of her head, Holly watched their uncle go out the door to his chores.

"Be sure to slice off some thin slabs of that beef, Holly," Priscilla said, taking her seat again. "Ethan's goin' wolf huntin' with some o' the other men. He'll need a good lunch. They could be gone for days."

"Yes, Auntie."

Beth crossed to the sink and poured hot water into the tub of dirty dishes. She tied on a work apron and shuddered. "That sounds scary, going after wolves. I'd never do it."

Priscilla sipped her coffee. "Nor me. But somebody has to. Specially in a bad year like this'n."

"Is Uncle Matt going too?" Holly asked, reaching for the kitchen towel.

"Don't rightly know. Usually does."

"It'll be pretty lonely for Aunt Hannah, then," Holly added wistfully, "with both her men away. Maybe I'll run over for a visit."

"Jest don't forget yer chores. After all, Mr. Harris'll be comin' by fer ya after while. Never heard tell of such foolishness. Goin' fer a store-bought meal, when there's decent cookin' to be had right here."

Drying the pewter plates, Holly shrugged. "I think it might be interesting, Aunt Pris. Lots of people eat at restaurants."

"So I hear tell."

Dark clouds were drifting in from the west by midday, and a cool breeze ruffled the trees and made waves across the meadow grasses as Holly ran toward the Banister house. At the edge of the grove she tiptoed, trying to sneak up on the dog. He raised his head and sniffed the breeze, then bounded her way.

Holly knelt to hug his warm furry neck. "Hi, Shad. Lonesome for Rhon, old fellow?" With a kiss to the top of his head, she rose and continued walking. "You're not the only one." He panted along beside her the rest of the way. She mounted the porch steps and opened the door a crack. "Aunt Hannah?"

"In here, Holly girl," came her aunt's high-pitched voice from the next room.

Holly found her atop a chair in the parlor, rehanging the heavy curtains.

"Whew! What a chore." Easing herself down, the older woman wiped her pudgy hands on the sturdy apron that covered her olive cotton dress. "All aired out again."

"My goodness," Holly said with a smile. "You sure do keep a clean house, Aunt Hannah."

"Well, like they say, cleanliness is next to godliness. Can't abide it when things git behind." She pulled off her spectacles

and held them up to the light, then huffed on each lens and wiped them with a handkerchief from her pocket before hooking the gold side pieces behind her ears again. "What brings ya by?"

"Just thought I'd say hello. Uncle Matt off hunting with the others?"

"Yep. Figured he could go fer one day, but no longer. There's too much to be done here to waste time out admirin' the landscape." She untied her apron and tugged it off. "Come on, let's go set in the kitchen. I baked some cinnamon cookies this mornin'."

"I thought I smelled them when I came in."

Once in the next room, Hannah poured a glass of milk and brought it to the table, motioning for Holly to sit down. She took a seat herself on the opposite side and pushed the cookie jar Holly's way.

"Thanks." Neither spoke for a moment. "Sure is quiet here, with everyone gone."

"Yep. I git lots done when I'm by myself."

"Think Rhon will be away long?" asked Holly.

A curious expression crossed her face, and she averted her gaze. "Don't rightly know. Matt told him to see if Zed's needin' any help. Figured the man's prob'ly homesick, 'bout now. A visit'll do 'em both good."

Holly nodded, puzzled over her aunt's seemingly guilty expression. Even her voice sounded strained as she talked, and her speech seemed faster than normal.

"I see you've been keepin' company with that Mr. Harris lately."

"Yes. He's been coming by quite often for supper and taking me to church."

"Must be a hard workin' man, to be havin' such fine horses an' things."

Holly bit into a cookie.

"Ya could do lots worse, ya know, than marry up with the likes a him."

She stared at her aunt with shock. "Who said anything about marriage? I barely know him. We're hardly more than acquaintances."

"Still, he seems pretty regular around here."

Holly shrugged and looked away.

"You're comin' of age, ya know." She tapped a fingertip on

the table.

"Everything's happening so fast, Aunt Hannah," Holly said softly. "When people begin to consider marriage, shouldn't there be something else that's taken into account? Like love?"

"Hmph. Love. It ain't like it tells in books, honey. It ain't a mushy feelin' a'tall. It's a doin' fer somebody. Through good times an' bad. It's puttin' somebody else above yerself an' makin' a good home fer him."

Holly considered her aunt's words. "But Mama and Daddy loved each other. And you and Uncle Matt do too, don't you? I want that kind of marriage. With someone I love more than I do my own life."

Her aunt shrugged. "Sometimes the feelin' don't come till later on, child. But ya shouldn't let a good chance pass ya by." Reaching into the jar, she took out a cookie. "Think on it."

Holly sensed that everyone had conspired together to marry her off, ready or not. Willing or not? She swallowed her last mouthful and drained the glass, then rose and carried it to the sideboard. "Well, thanks . . . for the cookie and all." She stepped back to the table and kissed her aunt's round cheek. "I'd best be getting back."

"Was sweet of ya to come visit, honey."

Holly nodded and headed for the door. Outside, she shivered despite the still mild temperature. She had hoped for some word of Rhon, some date to look forward to for his return. Seeing his sad-eyed dog only made her feel worse. She brushed a lock of hair away from her face, surprised that her fingers were wet with tears.

"Warm enough?" Tyler Harris asked on the drive into town late that afternoon.

Holly nodded. "Yes. Thank you." She drew her shawl closer around her shirred cambric blouse and violet skirt and looked beyond the distant treetops at the ominous, leaden sky. Heavy clouds accelerated the waning of daylight with each mile. Was it dreary in Cheyenne too? she wondered. She sighed unconsciously.

"It appears that we're in for more rain," Tyler said. "By tomorrow for sure."

"I'm afraid you're right."

He reached into his breast pocket and held out a small, thin packet. "I bought you and your sister something."

Surprised, she turned to him and accepted the package. His eyes reflected the dusky sky and held a smile within their depths. The gift felt light in her hands, as though it were nothing except wrapping. Opening one end, she peeked inside, then drew out a pair of exquisite white silk handkerchiefs bordered with intricate lace. "Oh, Tyler. How beautiful! Thank you. I'm sure Beth will love hers." She ran her fingers along the delicate edging.

"It's Belgian lace. Best there is."

Holly searched his face. "Why do you always bring gifts? You really shouldn't, you know."

A smile lifted one side of Tyler's mustache. "Don't you like presents?"

"Of course. Who doesn't? But it brings back memories. Sad ones." She drew a fortifying breath and slid the soft cloths back inside the packet. "When Beth and I were little and our parents went for supplies or out on deliveries, they always came back with something for each of us. Special things they knew that we'd like."

His dark, even brows rose. "Have they been . . . gone long?"

Holly sighed. "Seems like forever." She hesitated for a moment before continuing. "It was March, three years ago. They were hauling a load of shingles across the river to Pittston. The bridge washed away."

"Oh, I'm terribly sorry. I shouldn't have asked. It must have been hard on you, I'm sure, and on your sister especially, being younger."

Hearing the concern in Tyler's voice, tears threatened, and she quickly blinked them away. She gazed into the distance and struggled to compose herself again.

He eased forward on the brake as the buggy began its descent down the last, steep hill into Dallas. "Well, you're a few gifts behind, then, I'd say. Someone has to take up where your folks left off."

Holly shook her head in wonder and smiled.

Moments later the carriage pulled up before Charlotte's Kitchen on Main Street, a low, square building immaculately painted white with dark green trim. Light glowed from the windows despite the early hour.

"We're here, my dear," Tyler said with a smile as he climbed out.

Holly tensed at the endearment and glared his way.

Tyler appeared not to have heard his own words. "I think you'll like this place. I found it to be quite charming." Assisting her down, he led her onto the landing and opened the door.

She stepped inside, blinking against the warm brightness.

Cheerful red-and-white gingham cloths covered the round maple tables, each with a tiny kerosene lamp in the center. The low, dancing flames made shadow patterns on the colored fabric.

Tyler removed his hat and her shawl and hung them both on a rack beside the door. He gestured to a vacant spot next to the front window, then seated her before taking a chair on the opposite side.

"Good evening, Mr. Harris and aren't you Holly Grant?" said the thin, aproned woman who approached them.

Holly looked up into Charlotte Benson's thin face, recognizing her from church, and nodded.

"Well then, how's Pris doin'? She beat me this year at the fair, with that pie of hers, tsk tsk." Wagging her head of dull brown hair back and forth, she smiled good-naturedly. "I'll win that ribbon again come next year, though."

"I'm sure you will," Holly said with a grin.

"Well, what'll you be havin', the two of you?" She looked from one to the other over her narrow, hooked nose.

"We'll have that splendid roast beef of yours," Tyler answered. "And coffee. Do you mind?" he asked Holly.

"Not at all. It sounds lovely." She had had no idea that there'd be more than one choice. It seemed an extravagant waste of food.

"Two roast beef dinners, then," Mrs. Benson said, pivoting on the heels of her serviceable shoes. "You'll have them right quick." She rushed off toward the kitchen, which emitted delectable aromas and cooking sounds.

Holly glanced around the establishment, noticing that there were only two other patrons, an elderly couple she had never seen before.

"Homey little place, isn't it?" Tyler asked pleasantly. "I come here quite often. When I'm not at home, of course."

She smiled, taking a second look at the efficient arrangement of the furniture. Unlike the mishmash at Aunt Priscilla's, every-

thing matched at Charlotte's Kitchen.

Within moments, Mrs. Benson returned. She set a heaping white china plate before each of them. "Here you be. Enjoy your meal. I'll be right back with your coffee."

Tyler nodded. "Thank you kindly, Miz Benson."

"Holler when you're ready for some dessert."

The door opened just then, and the woman turned to greet three newcomers before returning momentarily with two steaming cups of coffee.

"This looks delicious," Holly said after Mrs. Benson walked away. Automatically she bowed her head and clasped her hands.

Tyler cleared his throat. "Almighty God, we do thank you for this fine meal. Amen."

Holly sliced a piece of beef and chewed it slowly. It tasted even better than it smelled, she decided as she sampled the equally delicious mashed potatoes and gravy beside it.

"I knew you'd like it," Tyler said, his gaze penetrating her thoughts.

Embarrassed, she wondered if he also knew that she was still a bit nervous around him and that she worked hard to appear relaxed. His steady gaze was somewhat unsettling. Perhaps it was just his way, she told herself as she sampled the glazed string beans.

"There are a few other places in town that serve good food," he said, setting his cup down. "I'll have to take you around to them. Maybe Beth would enjoy coming along with us sometime."

"Yes, I'm sure she would." Tyler really was a thoughtful person, she thought. Her eyes widened as she tried to imagine making a circuit of all the eating establishments in Dallas, and she reminded herself to act like a lady.

"So tell me about all the years you spent growing up in Huntsville. Didn't you find it rather quiet?" he asked.

Holly lowered her gaze in thought and smiled. "I've always liked quiet places."

"But what did you do all that time as a child? Surely your life now must be quite a bit different from before."

"Yes, it is." She sipped her coffee and set down the cup. "Mostly I loved the outdoors. Uncle Zed took Rhon and me for long walks all the time. He's a great storyteller, and he used to entertain us for hours with stories. He was forever whittling figurines of

animals and birds for us. When he moved out to the Wyoming Territory it was hard for us to accept, after all the time the three of us had spent together. We really missed him." As she looked absently out the window, a sad smile crossed her face.

"Didn't your sister go along too?" Tyler asked.

"Oh, no." Holly tilted her head. "Beth is a homebody. She likes being inside and doing things like sewing. She's much better than I am at that sort of thing, really. I always wanted to be outside with Rhon. And Uncle Zed," she added quickly. "Rhon's visiting him right now." Holly was embarrassed again and took another drink to avoid Tyler's eyes.

In no time at all, Mrs. Benson whisked away their plates and poured second cups of coffee to go along with her fresh blackberry pie. Holly could barely finish hers.

"Did you have enough to eat?" Tyler asked, leaning his head slightly in question.

She nodded and replied, "I couldn't eat another bite. It was scrumptious." She set down her cup and glanced outside. "Oh, dear. Aunt Priscilla expects me home before dark. Perhaps we'd better be going."

"You're quite right. We wouldn't want the dear lady to worry." Taking some coins out of his pocket, Tyler placed several on the table and got up, offering his hand.

Beth burst into the room, breathless from flying up the stairs. Flopping onto the bed, she propped her chin in her cupped hands. "I just put the kids down for tonight, and I'm dying to hear about it. Tell me everything!"

Tying the bow of her nightgown, Holly grinned impishly. She bent forward, brushing her hair in long strokes from the underside. "Well, there's not much to tell."

"Hol-ly," Beth coaxed, her voice drawing out the name like molasses. "Come on. Where did he take you? What did he say? What did you say? Did he . . . kiss you goodnight?"

Laughing, Holly straightened, flipping her sable locks back into place. She leaned her head to one side and stroked that half of her hair. "Actually, we had supper at Mrs. Benson's restaurant in Dallas. It's a cute little place. She has it fixed up real nice."

"Was everything elegant?"

"You mean the food? It was very good, but not fancy. Kind

of like Aunt Priscilla makes, or Aunt Hannah. Tyler goes there because he says it's like home cooking. I had a nice time."

"And?" Beth prompted, her eyebrows rising in slender arches on her forehead.

"And, no, he's far too much of a gentleman to try to kiss me goodnight. He asked about Mama and Daddy, and he brought these." Reaching to the dressing table, Holly passed the silk handkerchiefs to her sister. "One is for you. Choose whichever one you like best."

"Oh," Beth breathed dreamily, considering them both for several moments. Then, placing one on the night stand, she stroked the other along her cheek. "He buys such pretty things. I've never felt anything so soft. He's so nice."

Holly nodded, her expression thoughtful. Was it her imagination or had Beth tucked her own handkerchief under her pillow?

Beth rose and began to undress. "So, do you . . . like him?" A faint pink glow settled over her delicate face, and her eyes widened in question.

A smile tugged at Holly's lips as she stooped for her journal and pencil, then sat on the bed. "Well, I don't hate him, anyway. I suppose that's something." Her fingers opened the book to a blank page, and she began to write.

> Tonight Tyler took me to Charlotte's Kitchen, the first time in my life I've ever eaten in a restaurant. He says he often eats there, but I can't even imagine such a thing. He brought Beth and me more lovely gifts tonight, white silk handkerchiefs with the most fragile lace I've ever seen. He said they came from Belgium. He was a perfect gentleman. Aunt Hannah thinks he wants to marry me. I don't know if I could ever really love him. But at least he seems concerned about us, Beth and me.

Absently, Holly watched as her sister finished dressing for bed and knelt for her nightly prayers as the first light raindrops pattered against the roof.

> Sure wish I could talk to Rhon.

8

The incessant chugging of the Union Pacific locomotive slowed as it pulled into the station at Cheyenne and clanged to a stop in a whoosh of white steam. Rhon picked up his hat on the seat beside him and tucked it under his arm as he stood and made his way toward the door.

He grinned at Rusty as he started past the row where the child sat with his mother. Huge brown eyes brimmed with tears as the lad attempted a brave smile. He jumped down and threw his arms around Rhon's long legs. "Wish you didn't have to go."

Rhon stooped and hugged him hard. "Me too, pal. But you'll have lots of fun at Yellowstone Park, right?"

The curly red-haired boy's head bobbed up and down grudgingly.

"Well, tell you what. While you're there, look at everything twice. Once for you, and once for me. Will you do that?"

Rusty nodded again.

"And be sure to stay with your folks, don't wander off anywhere. Promise?"

With a sniff, the lad smiled. "Promise."

"Good. I hope that someday I have a boy like you." Rhon tousled the soft curls. "Might even name him Rusty."

"And I'll have a dog named Shadow," came the half-laugh, half-sob.

Rhon gave a last strong hug. "Well, goodbye, pal. God be with you."

"Bye, pal."

A throng of people were milling about the depot in clusters, some bestowing laughing, excited hugs of greeting, and others tearful, halting farewell embraces. As Rhon carried his satchel down the steps onto the wooden platform, he noticed that the freight from two cars back was being unloaded onto the landing. He tightened his grip and started in that direction, lifting a hand in passing to touch the rectangular train window where a little

freckled nose flattened against the glass. Cute little tyke, Rhon thought with a smile. Then, turning away, he strode toward the stacked crates.

Just beyond them his eyes picked out a familiar figure, bareheaded and tall, approaching from the other side in typical long, sweeping strides. "Uncle Zed!" Rhon released the bag, and it plopped onto the planks at his feet.

"Greetings, lad." In seconds two strong arms wrapped him so tightly he could barely breathe, and his uncle's big hand thumped him exuberantly on the back. "Welcome to our fair town," he boomed. "Good trip?"

"I'm a little tired from sitting forever. Otherwise it wasn't bad, give or take changing from one line to the next all the time."

"Yep, seems I recall a ride of my own like that." Zed's broad grin deepened the creases alongside his mouth as he let go and stepped back. "Well, I'll say. It's good to see you, boy."

"How'd you know I was arriving today, Uncle Zed?" Rhon asked, raising his brows in question.

His uncle's blue eyes crinkled at the corners. "Didn't. Been meetin' every train for the last week, ever since I got a letter from your pa." He clamped a hand onto Rhon's shoulder and gave an affectionate squeeze, then cast a gaze toward the traveling case at their feet. "This all the luggage you brought?"

"That and your box," he answered. "It's right this way." Grabbing his bag, he turned and led the way to the unloading platform.

Uncle Zed bent and hoisted the heavy chest up onto one shoulder with a grin. "Say, I sure appreciate you bringin' this out. Don't know how in the world I managed to go off without it."

Returning the grin, Rhon glanced around. "Your wagon nearby?"

"Naw. Didn't need one. My place is right up the street." He motioned with his head. "Come on, that's where we're headin'."

The commotion of the train station was nothing compared to the bustle and noise beyond it, Rhon decided. Lazy sunshine warmed the powdery dust coating on the wooden sidewalk and drew misshapen shadows on it as they walked. He noticed the jumble of brick and wooden buildings lining both sides of the wide main street. Luminous white letters advertising "Faro" and "Keno" seemed to decorate every other structure.

Turning his head this way and that as they wove through the strolling crowd, Rhon nearly tripped over a man dozing against

one such place, legs stretched out into the walkway. Raucous laughter and tinkling piano music echoed from inside swinging partial doors. A young woman in a gawdy red dress with a black feathery boa draped casually over her arms smiled suggestively through a large front window. "Not much like Huntsville, huh?" Zed teased.

Rhon's cheeks reddened, and he grinned at his uncle. "I'll say." He took a second look as Zed stopped at the side of the road to wait for a wagon and several men on horseback to go by.

His uncle chuckled. "No shortage of drinkin' spots around here, that's a fact. They entertain cattlemen, miners, and drifters mostly. Sometimes you might see a few Mexes in town, or a scout or two. Once in a while even some soldiers."

"Is there a fort nearby?" Rhon asked.

"Yep, Fort Carlin." He checked up and down the street and continued to walk. "But we've a fair share of churches, too, and decent folk. The saloons and gamblin' dens close up on Sundays from ten o'clock in the mornin' until two in the afternoon."

A stagecoach rumbled past in a swirl of dust, and they crossed the wide thoroughfare. A gust of wind caught the brim of his hat. He reached to press it more firmly on his head.

"That's somethin' you'll notice right off," Zed said, his voice barely audible above the noise of the wagons and horses. "Hats are more trouble than they're worth out here, with the wind blowin' the way it likes to. I don't bother with 'em unless I'm goin' someplace."

Zed stopped before a one-story, square, masonry establishment with a storefront and an overhead sign that read, "Banister's Woodworking, Zed Banister, Prop." "Well, here we are," he announced. Two large windows flanked the front door. Zed set down his burden and took a key out of his pocket, inserting it into the lock with a twist. Then he swung the door wide and motioned for Rhon to go in.

Out of the bright sun, it took a moment for Rhon's eyes to adjust. But as his uncle closed the door behind them, the open area quickly took shape. Rhon set down his bag and took off his hat, putting it on a massive pigeonholed desk by the door. He inhaled the aromatic fragrances of resin, new wood, and sawdust, some of his most favorite smells.

Zed's lopsided grin flashed beside him. "Well, this is my shop."

He made a wide gesture to his left. "Over here's where I do most of my work."

Rhon, noticing that the work counter was cluttered with tools and with projects in progress, admired the fine lathe work and smooth grain of a partially built chair. Stepping to the table where a ray of sunlight glinted off the teeth of several steel saw blades, he made a visual circuit of the efficient work area. Each tool had its place and the supply shelves were stocked with hinges, nails, varnishes, and other items. "Not bad, Uncle Zed. Not bad at all."

"There's a shed outside where I keep the extra lumber I've had shipped in," his uncle said. "Keep pretty busy, most of the time."

Stifling a yawn, Rhon smiled.

"Say, I bet you're hungry, after that long trip. There's a room back here," he motioned for Rhon to follow, "where you can wash up a bit. Then we'll go get some supper."

Within the hour they were seated on sturdy pine chairs at The Blue Bird. Rhon cut a chunk of beefsteak and forked it into his mouth. His gaze wandered casually over his uncle's jovial features, noting the liberal sprinkling of gray among the closely cropped head of brown, curly waves. There were new lines around his eyes, Rhon noticed. But he looked less tired than when he'd lost his beloved Ellen and left Pennsylvania seven months before.

His uncle grinned from across the table. "Say, it's good to have you out here, lad. Been thinkin' a lot about you and the folks back home. Everybody doin' okay, are they?"

Rhon nodded. "Pa's got his hands full running two businesses since he took over Uncle Will's sawmill along with his own coopering, but you know him. He likes being busy." He chuckled and continued, "Last month he took Holly and me to see President Hayes at a centennial celebration down in the valley. It was great." Having spoken her name, Rhon sighed and settled back in his chair, envisioning his cousin in a gown of midnight blue. The mental picture had distracted him throughout the trip; her face had superimposed itself over the passing landscapes, diminishing their blurred beauty to pale transparency. For one brief instant he could feel her soft kiss again, and he began to perspire under the collar of his shirt.

"Say, I read about that in *The New York Daily*, the festivities you had honoring the Wyoming Massacre." Zed's eyes twinkled. "Seems strange to be livin' now in a place with the same name."

A smile spread slowly across Rhon's lips. "Yeah, Holly's always saying how empty Huntsville seems since you left." Surprised to hear he'd voiced the quiet thought aloud, he shifted in his seat. Somehow he'd have to squelch the impulse to talk about his cousin every time he opened his mouth, he realized. He cleared this throat. "How did you come to choose Wyoming, Uncle Zed?"

Quirking his mouth in thought, Zed reached for the bread on the table between them. "Guess I wanted to see how it compared to the place it was named for. Must say it took me off balance, at first, bein' so open, so empty of trees around Cheyenne. But it grows on you. You'll see."

Holly tried once more to read the psalm before her as she leaned back against the boulder and raised her knees, propping the book closer, but the words kept running together before her eyes. With a sigh, she closed her Bible and set it down. The days seemed so interminably long without Rhon's usual visits, she mused. He'd been gone for almost two months already, and even his own mother seemed to have no idea of when he'd be coming home again. Her mind pictured their parting again, and as always, her emotions reacted at the bittersweet memory. How could she have been so bold as to kiss him?

"Hol-ly!" came Aunt Priscilla's faraway call.

She grimaced. Not even the glen was much of an escape when the wind blew from the east.

"Hol-ly!"

Reluctantly, she picked up her book and ran back to the house.

Holly rounded the necessary a few moments later and ran up the porch steps, skirts flying. "Well, it's high time ya got here," her aunt chided. "Uncle Ethan picked up a letter in town today. Says it's fer you." She squinted at the markings on the envelope. "It does look like yer name, but I can't read them other words."

"A letter!" Holly gasped, still panting from the run. Unceremoniously she grabbed it out of her aunt's fingers and scanned the sender's name. "Oh! It's from Rhon!" she blurted. "I—I mean," she said, forcing a calmer voice, "It's from Rhon. How nice. I'll read it up in my room." Turning, she threw open the door and bounded inside. "Thanks, Aunt Pris."

"Wait," her aunt called. "I wanna hear it, too."

Pretending not to hear, Holly hugged the missive to herself as she flew up the stairs and plopped onto the bed. She tore the envelope open. As she did, her heart pounded so hard that she wondered if everyone in the house could hear it.

> Cheyenne, Wyoming Territory
> 20 September 1878
>
> Dear Holly,
> Uncle Zed had to go to a town meeting at the church tonight, so I have some time to write. I arrived here on the first of last month, after a long and jolting train ride. It was good to set foot on the ground again.

Her mouth softened in a smile as she turned over onto her back. He wrote just the way he talked, and she could hear his voice inside her head. It made her all the more lonely. She held the letter up and read on.

> I wish you could have seen the beautiful scenery I passed. Ohio and Indiana reminded me of home, with woods and lakes and rolling hills and pastures. But Illinois and Nebraska were much flatter and open and unending, with the sky so big and so close it felt like I could reach up and touch it. Here in Cheyenne it is open too, with real gentle hills, practically without a tree. Uncle Zed must ship his lumber in from other parts.
> He looks good, rested and robust, almost like before Aunt Ellen died. He has a great shop right in the town and a four-room house about two miles out. It seems big enough for him, and it is full of the good furniture he builds. He still likes to walk most everywhere, so he never bought himself a horse.
> It's been good being with him again. We talk about the old days quite a lot, and it seems funny that you're not around. While we ·work together in the shop, he tells me stories about Wyoming and his trip out this way. He has even offered me a permanent job. We are in the middle of a big project he is trying to get done before winter—pews and a pulpit for a new church being built in Cheyenne. We

go to bed tired and aching every night, but it is coming along with both of us working at it.

I hope you are keeping well. I will have much to tell you the next time I see you. Until then, you are in my thoughts and prayers. Tell Beth and everyone I send my best.

Affectionately,
Your cousin, Rhon

Holly didn't breathe for a moment. She turned the pages over to look for more writing on the back, but they were empty, like she felt inside. *When are you coming home, Rhon?* Bitterly she crumpled the paper in her hands. *I knew when you went out there that you'd never come back; no one ever comes back.* Her head sank onto the pillow. *He didn't even ask me to write.* She lay staring at the ceiling, and it blurred before her. Maybe she'd been asking the wrong person about her cousin. Maybe she should have asked snippy Jenny Spencer when he planned his return trip. He'd probably written to her, too. He'd bought her that cameo, after all.

Zed stomped his boots just outside the cabin door and stepped inside. "Rhon? I'm home."

"Out here, Uncle Zed," Rhon called from the back porch. He swung his legs down from where they'd been propped against the railing and stood, shaking the listlessness from his head. He'd fallen asleep thinking about Holly, seeing her again with the sun on her shiny hair, feeling her soft body in his arms. A longing ache filled him from his toes to his head, and especially deep inside his gut. Then came the familiar sense of reproach. How could he be having these feelings for his own cousin? he wondered. His lungs deflated as he cast a despairing gaze at the rose-colored evening sky streaked with deep purple clouds.

His uncle's big feet clomped across the cabin floor. "Worked myself up a big appetite," he said, leaning out the door. "Like to go into town for supper, or just have some beefsteak here?"

"Here's fine."

"I'll have 'em on in a jiffy," the older man said with a grin. "See you've chopped the wood already."

Rhon nodded.

Zed studied his nephew for a few seconds, then went back inside to the stove, where he got out the big iron skillet and set it on the hottest part of the stove. The boy had been pretty quiet the last few weeks, although he'd tried to hide it, Zed realized. It looked like more than plain old homesickness, too, and it was eating away at his nephew. It was great having some company around again, after being alone since leaving Pennsylvania and all the sad memories. At times he'd regretted the decision, but somehow he knew that he'd done the smart thing.

He opened the trap door to the root cellar under his kitchen and descended the ladder into the dark cold storeroom, choosing some choice cuts he'd brought in from the smokehouse that morning. He also picked out a few turnips and radishes. He ascended the steps again and lowered the hinged door, then unwrapped the meat and flopped it, sizzling, into the pan.

Rhon ambled in at that moment and filled the wood box with kindling, then took a seat at the table. Zed watched him sit there with his chin in his hand, moping like a young buck in love. *Was that it*? he wondered. The boy hadn't so much as mentioned a young lady since he'd come, except for Holly. But now that he thought about it, her name somehow popped into every conversation one way or another. Zed drew his bushy eyebrows together in thought and cleaned the turnips. Taking a pot from a shelf by the sink, he chopped the vegetables and put them on to cook. "You say the girls been gettin' by okay since I've been gone?" he asked casually.

Rhon's expression brightened considerably, and a hint of a smile played across his mouth. "Yeah. Sometimes it gets to me the way Aunt Pris works them like there's no tomorrow, but they don't seem to mind." He smiled and shook his head. "Holly has that house almost as clean as Ma keeps ours. Beth looks after the little ones most of the time."

Zed wrinkled his forehead as he studied his nephew. "Have enough to live on, do they?"

"Well, Pa sends over some money from the mill for them every month. But I don't know. They don't seem to get new clothes very often." He paused for a moment. "You know, they should have it better than they do. Think I'll talk to Pa about it when I get back."

Zed flipped the meat with a fork, and the pleasing smell made

his stomach growl. He returned his attention to his nephew. "Can't help noticin' you've filled out some since you've been helpin' your pa at the mill. Guess all the gals back home must be flockin' after you, huh?" he teased.

Cocking his head, Rhon grimaced. "One or two. But they're not like—" He paused abruptly. "They're not easy to talk to . . . or even to be with." He traced the grain of the walnut table idly with a finger. "Guess I thought I'd find someone who'd fit right in, who'd feel right. Know what I mean? Someone I could be natural with . . . like Holly." A guilty expression crossed Rhon's features.

Zed smiled to himself. No wonder Matt had sent him out with the request to keep him occupied for awhile, he realized. Rhon had gotten a bit too attached to his spirited little cousin. But how could he blame the boy? He himself had relished the girl's spunk and impetuous nature since the first time he'd picked her up and set her on his shoulder, only to have her jab a finger into his ear. If Ellen hadn't been so poorly when Will and Sarah died, they could've taken the girls in themselves and made a life for them, he reflected. He'd have liked that.

He looked back over at Rhon. "Seems I recall a little gal I had my eye on back when I was your age," he said, liberally peppering the beefsteak. "Prettiest thing I ever laid eyes on. Couldn't so much as walk past her on the street without my knees turnin' to jelly."

"Aunt Ellen?" Rhon asked.

Zed shook his head and leaned back against the sideboard. "No, she came along a bit later. After I'd had my heart broke. This little gal had grand dreams, of money and all the nice trappin's it can buy. What she didn't want was an ordinary man who worked with his hands. Ran off with a highfalutin' city fella one day, she did."

He paused, his mouth compressed in thought. "My Ellen was nothin' like that." Nodding to himself, he smiled sadly. "She was simple and quiet, and right pretty in her own way. Took all thoughts of that other lass clean out of my head. There was only one Ellen, and I thank the good Lord He saw fit to bring her to me."

The smile broadened into a grin as he lifted the lid to check the turnips. "Well, these're a bit firm, yet. But the meat's done. Let's eat." Grabbing the plates and utensils, he plunked them onto

the table and set the pots on a towel in the middle. Folding his long legs, he lowered himself onto a seat, then bowed his head. "Dear Lord, we thank you for what's been provided and ask your blessin', in Jesus' name. Amen."

"Amen."

Later that night, in the bed in the spare room, Rhon let his thoughts drift back to Pennsylvania. He wondered whether Holly had received his letter yet. *She must have been thrilled to get mail of her own,* he thought. With a grim smile he remembered the finished product and how it differed from his first few attempts at writing that night. If only he could have written what he'd wanted to, it would've been much easier.

What was the matter with him? he wondered. She couldn't possibly be having the same feelings that were waging a war within his own heart each day and night. After all, they *were* related. She'd never done anything to even hint she'd so much as thought that they could be more than best friends. Not ever. It was just a kiss goodbye, he rationalized. People kissed goodbye every day. She'd probably forgotten about the whole thing by now . . . or worse, regretted it. He ground his teeth together. Maybe she was relieved that he'd left.

He thought of that new bounder . . . Harris, wasn't it? He certainly made no attempt to conceal his attraction for Holly. *Was he taking advantage of her loneliness already?* Rhon wondered. *Was she lonely?*

When he closed his eyes Rhon could see her again, in gingham, in ivory with pale violets, in indigo blue. For the flicker of a second, when he inhaled, he could smell the summer roses she wore. And his longing became a dull ache.

Holly knelt in a dim corner of the barn and pushed the folds of the burlap sack aside, scooping chicken feed into the pan she held in her other hand. Three should do it, she thought, allowing the mouth of the bag to close again over the dusty contents. Suddenly the fine hairs on the back of her neck prickled. A shadow fell over her. She jumped to her feet and quickly turned around. The hulking form of her Uncle Ethan bumped into her. "Oh!" she exclaimed.

"Think ya need a bit more, lass." His leering grin revealed a gap next to his front teeth that he rarely displayed.

Taking a step to one side, she laughed nervously. "I—I didn't hear you come in, Uncle Ethan." Her heart thumped crazily as he moved into her path.

Beady eyes imprisoned her with a vile gleam.

She looked toward the closed door. Only moments ago she had left it open, and now the heavy plank had been dropped into place. She swallowed, trying to remain calm. "Well, Aunt Pris told me to hurry with this, so I'll just—"

His hand closed over hers as he slowly swept a feral gaze over her body. His foul, whiskey-thick breath assaulted her.

"No!" she screamed. Holly twisted out of his grasp, painfully wrenching her wrist in the process. The tin clanged to the floor, spilling kernels of feed in a wide arc. She darted behind a support beam, searching for a means of escape. "Aunt Priscilla!"

Ethan's sneer twisted maliciously as he took slow, calculated steps toward her. "Have to yell a bit louder, lass. No one else here," he cackled.

The words barely registered over the pounding of Holly's heart. Her knees shook as she clutched the post. He was right, she realized. Over an hour ago Beth and Aunt Priscilla had taken the children with them to deliver cream and butter to Aunt Hannah and the Widow James.

"Aw, come on, girl. I jest wanna li'l touch." Her uncle's rough hand reached out and brushed her cheek.

With a shudder of revulsion, Holly shrank away. She cast a frantic eye toward the barred door. Her only recourse was the ladder to the loft . . . if she could beat him to it. She forced herself to speak calmly. "If you touch me, Aunt Pris'll skin you alive. You know that." As she spoke, she inched her way toward a stack of crates in the opposite direction, hoping to throw him off.

His coarse chuckle mocked her. "She thinks I left at dawn to git supplies."

With a desperate lunge, Holly dashed behind the crates to make a run for the loft.

Ethan charged after her, his heavy footfalls thudding against the packed dirt floor. He clamped a hand on her shoulder.

Holly gasped. Jerking free, she heard her sleeve tear. With all her might she yanked at an empty barrel, and it crashed into her uncle. She heard him swear as she hurled herself at the ladder and started up.

He caught one of her ankles, and a raspy laugh rumbled from his chest.

Holly kicked wildly with her other foot, striking an intense blow to his nose.

"Awk!" Reacting to the kick, he released her ankle and stepped back, clutching his face. Blood trickled between his fingers.

Her teeth clenched in grim victory, Holly flew up the last few rungs, not daring to look behind her. But as she ran for the hay window she heard him clumping up the ladder. She grabbed the rope and leaped out, sliding down its length.

The moment her feet touched the ground, she sped from the barn, not knowing or caring where she was headed. Reaching the sanctity of the shrouded woods, she darted behind a tree trunk and dared to look back. Uncle Ethan was driving away in his empty wagon. She collapsed in tears.

As her sobs quieted, Holly heard the sound of horse hooves. He was coming back! She crouched behind a bush and slowly peered around it. But instead, she saw Tyler's buggy. Releasing her breath in a sob of relief, she shakily rose and came out.

"Holly! I just passed your uncle a minute ago—" His eyes widened as he drew near, and he jumped out even before the carriage stopped. "My dear! What on earth has happened?" He gathered her into his arms.

With a little cry, Holly crumpled against his chest. "I . . . Uncle Ethan . . . He . . ."

"What are you saying?" Tyler tightened his embrace and rocked her back and forth, stroking her hair. Then he gently pushed her away to arm's length. "Did that wretch harm you? I swear I'll kill him, if he did."

His words appalled Holly. She lifted her reddened eyes and searched Tyler's face, then she shook her head. "He . . . only tried. He'd been drinking. Everybody was gone. He came into the barn, and . . ." She couldn't continue. She shuddered and pressed against the comfort of Tyler's chest. "I'm afraid of him."

"It's all right, my dear. He's gone, at least for now." Bending, he scooped her up into his arms and carried her to the carriage.

Holly felt safe again. Drawing comfort from Tyler's strength, she relaxed and leaned her head against his shoulder. She was almost disappointed when he set her onto the seat.

He climbed in beside her and took the reins. "I can't tell you

how shocked I am about this. How could your aunt allow such a thing, when you and your sister are in her care? I'm going to have a talk with her—after I deal with your uncle, that is." He clucked his tongue, and the buggy lurched forward.

Holly put a hand on his arm and tilted her head. "No, Tyler. Please. You mustn't say anything about this to anyone."

"But the man needs to be punished. I should think you'd want that, after what he put you through." Taking her hand in his, he turned up her palm and drew it to his mouth. He stopped short and held it out with a frown. He took her other wrist, and she winced. "How on earth did this happen?"

The sight of her raw, bloodied hands caught Holly by surprise, and for the first time she became aware of how much they hurt. "It . . . must have been the rope. When I slid down from the hay window."

Tyler mumbled something under his breath and shook his head. "Well, we'll take you home, anyway, and tend your battle wounds, my brave little one." His expression softened. "Then you can tell me why all of this must be kept secret." Turning the horse, he headed for the house.

"Don't you see, Tyler? It's because I still have to live there. This could cause a lot of trouble. Aunt Pris could send me away. And there's Beth to consider. I don't want her to live here by herself, or to live in fear. I'm responsible for her." Holly avoided looking at the barn as they drove past it. "I have nowhere else to go."

Tyler put an arm around her shoulders and drew her close. His expression became serious. Then he smiled. "Oh, but perhaps you do."

9

Holly stared at Tyler from within his protective hold, and her lips parted in surprise. Her back stiffened as she eased herself upright. "I beg your pardon?"

Tyler's smile faded and he grew solemn. Although he did not lower his arm, he relaxed and rested it on the seat back. "Surely you know that my intentions toward you are honorable, my dear Holly. That first day your aunt invited me to Sunday dinner she gave me permission to call on you, and I've been courting you ever since." He smiled and removed his hat. "However, if you prefer that I kneel at your feet and beg for your hand, I would be more than happy to oblige."

The mere thought of it almost made Holly laugh. "You really are serious about this!" she said in wonder.

"Yes. Quite serious."

"Why, Tyler? With all the eligible young women in this area— all of whom seem inclined to throw themselves your way every time you pass—why would you want to marry me?"

Tyler considered his answer thoughtfully. Holly Grant was a beautiful, sensitive young woman, and from today's encounter with her uncle, she obviously had spirit, he realized. Despite her youth, she wasn't the naive, empty-headed child so many girls her age tended to be. Even her flaxen-haired younger sister seemed to have a serious way about her. If their aunt hadn't been pushing the older sister toward him he could quite easily have been drawn to little Beth, the selfless homebody. Something about her brought out a desire within him to protect and provide for her. And if by marrying Holly, he reasoned, he could look out for her younger sister as well, he was quite willing and able to do just that.

He tipped his head and smiled. "Because I need someone in my life . . . and so do you. I have a huge house where my every footstep echoes from one end to the other, and money enough to provide a fine life for you—and Beth, too, if you like. She

could live with us and be safe."

He watched Holly struggle with her own thoughts, watched her cast a furtive glance every so often toward the barn. Her hands still trembled from her frightful experience, and the usual sparkle was missing from her eyes when she raised them to him. "I . . . don't know what to say."

"Well, then," he said, stepping out and hurrying around to her side, "at least say that you'll think about it."

With a sigh, Holly stood. Her fingers curled into her palm and she flinched unconsciously. "I will. Truly."

"Good. That's all I can ask." Taking hold of her slender waist, Tyler swung her to the ground. "Now let's go inside and see what we can do for those poor hands of yours. I'll stay with you until your aunt returns."

When Priscilla and Beth came home some time later, Holly heard their voices drift up from downstairs. She heard Tyler tell them that she had taken ill and had retired to bed. She was grateful that he had insisted on staying. She didn't want to talk to anyone at the moment, and when Beth tiptoed into the bedroom, she pretended to be asleep.

"Well, that finishes another one," Zed said as he and Rhon set another church pew with the others along the wall.

Rhon grinned broadly. "That's half of them, anyway." Stretching the kinks out of his back, he yawned. "What do you say we go have some coffee, Uncle Zed?"

"Just what I was thinkin' myself, lad. That cute little blond-haired lass over at The Blue Bird's probably pinin' for the sight of you by now."

With a sideways glance at his uncle, Rhon stifled the impulse to reply. Grabbing his hat, he jammed it on his head and led the way, waiting outside while his uncle locked up.

Their usual pine table beside the window was empty and waiting, with two places already set. Zed folded himself up to fit the confines of the spindly chair, and Rhon took the opposite one.

A young woman, with long curls the color of sun-ripened wheat and a smile full of even, white teeth, appeared at their table and poured coffee into their mugs.

"Thanks, Amanda," Zed said.

"What might I get for you gentlemen?" she asked, with a shy,

furtive glance toward Rhon and a pale blush coloring her fair skin.

"Oh, let me think." Zed kneaded his chin thoughtfully as though he hadn't noticed anything unusual. "Got any of that good apple pan dowdy?"

She nodded. "We just baked some this morning. I'll be right back." In a swirl of her burgundy skirt, she left.

Zed winked at Rhon. "See?

Rhon chuckled, trying to keep a straight face. "How do you know she's not interested in you, Uncle Zed?"

The older man laughed softly and shook his head. "Young fellas just don't know when they got it good. Between her and that Margie over at Foley's, you got a fair pick of company. If you're of a mind to be interested, of course."

Amanda returned with their plates and glasses of water. After setting Zed's in place, she straightened, and the edge of her tray bumped Rhon's drink over. "Oh!" she gasped, turning scarlet up to her ears. "I'm so sorry." Grabbing at the ties of her long apron, she tore it off and mopped at the cool liquid puddling over everything.

Rhon and Zed leaned back watching her flustered motions, not daring to meet each other's eyes.

"I—I'll bring you some new pie," she blurted. "I'll just take these away." Removing the soaked food, she stumbled away, barely missing the chair directly behind her.

"Ah, the power we hold over the fair sex," Zed teased. "It's frightening."

Rhon leaned an elbow on the table and covered his mouth as Amanda brought fresh servings and set them down with extreme care. He smiled at her, noticing that her face and neck were now mottled. "No harm done. Thanks."

She nodded quickly and hurried off, ducking into the kitchen.

Zed took a gulp of coffee and cut into his pie. "Saw her lookin' your way a lot at church, too."

Rhon exhaled slowly. "Yeah."

"Seems pretty nice. She's a sweet gal."

"Yeah. Only . . ."

"Only there's Holly," Zed finished.

Rhon looked at his uncle straight on. "It shows that much?"

"Does to someone who knows you."

Chewing a mouthful of his dessert, Rhon lifted his shoulders in a resigned gesture. "The thing is, it's hopeless. We're related. There's no way around it."

"Holly feel the same way about you, does she?"

"Sometimes I'm almost sure of it. Other times I just wonder."

Zed had to force down his last bite. His appetite had suddenly evaporated. He remembered enough of his own youth to know how much pain accompanied first love, and his heart went out to his nephew. A long-ago promise flashed into his mind. He was torn between a vow he'd made his brother and the knowledge that he could eliminate the constant torture Rhon brought upon himself. Surely the lad was of an age to know the truth, he reasoned. But by rights the story should come from his own father. He'd have to give the matter some deep thought. And he'd have to do some praying about it as well.

Holly winced as Beth accidentally pricked her while adjusting a seam. "Sorry."

"Would you please hurry?" Holly snapped. "I'm tired of being your pincushion."

Beth flushed. "I said I was sorry."

Her expression softening, Holly sighed. "Oh, I didn't mean to be short with you, Bethy. I just have a lot on my mind right now."

"Well, that's the last one, anyway," the younger girl said, straightening up. "I think I can finish it now. Sure is pretty material, isn't it? I almost fainted dead away when Uncle Ethan brought the new dress lengths home for us."

With a scathing grimace, Holly let her eyes wander over the raspberry muslin, then looked away.

"Aunt Pris said he was real worried about you when you got sick the other day. He kept asking about you when you took to your bed."

"Well, I'm okay now. And a lot smarter than I used to be."

Beth tilted her head questioningly. "What do you mean?"

Clenching her teeth, Holly assessed her situation. How could she tell Beth the truth about her scare and have her afraid to step outside the house? She'd let her sister and Aunt Pris believe the story that she had begged Tyler to pass on, that she'd burned her hands on the handle of the iron skillet. But she'd been especially careful not to be alone anywhere near Uncle Ethan,

and she had not spoken to him once since the incident in the barn. She knew that Tyler had stayed long after supper that night and had made sure he'd had a few choice words with her uncle before he went home. "I just grew up a little, that's all," she finally replied.

"What kind of answer is that?" Beth carefully slid the bodice of the dress off Holly's shoulders and down to the floor while Holly stepped out of it. Then she gathered it again and smoothed the fabric, draping it over the edge of the bed.

Holly forced a smile. "Well, aren't we going to try yours on, too? I'd sort of like a turn at you with those dressmaker pins of yours."

With a giggle, Beth tugged at her own buttons and quickly removed her worn cotton skirt and blouse. "I just need the hem pinned."

Grabbing the stool, Holly pulled it over and motioned with her head toward the seat. "Up, then."

Beth pulled on the new sky blue muslin frock and stepped up, straightening her shoulders while Holly folded up the length. "Tyler hasn't been around for awhile, now, has he?"

"He had some business to take care of for a few days. Turn."

Beth shifted her position slightly. "Horse business?"

Holly glanced upward. "He didn't say. Turn."

"Does he go away very often?"

"I have no idea."

"Will he be back soon?"

"Most likely. Why?"

"Oh, I just wondered." Beth rotated again. "Are your hands any better today? Now that the bandages are off, do they still hurt?"

"Not very much." Holly peered around with a wry grin. "Don't worry, I should be able to dry dishes tonight."

Zed peeled off his work shirt and took a fresh one out of his drawer. Buttoning it, he strode to the kitchen and poured two sarsaparillas. Then he carried them out to the porch where Rhon was relaxing on the bottom step chewing on jerked beef, his legs stretched out in front of him. "Looks like another nice night." He handed Rhon a glass.

"Thanks." Rhon shifted his attention to the evening sky that

was paling into peach and mauve tones. The edges of the clouds shimmered with gold. "Yeah, looks real peaceful."

"I . . . wanted to talk to you about somethin'," Zed said casually, taking a seat in one of the big chairs he'd built.

Warily, his nephew looked up at him. "A sermon about cousins?" he asked sarcastically. "And why they should never love each other?"

"Never lectured you before, did I?" Zed's tone was even.

"No. Sorry." Standing, Rhon brushed off his backside and mounted the steps, perching on the rail. Idly he bent the jerky back and forth in the fingers of one hand. "Most lectures come from inside, actually. Nobody has to tell me when I'm in trouble."

Neither spoke for a few moments. The whisper of the evening breeze and the shrill cry of a hawk in the sky were the only sounds.

Zed fortified himself with a gulp of sarsaparilla. "You know, I don't believe that it's against the law in Pennsylvania for first cousins to marry."

"Maybe not." Rhon drained his glass and set it down on the floor. "But that's not the way most folks see it. Some people act like it's incest. They talk behind your back, look at you funny. People who used to be friends start making themselves scarce. It's not much of a life to offer Holly. She'd end up hating me."

"Guess it would ease things some if you had no blood ties to the girl, wouldn't it?"

Rhon grimaced. "I'd give anything in this world if we weren't related, if she were just another person in Huntsville who I'd met at school or in town. But that's just wishful thinking." Hurling the shredded jerky as far as he could, he stood and shoved his hands into his pockets. He leaned against the pole that supported the roof, his gaze far away and unseeing.

Zed cleared his throat. *Why hadn't Matt just been honest with the boy instead of trying to separate them?* he wondered. What difference would it have made at this point for Rhon to know the truth? After all, he was grown and he was level-headed. Zed tried to quiet his thoughts. He had no right to be the one to tell him, he mused. It should come from his father. But Matt was hesitant to break his vow to Hannah and had left it up to him. Why else would he have written a week ago with the news that Hannah and Pris were planning to marry Holly off in the near future? Was it so that Zed would weaken and tell Rhon the whole

story? Was a vow of silence binding forever in a circumstance such as this? *Didn't the lad have the right to make a life with the woman of his choice?* he wondered. He studied his nephew. One look at the slump of Rhon's shoulders, the trouble in his eyes. . . . How could he *not* tell him the truth?

"Rhon."

Something in his uncle's voice made Rhon snap out of his reverie. He turned.

Zed's face was shaded in the waning evening light. Deep shadows drew craggy shadows around his nose and chin. Even his eyes were hidden. "I have somethin' to tell you. Don't know if it's right or not that it come from me. But it's somethin' I feel is your right to know."

An eerie feeling wrapped chilly fingers around Rhon's insides. "Has something happened to Holly?" he gasped.

"No, no, nothing like that." Zed scratched his head. "This has to do with your ma."

"Something's happened to her then?" Rhon asked. He hadn't even thought of that. He sank down onto the porch rail.

Zed rubbed his chin with one hand and shook his head. "Look, I tried all day to think up a big, proper speech, but nothin' worked. I'm gonna just say this straight out, however it comes. But one thing I wanna make clear from the top," he jabbed a finger into the air for emphasis, "and that's that they both love you, your ma and pa. And they kept this from you because of that love. They didn't want you ever to know, in case the knowin' hurt you."

Flabbergasted, Rhon just stared at him. "What in the world are you trying to say, Uncle Zed?"

"Just this. Your ma, she . . . well, she isn't . . . your ma."

Rhon felt his mouth drop open at the ridiculous statement, and his brows drew together in a frown. "Why in the world would you say such a crazy thing?"

"Because it's the truth. I said this wasn't gonna be easy. Please, just listen to me. A long time ago, when your folks were living in Connecticut, your pa, he—he made a mistake with a little gal. She was a purty, red-haired lass from Wales, an' she had these big eyes as green as emeralds. Worked as a teacher in a school-house where he was doin' some repairs. She was a little bit of a thing, all moon-eyed over your pa. He never encouraged it, mind you, but all the same, he knew of her feelin's. One day she

received word that her only sister had died of cholera, and it hit her awful hard. She tried the best she could to go on with the lessons. But when she heard that there was a blizzard blowin' in, she sent the school kids home early and just gave in to her grief. Your pa came by to put his tools away and ready the place for the storm. When he walked in, she was lyin' in a heap on the floor. He picked her up and held her, and she . . . well, she . . . turned to him."

Nothing in that jumble made any sense in Rhon's mind, but he didn't interrupt. It had to mean something sooner or later, he thought.

Zed stopped and changed position in his chair. "Anyway, your pa was concerned that she get home safe before it got too late, with the storm comin' an' all. He checked outside, and it was whiter than a dandelion gone to seed. He couldn't see past the steps of the schoolhouse, and the wind was whippin' snow around so hard that it near blew the door right off its hinges. He went back inside and stoked up the fire in the stove, 'cause he knew the two of them would be spendin' the night."

"Are you saying what it sounds like you're saying?" Rhon asked incredulously, his voice squeaking like he was thirteen again. "That Pa and some—some little—"

Zed gave a calming squeeze to Rhon's knee. "Now, I never said anythin' about blamin' either one of 'em, did I? Your pa took most of the fault on himself in the end. It wasn't any kind of planned thing. It just happened. And if he hadn't had a fight with your ma earlier that day he wouldn't even have gone to the schoolhouse in the first place. It wouldn't have hurt his supplies to get some snow on 'em."

A heaviness like a punch in the stomach clutched at Rhon. If anyone but his Uncle Zed had even tried to palm off such an insane tale, they would have come to blows by now. With supreme effort, he forced himself to listen, but he knew he wouldn't believe what was coming.

"In his younger days, before he met the Lord, your pa was wilder than a range horse. From the time he was housebroke he didn't take kindly to discipline or rules. When your ma came along they moved up north and he settled down some, but he still thought mostly of his own self and nobody else. It hit him hard when Hannah found out that she could never have children. On his bad

days he'd say terrible, hurtful things to her, and she'd shut herself in her room and cry."

This picture of his steady, reliable father was totally foreign to Rhon's mind, and he tried to make it fit the image he'd grown up with. They were like two different men. He kneaded his throbbing temples, but the pain in his head was nothing compared to the hollowness inside. New feelings began to emerge: anger, shock, disbelief. He couldn't decide which was the strongest.

Zed droned on steadily. "When the little lass found out that she was with child, she had to resign from the school, of course, and move to another place not too far away. Your pa planned from the start to pay for your keep and help in whatever way he could. But he never told your ma about her. Not until he had to."

Rhon tipped his head. "What do you mean?" He couldn't even see his uncle now; darkness had enveloped the porch.

"The birthin' was a hard one. The lass lived just long enough to hold you, no more. Her name was Rhonwyn, by the way. You were named for her. It was her wish."

"Whatever possessed you to tell me this, Uncle Zed?" Rhon asked. Anguish clutched his throat, making it almost impossible to force words out. "All these years, livin' with Ma . . . thinking she was my mother . . . that I belonged to her. I wish you'd never told me any of it! What was the point?" Springing to his feet, Rhon stumbled blindly down the steps.

Zed leaped from his chair, barely catching Rhon's arm in the dark. Gently he turned him around and took his other arm. "I'm hopin' you'll figure that out, when you've had some time to think it through. And I'll let you go and do just that, after I've said one more thing."

"Oh? And what is that?" Rhon asked bitterly.

"There's more to bein' a mother than just givin' birth. Hannah took you in because you were her husband's son, and she promised to *be* your mother. She had a heart big enough to forgive her husband and big enough to love another woman's babe. No one knows about any of this except Matt, Hannah, and me. They moved back to Pennsylvania soon after you were born. We wanted you to be secure in bein' part of the family. We didn't want anyone to treat you differently than that."

Rhon pulled free of his uncle's grip. "Well, that was awfully big of the three of you, wasn't it? Thank you for the *interesting*

story, Uncle Zed. Now, if you don't mind, I'm going for a walk."

Sometime during his wanderings in the dark, the breeze became wind, and Rhon shivered. *What had his uncle been thinking of, to come right out and ruin his whole life like that?* he wondered. Whoever heard of a stupid name like Rhonwyn? Or a stupid name like Rhon, for that matter? He kicked at a clump of something black and stubbed his toe right through his boot. Good, he thought with a perverse measure of satisfaction. Up until then he'd been numb, too numb even to know how cold he was. He'd have to go back, he realized.

He turned and looked in the direction of his uncle's house, barely a speck in the distance. Good thing Cheyenne was so wide open, or he'd have gotten lost until tomorrow, he thought. With his hands in his pockets, he trudged back toward the light.

Well, that certainly would explain all the strange looks he'd noticed between his parents—well, *one* of his parents anyway, he thought with contempt. They must've been assuring each other that the deep, dark secret would never be uttered aloud. Well, it had come to light now. What reason was there to even go home? Why had Uncle Zed done this?

The only good thing back there was Holly, his cousin. He let the warm thought of her soothe his jagged nerves and wrap around him like a comforting blanket, shielding him from the cold wind, from the pain of betrayal. Beautiful, exquisite, impulsive Holly, related to him because of some quirk of fate. One simple line of blood. Because her father was his mother's brother. His mother's . . .

Rhon halted. For a moment he couldn't feel his own heartbeat. *"I'd give anything in this world if we weren't related."*
"Your ma isn't your ma."

The anguish inside of him blew away on the night wind. A smile slowly spread across his face. Glancing up at the sky, he noticed for the first time the sprinkling of a million brilliant stars twinkling like diamonds on indigo satin. Somewhere under those same stars there was a beautiful woman who wasn't really his cousin.

He broke into a run.

10

Beneath a scattering of afternoon clouds, Holly took down the wash, folding each piece before putting it in the basket. She hoped that Aunt Priscilla had dressed the children warmly for the walk back from the old Widow James's place. Already the days were cool more often than warm, and soon the trees would be ablaze in all their brilliant fall hues. She looked forward to the beautiful display and the joy of seeing her glen carpeted in multicolored leaves until the first snow came. With a toss of her hair, she carried the heaping basket up the back porch steps.

Catching a movement beside the barn, she turned.

Her Uncle Ethan peered around the corner, looked to the right and left, then slowly crept toward the chicken coop, where her sister had gone scant moments before.

Beth! Dropping the clothes, Holly flew through the haphazard piles down the stairs. "Beth!" Her heart pounded as she raced for the henhouse.

Her uncle stopped abruptly and turned, going instead into the wide barn door.

"What do you want?" Beth asked, emerging with the egg basket on one arm.

Breathless, Holly stopped just outside the rectangle of chicken wire. "I—um—need some help. Back at the house."

Beth was puzzled as she closed the gate. "But we're finished in there, aren't we?"

"Yes, but . . . I dropped the clothes all over the back porch. Would you mind helping me pick them up?" She glanced warily toward the barn.

"You came running all the way over here for that?"

"I . . . just come on, will you?"

"At least let me put the eggs away." With a disbelieving look at Holly, Beth ran up the creaking steps and into the kitchen. The door slammed behind her, then protested with a loud squeal as she came back out. "I can't believe that you need help with

this." Stooping down, she began gathering the garments near her feet.

Holly sighed. "Since Aunt Pris isn't back yet, we should probably start supper, too. What do you think we should have?"

"How should I know? Really, Holly, you've been acting very strange lately."

"What do you mean?" She reached down and folded a gingham skirt, adding it to the stack.

With a curious smile, her sister shook her head. "You're jumpy, touchy. You drop things. And you spend most of the time after chores upstairs in the bedroom . . . except when you go out with Tyler." Grabbing the last item, she shook it out and put it on top. "Sound familiar?"

Holly rolled her eyes heavenward. "I have a lot of things on my mind right now. I wish Rhon were here. I need to talk to him."

"You can talk to me, you know. I'm not a little girl anymore. I might be able to help you." Tipping her head, Beth opened the door.

Holly considered her sister for a moment, then bent and retrieved the basket. She carried it inside and set it down, turning as Beth followed. "Maybe not . . . but this is the one thing I can't talk to you about, Bethy. It's something I have to figure out on my own."

Opening her Bible early the next morning, Holly pulled her shawl tighter and leafed through the pages, stopping to read underlined verses.

> If any of you lack wisdom, let him ask of God.

With a sigh, she scanned a few more.

> If ye, then, being evil, know how to give good gifts unto your children, how much more shall your Father which is in heaven give good things to them that ask him?
> Ask, and it shall be given you.

She bowed her head. *Father, please help me. What should I do? The Bible says that you will answer those who ask, and I need your wisdom. Tyler's offered to marry me. He's been very*

nice and has treated me with kindness. I've always thought that
I would spend my life with someone for whom I cared very deeply.
But the one person I truly love can never be mine.

Holly opened her eyes and tried to look through the leafy boughs
above, wishing she could see all the way to Heaven and find the
guidance she so desperately sought. *Please, give me some kind*
of sign, Father. I must make an important choice, right now, and
I'm so mixed up.

In the silence, jumbled thoughts paraded through her mind.
When are you coming home, Rhon? Would you approve of Tyler
once you got to know him? Even if you don't, I have Beth and
her safety to consider. Tyler seems genuinely fond of us both,
and he does have a lot of money, so we wouldn't want for anything.
There'd be no Uncle Ethan to worry about. There really was only
one choice. She had to get Beth away from Uncle Ethan. Slowly
Holly walked back to the house and up to her attic room.

Beth lay awake, with her head resting on her arm. "No one's
up yet?"

"No, but I heard them stirring." Letting her wrap slip to the
floor, Holly lifted the blanket and got back into bed. "It's getting
too cool to go out for my devotions so early in the morning. I'll
hate it when I can't go."

"Something's still bothering you, isn't it?"

Holly turned to her sister. She nodded. "I . . . think I'll tell
Tyler that I'll marry him."

"What?" Beth sat up. "Do you love him?"

"I don't know. Anyway, I thought you were the one who was
so enchanted by him and happy that he was courting me."

A frown wrinkled Beth's smooth forehead. "Well, does he love
you?"

Holly wondered as much herself, since he'd never actually said
the words. But then, according to Aunt Hannah, sometimes the
feelings came afterward. Maybe it would be that way for both
of them. She looked at Beth and shrugged.

"I think you should wait until Rhon comes home and see what
he has to say about this."

"Why?" Holly asked petulantly. "Seems to me that if he cared
about what happens to us he wouldn't have stayed away so long.
For all I know he may never come back."

Beth reached under the bed and pulled out her sketch pad. "All

the times I've ever seen you with Tyler you never once looked at him like this," she said, shuffling through the pages and turning to one in particular. She thrust it at Holly.

Taking the tablet in her hand, Holly sat up and stared at the drawing. Her eyes widened. Obviously done on the day of the picnic, it was a sketch of her and Rhon on the wagon seat. Beth had captured the curve of his mouth, the tip of his head, and the gentleness in his face. Then Holly's eyes moved to the rendition of her figure in the drawing and to her own expression, a look of longing.

Swallowing, she turned to another page. Between likenesses of Amy Sue and Aaron and the house and surrounding scenery, were other sketches of Rhon and herself: on the porch steps, standing in the yard, visiting over the stone wall. All depicted the secret feelings of which they, themselves, hadn't even been aware. Idly flipping pages, Holly noticed the last several were of Tyler. Skipping quickly over them, she turned back to a sketch of Rhon.

A flood of bittersweet memories brought unbidden emotions to the surface, and Holly's eyes welled. She blinked quickly and raised her chin. "Rhon is very special to me, you know that. He always has been. But he and I can never be together, Bethy. Not ever. And Tyler is offering us a good life. Both of us." And, came her resigned thought, *it's the only way out of here I've been able to find.* "I'm going to accept his proposal tonight."

Beth opened her mouth as if she were going to say something, but didn't. Her eyes became unusually bright, then she turned away.

Whoever said that the ride home was always shorter had never endured a week traveling by railroad, that was for sure, Rhon thought. He could hardly stand the thought of one more hour in a passenger car, and the dining stops made him jittery. *Please, Lord, let me be in time. I have to be in time.*

When he finally set foot again in Wilkes-Barre and hitched a ride on a wagon bound for Dallas, the first touch of autumn was already upon the woodlands of northeastern Pennsylvania. Rhon forced himself to concentrate on the bright yellow already painting the poplar and birch trees and the red, orange, and gold of the maples. The Indian summer afternoon was mild and clear.

The last clouds of substance had been left behind in Ohio.

Reaching Huntsville and, at last, his own lane, he gave a soft whistle. Shadow leaped up and darted toward him over the ruts in a streak of black, yelping excited little barks the entire distance. Kneeling down, Rhon opened his arms, and the dog hurled himself against his master, licking his face. "How are you, fella? Missed me, huh? I'm glad to see you, too." Rhon scratched behind Shadow's ears and stood, ruffling the black fur one more time. He picked up his satchel. "Let's go, boy. There's something I have to do."

Approaching his family's neat, white house, Rhon took a deep breath and mounted the porch steps. It was suppertime, and he could smell roast beef. His folks would both be home. He said a quick prayer that the Lord would give him the right words for what he knew lay ahead. Opening the door, he stepped inside and set down his bag, then he walked toward the sound of their voices. "Ma? Pa?"

A chair scraped loudly over the floorboards. His father laughed and met him in the kitchen doorway with an exuberant embrace. "Son! You're back!"

Somewhat more restrained, his mother rose at her chair, her cheeks slightly flushed as Rhon smiled over his father's shoulder at her. "Ya must be hungry. I'll set another place." Hurriedly she went to the cupboard and returned with a plate and utensils.

"Well, come sit down, son," his father said, putting an arm around Rhon's shoulders. "Tell us about your trip. How's Uncle Zed?"

"He's fine, Wyoming's fine, and so am I." Meeting his father's eyes with a level, steady gaze, he joined his parents.

His mother passed him the platter. "We, um, didn't expect ya back, jest yet." She pushed a few straggly hairs away from her eyeglasses.

Rhon nodded slowly. "I know." A glimmer of hope began to burn brightly in his heart as he watched her push her spectacles higher on her nose. Fidgeting the way she was, he knew that the wedding couldn't have taken place yet. There had to be some time left for him to convince Holly not to go through with it. He smiled inwardly, forked a slab of beef, and added some boiled potatoes to his plate. "I had to come home."

"Ya must've seen some real purty gals out west, I'll bet." His

mother lifted her eyebrows, her expression hopeful. "Hear tell there's good pickin's."

He let the remark pass. He knew that she meant well. "Holly been by lately?" he asked casually.

His mother's face turned scarlet. "Uh, well, not too awful much. She's been busy."

Rhon felt his pulse quicken as he tried to remember how he'd planned to bring up the subject uppermost in his mind. Maybe Uncle Zed's way was best after all, he thought. *I'm just gonna say this straight out, however it comes.* He swallowed a mouthful and looked straight at her. "Ma, I have to tell you something. I . . . know . . . everything."

Her fork clattered onto her dish. Heavy silence followed. Finally she said, "What? I don't know what ya mean."

"Yes you do," he said gently. "I know the whole story."

All color drained from Hannah's face. "What story?" Her hands began to shake visibly.

Inhaling deeply for strength, Rhon looked in his father's direction and saw a nervous smile play across his mouth. Uncle Zed was right, he realized. If it hadn't been for the vow that his parents had taken long ago, his father would have explained the whole story himself, in time. Only time had run out. He averted his attention from his father and turned to his mother. "Look, Ma, I want you to know right off that I don't hold anything against you or Pa or anyone else. You have to believe that."

She opened her mouth as if to speak, but he gave her no time. "I love Holly. I've always loved her. You couldn't expect me to stay away forever while everybody tries to arrange her life, and mine as well. We're not kids anymore. We should have some say about it."

"But it ain't fittin' fer cousins—"

"Ma, I said I know *everything*. I know about what happened all those years ago . . . and about my birth."

His mother gasped. "But we took a vow." Her face contorted with anguish as she turned it toward his father, then back to Rhon. Her breath came out in a huff. "Oh. So now ya hate me, since I wasn't the one who gave birth to ya. An' it's time to shame me, is that it?" The tip of her nose began to redden as her eyes glistened with tears. "An' now ya'd tell the world how yer Pa spited me after we was married, seein' as how I couldn't bear

him children of my own, like a good wife?"

Resting an elbow on the table, his father leaned his head into his hand. "Now, Hannah, I'm sure the boy's not trying to hurt you—"

"An' *you*!" she shrieked. Anger sparked from her narrowed eyes as she glared and stood, heading straight for him. "Some good yer fine promises turned out to be."

His father shot up from his seat and grasped her wrist, warding off her blow. Taking her other one, he held them together between their chests and spoke in a calming tone. "It was time for him to be told. We've been livin' this lie his whole life. It wasn't right. I prayed that Zed would tell him. The children should not be made to suffer because of us, Hannah. We've no right to forbid their happiness."

Grimacing, his mother stared into his father's blue eyes for several moments. Gradually, her breathing slowed and a resigned expression settled over her face.

"Everything will be all right," Matthew said gently. "Come, sit back down." He led her to her chair. Once she was settled, he returned to his own.

Rhon got up and moved beside his mother. Kneeling, he put his arms around her. "I love you, Ma. I always will. Don't you think I know how much love it must've taken for you to raise me all these years like I was your own?" He tightened his embrace. "I never knew anyone else but you. To me, you'll always be my mother. And I promise, nobody has to know anything about this . . . only Holly. It won't change anything for you at all. You do love me, too, don't you?"

Nodding, she sniffed. "But I thought—"

"I know, Ma." He drew her up into a hug. "I've had a lot of time to think about it, you know. And I understand you and Pa doing what seemed best for all of us, back then, when the truth would've hurt a lot of people. I am thankful to both of you for that. I really am. But now things have changed. And trying to keep that truth to ourselves could cause me even worse pain for the rest of my life." He rocked her gently in his arms and tipped up her chin. "Going away showed me what it was like to be without Holly, and I don't want to spend the rest of my life like that. She's the one I want to be with forever. I have to see if she feels the same way I do, before it's too late."

"It . . . it's too late already," she said. Tears coursed down her face.

A stab of dread choked off Rhon's breath.

"I'm—I'm . . . sorry, son," came his father's voice. "The wedding's the day after tomorrow."

Despite the finality of those words, Rhon saw them as a reprieve, however small. He was home. He still had one day. He kissed his mother's cheek. "Well, I'd better go see Holly. Now."

He was out the door in seconds. "Stay," he commanded as Shadow bolted up beside him. "I can't take you along. Not this time." With a soft whine, the dog obediently lay back down, resting his jaw on his paws.

Taking the shortcut across the meadow, Rhon vaulted over the stone wall at the boundary of Aunt Priscilla's property. The house appeared to be quiet, and golden light from the lamps filled the windows as daylight began to wane. He picked up a few pebbles and tossed them at the attic window.

Holly appeared almost instantly. She flung open the glass and leaned out, her face alight with surprise. "Rhon!" she gasped.

"Hi, cousin." He motioned with his head toward the glen, and at her nod, he raced there, hoping that he could calm his thoughts while he paced between the boulder and the creek. Convincing Holly to jilt Harris at this late date would take a miracle, of that he had no doubt. He said another silent prayer. *If this is Your will for us, Father, I sure could use Your help to make her see it too.*

He heard the light sound of Holly's running footsteps even before she came into view. His heart beat furiously at the sight of her. Dressed all in white lace, she looked even more beautiful than he had remembered. He watched her release her skirts and stop as she panted through slightly parted lips. It took two tries before he could force her name past the tightness in his throat. "H—Holly."

"Hi. What are you doing here?"

He swallowed and forced himself to speak casually. "I live here, remember?" He could not take his eyes off her. And with every blink his spirit sank lower. Why was she wearing her wedding dress? he wondered. Hadn't Pa said that the wedding wasn't for another day? He ground his teeth together, his long, practiced speech forgotten.

She gave an incredulous toss of her head, and her sable curls danced with the movement. "Oh, I thought maybe you came to say goodbye, again," she said coolly. "Like the last time I saw you. Do you remember that?"

Did he remember it? He could feel her body in his arms even now, and the imprint of her full, exquisite lips still warmed his. He nodded slowly as the fading light played over the seed pearls decorating the elegant lace of her bodice and flounced skirt. "You look . . . beautiful."

Holly smiled. She'd been spending more time than usual lately in this special place, dwelling on bygone days and secret, hopeless dreams. She had hungered for the sight of him for such a long time that at her first glimpse moments ago she'd been certain he was a vision she'd conjured up from sheer wishing. But he was quite real. She felt lost in the depths of his gaze. She tried to still the pounding of her heart and keep her hands from trembling. Tangled emotions nearly rendered her speechless. "Beth was just fixing my—" She cleared her throat and attempted a joke. "Did you come to give me away?"

Rhon's eyes sparked with anger. "What? Are you crazy?" His voice squeaked on the last word, and disgustedly he turned away, shoving his hands into his pockets. His head fell back for a second as he inhaled deeply. He spun around. "Holly, how can you even think of doing this?"

"Beth and I—"

"I wasn't gone that long."

"That long?" she cried. "That long, you say? You were gone forever, Rhon Banister. With one letter in all that time, never even mentioning when—or if, for that matter—you'd deign to return. For all I knew, you were going to take Uncle Zed up on his precious job offer!" She stamped her white slipper and turned her back. "I wasn't about to check with that snip, Jenny Spencer, to find out when you were coming home."

He stepped around to her face. "What are you talking about?"

As if he didn't know, she thought. She turned up her nose. "Oh, she's sporting that stupid cameo you bought her and bragging about how you want to talk to her as soon as you get back. I shouldn't have to tell *you* that."

Rhon blinked in surprise, his brows rising high. "I don't have the foggiest notion of what you're talking about. I never bought

a cameo for—" He kneaded his temples for an instant. "Wait a minute. I *almost* bought a necklace the day I went away. But I didn't have enough money, so I put it back. And if I'd gotten it, it would have been for you, not for Jenny."

Only slightly appeased, Holly stared at him.

Rhon shook his head, and the tranquil green of his eyes twinkled with a hint of a smile. He took hold of her arms and drew her nearer, coaxing her gaze until it locked with his. "Holly, I could never make promises to anyone but you. Don't you know that by now?"

She grimaced. "Well, that's all very nice," she said quietly. "Too bad you never mentioned it before."

"Yeah, I see that. I probably should never have gone away when I did. Or stayed away so many weeks." Letting her go, he shook his head. "But, *Harris*. How could you consider him, of all—"

Holly felt the flare of a blush and struggled to keep her voice even. "You want to know how I could possibly have chosen him? Well, I'll tell you how, Rhon Banister. Tyler was here when I needed someone to turn to."

"And how is that, if I might ask?"

She lowered her gaze and looked off into the distance. Unexpected tears threatened at the memory of the frightful experience she had tried to shut out of her mind, and she trembled. "It—it was . . ." her words lowered to a whisper, "because of . . . Uncle Ethan."

Rhon grabbed her. "What?" He searched her face.

Nodding, Holly sank against him. "I was . . . alone, and . . . he—he—tried to . . . touch me." Rhon's hold tightened so much that she could barely breathe for a moment. She felt the surge of his heartbeat, and drawing strength from that, she continued. "Somehow I managed to . . . get away before—" She hesitated, then slowly continued. "I knew then that I needed to find somewhere else to go, someplace where Beth and I could both live and be safe."

"My poor love," he breathed. "I am so very sorry I wasn't here then. I'd have crippled him."

"But you weren't."

"I'll never forgive myself for that, believe me." He eased her gently away. "Surely you told Aunt Pris, at least."

Holly shook her head. "How could I? She might have sent me

away. No one knows but Tyler. He came along at just the right time." She watched Rhon's jaw tighten. "I didn't even tell Beth, because I didn't want her to live in fear. I thought that I could keep watch over her. But—"

"You mean that cur tried a second time?" he spat. Rhon's hands curled into fists. He didn't speak for several moments, then he blew a resigned breath. "So you . . . turned to Harris. I . . . suppose I can understand that. *If* you love the guy." He drew her into his embrace.

She did not respond.

"Do you, Holly? Because if you don't, *I* want to make a life for you. I came back to ask you to marry me."

Holly almost stopped breathing. How she had longed to hear those very words from his lips. Impossible though she knew her daydreams to be, she had wished anyway. For a brief second she pressed against him, reveling in the feel of the strong arms that enfolded her. But she knew, and so did Rhon, that it was hopeless for them ever to love. They'd already had all the time together that they were meant to have in this life, she reasoned, and now things were happening that would cause even more distance between them.

She drew back and lifted her face, keeping tears at bay by sheer force of will. "You shouldn't be saying that. We can never say *or* feel those kinds of things for each other. It's forbidden to us." The evening breeze stirred the ribbons in her hair, and unconsciously she shivered.

"No." He gripped her arms. "It's not. Come here. I have something amazing to tell you. I hope you have time for a story."

She nodded. "Aunt Pris is lying down with a headache, and Beth is watching the children."

"Good." Reaching for her hand, he led her to the boulder. He spread out his neckerchief on the rock, gesturing for her to sit down, then removed his jacket and put it around her shoulders.

The doeskin was still warm from his body, and Holly snuggled into it as she studied him.

"Uncle Zed told me something just before I left. In fact, that's what finally made me decide to come home. The deep, dark family secret. I found it quite interesting."

"I didn't know there was one."

"No one was ever supposed to know. And no one would have,

if Pa and Uncle Zed hadn't taken pity on me."

Holly frowned. "What in the world are you talking about?" she asked.

"I'll tell you." He paused for a few seconds. "I didn't want to go out to Cheyenne. It was all arranged by Ma and Pa, and maybe even Aunt Pris."

"What?"

"They noticed that you and I were becoming a bit too close lately. And they decided to put some space between us, hoping that we'd both find somebody else."

"Well, it shouldn't surprise us. We're cousins after all," she said.

"Cousins can marry, Holly. If we really wanted to, they couldn't stop us."

"Only they'd hate us. They'd never accept it. A lot of people think that it's wrong."

"And why do you suppose that is?" he asked with the merest pause. "Because there's no real reason why it should be frowned upon." Bending down, he picked up a flat pebble and skipped it across the shallows of the stream. "I was miserable in Wyoming."

Holly managed to contain the measure of satisfaction that flickered through her. It served him right, she thought, for all the times she'd been lonely without him.

"Uncle Zed went out of his way to keep me busy, tried to steer me toward one of the cute town girls—"

She hadn't thought of that. Exactly how hard had *dear* Uncle Zed worked at it? she wondered. Her eyes assessed her handsome cousin as he picked up a few more stones and tossed them lightly across the ripples.

"—but I kept talking about you. It didn't take him long to figure out why." He dropped the last rock into the water, and delicate rings appeared and spread outward in the stillness. Brushing his hands on his pants, he turned and faced her. "I love you, Holly."

Her breath stopped suddenly. "But . . . that doesn't change things," she said softly. "Not for us."

A tentative smile teased his mouth. "Maybe. But then again, it doesn't matter."

With a deep sigh, Holly looked away. In the last half hour or so, Rhon had said more—and less—than he'd ever said in all the times they'd been together. It was certainly a curious con-

versation. "Rhon, could you actually be trying to tell me something in all of this?"

He grinned. She looked so lovely as dusk settled over the glen,
so fragile in white lace. Her dark eyes reflected the dim remaining
light. He wanted to keep her here forever and never let her go
back home. He clenched his teeth at the thought of Uncle Ethan
and his unspeakable actions. No one would *ever* harm Holly
again, he vowed to himself. He had to make her understand that
there was nothing standing between them now . . . except that
bounder, Harris. As her gaze returned to him, he nodded.

"Well, I can't imagine what you're trying to say." Holly prompted.

"This is beyond imagining."

"Oh?"

"Yep." *Please give me the right words, Father*. Striding over
to where she sat, Rhon stooped beside her and took her hand.
"A lot of years ago, Pa and Ma made a vow with Uncle Zed.
It was a vow of silence, really."

Holly tilted her head. "What would they have to keep silent
about?"

"Me." He saw her expression turn to one of confusion. "Listen,
I know this is going to sound unbelievable to you, but I swear
it's all true."

She eyed him suspiciously, but remained silent.

He laced his fingers with hers. "There is . . . no blood tie between
us, Holly."

"What? Daddy and Aunt Hannah are—"

"Brother and sister," he finished. "But as it turns out, Ma—
Hannah—is not my real mother."

Holly pulled her hand free and stood, a frown drawing her brows
together. "That has to be the dumbest thing I have ever heard!"
She took a few steps away and stopped.

"But it's still true."

"I don't understand this at all. It just isn't possible."

"Why not?" he asked gently. "Things happen, sometimes, that
no one expected ahead of time. People fall in love, make mistakes,
go on." He stood and walked to her. Placing his hands on her
shoulders he drew her back to his chest. "The woman who gave
birth to me was a schoolteacher in Connecticut who loved my
Pa even though he was married. Through a weird twist of cir-
cumstances, she and Pa ended up spending one night together.

And I was conceived. My mother died after giving birth, and Pa took me home. Hannah took me in at once and raised me as her own. She was unable to have children."

Holly turned to face him, and a perplexed look met his eyes. He put his arms around her.

"I know just how you feel. I went through a hard time with it when Uncle Zed told me. I couldn't imagine why he'd pull my whole world out from under my feet like that, out of the blue. It took me a while to sort through it all and see why. I'd been reciting the usual cousin speech we've heard so many times, why good little cousins don't get involved. And he decided to put all that to rest."

She eased away slightly and tilted her head back. "Do your parents know?"

He nodded. "I had a real good talk with both of them right before I came here." He let out a whoosh of breath and grinned. "Actually, Pa's been wanting to tell me the truth for some time. When he saw how quickly things were being . . . *arranged* for you, he wrote to Uncle Zed and as much as gave him approval to do what he thought best. And here I am." With the back of his fingers he tenderly caressed the rise of her cheekbone.

Yes, here you are. Holly knew that she should be the happiest person alive at that moment, but she felt just the opposite. In fact, she doubted if she'd ever been more miserable in her entire life. She tried to fathom the whole story, but the tempo of her heartbeat made that impossible. This had to be a dream. It couldn't be real. So many things flashed in her mind: her promise to Tyler, their wedding plans, Beth . . . Uncle Ethan. A few months ago, things had only been hopeless for her and Rhon. Now they were beyond even that; they were completely impossible.

She sighed. "I know what you've told me must be true. It's too incredible for it to be something someone made up. But things are still the same for us. Our families would probably never accept us. Neither would our friends. And anyway, it's . . . too late."

Locking his hands behind her waist, Rhon pulled her close again. "Don't say that, Holly. Please, don't."

She felt his heart thundering against hers. Tears stung her eyes, and her breath caught on a sob. "How can I not say it? It's true, and you know it as well as I do." She tried to pull away, but he would not release her.

"You mean that you would still go through with the wedding? Even though I just told you that I love you? And that nothing stands between us?" Despite the pale light, his expression pierced her soul.

Holly ached inside at the pain she saw on his face, pain she knew that she had inflicted herself on the dearest person in her whole world. Her vision blurred with tears that brimmed and spilled over. "I—I have to. If you had come home before this, maybe things could have . . . worked out for us somehow. But it's too late now! Everything has been planned. Don't you see? I can't back out. Tyler's been really good to Beth and me. He knows about Uncle Ethan. He— no, I—couldn't do that to him."

Rhon exhaled a shaken breath, and a muscle twitched in his jaw. "But you could do it to me?" He let his arms fall to his sides. "How stupid of me. I actually thought you loved me, too."

"But I do. . . . I always have."

Rhon's mouth dropped open in disbelief. "Yeah, but not enough. I see that now."

Holly sobbed openly at the despair in his tone. Not even attempting to stem her tears, she turned to leave.

"Wait," he whispered, catching her arm. "There's something I owe you. A kiss goodbye. Remember?" Lowering his head, he covered her lips with his.

As the kiss deepened, she melted against him, no longer conscious of whether it was her own legs or the power of his arms that held her up. Fleetingly she thought of Tyler's chaste embraces, his polite kisses. How could she settle for that kind of existence when she'd been offered all that she'd ever dreamed of? When Rhon eased away too soon, she raised her lashes. Even in the dusk of the glade his love shimmered in his eyes.

She lingered in his embrace for several moments, and her resolve evaporated like dew on a rose petal. She searched his face, then glanced away. "Maybe I *could* have a talk with Tyler," she whispered.

11

"There, that's the last one." Beth stepped back and scrutinized the satin bow she had just fastened to the end of a pew. "Pretty, huh?"

Holly feigned an enthusiastic expression. Tyler would be arriving for the rehearsal any minute now. *She had to tell him about Rhon. But how?* she wondered. Even after lying awake most of the night she hadn't been able to decide how to break the news to him. Every time she so much as thought about it, her heart thudded erratically against her ribs, leaving her breathless.

"Sure was nice of Rhon to bring us here early," her sister said. "Is he over talking to the pastor?"

"Hm?" Holly turned with a blank look.

"My goodness. You are in a state," Beth said, a teasing note in her voice. "You're only getting married, not being hanged by the neck until dead. Everything will be all right. You'll see. He's such a fine man. You're so lucky, Holly," she added wistfully. "I wish—"

Holly looked toward the back of the sanctuary, sure that she had heard hoofbeats growing closer. Anxiously, she walked to the door and opened it a crack as Tyler's buggy came into view. She cleared her throat. "I, um, will be back in a second." Ignoring her sister's puzzled frown, she pulled on her shawl and stepped outside. Chin high, she waited on the bottom step until he pulled up.

Tyler thumbed his hat and grinned. "Good day, my dear Holly. All ready for tomorrow?"

"Almost." She forced a smile. "Tyler, I . . . have to talk to you. Could we please go for a ride?"

Bewilderment settled over his features. "Anything you like," he said, getting down and helping her in. Then he climbed back into his seat and clucked his tongue, urging the horse forward.

It took all the determination she could gather not to look around to see if Rhon was watching. She stared straight ahead, hardly

breathing as they maneuvered beneath the over hanging branches of a golden poplar and followed the tree-dotted curvature of the church pond.

"Lovely day, isn't it?" Tyler said.

The sound of his voice in the stillness startled her. "It's my favorite time of year." Why had her own voice sounded unnaturally high with a tremor? Her hands shook as she pulled her wrap tighter.

"Mine, too. I only wish it would last a bit longer." Tyler stopped at the far side of the pond by a stand of bright maples with leaves of the rich, leathery red of autumn. He draped the traces over the front of the buggy and leaned back against the seat again. "Did we come out here to discuss the weather?"

Holly moistened her lips and brushed an imaginary bit of lint from her emerald skirt. "No." Unable to meet his eyes, she lowered her head.

"Then, what is it, my dear?"

"I . . . um . . ." The pounding of her heart sent a rushing sound into her ears, and she suddenly felt dizzy. *Please, don't let me be sick now.*

With a gentle smile, Tyler stroked her cheek with one hand and studied her. "I see. A case of wedding jitters, is that it?"

If only it were as simple as that, she wanted to say. Twisting the end of her shawl with trembling fingers, she gazed distractedly at the white clapboard structure mirrored in the rippling water. "This is a bit . . . different, I'm afraid."

A frown played across Tyler's forehead, but he rested an arm on the upholstered seat back and appeared to relax slightly. "How different?" His low tone emitted concern.

"Well, I—I . . . don't know how to say this, really. I thought I would. But I don't." How did one go about jilting a person she truly did care about? How could one inflict pain gently? Say something, she told herself. *Anything.*

He inclined his head. "Oh, I see. This is a guessing game. Well, tell me when I get close, will you?" He rubbed his mustache with an index finger. "You aren't in such a hurry to get married. Your uncle has repented of his sins and begged your forgiveness. He assures you that you will be quite safe under his roof after all."

Although on the verge of tears, that absurd image almost made Holly smile. But her throat tightened instead.

"Hm. Well, let's see. You've just learned you have some horrible, deadly disease, and you don't want to burden me with your care as you waste away."

A light laugh came out in a cough. She shook her head. This was going to be even harder than she'd thought, much harder, she realized. Would she really be able to go through with this?

"Oh. Worse than that, then." He drew in a deep breath. "You've . . . had a better offer?" Although the note of absurdity in his voice left no doubt that in his mind the suggestion was quite farfetched, Holly's eyes widened in shock.

Tyler exhaled all at once, feeling as if he'd been punched in the stomach. "That's it, isn't it?" This couldn't be happening, he thought, not at this late date, not after everything was set for their marriage on the morrow. Anger and disbelief shot through him. He lifted her chin so that he could look into her eyes. "Do you mean that someone else has been courting you? That all this time that we've been keeping company with one another you were—"

"No. No, it wasn't like that." A pink flush colored Holly's cheeks, and she averted her gaze. "Not at all."

"People have seen us together for weeks," he prodded, trying to make some sense out of it. "Arrangements for our wedding have been made. I thought that you wanted to marry me."

Nervously she glanced back toward the church. "I did. But—"

"But not now?" He followed her gaze and noticed the pastor on the landing of the building with a young man at his side. So that was it, he realized. "Banister has come back," he said flatly.

Hesitantly, Holly nodded.

"And you've decided you'd rather marry him, is that it?" he asked, although he already knew the answer. She'd spoken of the kid often enough when they'd been together, and from the way her eyes and voice would soften, he knew that there had to be something serious between them. "But you're cousins," he said.

"Yes, but not in the way we thought," she blurted. "I know this sounds unbelievable, Tyler, but I promise it's true."

"What are you saying, exactly?"

"We've just learned that there's no blood relationship between us at all. My aunt is not Rhon's real mother." She placed a hand on his sleeve, and words gushed forth in a torrent. "I'm sorry.

Truly. If there's anything I never wanted, it was to hurt or embarrass you."

He stiffened and turned away.

A sob clogged her throat. She swallowed. "You've been so kind and considerate to Beth and me. You're such a thoughtful and generous person, and I've enjoyed being with you, getting to know you. I don't blame you if you never forgive me."

Tyler rubbed his jaw and watched Holly mangling the fringe of her shawl. This was certainly one bizarre turn of events. But he wondered if it was really all that bad. He nodded his head slowly, thoughtfully. He should have been devastated at her news or, at the very least, angry. But oddly enough, as he mulled things over in his mind, an amazing relief flickered through him, and an astonished smile worked its way across his face. He didn't really love Holly, that was a fact. Her need to escape from her uncle had accelerated their relationship, when, by rights, things should have been allowed to develop at a far more leisurely pace, if, indeed, they would have at all.

He cleared his throat self-consciously and gathered his thoughts. "Of course I forgive you. After all, this was just my humble attempt at saving a damsel in distress, right?" Removing a handkerchief from his pocket, he dried Holly's tears and placed the cloth in her hand.

"Oh, Tyler," she moaned miserably, "now I really hate myself. You've been wonderful, right from the beginning. I shall never forget you."

He shrugged. After a moment he turned and stared in the direction of the church. "May I at least ask, my dear Holly, how this almost-cousin of yours plans to support you—and, I certainly would hope, Beth? And what about the gossip? Won't that affect your relatives, and hurt your sister especially?"

Holly blotted her eyes again and looked at him. "If our own family accepts our marriage—and, considering everything, so far I believe they will—I don't think there'll be much of a problem with other people." Her expression grew brighter. "After all, how long could we be an item?"

"That's something you'll have to wait to find out for yourselves, I suppose. But you mustn't forget Beth's feelings."

Lowering her head, Holly grimaced. "If things got too bad, we could always make a new start in Wyoming. Our uncle offered

Rhon a job while he was there."

"Wyoming!" That thought hit with a jolt. "You mean you'd take that dear, defenseless girl to Wyoming, to a wild, half-civilized place like that?"

Beth? she wondered in surprise. How dear of Tyler to be so concerned about her sister. Squeezing his hand, Holly searched his face. Suddenly she saw something revealed within the depths of his gray eyes, and some random fragments began to fit together extremely well in her mind. Tyler was certainly more than just concerned for her younger sister. And Beth. Holly's memory recalled up the last sketches in Beth's tablet, touching, tender portraits of Tyler Harris. How could she have missed it before? Her sister was in love with Tyler herself. "You love her, too," she said in awe.

"What? Are you telling me someone else is already calling on her?"

Holly's smile widened. "No, I didn't say that at all."

"Whew!" Tyler reddened around the ears, and his mouth twisted into a guilty smile. Flustered, he pushed his bowler back a few inches. "I confess that there's something I find quite irresistible about her."

"Well, why on earth didn't you court *her* instead of me?"

He shrugged. "She wasn't offered to me, you were. Besides, she's young and all. How could I even hope that she might consider having callers already, much less someone of my age?"

Holly's emotions toppled absurdly from her earlier panic, and she now felt as if she were in some comical dream. She struggled to maintain her composure. "Actually, she's fifteen, the same age as our mother when she married. And in many ways, Beth's older than I am. Oh, Tyler!" Taking hold of his shoulders, she leaned over and lightly kissed his cheek. "This is perfect!"

"Do ya think he's really fergiven us?" Hannah asked, looking up from the pie crust she was rolling out.

Matthew put an arm around her cushiony shoulder and squeezed. " 'Course. He's got a level head. I tried to tell you that before."

She brushed away a stray tear. "I was sure he'd hate me fer not bein' the one who bore him. An' fer lyin' to him all these years. More'n anythin', that's what I feared. What's the difference if Pris found out I couldn't have children of my own? It

was bein' afraid of what *he'd* think that made me forgit what was most important."

"Well, it's all out in the open now, Hannah, my love," he said gently. He paused, indenting a finger into a scrap of dough. "If things do work out for them, think you'll be able to accept Holly as your daughter-in-law?"

Hannah frowned in thought. "Well, she's a durn sight less persnickety than that Spencer gal, that's fer sure, even with all that money an' bein' well off." She cocked her head to the side. "Yep, I've always liked that Holly. She keeps a clean house."

Matthew sputtered into a laugh. "What more could a man want, huh?" Brushing a dab of flour from the end of her round nose, he kissed it, then swiftly glanced around the spotless kitchen. He put his arms around her. "I always did love a clean house."

Holly looked at Rhon with a smile as the buckboard rumbled homeward in the mid-afternoon sunshine. "I never would have dreamed the way things have worked out today. Not in a thousand years."

He pulled her against his side and shook his head in wonder. "Yeah. Somebody *always* ends up hurt in a situation like this. It's nothing short of a miracle. You don't know how hard I prayed for one last night."

"You did?" She lifted questioning eyes toward him.

"Mm-hm. In fact," he added with a grin, "that's all I've been praying for the last week." His expression turned serious. "Things could have turned out the opposite way so easily. Think about it. The four of us could have all ended up living with the wrong people for the rest of our lives, all because of a family secret."

Holly sighed, then snuggled even closer. "And to think my little sister has been in love with *my intended* all this time. Isn't it the most incredible thing you've ever heard?"

"Are you sorry?"

"How could I be?" She gushed and kissed his cheek. She felt his gasp. "And," she continued in joyous chatter, "imagine his suggestion that we make tomorrow's wedding a double one! I can hardly make myself believe it."

Giving her an extra hug, Rhon chuckled. "Wonder what Aunt Pris is going to think about it."

Holly laughed lightly. "If you'd hurry, maybe we could see her

reaction."

"I don't think it's dawned on her that she's about to lose both of her housekeepers," he said teasingly. "It might take some convincing."

"Well, it would've happened anyway. I was planning to take Beth with me when I left."

"Did you tell her that?"

"Not in so many words. I hinted at it once, though. She was really counting on my marrying Tyler." She paused. "You'd have liked him, by the way, if you two had ever gotten to know each other."

Rhon gave a disbelieving smirk. "Not if he had you, I wouldn't." Bending his head, he lightly touched her lips with his.

Her heart went skittering. She took a calming breath. "But now?"

"Now, I figure I'll give the guy a chance."

Holly smiled. "He'll be good to Beth, I just know it. He'll make a fine life for her. He has a beautiful, big house, and he's quite well off." Her shoulders shook as she tried to control her laughter.

"What's so funny?"

She curled her lips inward, trying unsuccessfully to contain her mirth, then gave up. "I once thought—" She turned to gaze off in another direction. He'd never believe this, she said to herself. On second thought, maybe he would. She met his twinkling green eyes. "I once thought that all it would take to make me happy was . . . money."

"Well," he said with a nod, "I suppose there are quite a few people who'd agree with that." He paused for several moments. "I hope you won't regret what you've given up to marry me."

She considered his statement for only a scant few seconds as Nan's rhythmic hoofbeats clopped along the dirt road. "How could I?"

"That's a relief," he teased, toying with one of her long curls. "I—that is, *we*—don't have a heck of a lot at the moment. I did save all my earnings from Cheyenne, but other than that—"

"Shh." Holly silenced him with a rather adventurous kiss.

Releasing the leather straps, Rhon forced himself to pull away from her and held her at arm's length. He'd never seen her wide chestnut eyes so aglow with love, and in his wildest dreams he'd never thought that she'd truly be his for all time. He had an

incredible urge to kiss her and kiss her forever. Reluctantly he
touched the tip of her nose with his mouth, then moved her head
to rest on his shoulder again. He picked up the reins. "Holly?"

"Hm?"

"How would you like to go home? After the wedding, I mean."

She lifted her head and turned. "To your house?"

"No. Yours. Where you used to live." He swallowed, waiting
for her answer. Would she even consider going back to all the
old memories, some of which could undoubtedly be painful? he
wondered.

Her gaze had a faraway, misty quality, and it was several
moments before she even blinked. Her words came out in a
whisper. "I haven't ever gone back there."

"I know." He brushed a lock of hair from her face. "I checked
on it early this morning. It's still closed up and all. But it's in
good condition. Would you let me take you home, Holly?"

Even through shimmering tears, her smile lit his soul. "You
mean that we could live there? You and I?"

He nodded. "If you'd like to."

"It's a beautiful thought. But . . . it might be hard."

"Then again, it might be easy." he said gently. "You were all
very happy there. Perhaps we can build some good memories of
our own on the foundation your folks started."

Holly brightened. "And Beth and Tyler could come visit us."

"And we could visit them. At the *big* house," he said wryly.

She remained quiet for a few moments, then turned. "I never
asked what your parents had to say about all of this. An awful
lot of tongues are going to wag over this."

"So? Ma and Pa are for us, now that we talked it all out. They'll
stand behind us, you'll see. And as soon as something more
exciting happens, people will forget all about the two of us."

"I hope you're right." Holly nuzzled deeper into his warmth,
reveling in it before speaking again. "I've been thinking."

"About what, my love?"

A smile spread across her lips at his words. "It's only right
that Tyler's bride should wear the beautiful gown he bought."

He nodded. "Of course. But what will you wear, then?"

"Mama's white dress is in the bottom of her trunk. What could
be more special than wearing that? She looked so beautiful in
her wedding portrait with Daddy."

"You're sure this isn't too fast, Holly? It'll take some work to make the house livable again."

Holly eased back and turned her brightest smile his way. "I'd go there this minute . . . if we were married. It'll be such fun fixing it up."

Rhon drew her close again, back where she belonged. He lifted Holly's face and covered her mouth with his, fully aware that not long ago he couldn't let himself so much as dream that her satiny lips would tantalize his with their soft fullness. He coaxed them apart to taste her sweetness and wished for all the world that it was tomorrow. It was all he could do to contain his longing to claim all of her, to love her forever in their own private haven. After a long moment, he pulled back and inhaled an uneven breath. He looked deeply into her eyes. "I adore you, you know. I'll spend my life making you believe that." The autumn breeze rustled the rainbow of leaves overhead, and a handful of colors swirled lazily to the ground.

Holly felt as if some of those colors were also fluttering in her stomach as she beheld Rhon's dear face through her glistening eyes. In one more day she would marry the one person she loved more than her own life.

Suddenly another thought flashed, and her eyes sparkled with mischief. "Just promise me one thing."

"Anything."

"Don't ever kiss me goodbye again."

The corners of his mouth curved upward. "That's one thing you'll never have to worry about. Come here, *cousin*. Let me show you how I kiss hello."

Dear Reader:

Please let us know how you feel about Barbour Books' Christian Fiction.

1. What most influenced you to purchase **Romance Reader** #1, #2, #3, #4, #5, #6, #7, #8, #9, 10, #11, #12?

   _____ Author   _____ Recommendations

   _____ Subject matter   _____ Price

   _____ Cover / titles

2. Would you buy other books in the **Romance Series** by this author?

   _____ Yes   _____ No

3. Where did you purchase this book?

   _____ Christian book store   _____ Other

   _____ General book store   _____ Mail order

4. What is your overall rating of this **Romance Reader**?

   _____ Excellent _____ Very good _____ Good _____ Fair _____ Poor

5. How many hours a week do you spend reading books? _____ hrs.

6. Are you a member of a church? _____ Yes _____ No

   If yes, what denomination? _____

7. Please check age

   _____ Under 18   _____ 25-34   _____ 45-54

   _____ 18-24   _____ 35-44   _____ 55 and over

Mail to: **Fiction Editor**
Barbour Books
P.O. Box 719
Uhrichsville, OH 44683

NAME ——————————————————————————

ADDRESS ————————————————————————

CITY ———————————— STATE ——— ZIP —————

Thank you for helping us provide the best in Christian fiction!